Unsupervised

A Crabgrass Comics Adventure

TAUHID BONDIA

Andrews Mc
PUBLISHIN

D1286519

Crabgrass is distributed internationally by Andrews McMeel Syndication.

Andrews McMeel Publishing
a division of Andrews McMeel Universal
1130 Walnut Street, Kansas City, Missouri 64106

www.andrewsmcmeel.com

23 24 25 26 27 SDB 10 9 8 7 6 5 4 3 2 1

ISBN: 978-1-5248-8495-6

Library of Congress Control Number: 2023931224

Made by:
RR Donnelley (Guangdong) Printing Solutions Company Ltd
Address and location of manufacturer:
No. 2, Minzhu Road, Daning, Humen Town,
Dongguan City, Guangdong Province, China 523930
1st Printing – 4/24/23

THIS BOOK IS FOR
WALLACE JARVIS,
WHO WAS THERE FROM
THE VERY BEGINNING.

THANKS, POP

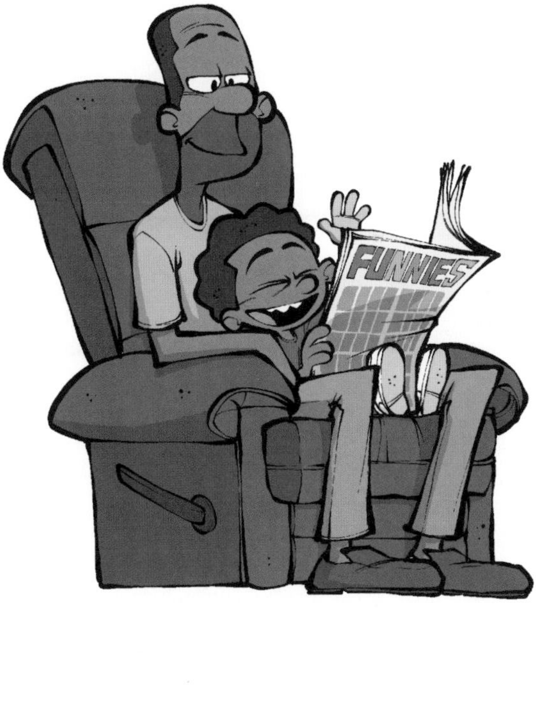
FUNNIES

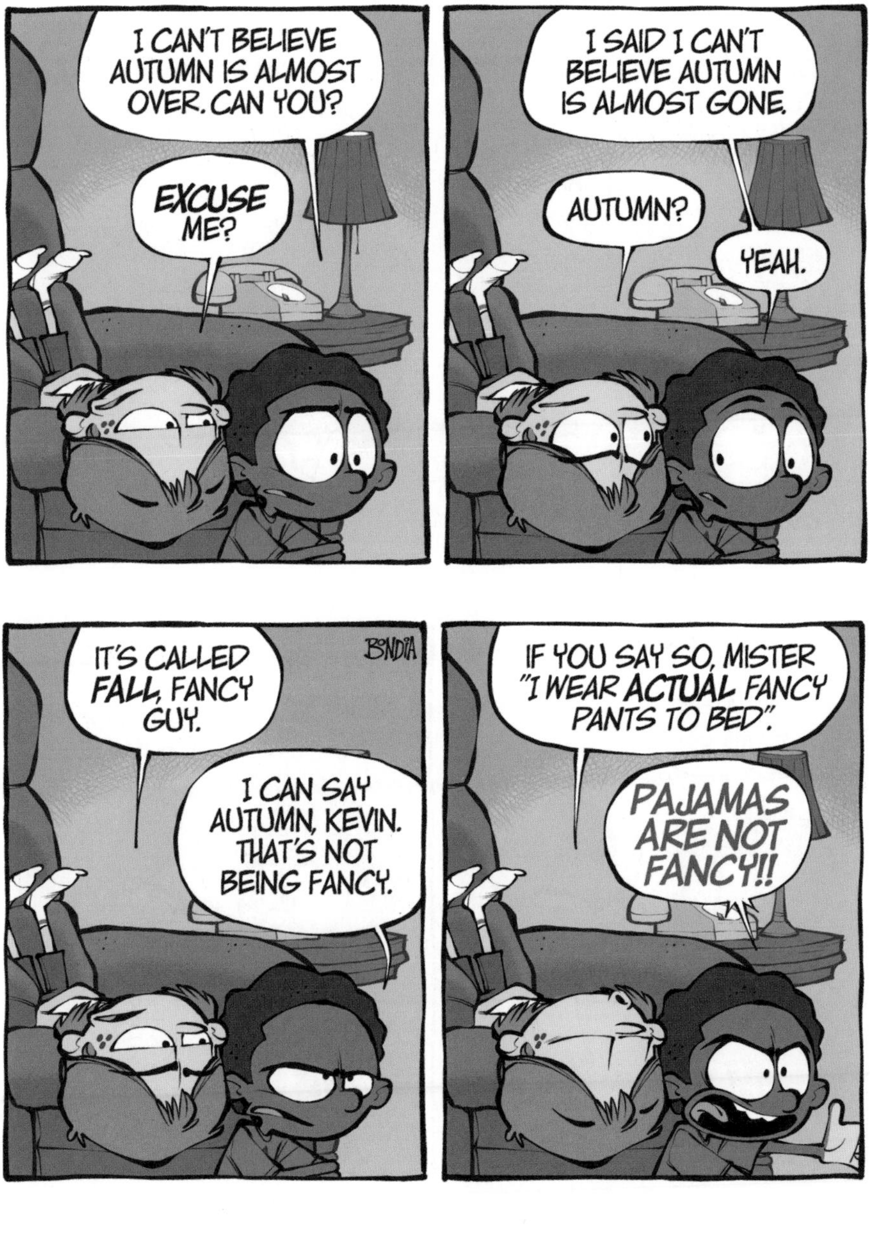
I CAN'T BELIEVE AUTUMN IS ALMOST OVER. CAN YOU?
EXCUSE ME?
I SAID I CAN'T BELIEVE AUTUMN IS ALMOST GONE.
AUTUMN?
YEAH.
IT'S CALLED FALL, FANCY GUY.
BONDIA
I CAN SAY AUTUMN, KEVIN. THAT'S NOT BEING FANCY.
IF YOU SAY SO, MISTER "I WEAR ACTUAL FANCY PANTS TO BED".
PAJAMAS ARE NOT FANCY!!

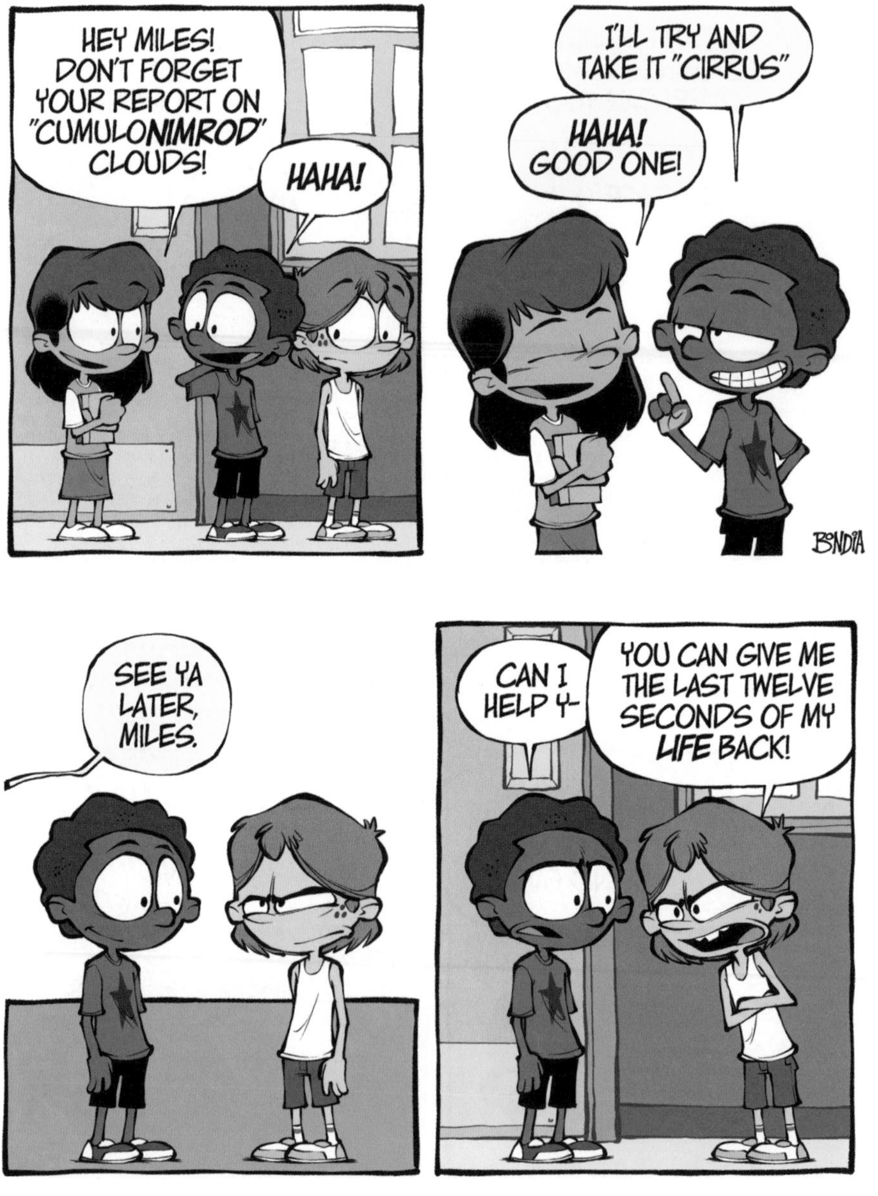
HEY MILES! DON'T FORGET YOUR REPORT ON "CUMULO**NIMROD**" CLOUDS!
HAHA!
I'LL TRY AND TAKE IT "CIRRUS"
HAHA! GOOD ONE!
BONDIA
SEE YA LATER, MILES.
CAN I HELP Y-
YOU CAN GIVE ME THE LAST TWELVE SECONDS OF MY ***LIFE*** BACK!

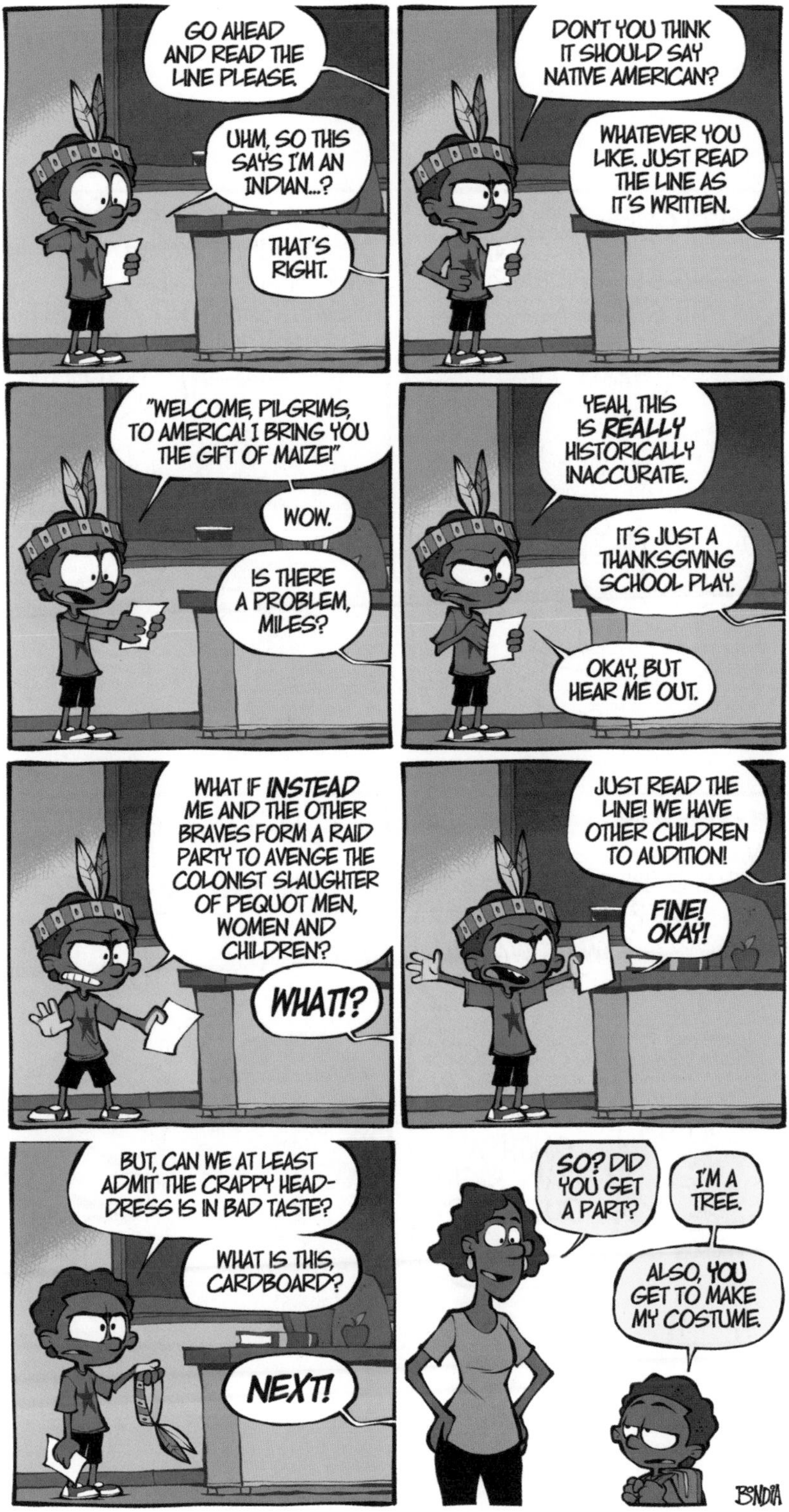
GO AHEAD AND READ THE LINE PLEASE.
UHM, SO THIS SAYS I'M AN INDIAN...?
THAT'S RIGHT.
DON'T YOU THINK IT SHOULD SAY NATIVE AMERICAN?
WHATEVER YOU LIKE. JUST READ THE LINE AS IT'S WRITTEN.
"WELCOME, PILGRIMS, TO AMERICA! I BRING YOU THE GIFT OF MAIZE!"
WOW.
IS THERE A PROBLEM, MILES?
YEAH, THIS IS **REALLY** HISTORICALLY INACCURATE.
IT'S JUST A THANKSGIVING SCHOOL PLAY.
OKAY, BUT HEAR ME OUT.
WHAT IF **INSTEAD** ME AND THE OTHER BRAVES FORM A RAID PARTY TO AVENGE THE COLONIST SLAUGHTER OF PEQUOT MEN, WOMEN AND CHILDREN?
WHAT!?
JUST READ THE LINE! WE HAVE OTHER CHILDREN TO AUDITION!
FINE! OKAY!
BUT, CAN WE AT LEAST ADMIT THE CRAPPY HEAD-DRESS IS IN BAD TASTE?
WHAT IS THIS, CARDBOARD?
NEXT!
SO? DID YOU GET A PART?
I'M A TREE.
ALSO, **YOU** GET TO MAKE MY COSTUME.
BONDIA

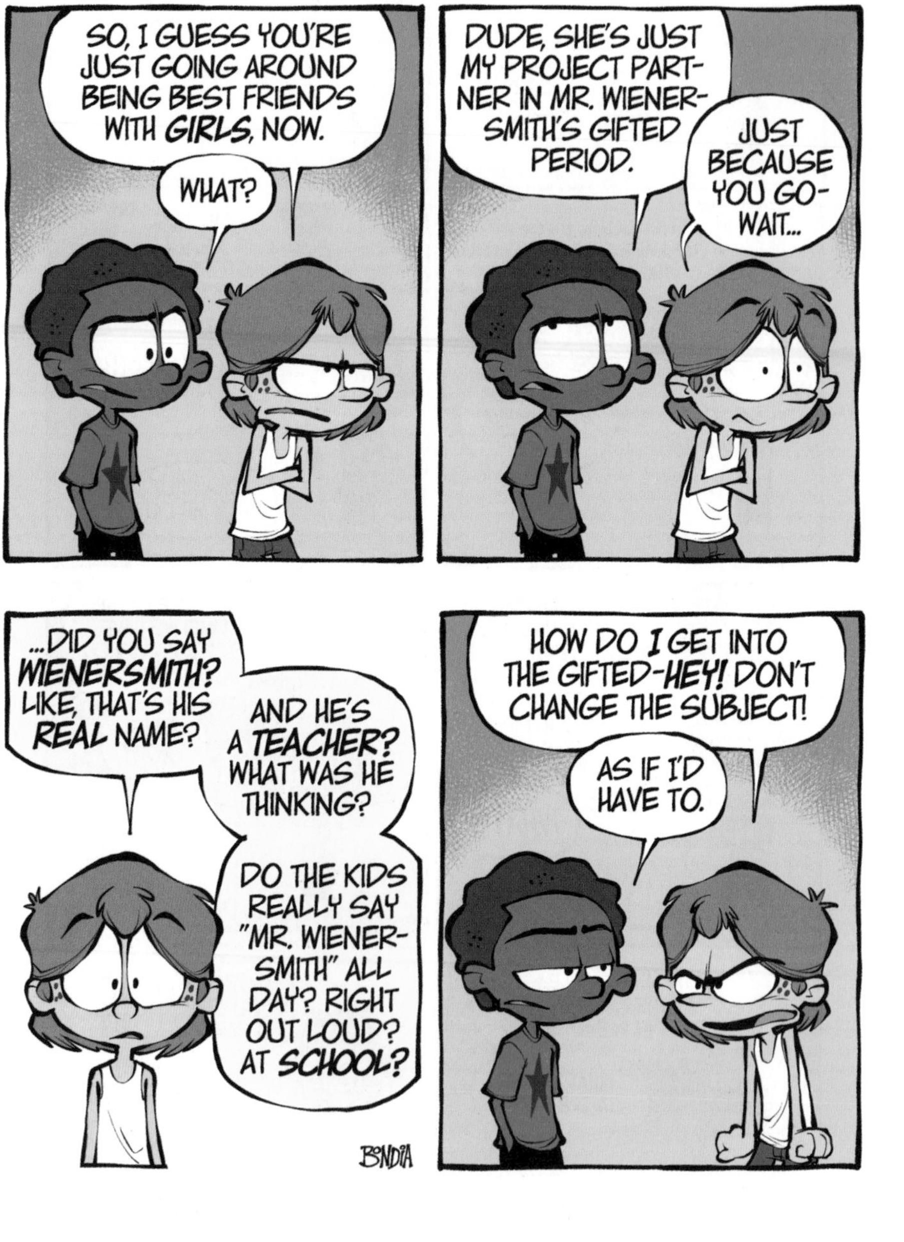
SO, I GUESS YOU'RE JUST GOING AROUND BEING BEST FRIENDS WITH GIRLS, NOW.
WHAT?
DUDE, SHE'S JUST MY PROJECT PARTNER IN MR. WIENERSMITH'S GIFTED PERIOD.
JUST BECAUSE YOU GO- WAIT...
...DID YOU SAY WIENERSMITH? LIKE, THAT'S HIS REAL NAME?
AND HE'S A TEACHER? WHAT WAS HE THINKING?
DO THE KIDS REALLY SAY "MR. WIENERSMITH" ALL DAY? RIGHT OUT LOUD? AT SCHOOL?
BONDIA
HOW DO I GET INTO THE GIFTED-HEY! DON'T CHANGE THE SUBJECT!
AS IF I'D HAVE TO.

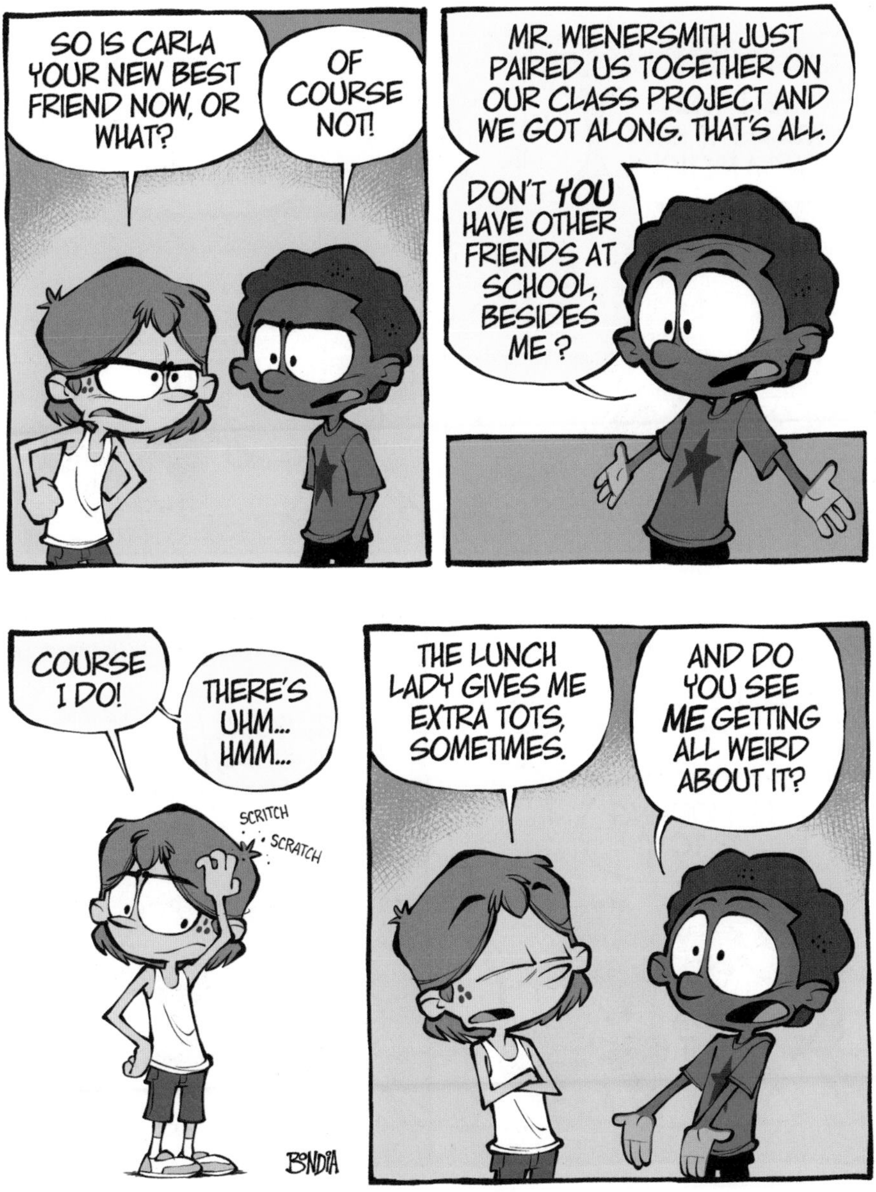
SO IS CARLA YOUR NEW BEST FRIEND NOW, OR WHAT?
OF COURSE NOT!
MR. WIENERSMITH JUST PAIRED US TOGETHER ON OUR CLASS PROJECT AND WE GOT ALONG. THAT'S ALL.
DON'T YOU HAVE OTHER FRIENDS AT SCHOOL, BESIDES ME ?
COURSE I DO!
THERE'S UHM... HMM...
SCRITCH
SCRATCH
BONDIA
THE LUNCH LADY GIVES ME EXTRA TOTS, SOMETIMES.
AND DO YOU SEE ME GETTING ALL WEIRD ABOUT IT?

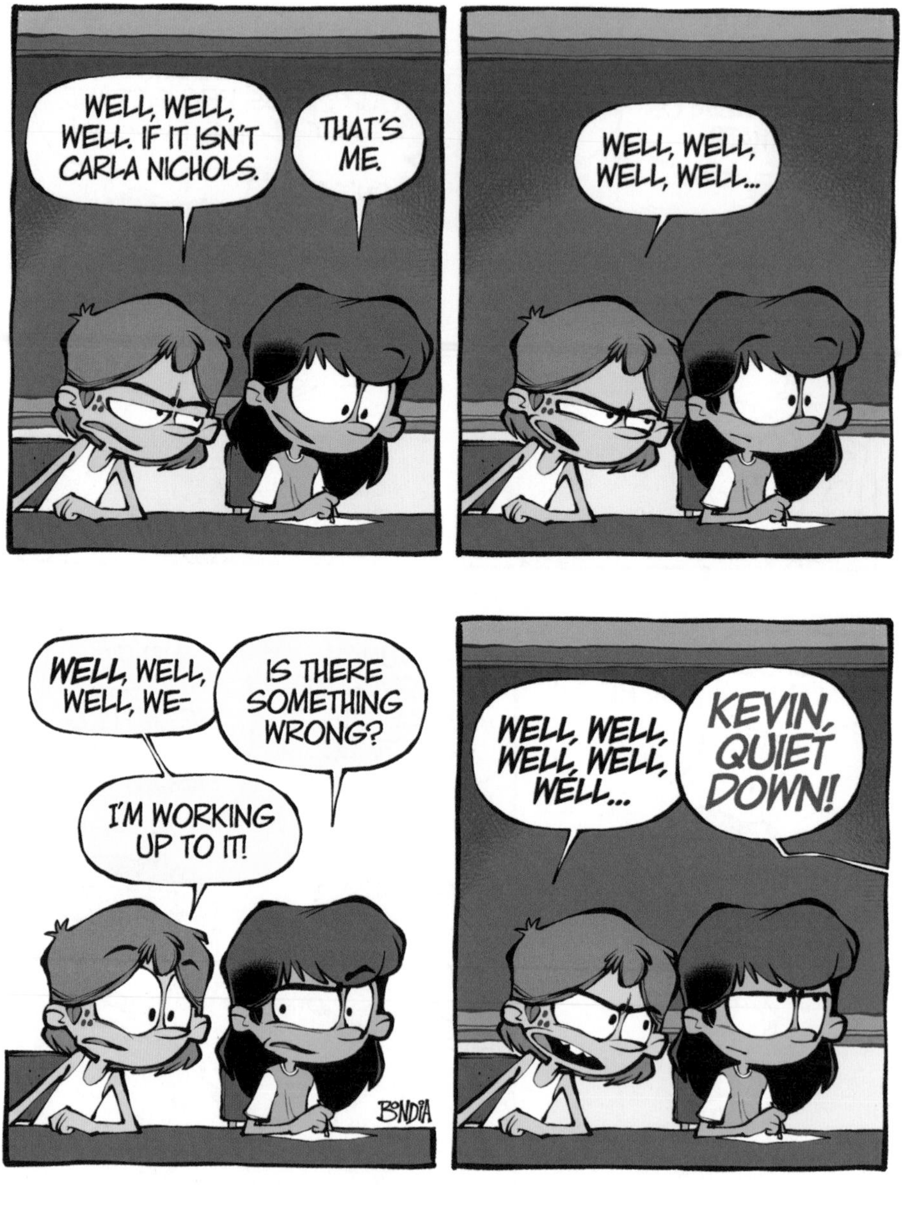

WELL, WELL, WELL. IF IT ISN'T CARLA NICHOLS.
THAT'S ME.
WELL, WELL, WELL, WELL...
WELL, WELL, WELL, WE-
IS THERE SOMETHING WRONG?
I'M WORKING UP TO IT!
BONDIA
WELL, WELL, WELL, WELL, WELL...
KEVIN, QUIET DOWN!

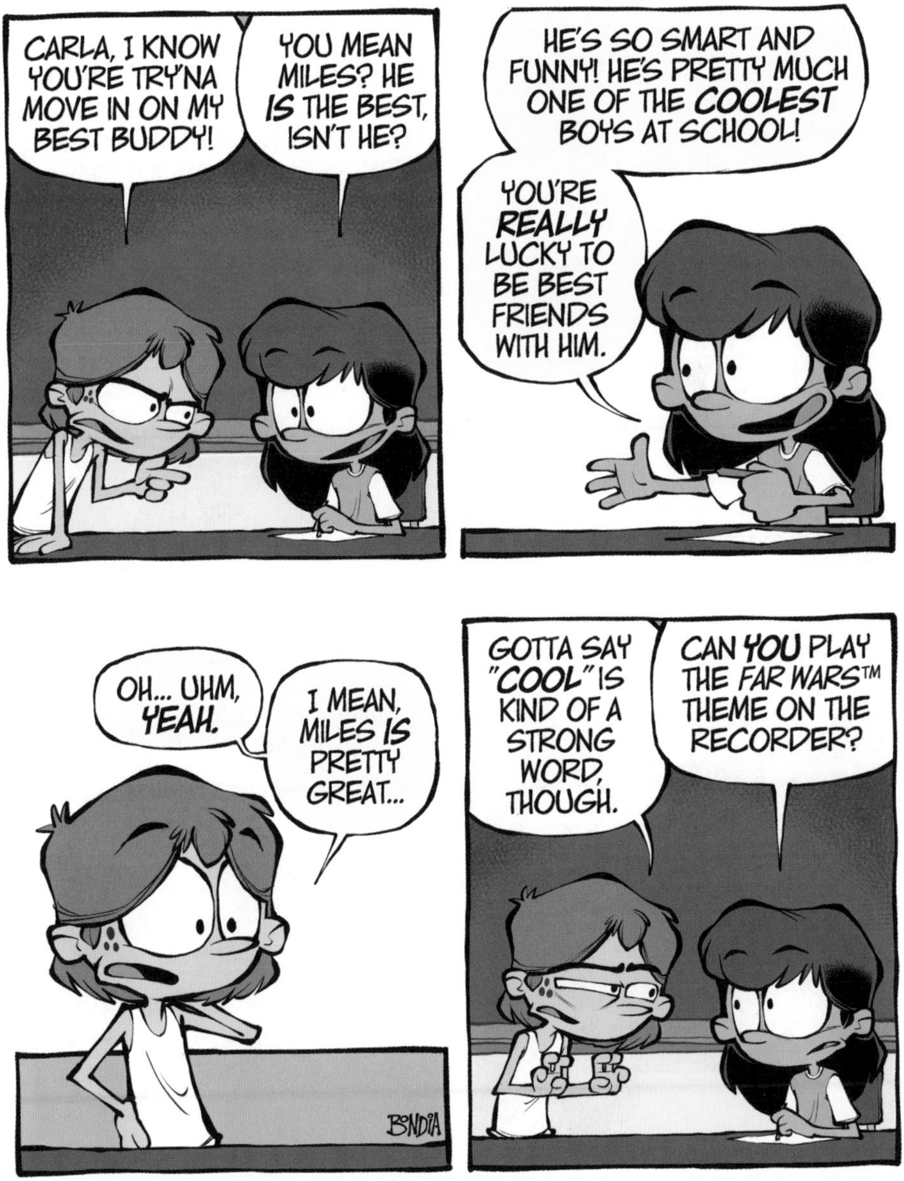
CARLA, I KNOW YOU'RE TRY'NA MOVE IN ON MY BEST BUDDY!
YOU MEAN MILES? HE **IS** THE BEST, ISN'T HE?
HE'S SO SMART AND FUNNY! HE'S PRETTY MUCH ONE OF THE **COOLEST** BOYS AT SCHOOL!
YOU'RE **REALLY** LUCKY TO BE BEST FRIENDS WITH HIM.
OH... UHM, **YEAH.**
I MEAN, MILES **IS** PRETTY GREAT...
BONDIA
GOTTA SAY "**COOL**" IS KIND OF A STRONG WORD, THOUGH.
CAN **YOU** PLAY THE *FAR WARS*™ THEME ON THE RECORDER?

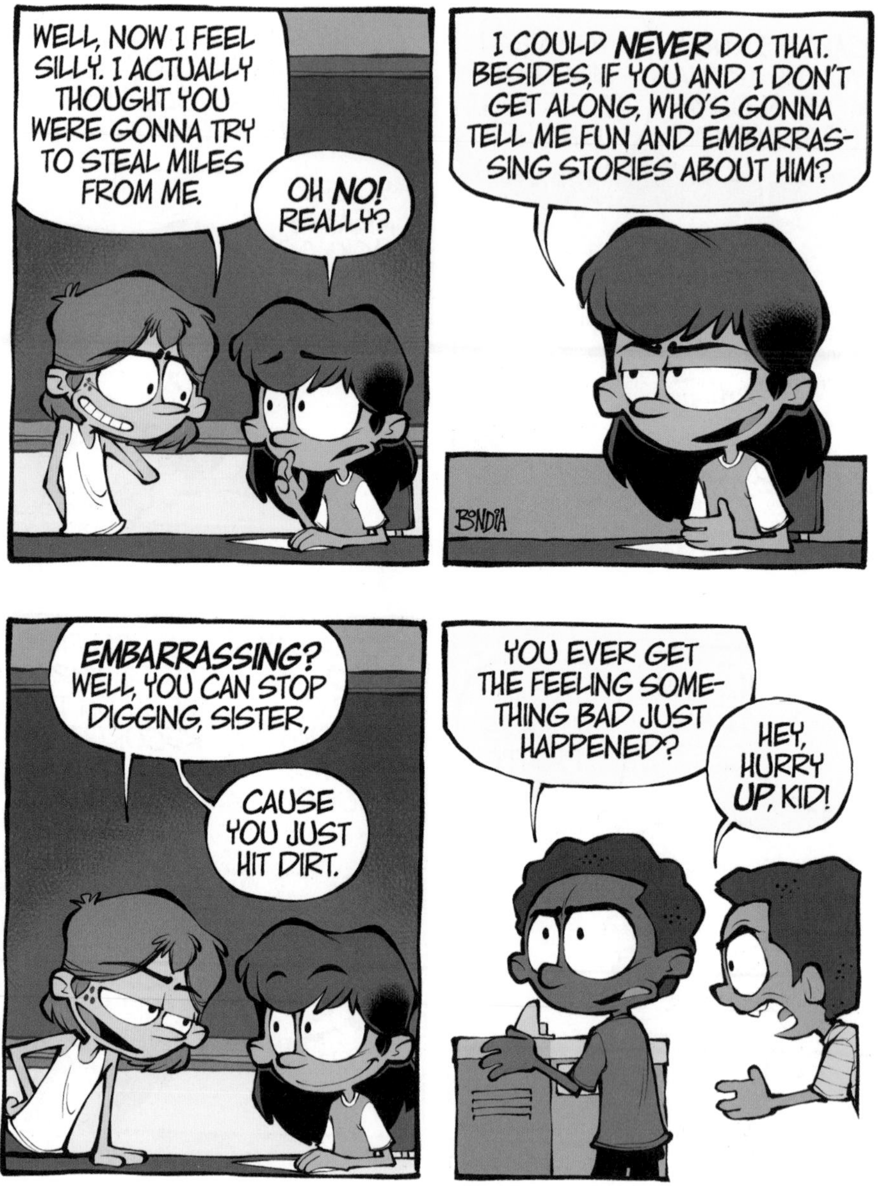
WELL, NOW I FEEL SILLY. I ACTUALLY THOUGHT YOU WERE GONNA TRY TO STEAL MILES FROM ME.
OH NO! REALLY?
I COULD NEVER DO THAT. BESIDES, IF YOU AND I DON'T GET ALONG, WHO'S GONNA TELL ME FUN AND EMBARRAS-SING STORIES ABOUT HIM?
BONDIA
EMBARRASSING? WELL, YOU CAN STOP DIGGING, SISTER,
CAUSE YOU JUST HIT DIRT.
YOU EVER GET THE FEELING SOME-THING BAD JUST HAPPENED?
HEY, HURRY UP, KID!

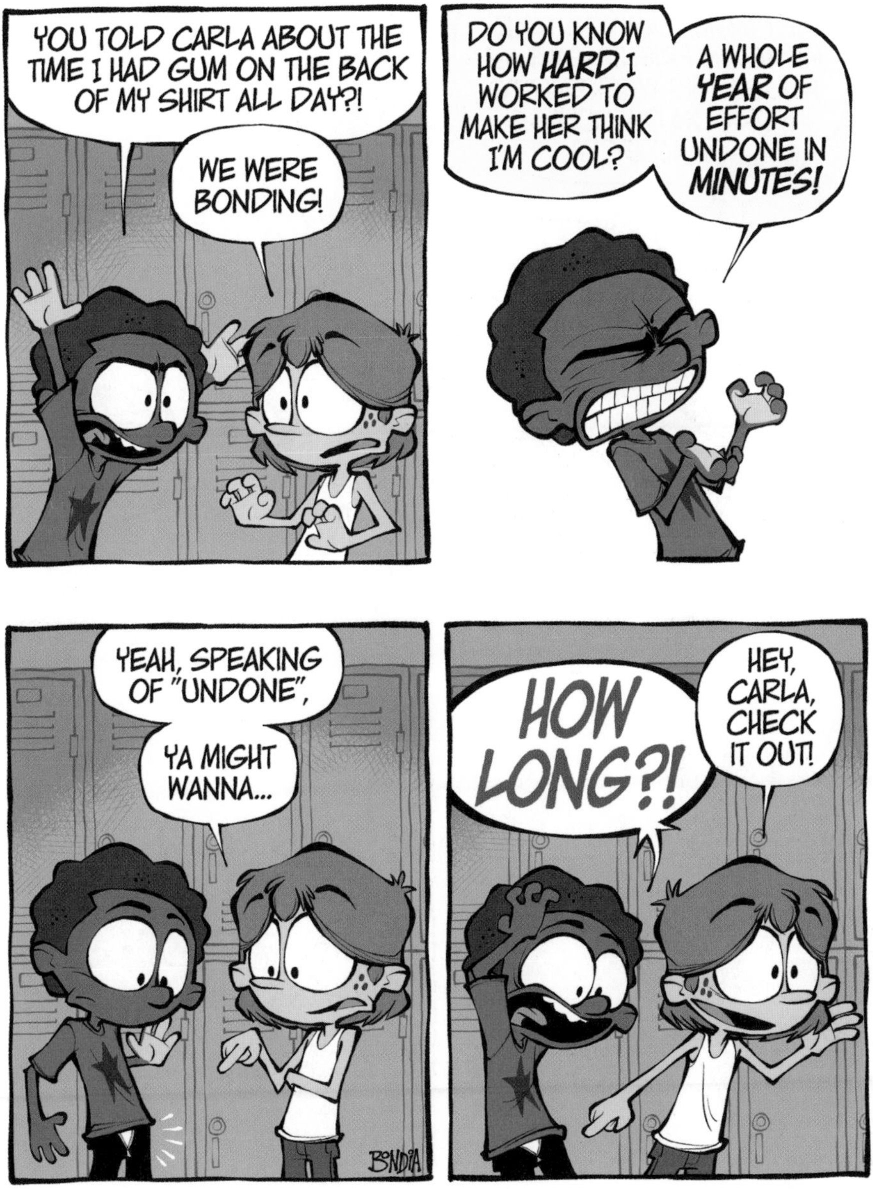
YOU TOLD CARLA ABOUT THE TIME I HAD GUM ON THE BACK OF MY SHIRT ALL DAY?!
WE WERE BONDING!
DO YOU KNOW HOW **HARD** I WORKED TO MAKE HER THINK I'M COOL?
A WHOLE **YEAR** OF EFFORT UNDONE IN **MINUTES!**
YEAH, SPEAKING OF "UNDONE",
YA MIGHT WANNA...
BONDIA
HOW LONG?!
HEY, CARLA, CHECK IT OUT!

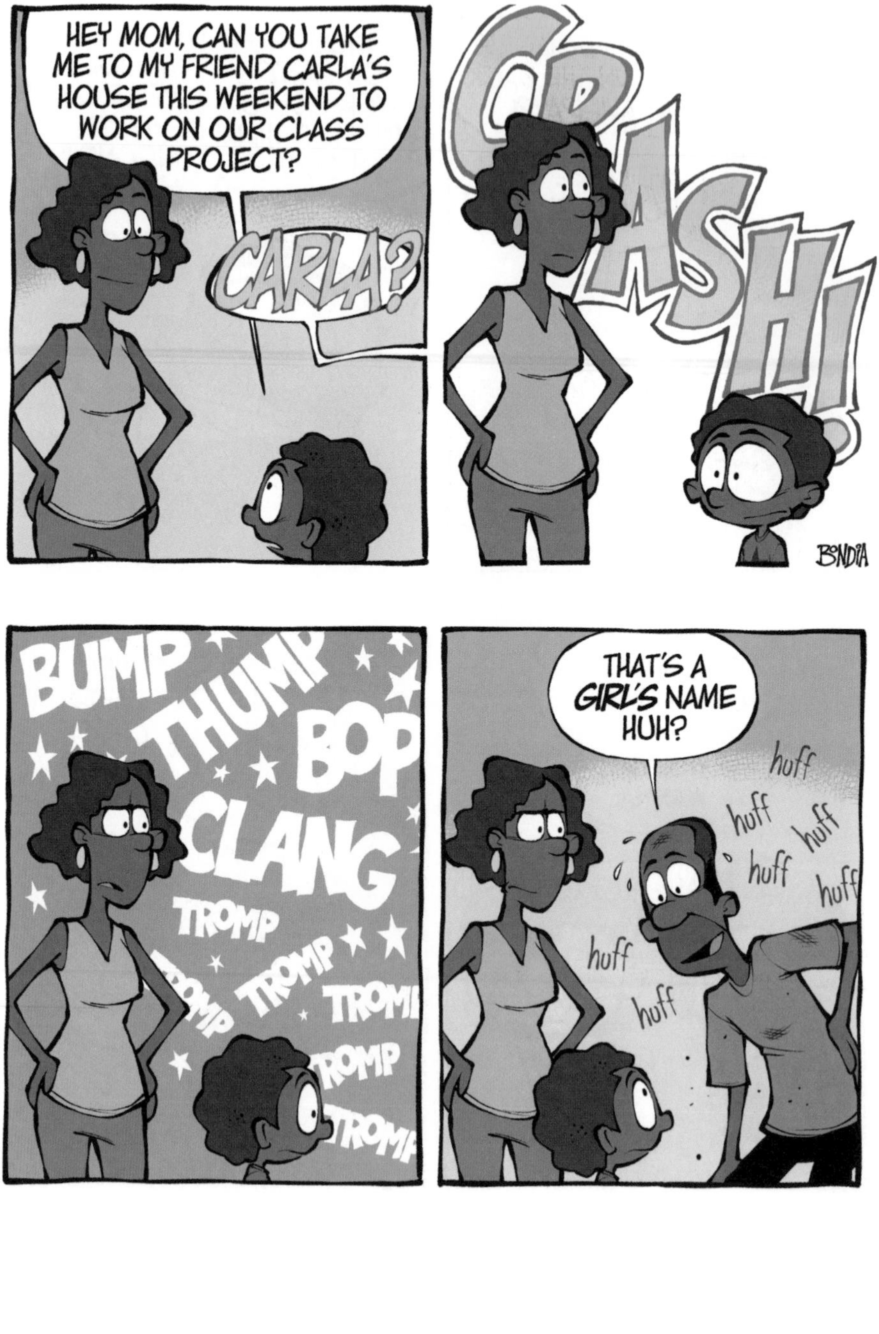
HEY MOM, CAN YOU TAKE ME TO MY FRIEND CARLA'S HOUSE THIS WEEKEND TO WORK ON OUR CLASS PROJECT?
CARLA?
CRASH!
BUMP
THUMP
BOP
CLANG
TROMP
TROMP
TROMP
THAT'S A *GIRL'S* NAME HUH?
huff
huff
huff
huff
huff
huff
huff

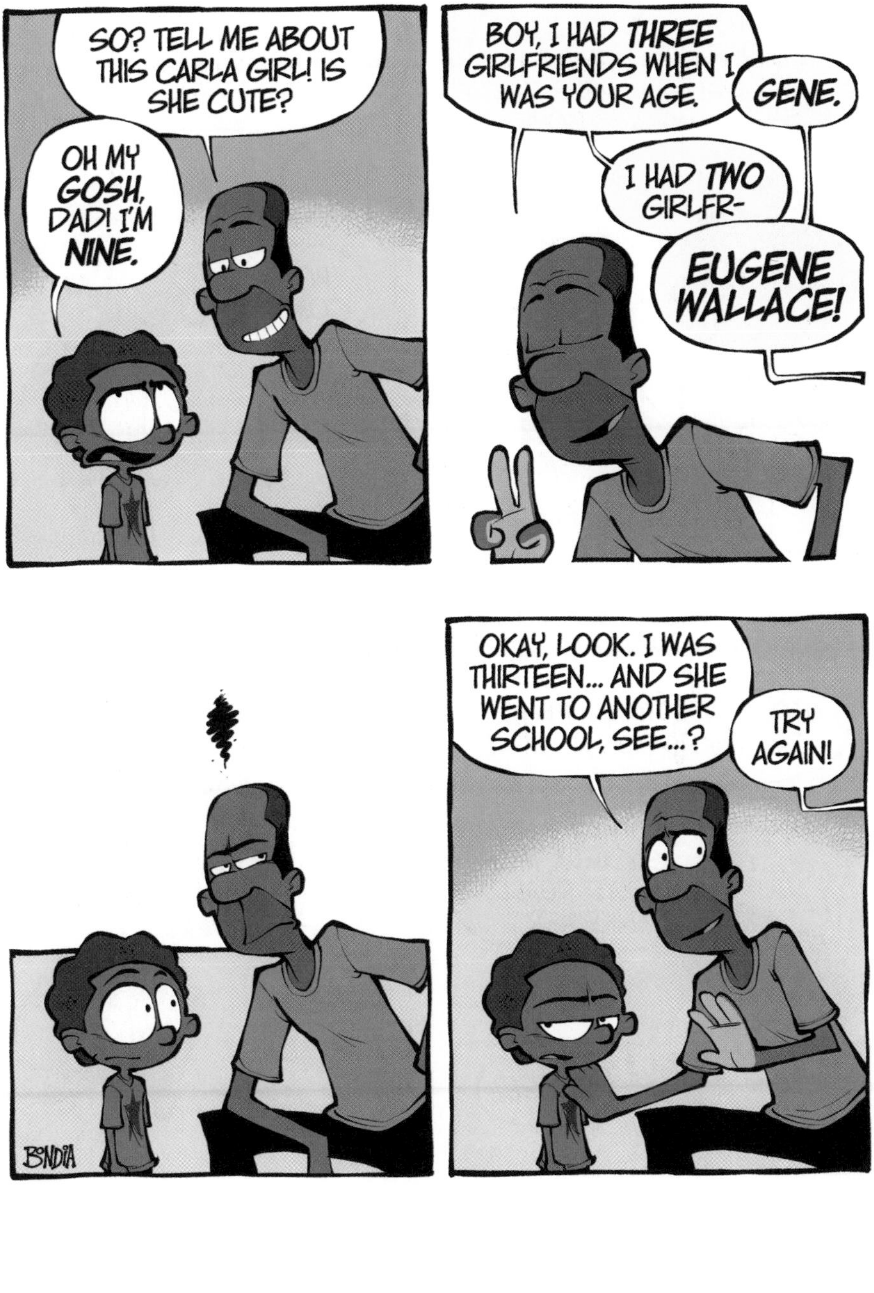
SO? TELL ME ABOUT THIS CARLA GIRL! IS SHE CUTE?
OH MY GOSH, DAD! I'M NINE.
BOY, I HAD THREE GIRLFRIENDS WHEN I WAS YOUR AGE.
I HAD TWO GIRLFR-
GENE.
EUGENE WALLACE!
OKAY, LOOK. I WAS THIRTEEN... AND SHE WENT TO ANOTHER SCHOOL, SEE...?
TRY AGAIN!
BONDIA

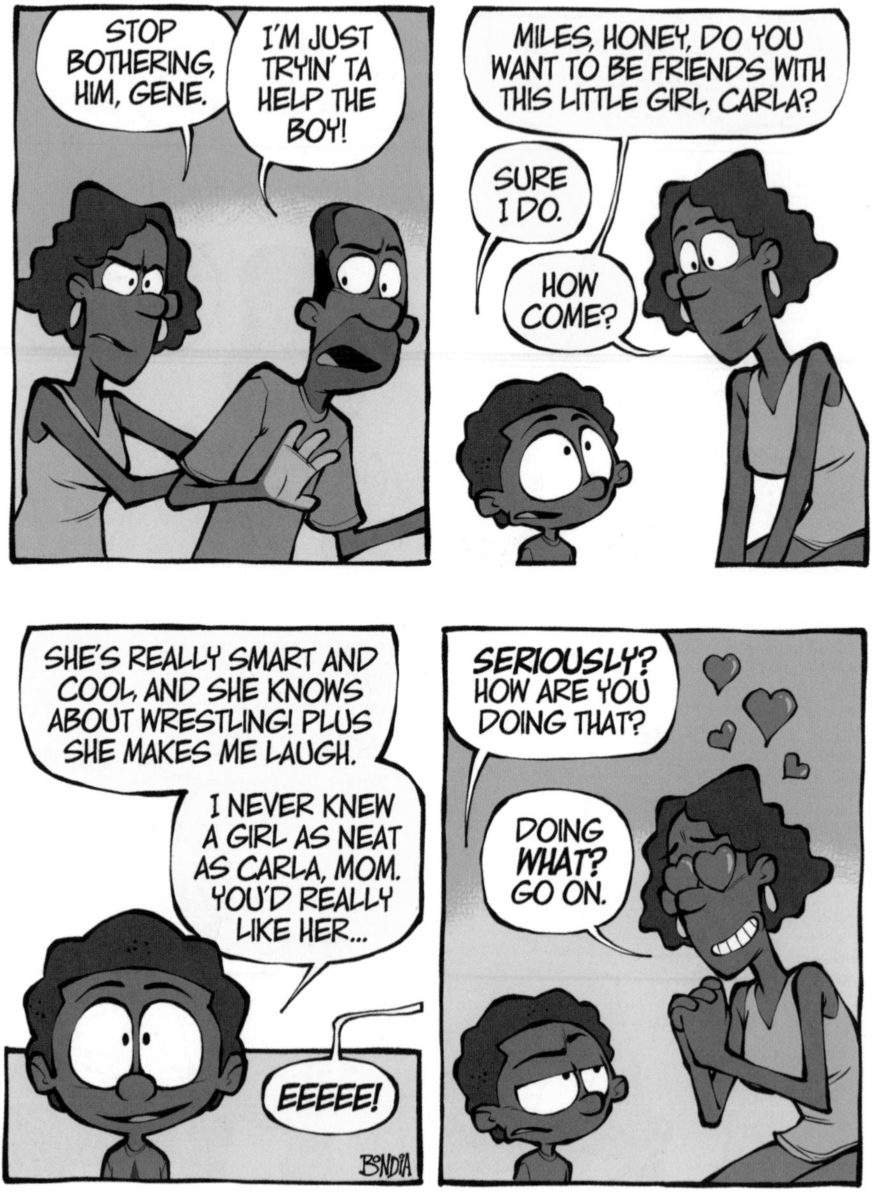

STOP BOTHERING, HIM, GENE.
I'M JUST TRYIN' TA HELP THE BOY!
MILES, HONEY, DO YOU WANT TO BE FRIENDS WITH THIS LITTLE GIRL, CARLA?
SURE I DO.
HOW COME?
SHE'S REALLY SMART AND COOL, AND SHE KNOWS ABOUT WRESTLING! PLUS SHE MAKES ME LAUGH.
I NEVER KNEW A GIRL AS NEAT AS CARLA, MOM. YOU'D REALLY LIKE HER...
EEEEE!
BONDIA
SERIOUSLY? HOW ARE YOU DOING THAT?
DOING WHAT? GO ON.

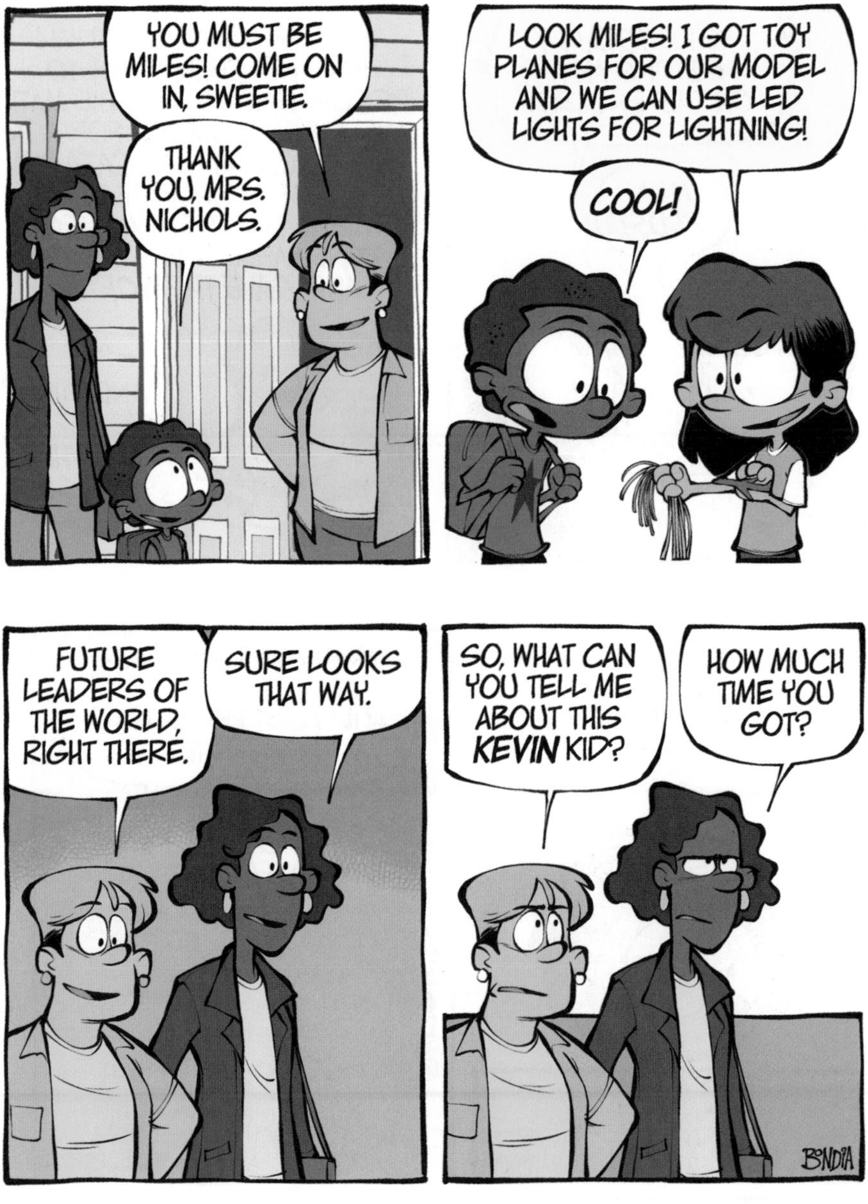
YOU MUST BE MILES! COME ON IN, SWEETIE.
THANK YOU, MRS. NICHOLS.
LOOK MILES! I GOT TOY PLANES FOR OUR MODEL AND WE CAN USE LED LIGHTS FOR LIGHTNING!
COOL!
FUTURE LEADERS OF THE WORLD, RIGHT THERE.
SURE LOOKS THAT WAY.
SO, WHAT CAN YOU TELL ME ABOUT THIS KEVIN KID?
HOW MUCH TIME YOU GOT?
BONDIA

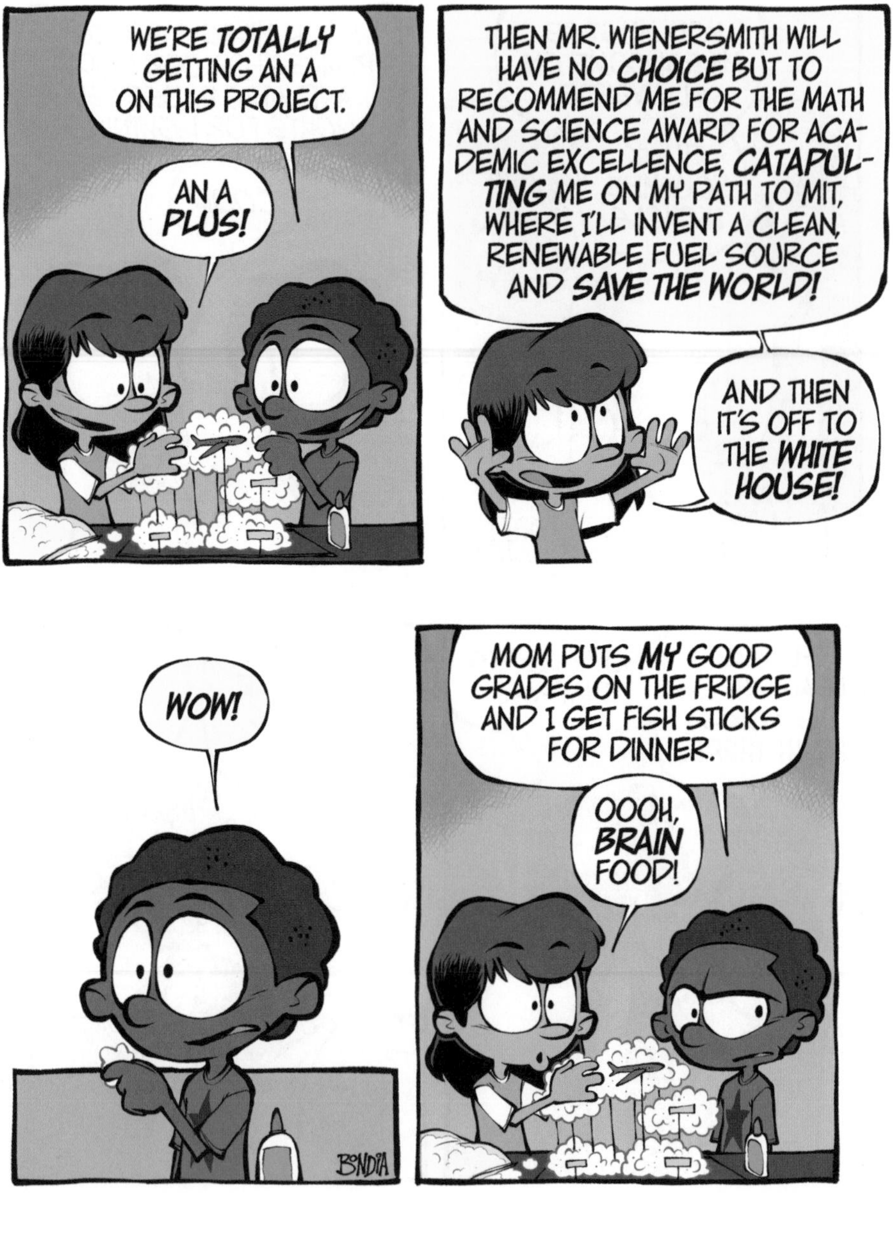

WE'RE TOTALLY GETTING AN A ON THIS PROJECT.
AN A PLUS!
THEN MR. WIENERSMITH WILL HAVE NO CHOICE BUT TO RECOMMEND ME FOR THE MATH AND SCIENCE AWARD FOR ACADEMIC EXCELLENCE, CATAPULTING ME ON MY PATH TO MIT, WHERE I'LL INVENT A CLEAN, RENEWABLE FUEL SOURCE AND SAVE THE WORLD!
AND THEN IT'S OFF TO THE WHITE HOUSE!
WOW!
BONDIA
MOM PUTS MY GOOD GRADES ON THE FRIDGE AND I GET FISH STICKS FOR DINNER.
OOOH, BRAIN FOOD!

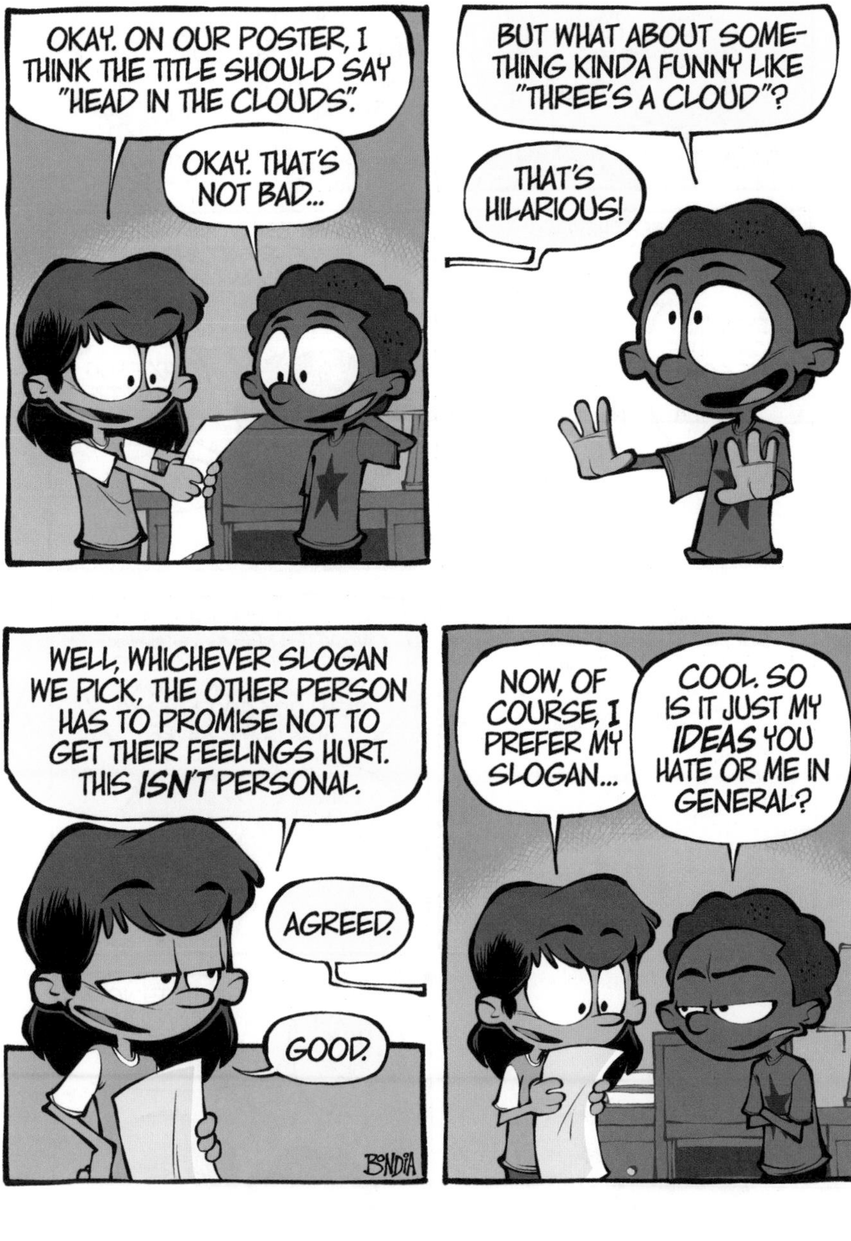

OKAY. ON OUR POSTER, I THINK THE TITLE SHOULD SAY "HEAD IN THE CLOUDS".
OKAY. THAT'S NOT BAD...
BUT WHAT ABOUT SOMETHING KINDA FUNNY LIKE "THREE'S A CLOUD"?
THAT'S HILARIOUS!
WELL, WHICHEVER SLOGAN WE PICK, THE OTHER PERSON HAS TO PROMISE NOT TO GET THEIR FEELINGS HURT. THIS *ISN'T* PERSONAL.
AGREED.
GOOD.
BONDIA
NOW, OF COURSE, *I* PREFER MY SLOGAN...
COOL. SO IS IT JUST MY *IDEAS* YOU HATE OR ME IN GENERAL?

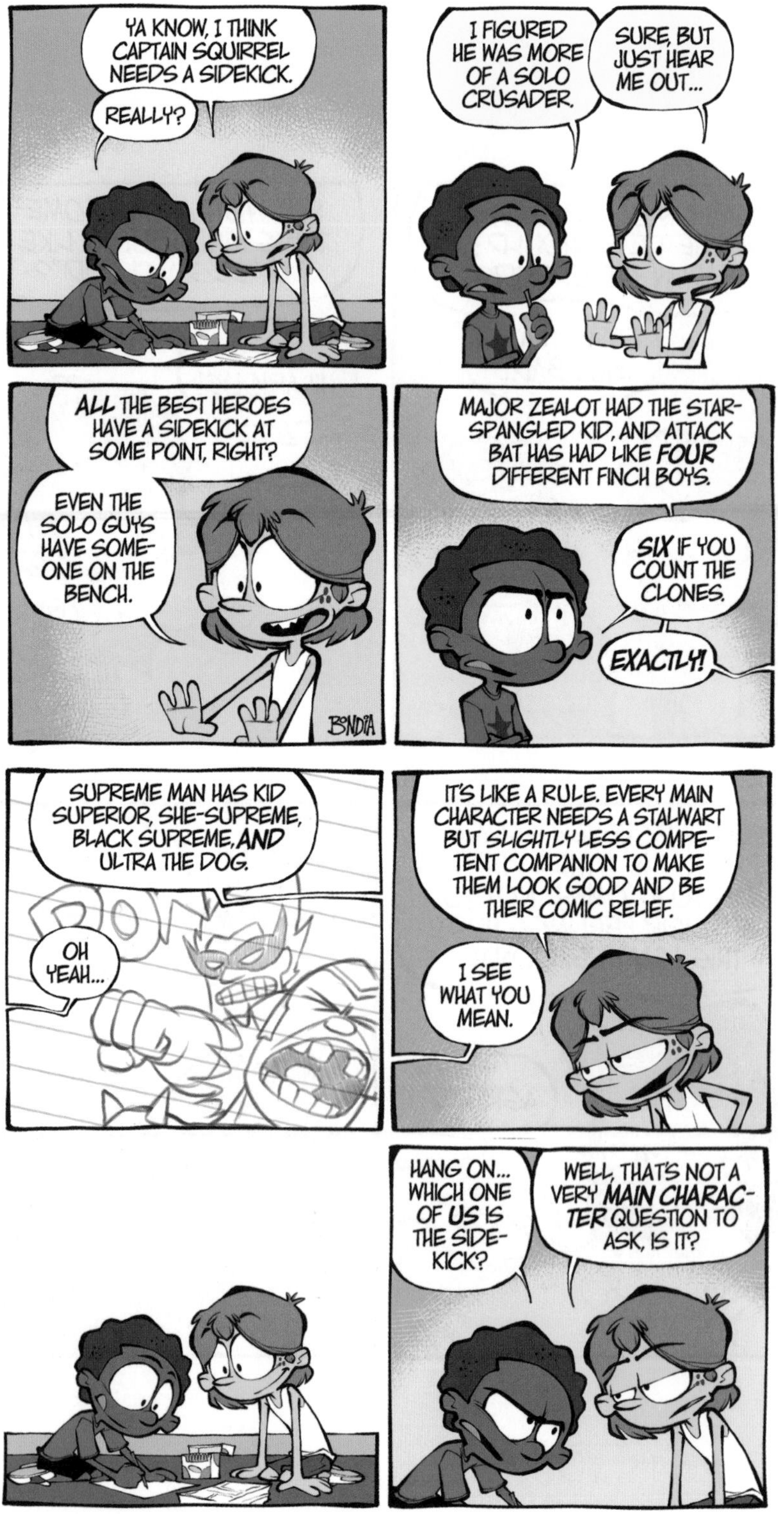
YA KNOW, I THINK CAPTAIN SQUIRREL NEEDS A SIDEKICK.
REALLY?
I FIGURED HE WAS MORE OF A SOLO CRUSADER.
SURE, BUT JUST HEAR ME OUT...
ALL THE BEST HEROES HAVE A SIDEKICK AT SOME POINT, RIGHT?
EVEN THE SOLO GUYS HAVE SOME-ONE ON THE BENCH.
BONDIA
MAJOR ZEALOT HAD THE STAR-SPANGLED KID, AND ATTACK BAT HAS HAD LIKE FOUR DIFFERENT FINCH BOYS.
SIX IF YOU COUNT THE CLONES.
EXACTLY!
SUPREME MAN HAS KID SUPERIOR, SHE-SUPREME, BLACK SUPREME, AND ULTRA THE DOG.
OH YEAH...
IT'S LIKE A RULE. EVERY MAIN CHARACTER NEEDS A STALWART BUT SLIGHTLY LESS COMPE-TENT COMPANION TO MAKE THEM LOOK GOOD AND BE THEIR COMIC RELIEF.
I SEE WHAT YOU MEAN.
HANG ON... WHICH ONE OF US IS THE SIDE-KICK?
WELL, THAT'S NOT A VERY MAIN CHARAC-TER QUESTION TO ASK, IS IT?

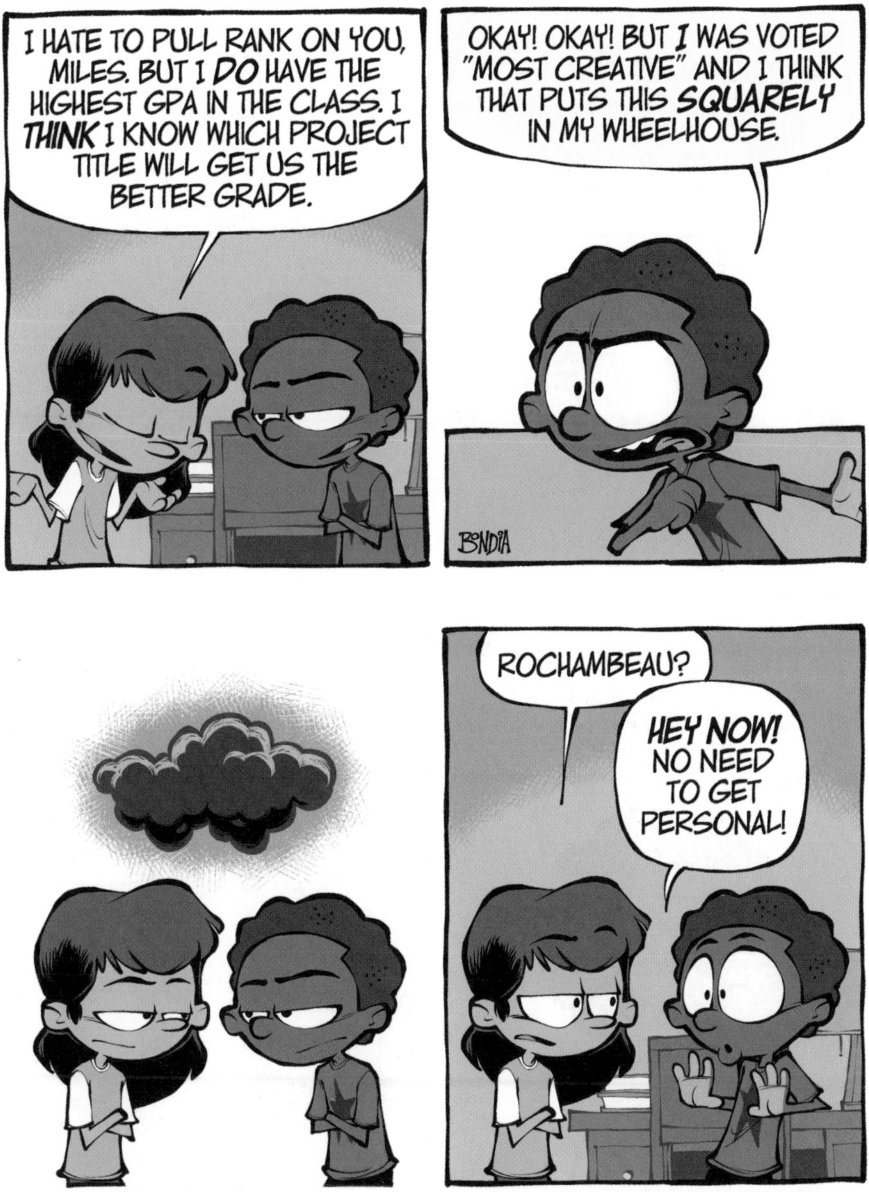
I HATE TO PULL RANK ON YOU, MILES. BUT I DO HAVE THE HIGHEST GPA IN THE CLASS. I THINK I KNOW WHICH PROJECT TITLE WILL GET US THE BETTER GRADE.
OKAY! OKAY! BUT I WAS VOTED "MOST CREATIVE" AND I THINK THAT PUTS THIS SQUARELY IN MY WHEELHOUSE.
ROCHAMBEAU?
HEY NOW! NO NEED TO GET PERSONAL!

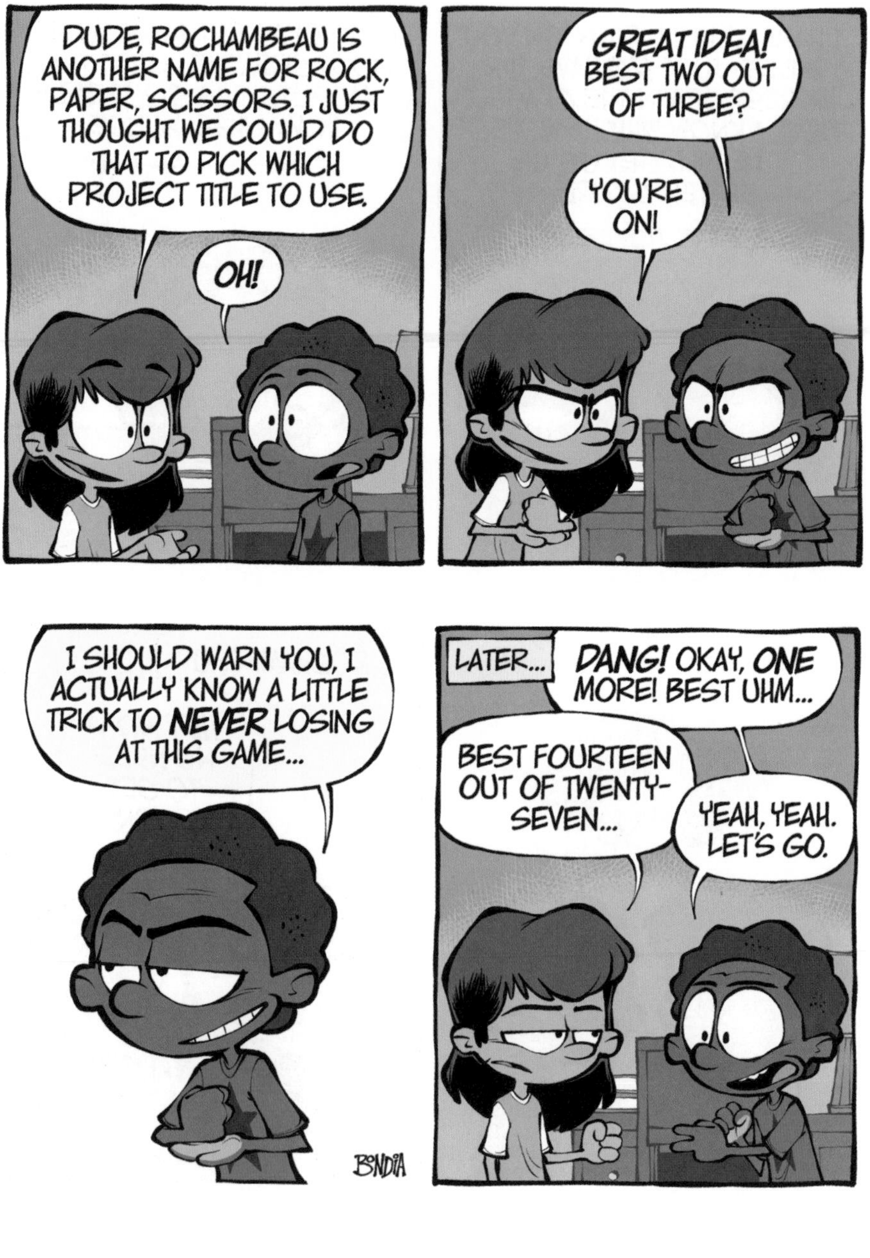
DUDE, ROCHAMBEAU IS ANOTHER NAME FOR ROCK, PAPER, SCISSORS. I JUST THOUGHT WE COULD DO THAT TO PICK WHICH PROJECT TITLE TO USE.
OH!
GREAT IDEA! BEST TWO OUT OF THREE?
YOU'RE ON!
I SHOULD WARN YOU, I ACTUALLY KNOW A LITTLE TRICK TO NEVER LOSING AT THIS GAME...
BONDIA
LATER...
DANG! OKAY, ONE MORE! BEST UHM...
BEST FOURTEEN OUT OF TWENTY-SEVEN...
YEAH, YEAH. LET'S GO.

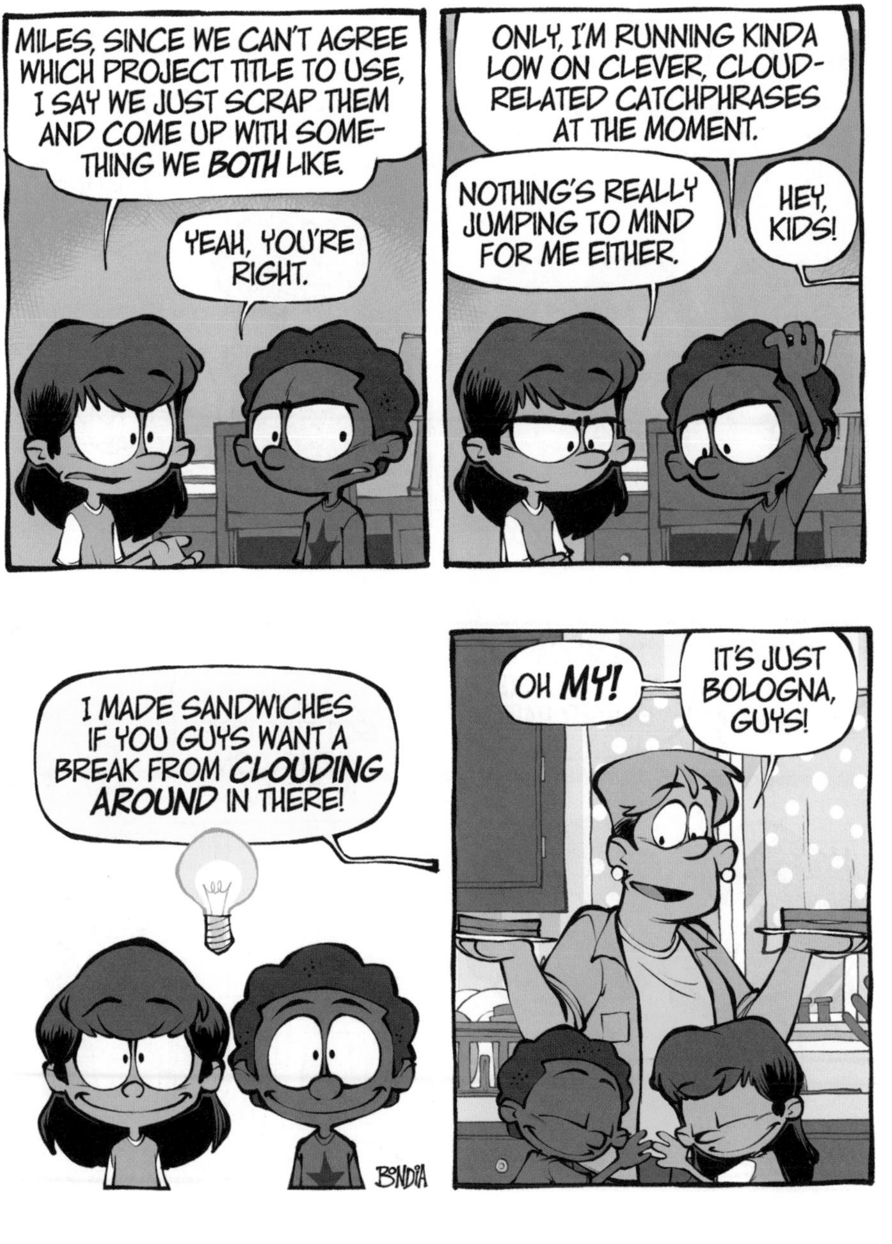

MILES, SINCE WE CAN'T AGREE WHICH PROJECT TITLE TO USE, I SAY WE JUST SCRAP THEM AND COME UP WITH SOME-THING WE **BOTH** LIKE.
YEAH, YOU'RE RIGHT.
ONLY, I'M RUNNING KINDA LOW ON CLEVER, CLOUD-RELATED CATCHPHRASES AT THE MOMENT.
NOTHING'S REALLY JUMPING TO MIND FOR ME EITHER.
HEY, KIDS!
I MADE SANDWICHES IF YOU GUYS WANT A BREAK FROM **CLOUDING AROUND** IN THERE!
BONDIA
OH **MY**!
IT'S JUST BOLOGNA, GUYS!

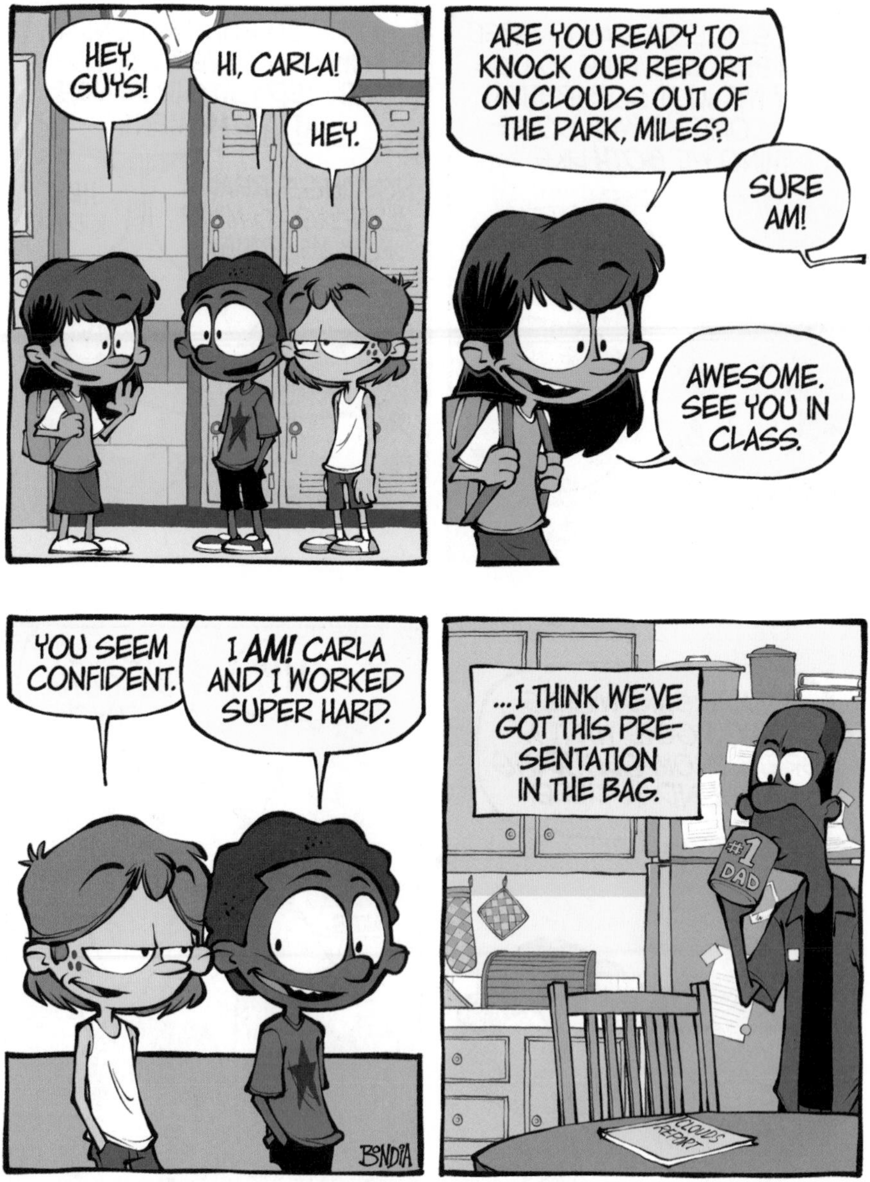
HEY, GUYS!
HI, CARLA!
HEY.
ARE YOU READY TO KNOCK OUR REPORT ON CLOUDS OUT OF THE PARK, MILES?
SURE AM!
AWESOME. SEE YOU IN CLASS.
YOU SEEM CONFIDENT.
I AM! CARLA AND I WORKED SUPER HARD.
BONDIA
...I THINK WE'VE GOT THIS PRESENTATION IN THE BAG.
#1 DAD
CLOUDS REPORT

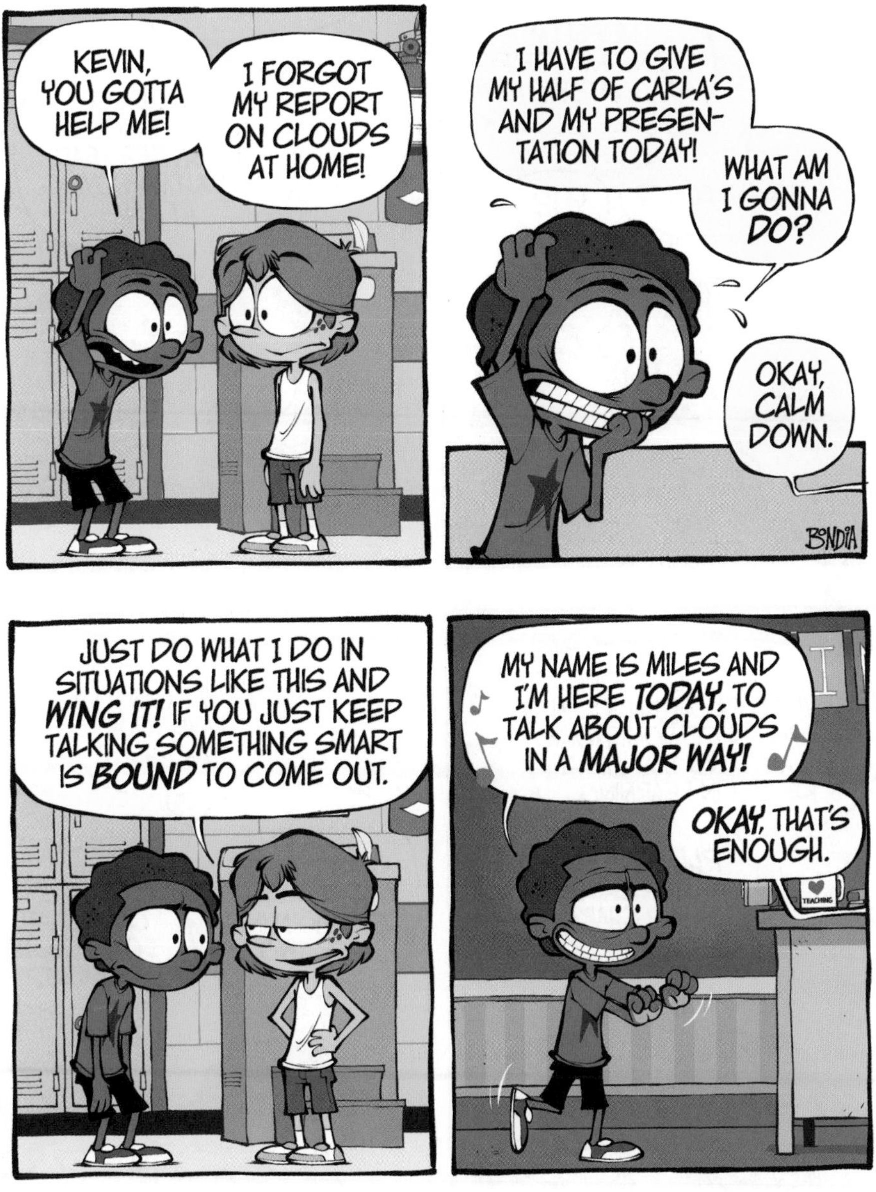
KEVIN, YOU GOTTA HELP ME!
I FORGOT MY REPORT ON CLOUDS AT HOME!
I HAVE TO GIVE MY HALF OF CARLA'S AND MY PRESEN-TATION TODAY!
WHAT AM I GONNA DO?
OKAY, CALM DOWN.
BONDIA
JUST DO WHAT I DO IN SITUATIONS LIKE THIS AND WING IT! IF YOU JUST KEEP TALKING SOMETHING SMART IS BOUND TO COME OUT.
MY NAME IS MILES AND I'M HERE TODAY, TO TALK ABOUT CLOUDS IN A MAJOR WAY!
OKAY, THAT'S ENOUGH.
TEACHING

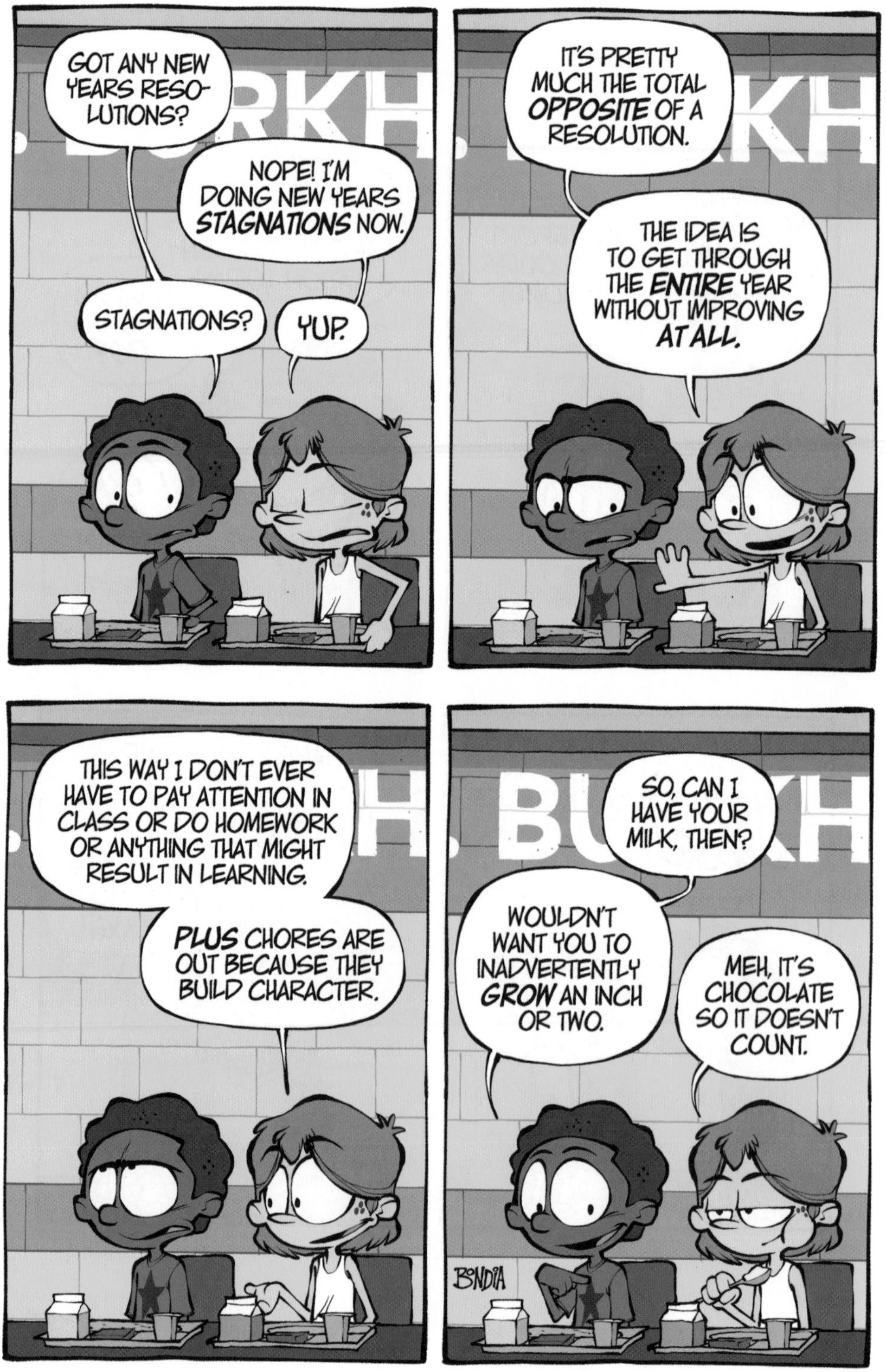
GOT ANY NEW YEARS RESO-LUTIONS?
NOPE! I'M DOING NEW YEARS STAGNATIONS NOW.
STAGNATIONS?
YUP.
IT'S PRETTY MUCH THE TOTAL OPPOSITE OF A RESOLUTION.
THE IDEA IS TO GET THROUGH THE ENTIRE YEAR WITHOUT IMPROVING AT ALL.
THIS WAY I DON'T EVER HAVE TO PAY ATTENTION IN CLASS OR DO HOMEWORK OR ANYTHING THAT MIGHT RESULT IN LEARNING.
PLUS CHORES ARE OUT BECAUSE THEY BUILD CHARACTER.
SO, CAN I HAVE YOUR MILK, THEN?
WOULDN'T WANT YOU TO INADVERTENTLY GROW AN INCH OR TWO.
MEH, IT'S CHOCOLATE SO IT DOESN'T COUNT.
BONDIA

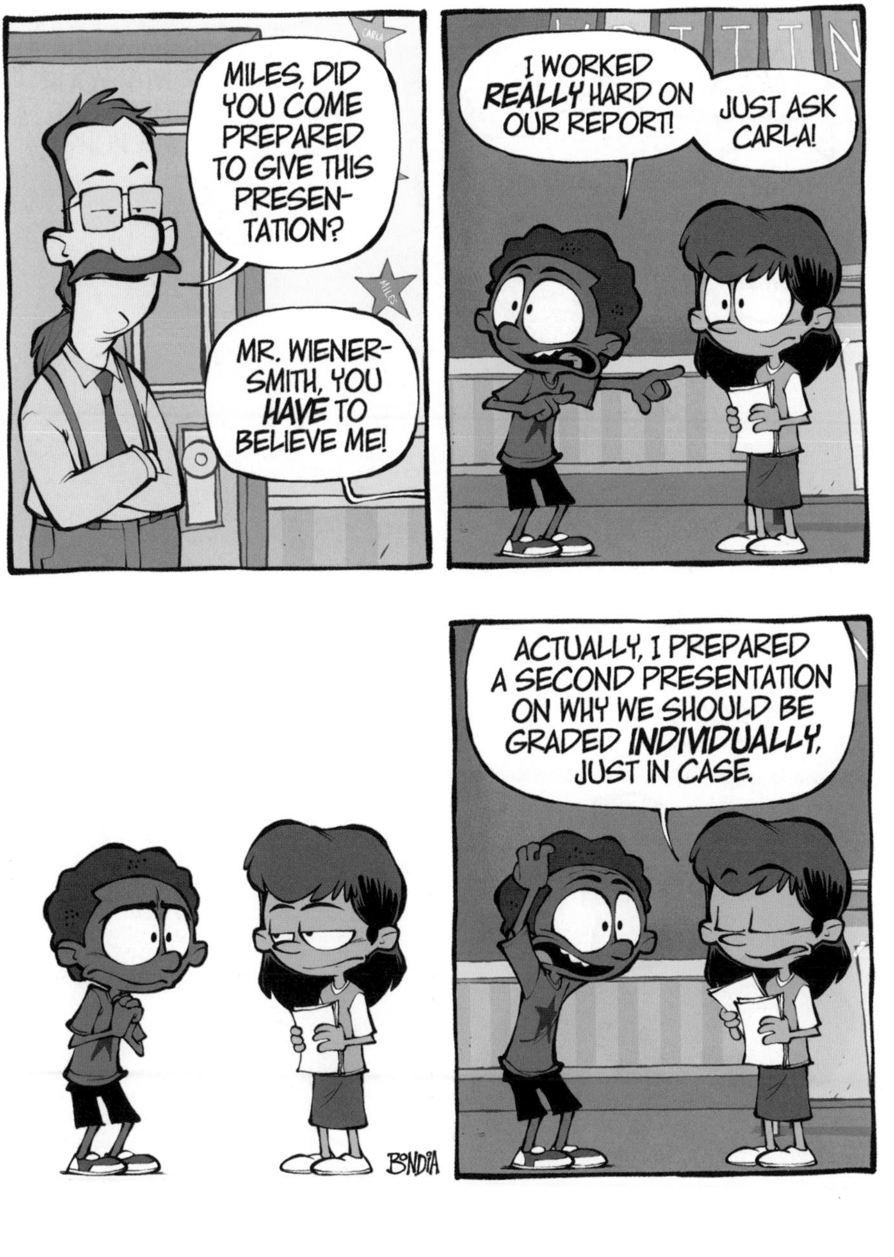
MILES, DID YOU COME PREPARED TO GIVE THIS PRESEN-TATION?
MR. WIENER-SMITH, YOU **HAVE** TO BELIEVE ME!
I WORKED **REALLY** HARD ON OUR REPORT!
JUST ASK CARLA!
ACTUALLY, I PREPARED A SECOND PRESENTATION ON WHY WE SHOULD BE GRADED **INDIVIDUALLY**, JUST IN CASE.
BONDIA

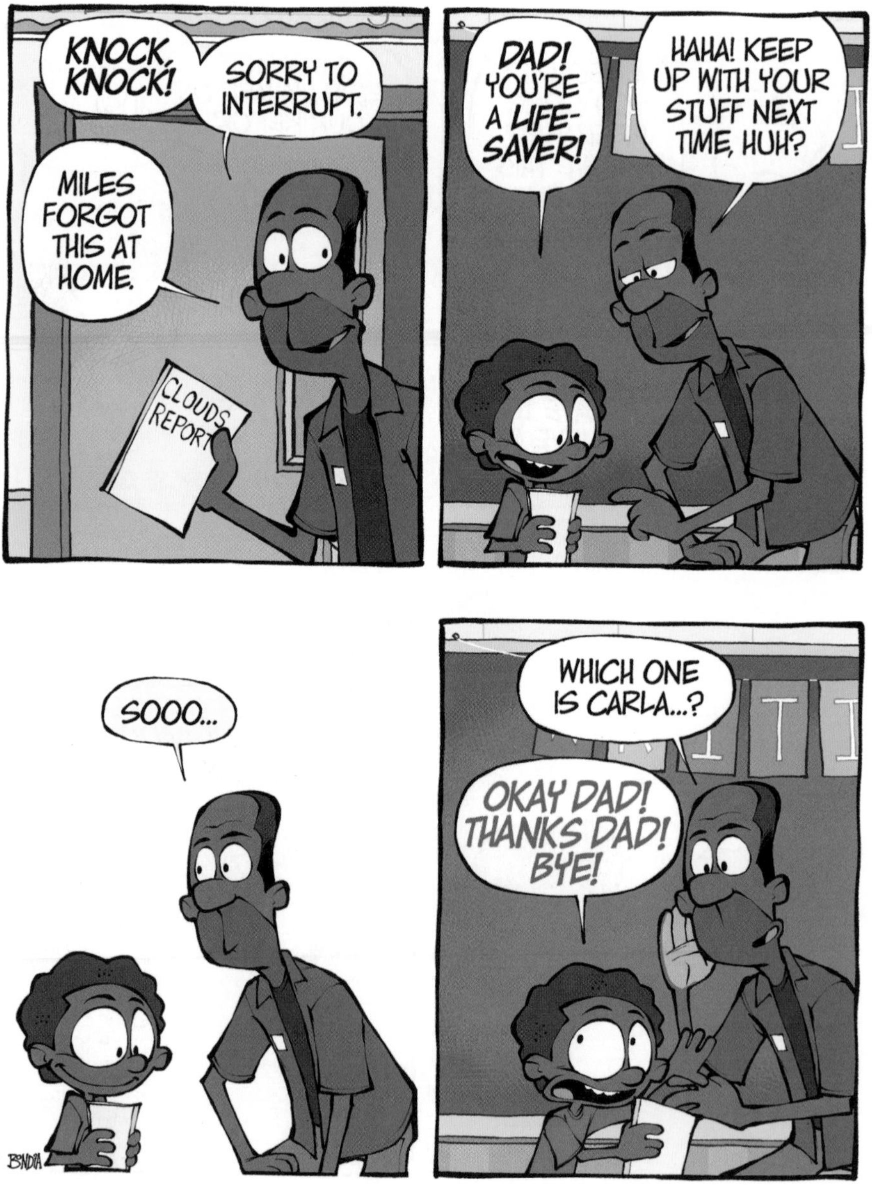
KNOCK, KNOCK!
SORRY TO INTERRUPT.
MILES FORGOT THIS AT HOME.
CLOUDS REPORT
DAD! YOU'RE A LIFE-SAVER!
HAHA! KEEP UP WITH YOUR STUFF NEXT TIME, HUH?
SOOO...
WHICH ONE IS CARLA...?
OKAY DAD! THANKS DAD! BYE!

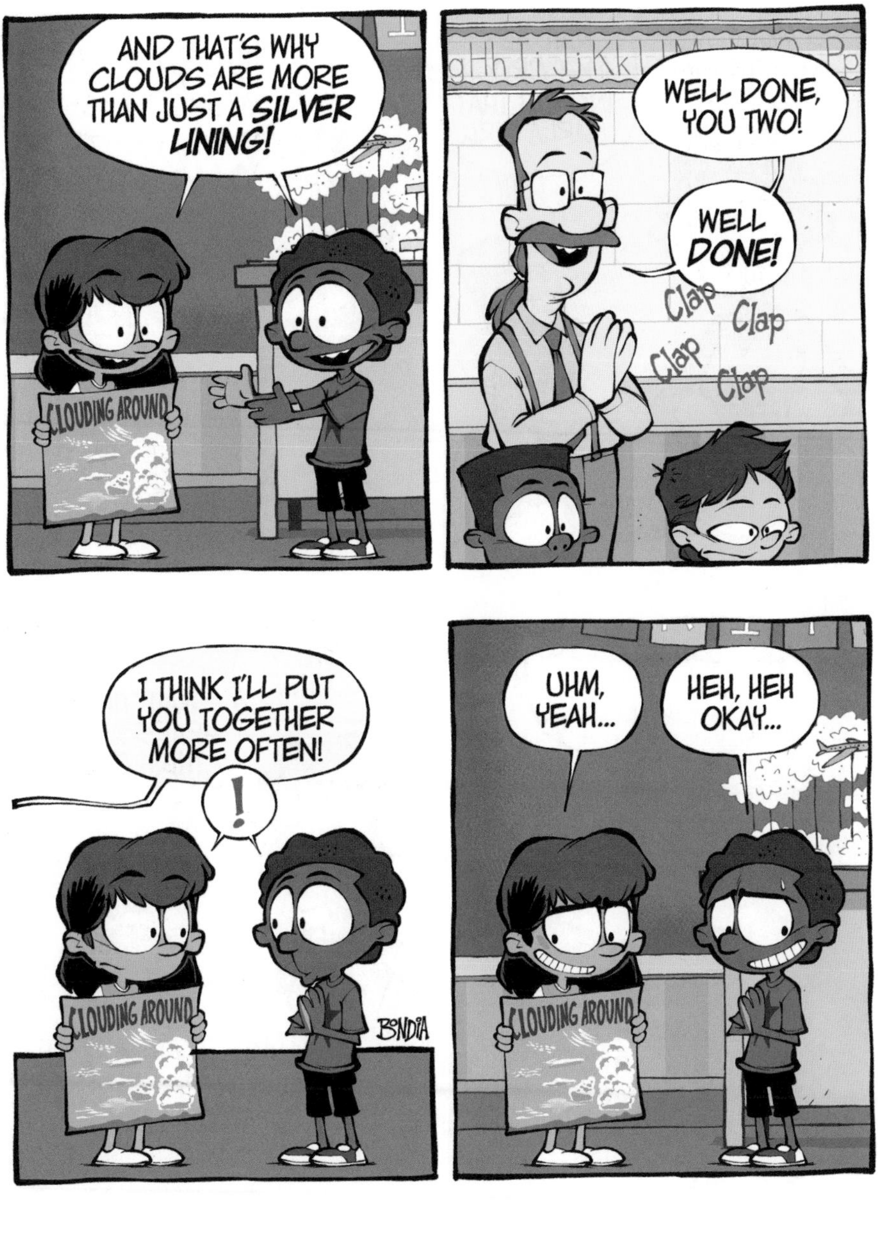
AND THAT'S WHY CLOUDS ARE MORE THAN JUST A SILVER LINING!
CLOUDING AROUND
gHh Ii Jj Kk
WELL DONE, YOU TWO!
WELL DONE!
Clap
Clap
Clap
Clap
I THINK I'LL PUT YOU TOGETHER MORE OFTEN!
!
CLOUDING AROUND
BONDIA
UHM, YEAH...
HEH, HEH OKAY...
CLOUDING AROUND

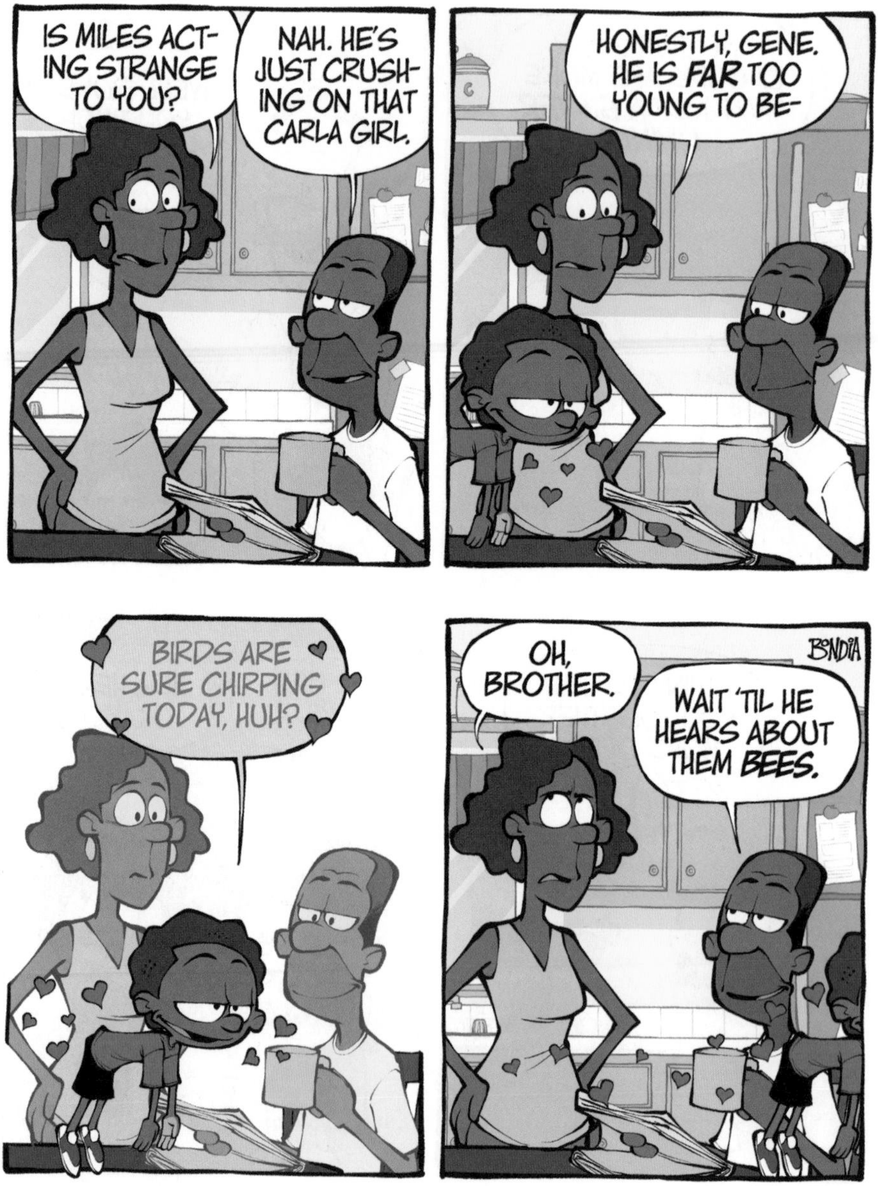
IS MILES ACTING STRANGE TO YOU?
NAH. HE'S JUST CRUSHING ON THAT CARLA GIRL.
HONESTLY, GENE. HE IS FAR TOO YOUNG TO BE-
BIRDS ARE SURE CHIRPING TODAY, HUH?
BONDIA
OH, BROTHER.
WAIT 'TIL HE HEARS ABOUT THEM BEES.

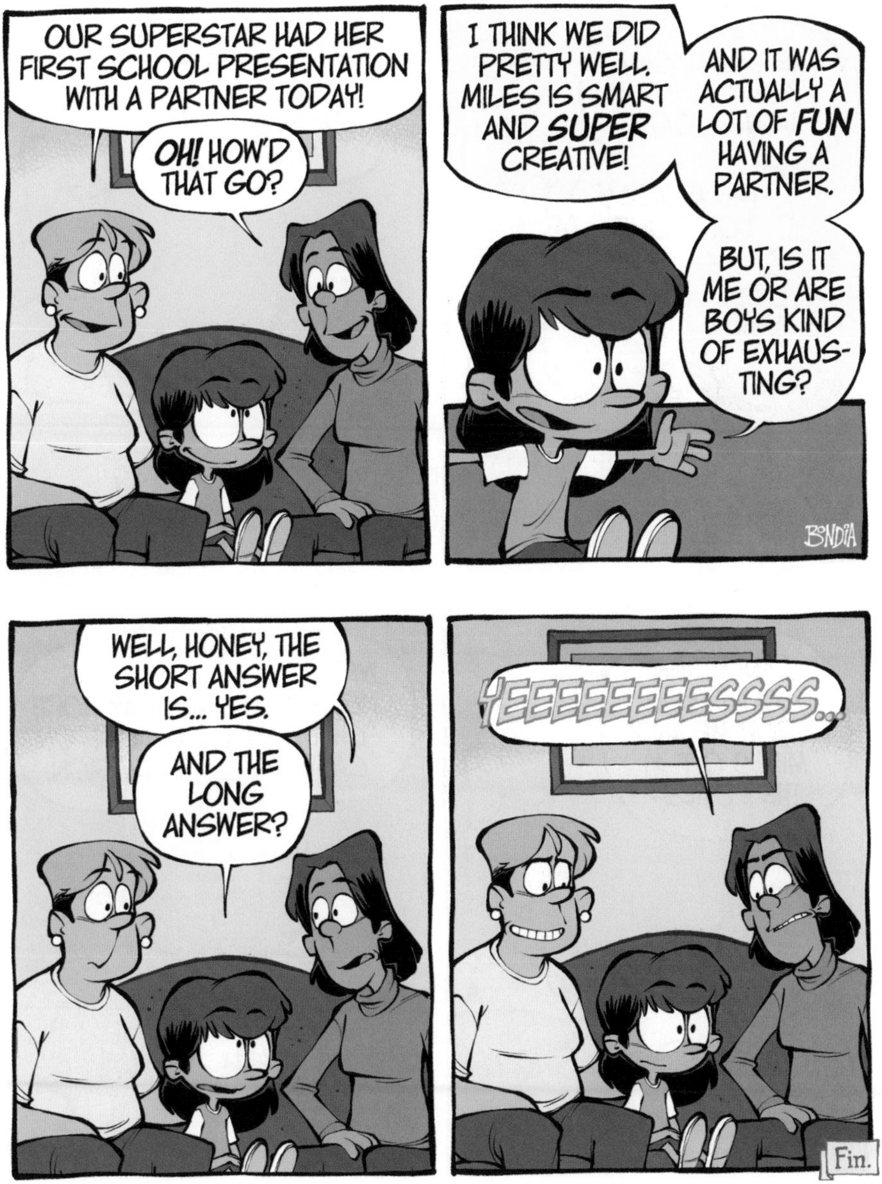
OUR SUPERSTAR HAD HER FIRST SCHOOL PRESENTATION WITH A PARTNER TODAY!
OH! HOW'D THAT GO?
I THINK WE DID PRETTY WELL. MILES IS SMART AND SUPER CREATIVE!
AND IT WAS ACTUALLY A LOT OF FUN HAVING A PARTNER.
BUT, IS IT ME OR ARE BOYS KIND OF EXHAUS-TING?
BONDIA
WELL, HONEY, THE SHORT ANSWER IS... YES.
AND THE LONG ANSWER?
YEEEEEEEEESSSS...
Fin.

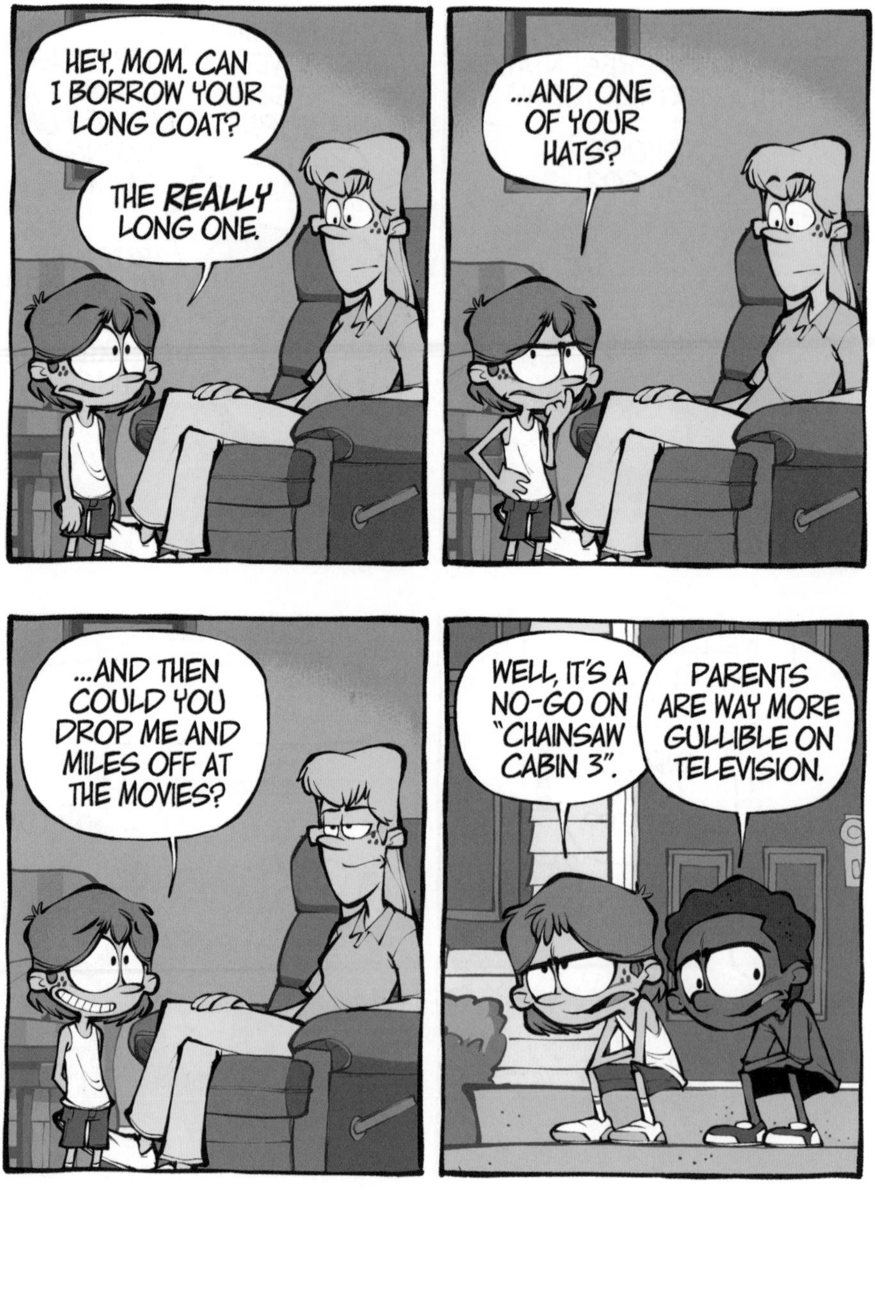
HEY, MOM. CAN I BORROW YOUR LONG COAT?
THE REALLY LONG ONE.
...AND ONE OF YOUR HATS?
...AND THEN COULD YOU DROP ME AND MILES OFF AT THE MOVIES?
WELL, IT'S A NO-GO ON "CHAINSAW CABIN 3".
PARENTS ARE WAY MORE GULLIBLE ON TELEVISION.

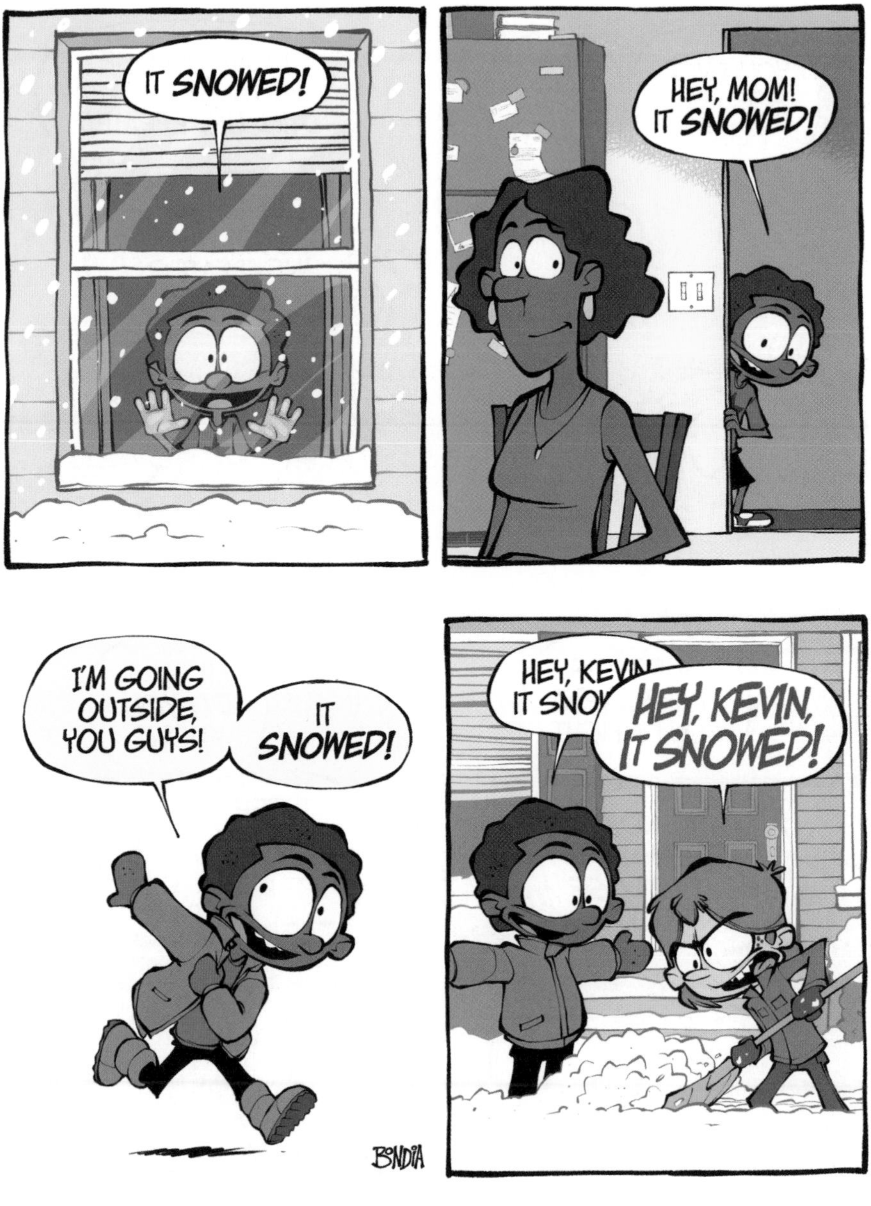
IT SNOWED!
HEY, MOM! IT SNOWED!
I'M GOING OUTSIDE, YOU GUYS!
IT SNOWED!
HEY, KEVIN, IT SNOWED!
BONDIA

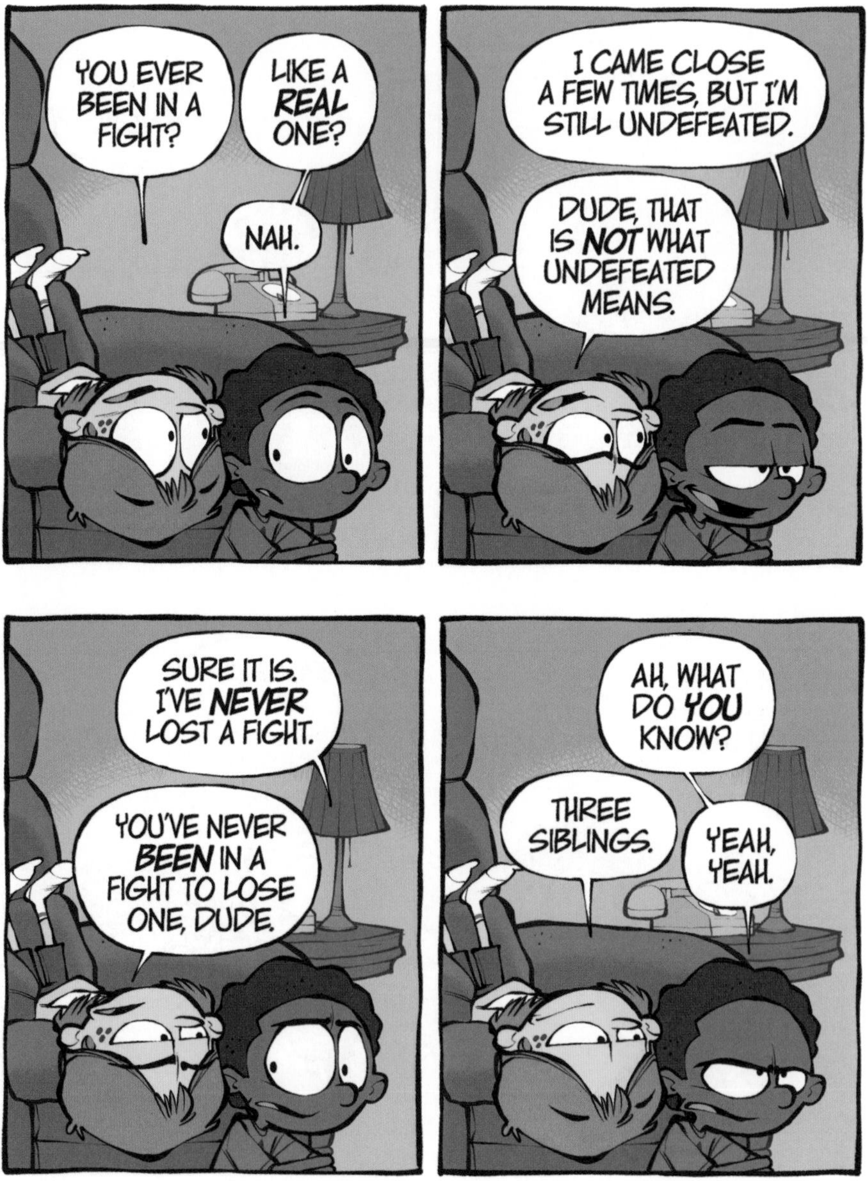
YOU EVER BEEN IN A FIGHT?
LIKE A **REAL** ONE?
NAH.
I CAME CLOSE A FEW TIMES, BUT I'M STILL UNDEFEATED.
DUDE, THAT IS **NOT** WHAT UNDEFEATED MEANS.
SURE IT IS. I'VE **NEVER** LOST A FIGHT.
YOU'VE NEVER **BEEN** IN A FIGHT TO LOSE ONE, DUDE.
AH, WHAT DO **YOU** KNOW?
THREE SIBLINGS.
YEAH, YEAH.

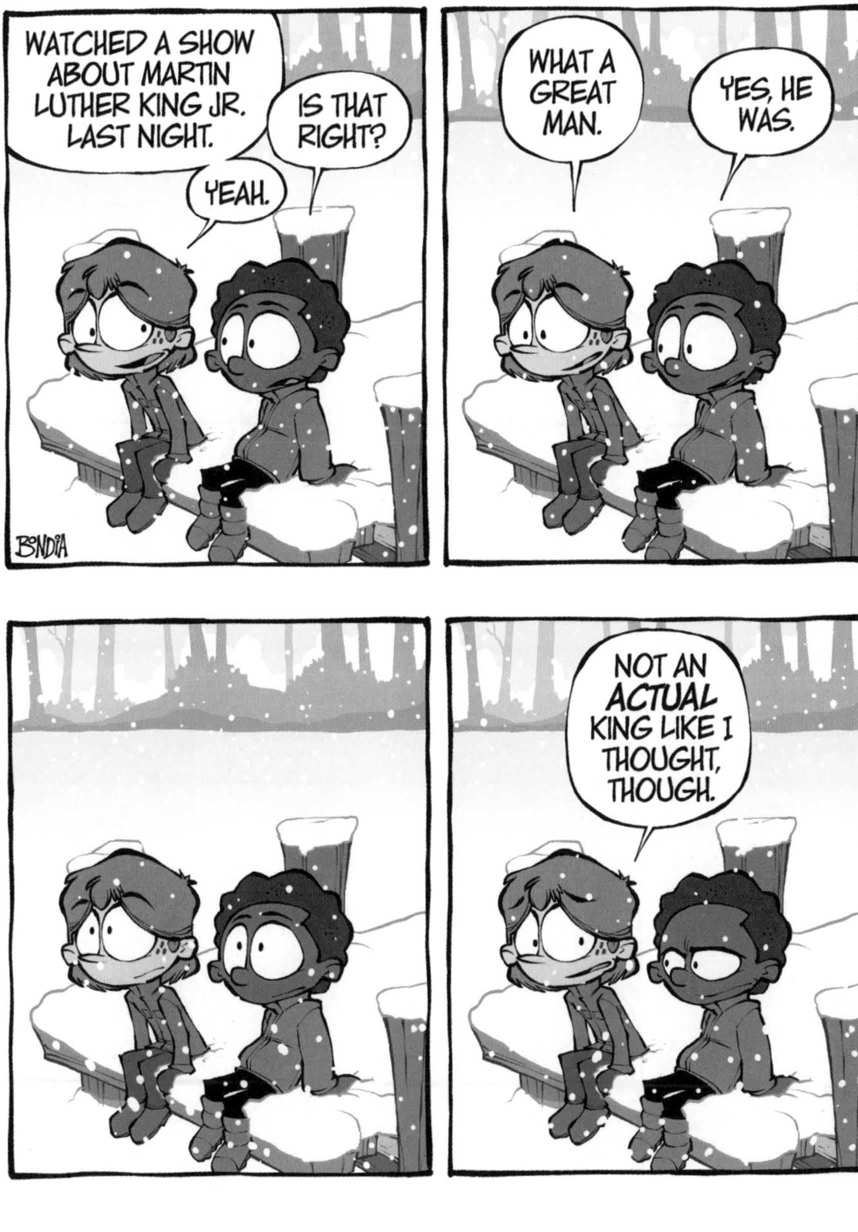
WATCHED A SHOW ABOUT MARTIN LUTHER KING JR. LAST NIGHT.
YEAH.
IS THAT RIGHT?
BONDIA
WHAT A GREAT MAN.
YES, HE WAS.
NOT AN ACTUAL KING LIKE I THOUGHT, THOUGH.

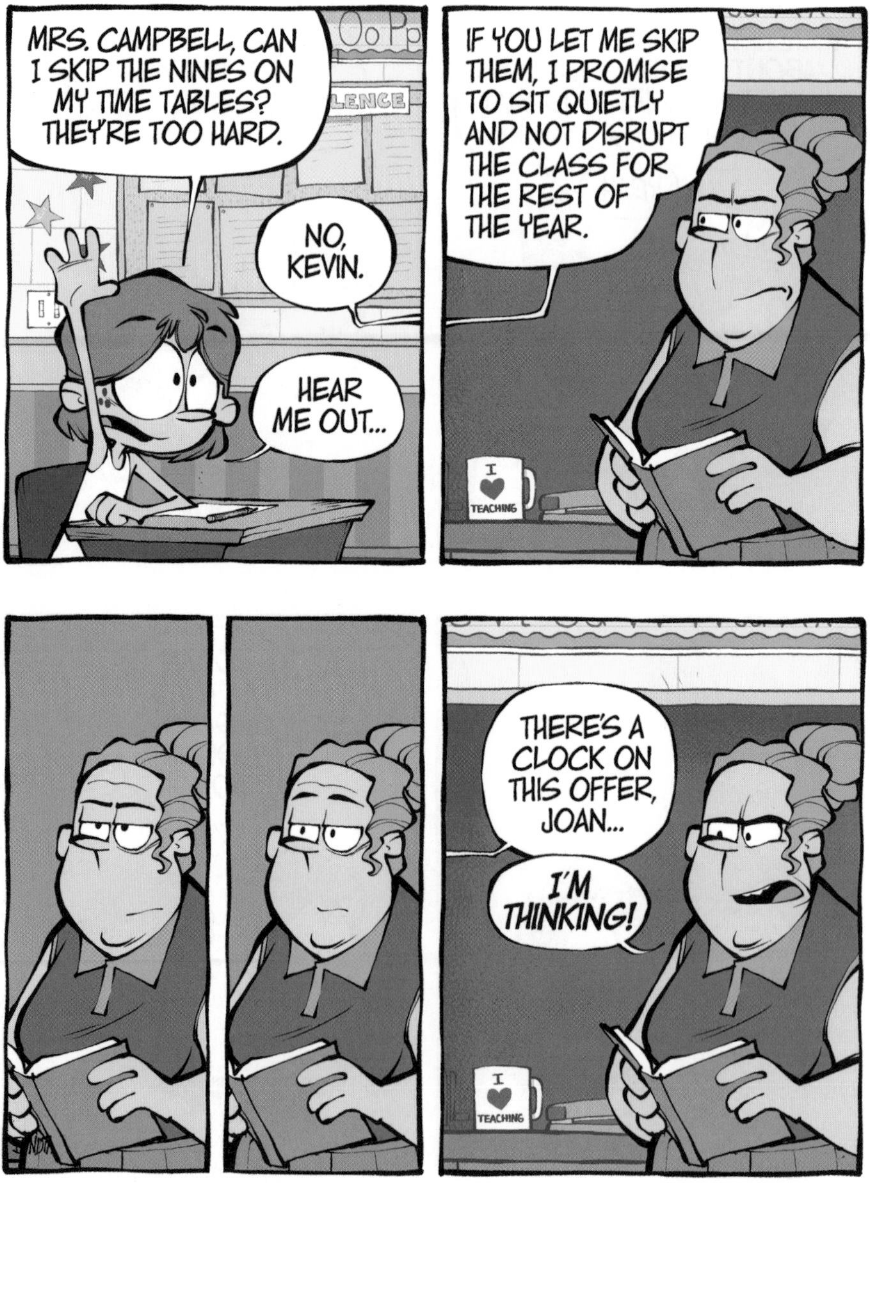
MRS. CAMPBELL, CAN I SKIP THE NINES ON MY TIME TABLES? THEY'RE TOO HARD.
NO, KEVIN.
HEAR ME OUT...
IF YOU LET ME SKIP THEM, I PROMISE TO SIT QUIETLY AND NOT DISRUPT THE CLASS FOR THE REST OF THE YEAR.
THERE'S A CLOCK ON THIS OFFER, JOAN...
I'M THINKING!

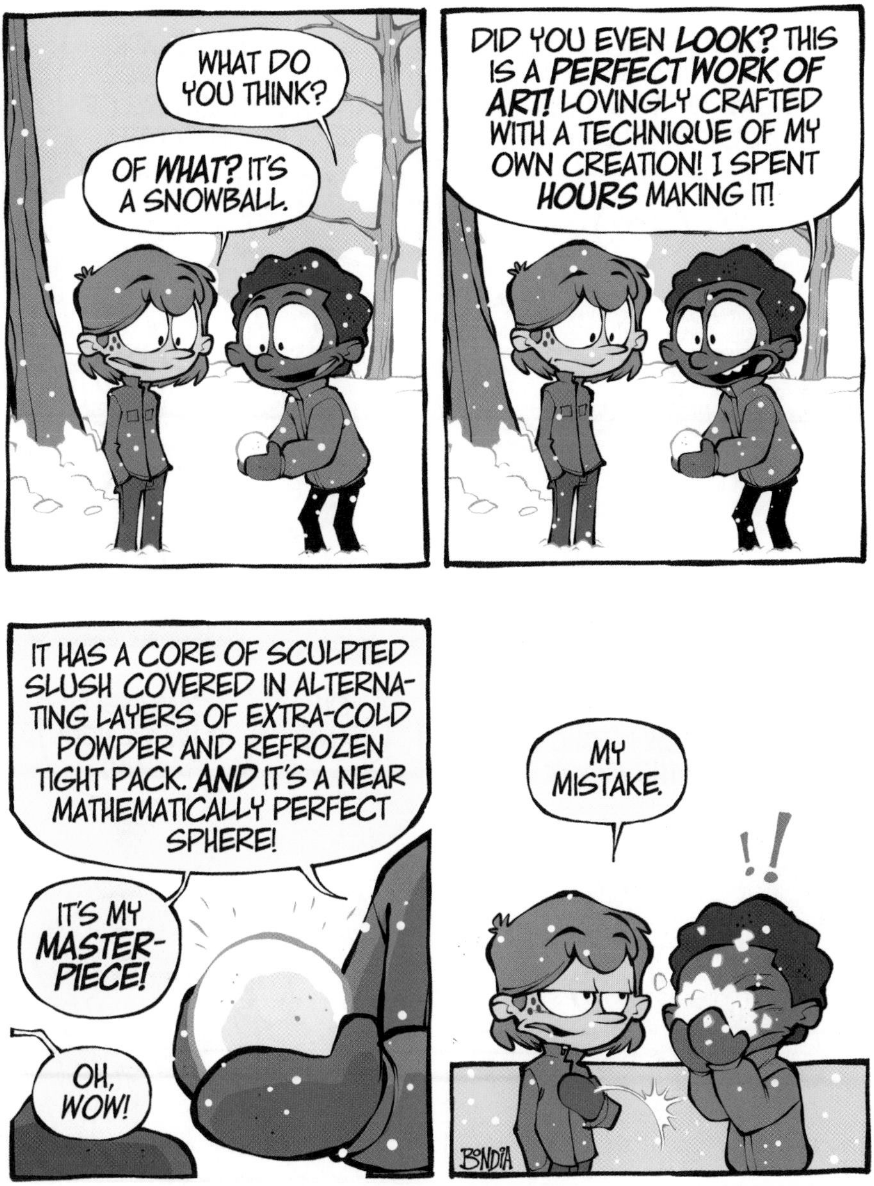
WHAT DO YOU THINK?
OF WHAT? IT'S A SNOWBALL.
DID YOU EVEN LOOK? THIS IS A PERFECT WORK OF ART! LOVINGLY CRAFTED WITH A TECHNIQUE OF MY OWN CREATION! I SPENT HOURS MAKING IT!
IT HAS A CORE OF SCULPTED SLUSH COVERED IN ALTERNATING LAYERS OF EXTRA-COLD POWDER AND REFROZEN TIGHT PACK. AND IT'S A NEAR MATHEMATICALLY PERFECT SPHERE!
IT'S MY MASTERPIECE!
OH, WOW!
MY MISTAKE.
!!
BONDIA

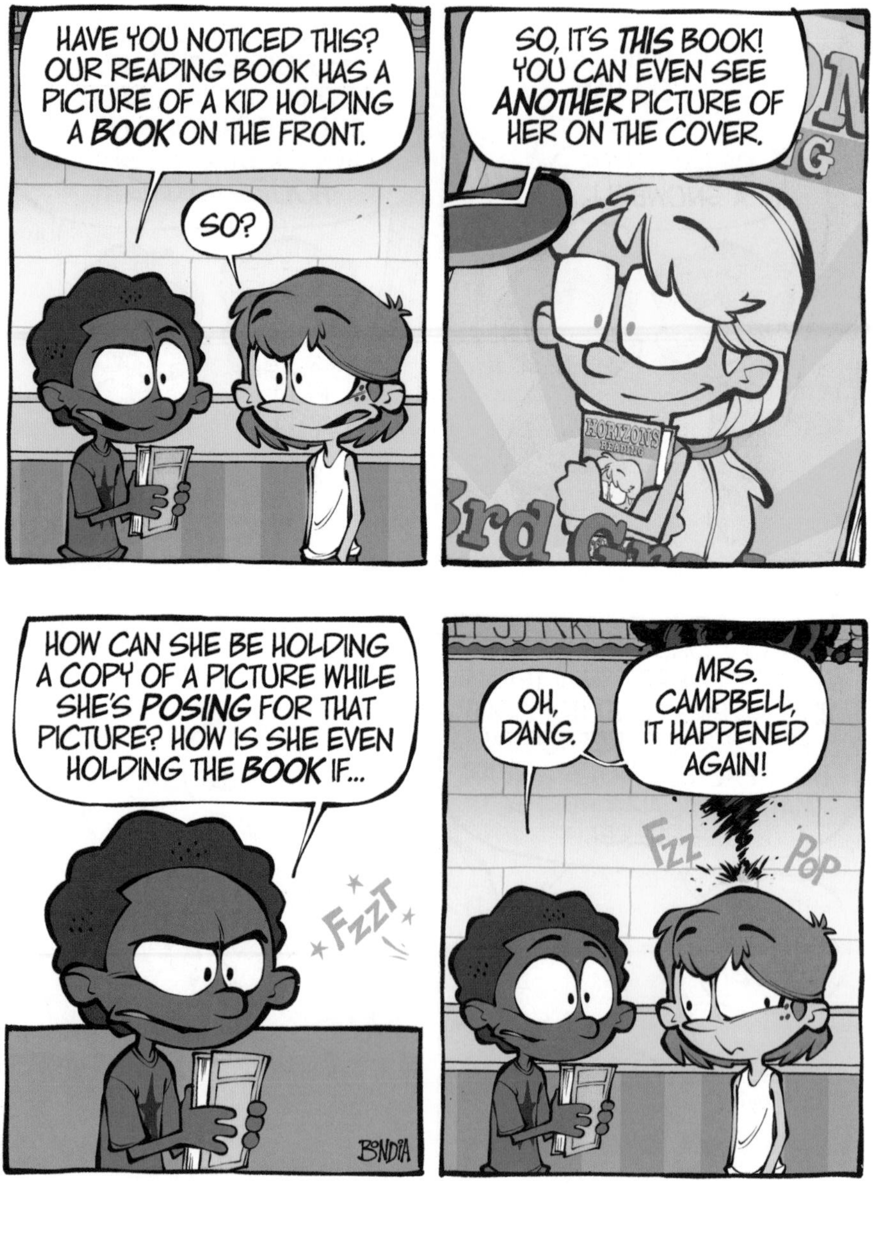
HAVE YOU NOTICED THIS? OUR READING BOOK HAS A PICTURE OF A KID HOLDING A BOOK ON THE FRONT.
SO?
SO, IT'S THIS BOOK! YOU CAN EVEN SEE ANOTHER PICTURE OF HER ON THE COVER.
HORIZONS READING
3rd
HOW CAN SHE BE HOLDING A COPY OF A PICTURE WHILE SHE'S POSING FOR THAT PICTURE? HOW IS SHE EVEN HOLDING THE BOOK IF...
FZZT
BONDIA
OH, DANG.
MRS. CAMPBELL, IT HAPPENED AGAIN!
FZZ
POP

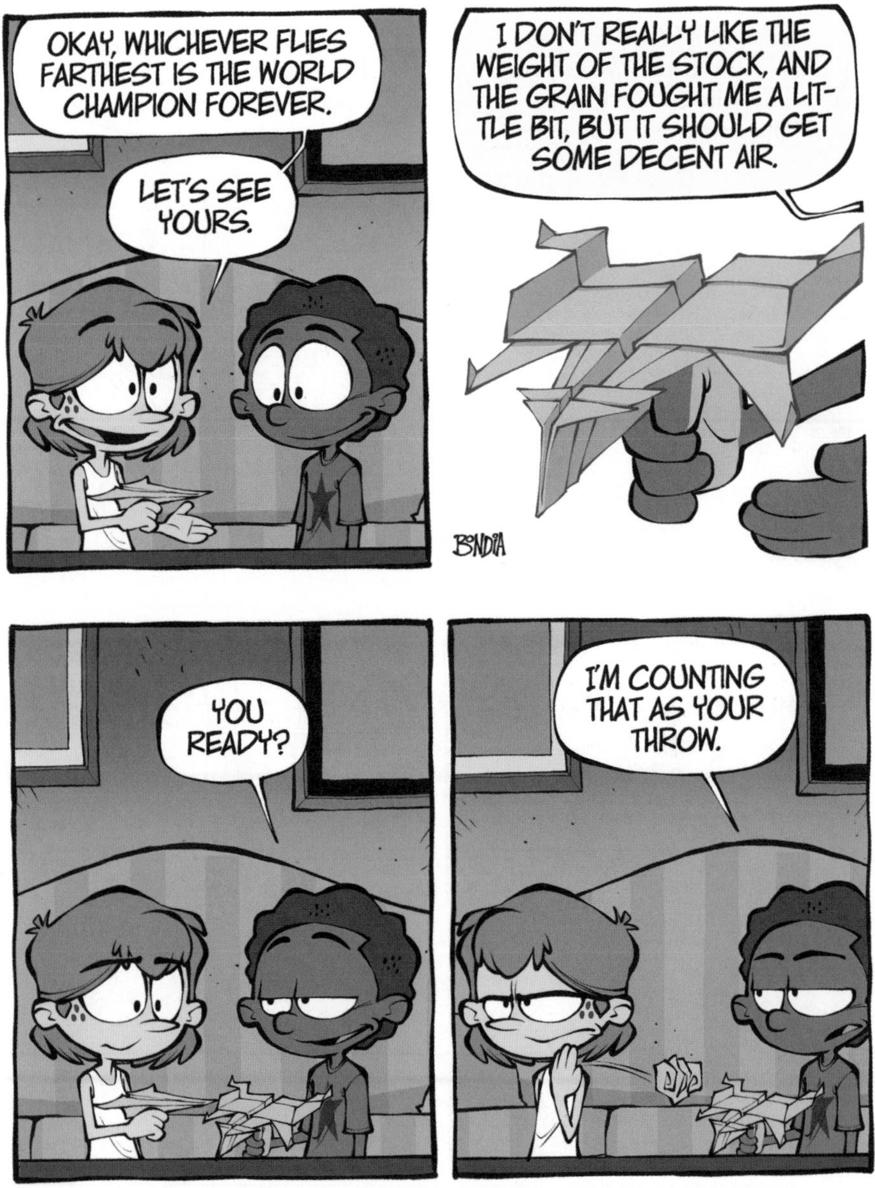
OKAY, WHICHEVER FLIES FARTHEST IS THE WORLD CHAMPION FOREVER.
LET'S SEE YOURS.
I DON'T REALLY LIKE THE WEIGHT OF THE STOCK, AND THE GRAIN FOUGHT ME A LITTLE BIT, BUT IT SHOULD GET SOME DECENT AIR.
BONDIA
YOU READY?
I'M COUNTING THAT AS YOUR THROW.

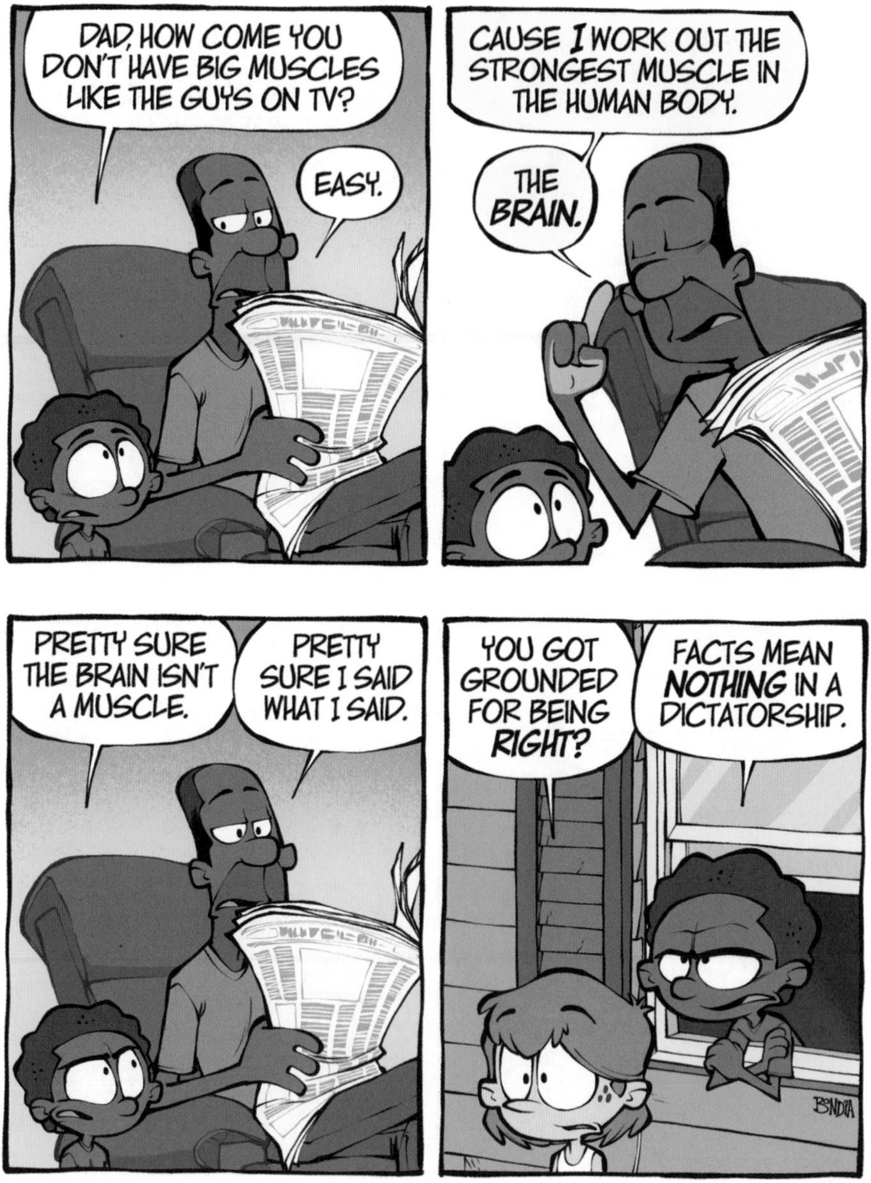
DAD, HOW COME YOU DON'T HAVE BIG MUSCLES LIKE THE GUYS ON TV?
EASY.
CAUSE I WORK OUT THE STRONGEST MUSCLE IN THE HUMAN BODY.
THE BRAIN.
PRETTY SURE THE BRAIN ISN'T A MUSCLE.
PRETTY SURE I SAID WHAT I SAID.
YOU GOT GROUNDED FOR BEING RIGHT?
FACTS MEAN NOTHING IN A DICTATORSHIP.
BONDIA

MAN, IT MUST BE GREAT TO HAVE A **WHOLE MONTH** TO CALL YOUR OWN.
BLACK HISTORY MONTH? I *GUESS.*
AT LEAST YOU STILL HAVE THE **ENTIRE** REST OF THE YEAR THOUGH, RIGHT?
YEAH, I KNOW...
BONDIA
IT JUST DOESN'T **FEEL** AS SPECIAL, YA KNOW?
IT'S THE **SHORTEST** MONTH, DUDE!

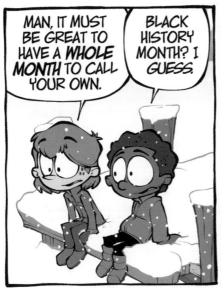

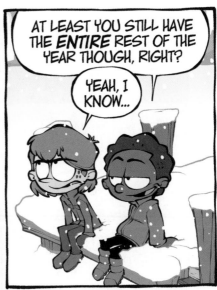

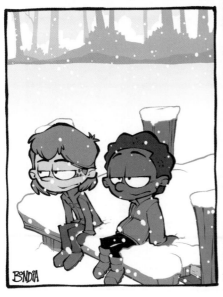

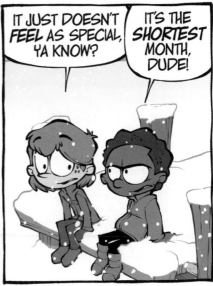

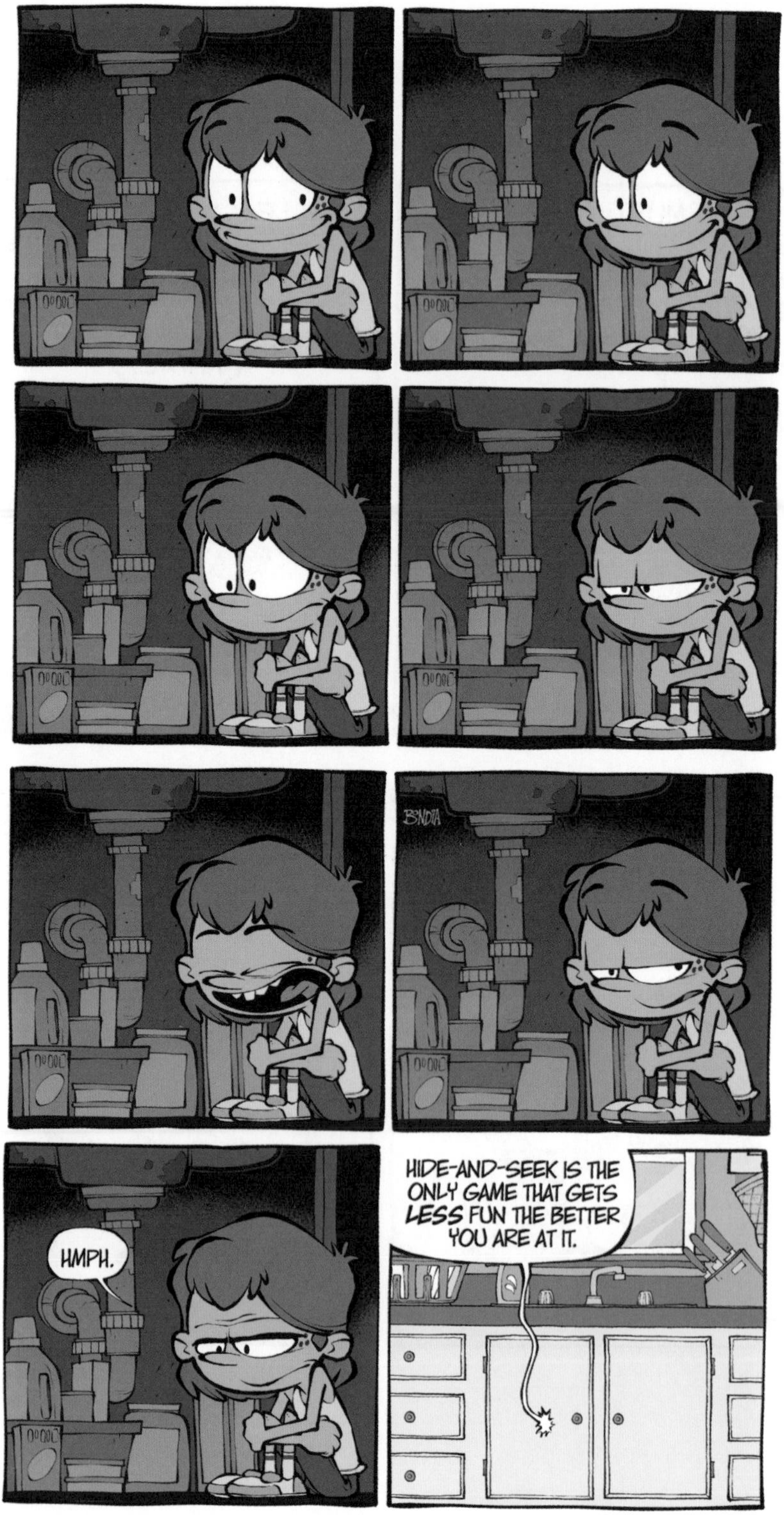
HMPH.
HIDE-AND-SEEK IS THE ONLY GAME THAT GETS LESS FUN THE BETTER YOU ARE AT IT.

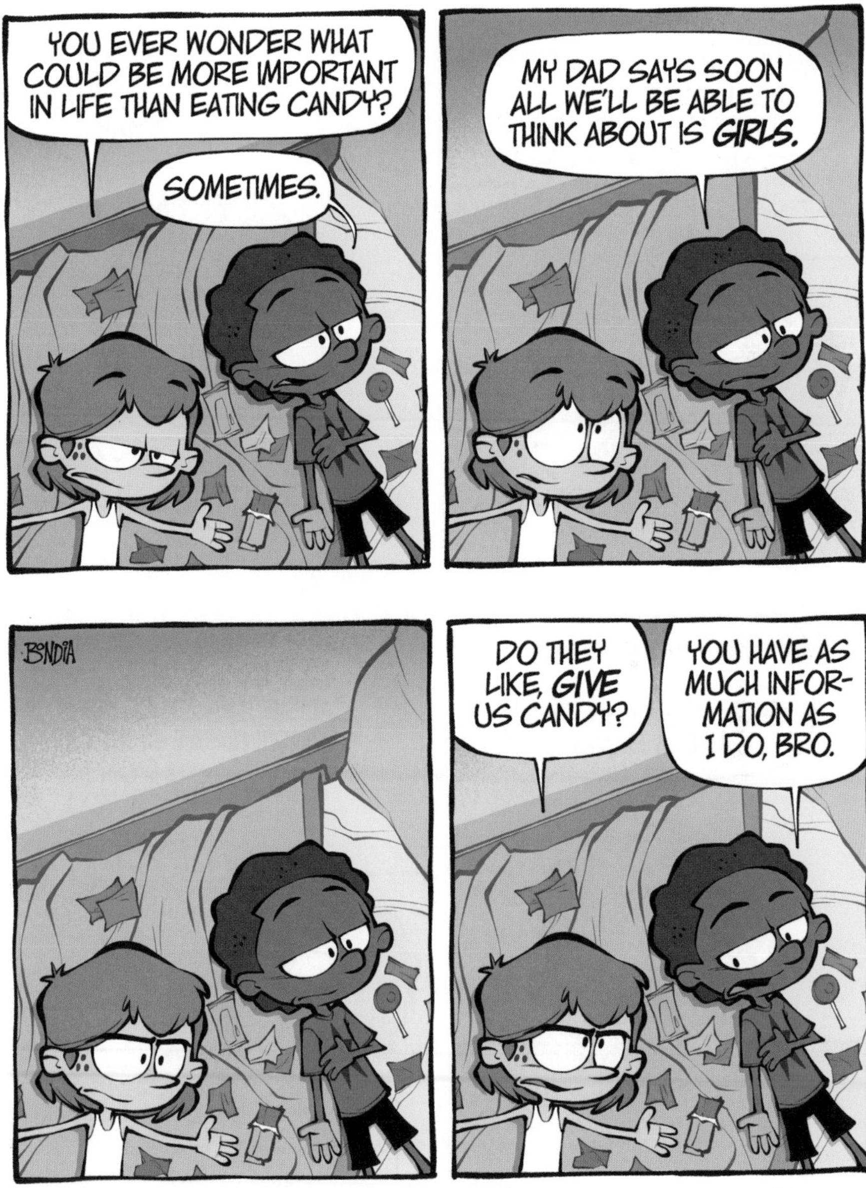
YOU EVER WONDER WHAT COULD BE MORE IMPORTANT IN LIFE THAN EATING CANDY?
SOMETIMES.
MY DAD SAYS SOON ALL WE'LL BE ABLE TO THINK ABOUT IS GIRLS.
BONDIA
DO THEY LIKE, GIVE US CANDY?
YOU HAVE AS MUCH INFORMATION AS I DO, BRO.

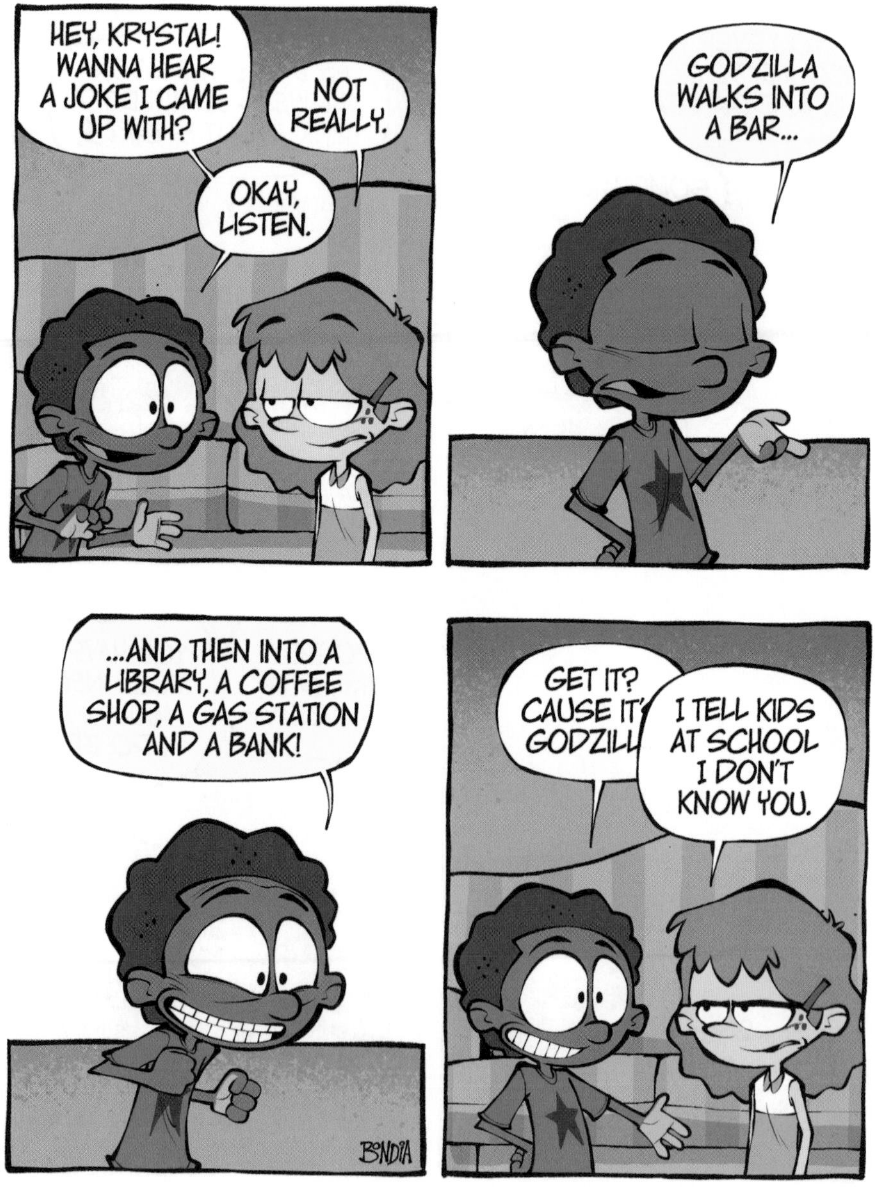

HEY, KRYSTAL! WANNA HEAR A JOKE I CAME UP WITH?
NOT REALLY.
OKAY, LISTEN.
GODZILLA WALKS INTO A BAR...
...AND THEN INTO A LIBRARY, A COFFEE SHOP, A GAS STATION AND A BANK!
BONDIA
GET IT? CAUSE IT'S GODZILL
I TELL KIDS AT SCHOOL I DON'T KNOW YOU.

KRYSTAL, I THINK WE SHOULD TRY TO BE FRIENDS.

CAUSE I WANNA GET ALONG WITH MY BEST BUD'S SISTER.

WHY?

WHY?

CAUSE... I DON'T *LIKE* IT WHEN PEOPLE DON'T LIKE ME?

WHY?

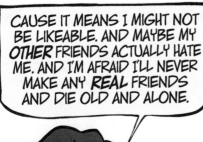

CAUSE IT MEANS I MIGHT NOT BE LIKEABLE. AND MAYBE MY *OTHER* FRIENDS ACTUALLY HATE ME. AND I'M AFRAID I'LL NEVER MAKE ANY *REAL* FRIENDS AND DIE OLD AND ALONE.

WOW.

BONDIA

THAT IS A *LOT* OF BAGGAGE FOR YOUR AGE.

I KNOW. THANKS FOR NOT SAYING WHY AGAIN.

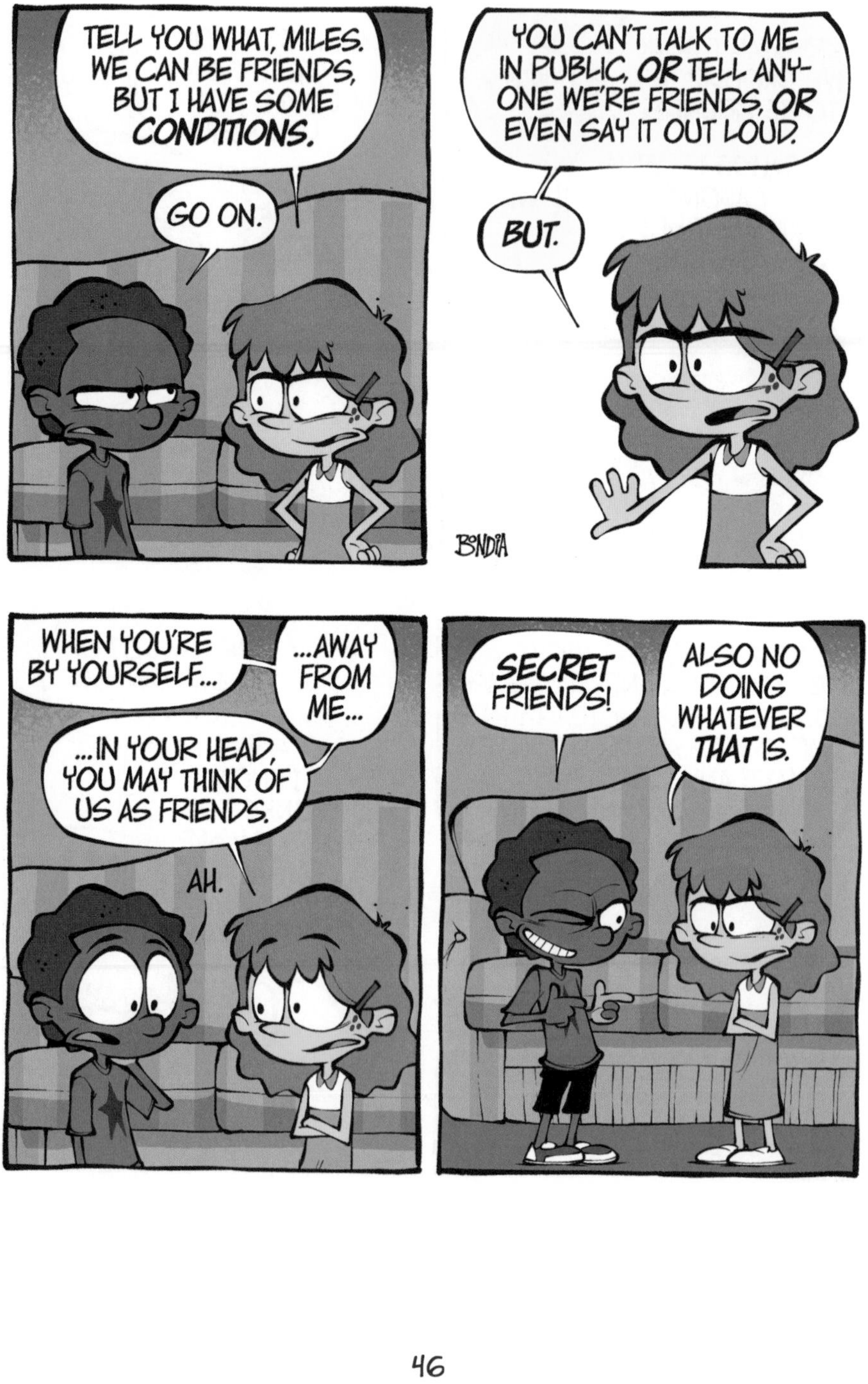
TELL YOU WHAT, MILES. WE CAN BE FRIENDS, BUT I HAVE SOME **CONDITIONS.**
GO ON.
YOU CAN'T TALK TO ME IN PUBLIC, **OR** TELL ANY-ONE WE'RE FRIENDS, **OR** EVEN SAY IT OUT LOUD.
BUT.
BONDIA
WHEN YOU'RE BY YOURSELF...
...AWAY FROM ME...
...IN YOUR HEAD, YOU MAY THINK OF US AS FRIENDS.
AH.
SECRET FRIENDS!
ALSO NO DOING WHATEVER ***THAT*** IS.

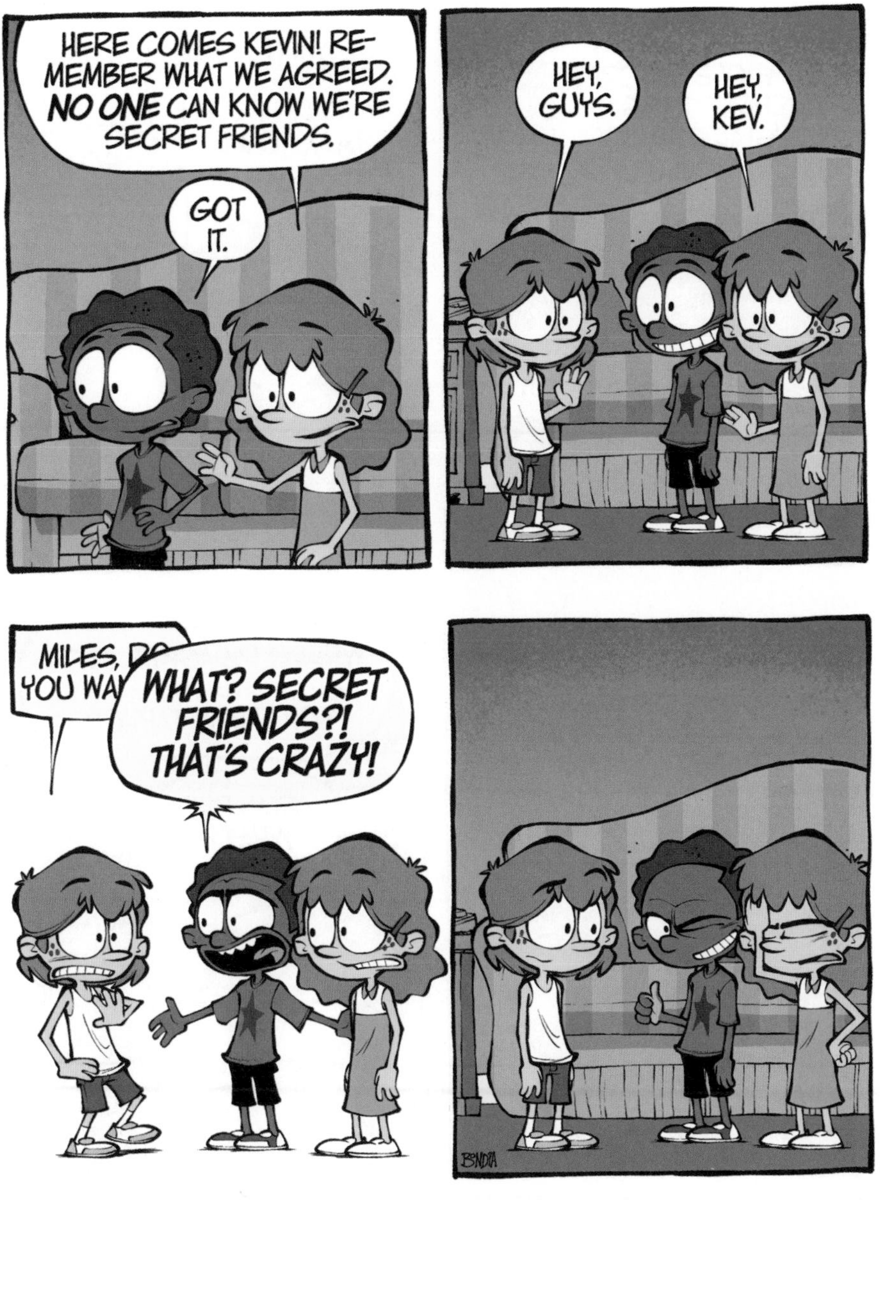
HERE COMES KEVIN! RE-
MEMBER WHAT WE AGREED.
NO ONE CAN KNOW WE'RE
SECRET FRIENDS.
GOT IT.
HEY, GUYS.
HEY, KEV.
MILES,
YOU WA
WHAT? SECRET FRIENDS?! THAT'S CRAZY!

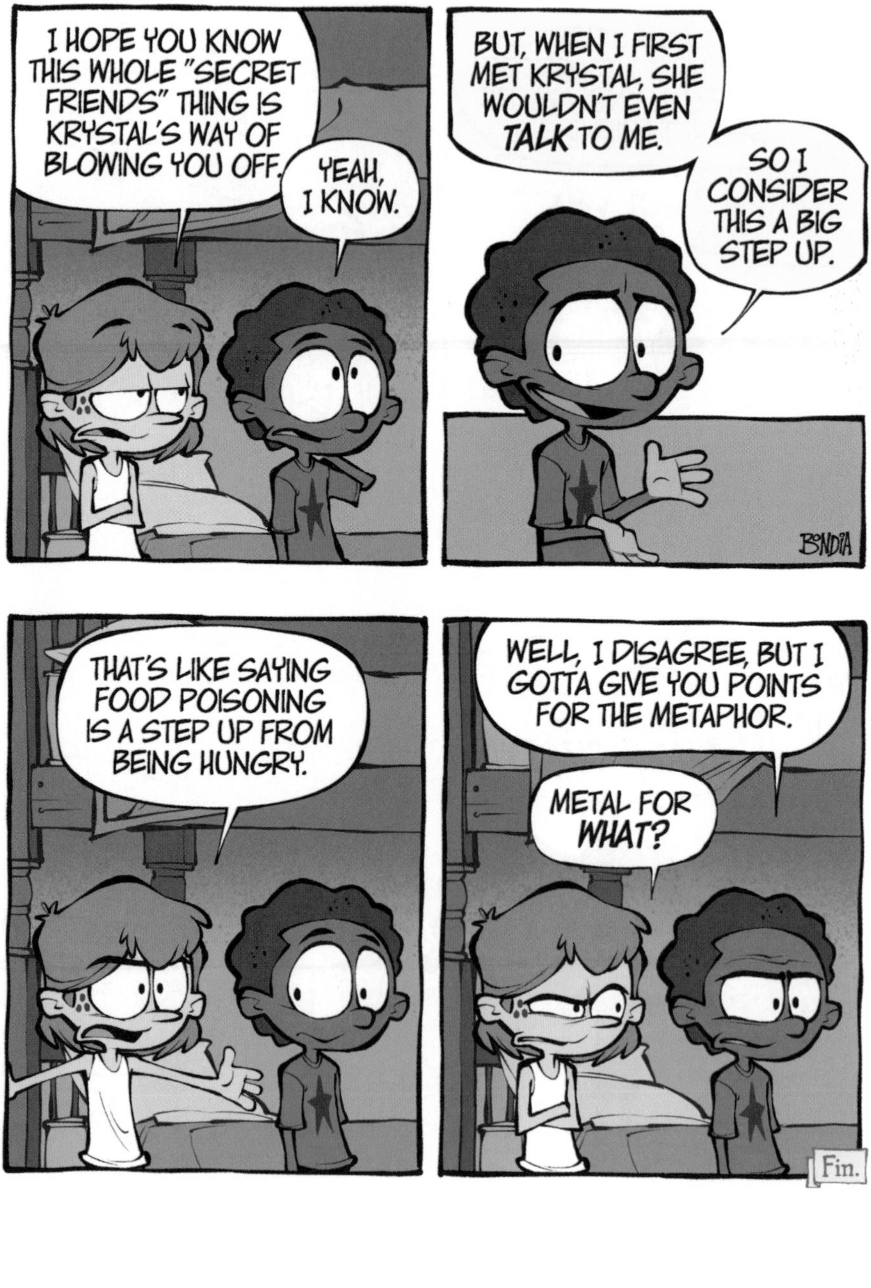

I HOPE YOU KNOW THIS WHOLE "SECRET FRIENDS" THING IS KRYSTAL'S WAY OF BLOWING YOU OFF.
YEAH, I KNOW.
BUT, WHEN I FIRST MET KRYSTAL, SHE WOULDN'T EVEN TALK TO ME.
SO I CONSIDER THIS A BIG STEP UP.
BONDIA
THAT'S LIKE SAYING FOOD POISONING IS A STEP UP FROM BEING HUNGRY.
WELL, I DISAGREE, BUT I GOTTA GIVE YOU POINTS FOR THE METAPHOR.
METAL FOR WHAT?
Fin.

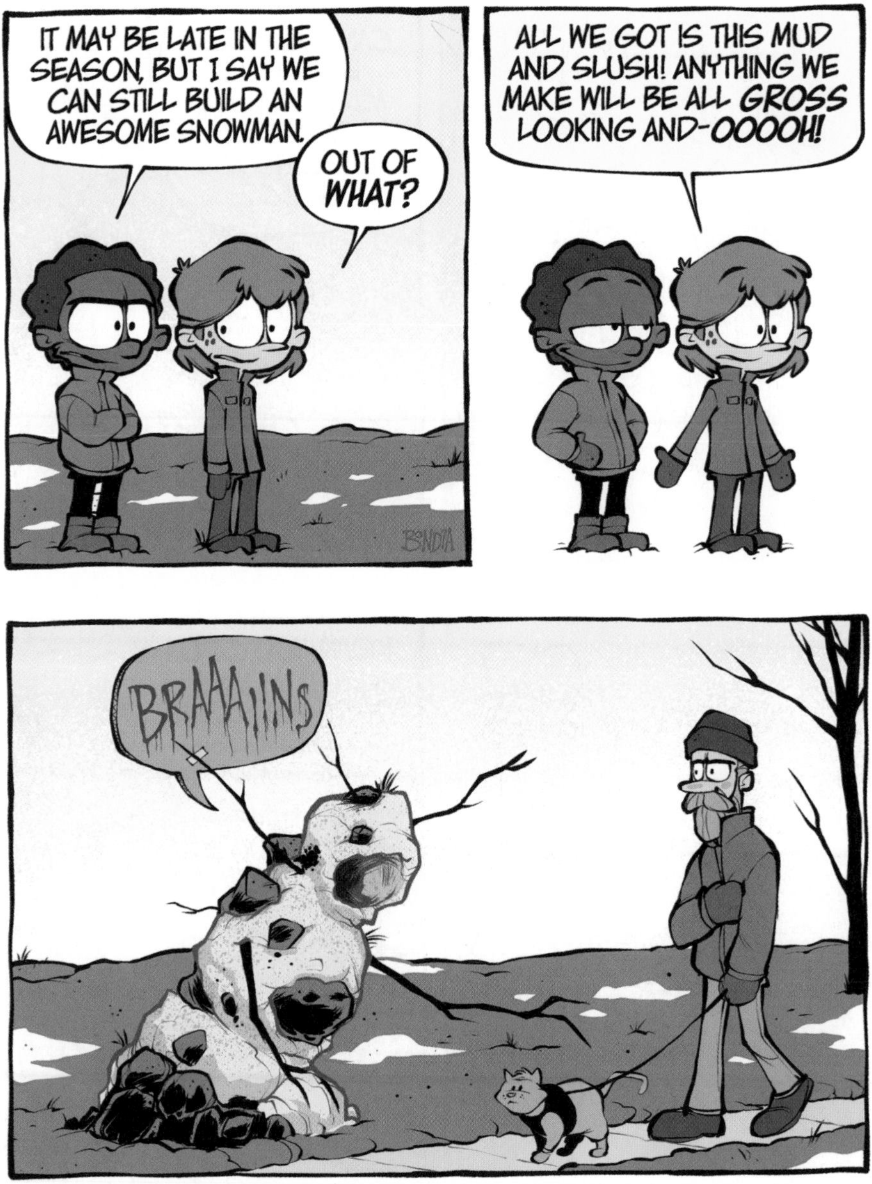
IT MAY BE LATE IN THE SEASON, BUT I SAY WE CAN STILL BUILD AN AWESOME SNOWMAN.
OUT OF WHAT?
ALL WE GOT IS THIS MUD AND SLUSH! ANYTHING WE MAKE WILL BE ALL GROSS LOOKING AND-OOOOH!
BRAAAIINS

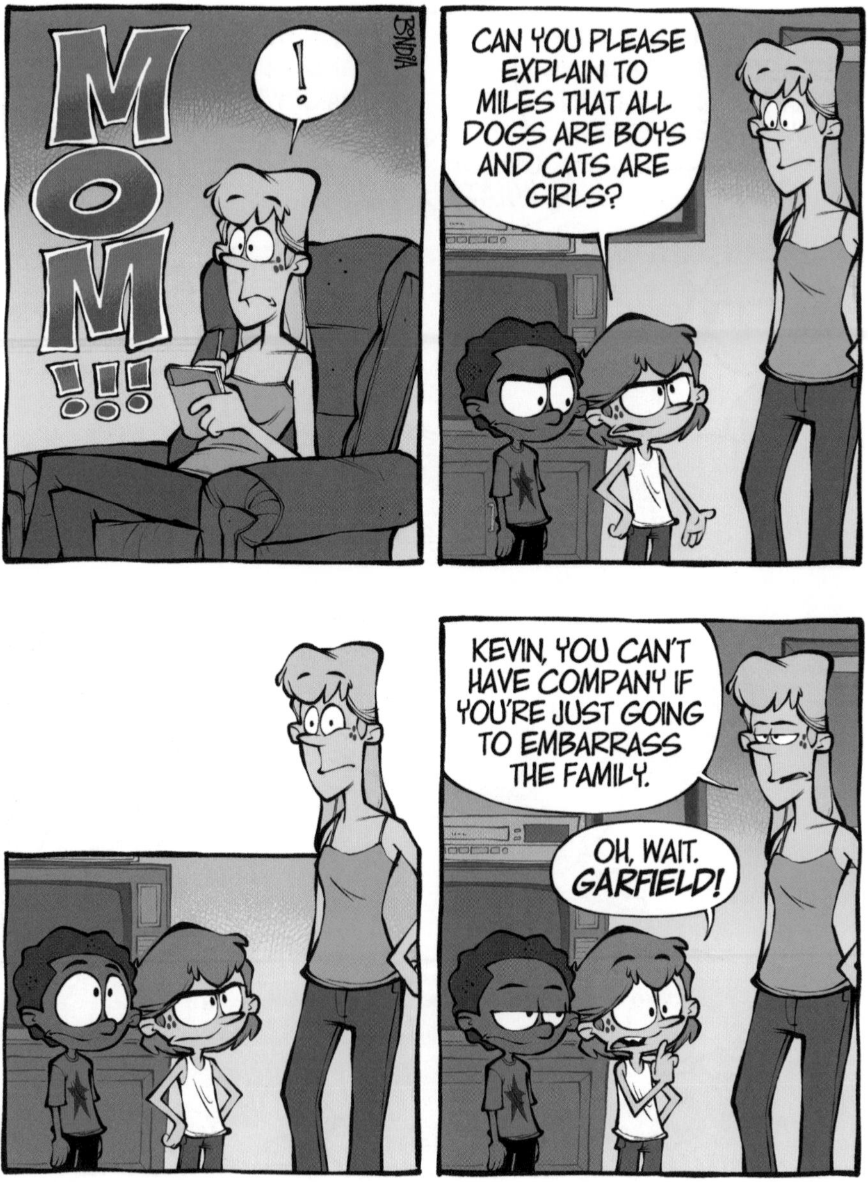
MOM!!!
!
CAN YOU PLEASE EXPLAIN TO MILES THAT ALL DOGS ARE BOYS AND CATS ARE GIRLS?
KEVIN, YOU CAN'T HAVE COMPANY IF YOU'RE JUST GOING TO EMBARRASS THE FAMILY.
OH, WAIT. **GARFIELD!**

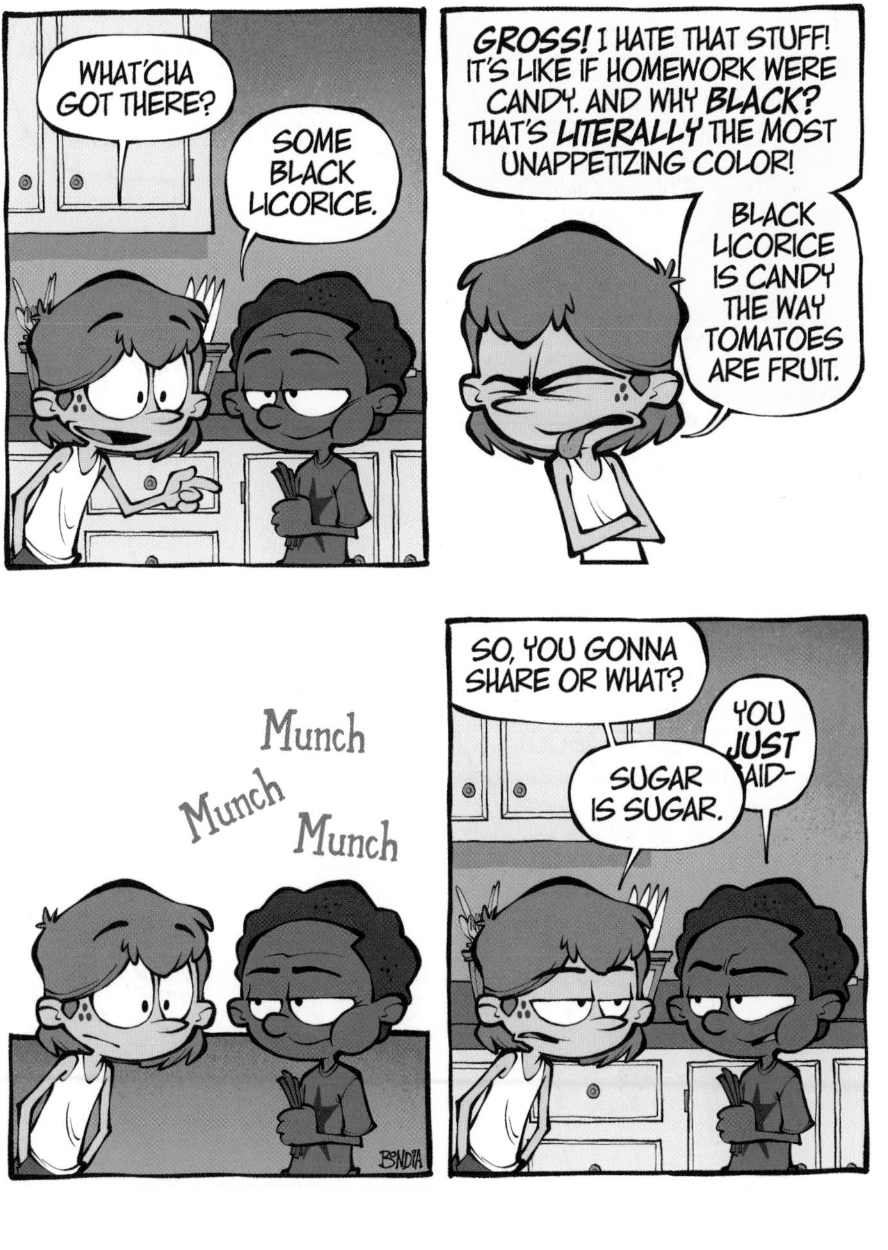
WHAT'CHA GOT THERE?
SOME BLACK LICORICE.
GROSS! I HATE THAT STUFF! IT'S LIKE IF HOMEWORK WERE CANDY. AND WHY BLACK? THAT'S LITERALLY THE MOST UNAPPETIZING COLOR!
BLACK LICORICE IS CANDY THE WAY TOMATOES ARE FRUIT.
Munch
Munch
Munch
SO, YOU GONNA SHARE OR WHAT?
YOU JUST AID-
SUGAR IS SUGAR.

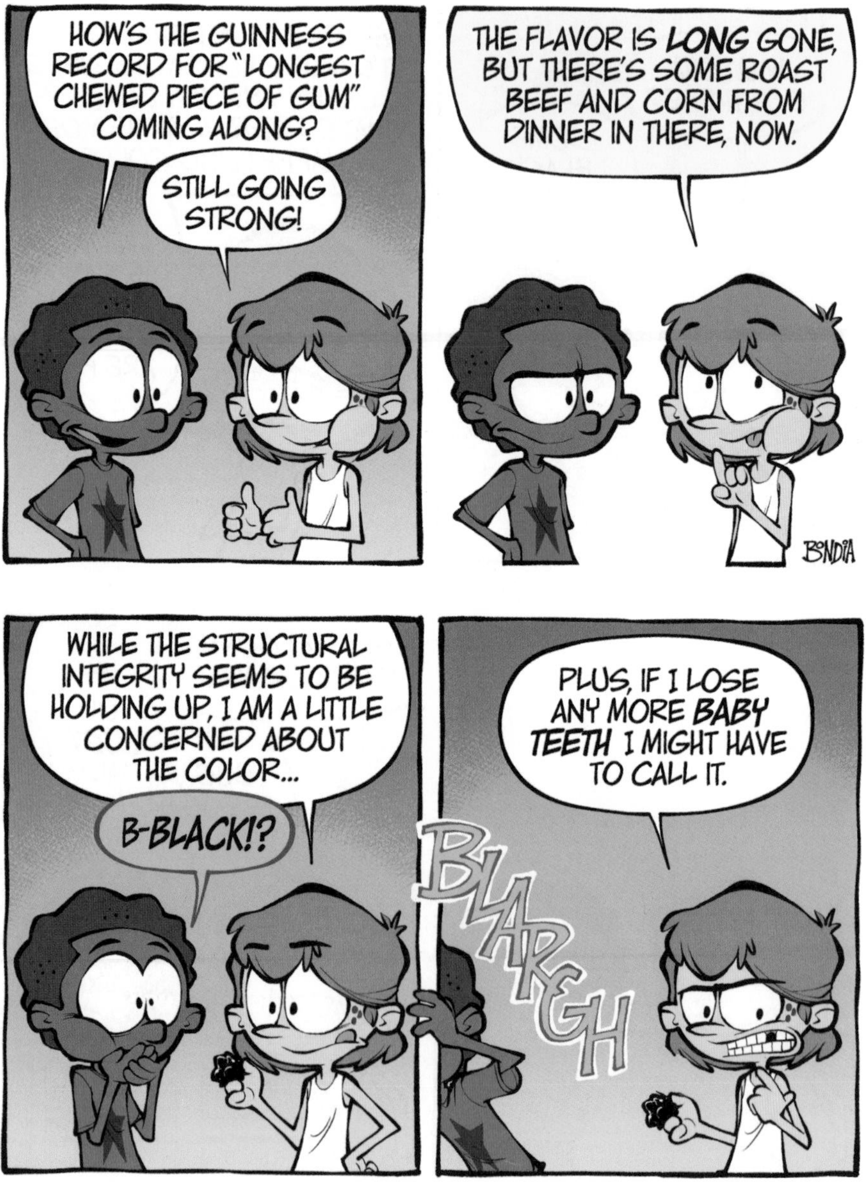
HOW'S THE GUINNESS RECORD FOR "LONGEST CHEWED PIECE OF GUM" COMING ALONG?
STILL GOING STRONG!
THE FLAVOR IS **LONG** GONE, BUT THERE'S SOME ROAST BEEF AND CORN FROM DINNER IN THERE, NOW.
BONDIA
WHILE THE STRUCTURAL INTEGRITY SEEMS TO BE HOLDING UP, I AM A LITTLE CONCERNED ABOUT THE COLOR...
B-BLACK!?
BLARGH
PLUS, IF I LOSE ANY MORE **BABY TEETH** I MIGHT HAVE TO CALL IT.

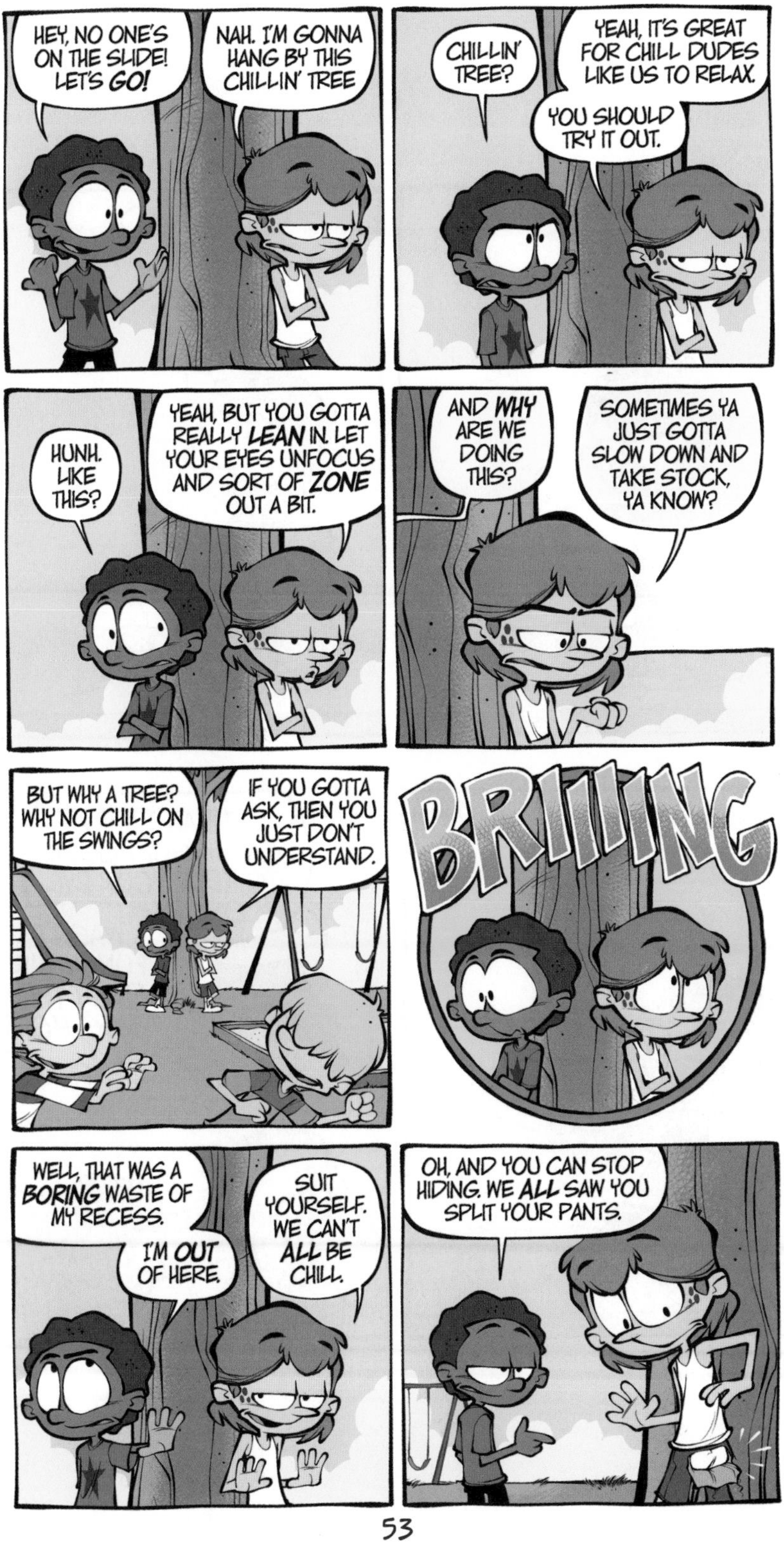
HEY, NO ONE'S ON THE SLIDE! LET'S GO!
NAH. I'M GONNA HANG BY THIS CHILLIN' TREE
CHILLIN' TREE?
YEAH, IT'S GREAT FOR CHILL DUDES LIKE US TO RELAX.
YOU SHOULD TRY IT OUT.
HUNH. LIKE THIS?
YEAH, BUT YOU GOTTA REALLY LEAN IN. LET YOUR EYES UNFOCUS AND SORT OF ZONE OUT A BIT.
AND WHY ARE WE DOING THIS?
SOMETIMES YA JUST GOTTA SLOW DOWN AND TAKE STOCK, YA KNOW?
BUT WHY A TREE? WHY NOT CHILL ON THE SWINGS?
IF YOU GOTTA ASK, THEN YOU JUST DON'T UNDERSTAND.
BRIIIING
WELL, THAT WAS A BORING WASTE OF MY RECESS.
I'M OUT OF HERE.
SUIT YOURSELF. WE CAN'T ALL BE CHILL.
OH, AND YOU CAN STOP HIDING. WE ALL SAW YOU SPLIT YOUR PANTS.

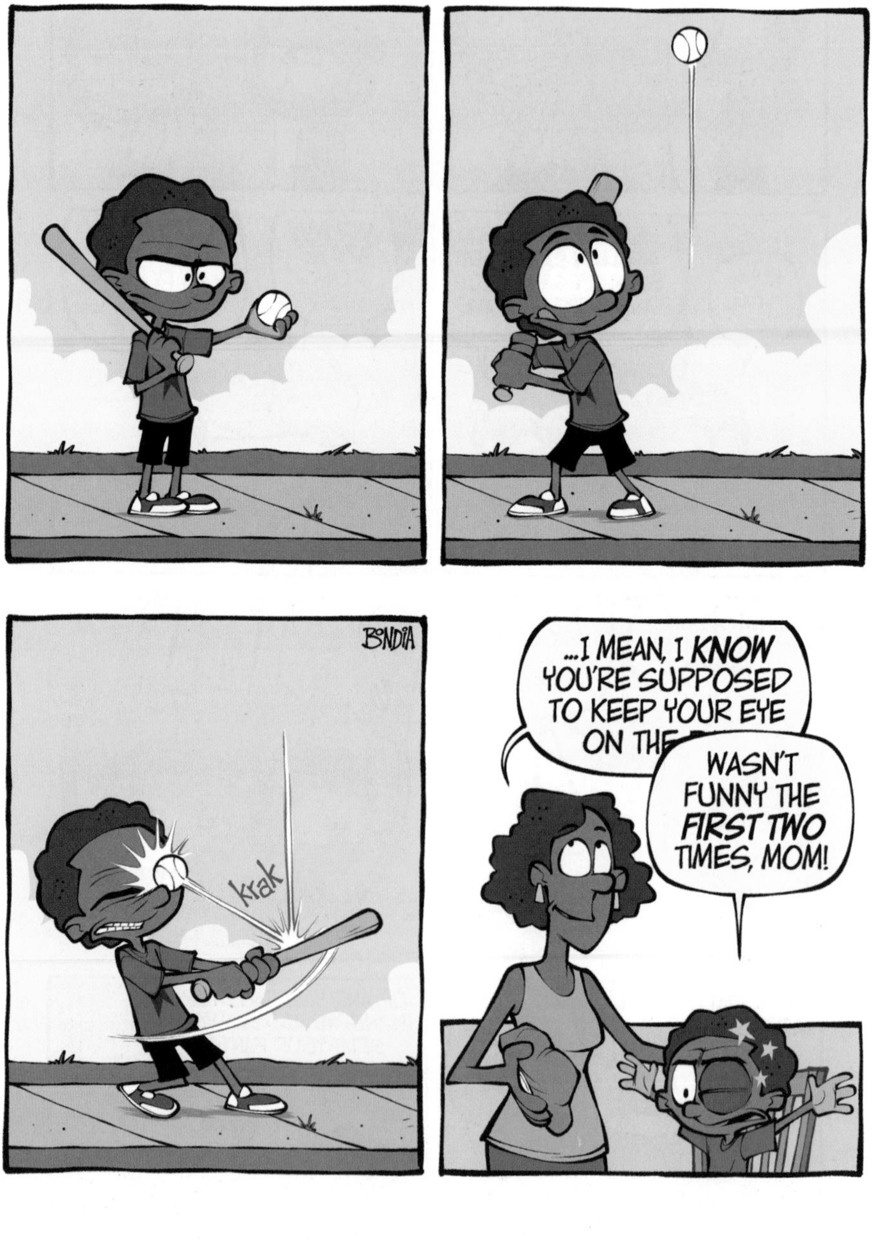
BONDIA
krak
...I MEAN, I KNOW YOU'RE SUPPOSED TO KEEP YOUR EYE ON THE
WASN'T FUNNY THE FIRST TWO TIMES, MOM!

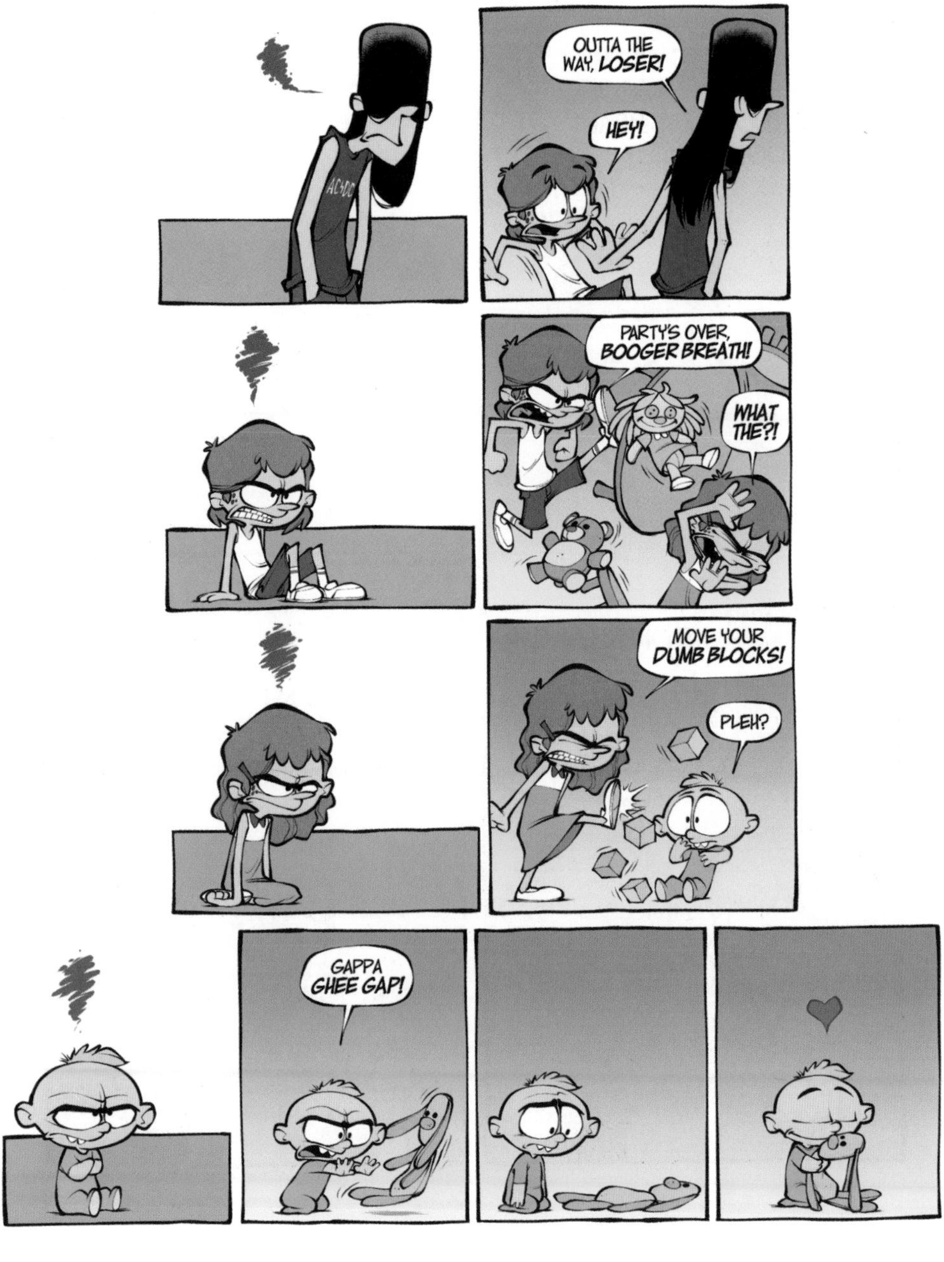
OUTTA THE WAY, LOSER!
HEY!
PARTY'S OVER, BOOGER BREATH!
WHAT THE?!
MOVE YOUR DUMB BLOCKS!
PLEH?
GAPPA GHEE GAP!

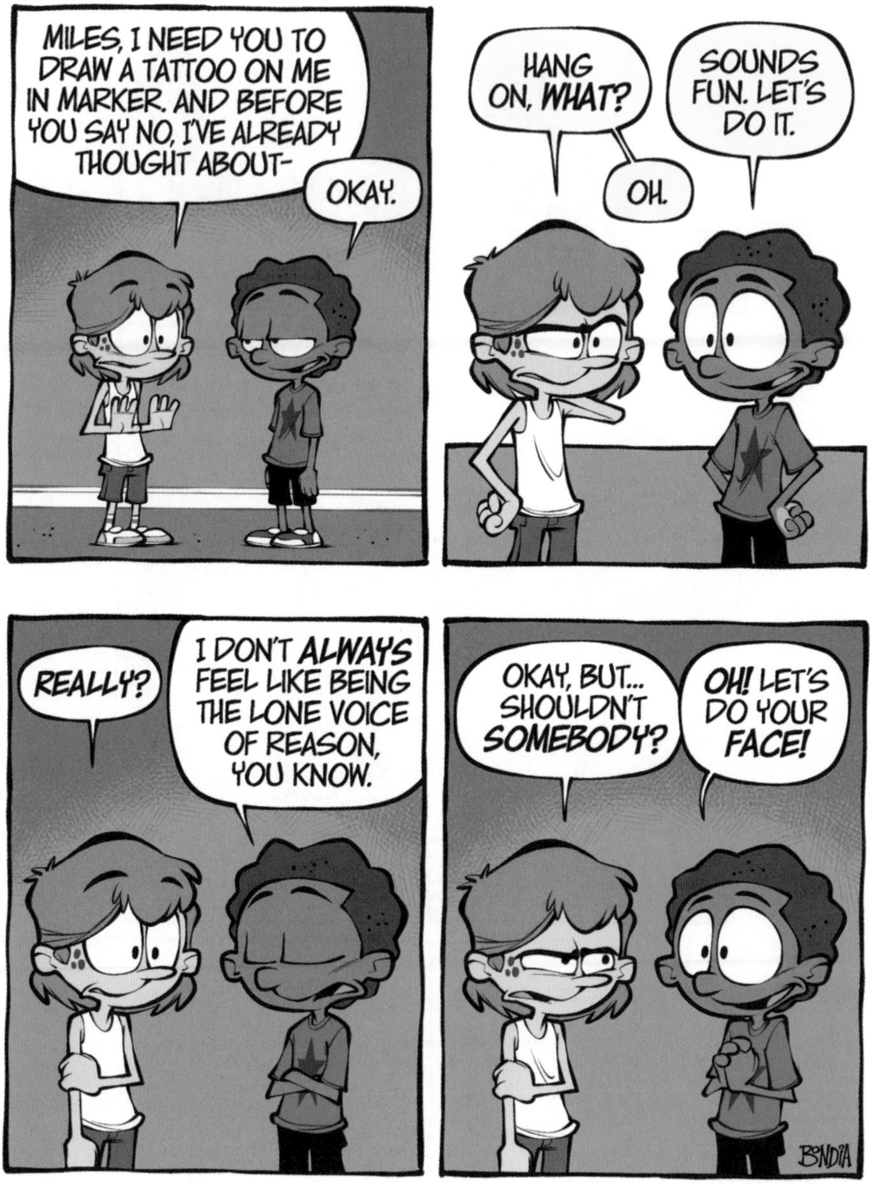
MILES, I NEED YOU TO DRAW A TATTOO ON ME IN MARKER. AND BEFORE YOU SAY NO, I'VE ALREADY THOUGHT ABOUT-
OKAY.
HANG ON, WHAT?
OH.
SOUNDS FUN. LET'S DO IT.
REALLY?
I DON'T ALWAYS FEEL LIKE BEING THE LONE VOICE OF REASON, YOU KNOW.
OKAY, BUT... SHOULDN'T SOMEBODY?
OH! LET'S DO YOUR FACE!
BONDIA

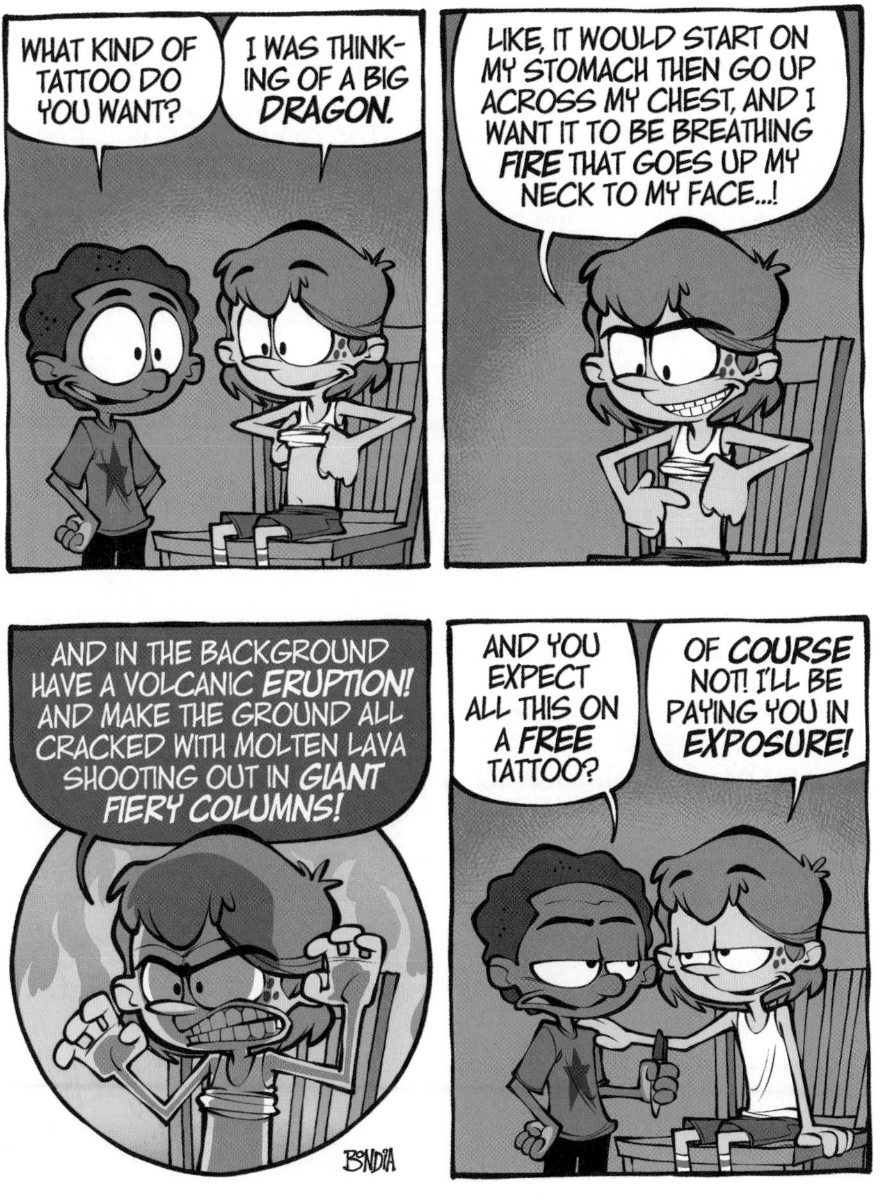
WHAT KIND OF TATTOO DO YOU WANT?
I WAS THINKING OF A BIG DRAGON.
LIKE, IT WOULD START ON MY STOMACH THEN GO UP ACROSS MY CHEST, AND I WANT IT TO BE BREATHING FIRE THAT GOES UP MY NECK TO MY FACE...!
AND IN THE BACKGROUND HAVE A VOLCANIC ERUPTION! AND MAKE THE GROUND ALL CRACKED WITH MOLTEN LAVA SHOOTING OUT IN GIANT FIERY COLUMNS!
AND YOU EXPECT ALL THIS ON A FREE TATTOO?
OF COURSE NOT! I'LL BE PAYING YOU IN EXPOSURE!
BONDIA

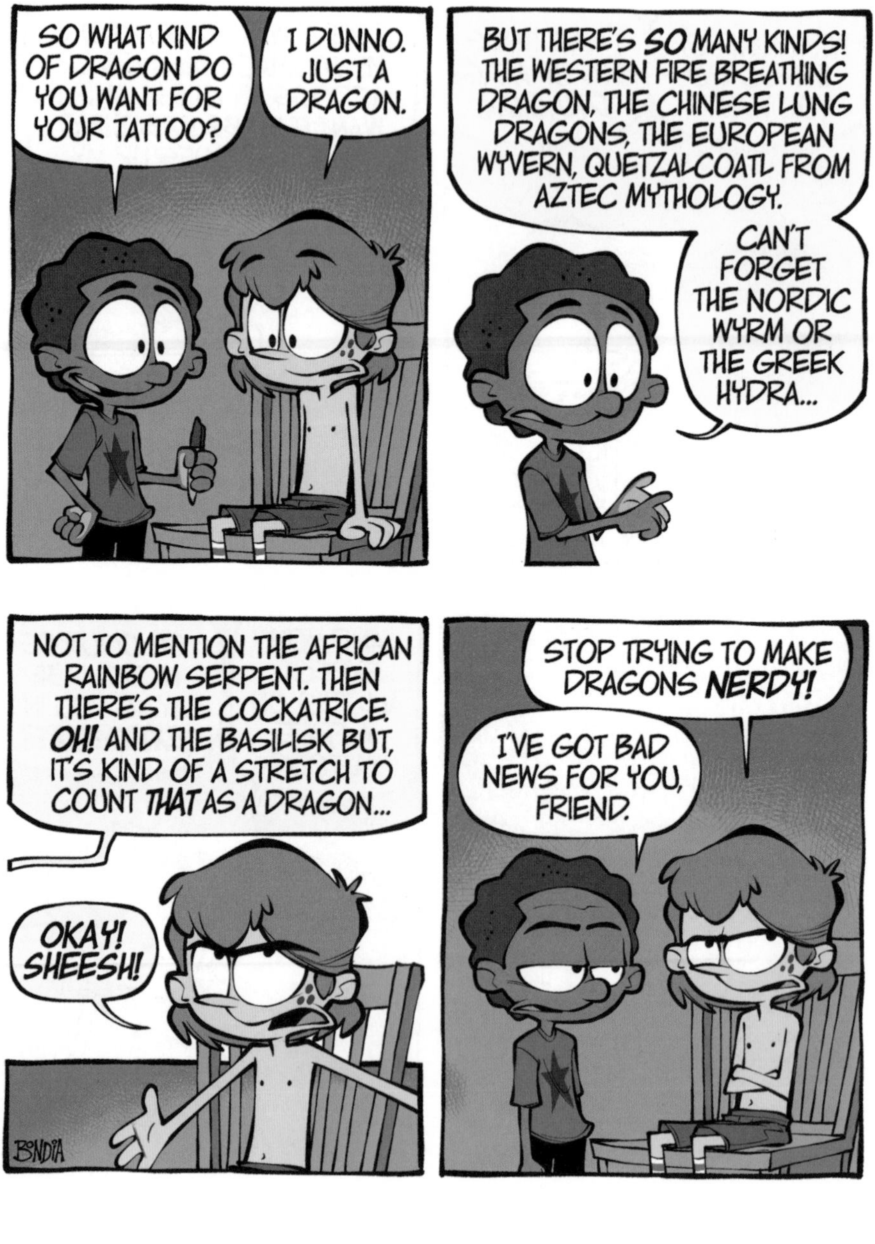
SO WHAT KIND OF DRAGON DO YOU WANT FOR YOUR TATTOO?
I DUNNO. JUST A DRAGON.
BUT THERE'S **SO** MANY KINDS! THE WESTERN FIRE BREATHING DRAGON, THE CHINESE LUNG DRAGONS, THE EUROPEAN WYVERN, QUETZALCOATL FROM AZTEC MYTHOLOGY.
CAN'T FORGET THE NORDIC WYRM OR THE GREEK HYDRA...
NOT TO MENTION THE AFRICAN RAINBOW SERPENT. THEN THERE'S THE COCKATRICE. **OH!** AND THE BASILISK BUT, IT'S KIND OF A STRETCH TO COUNT **THAT** AS A DRAGON...
OKAY! SHEESH!
BONDIA
STOP TRYING TO MAKE DRAGONS **NERDY!**
I'VE GOT BAD NEWS FOR YOU, FRIEND.

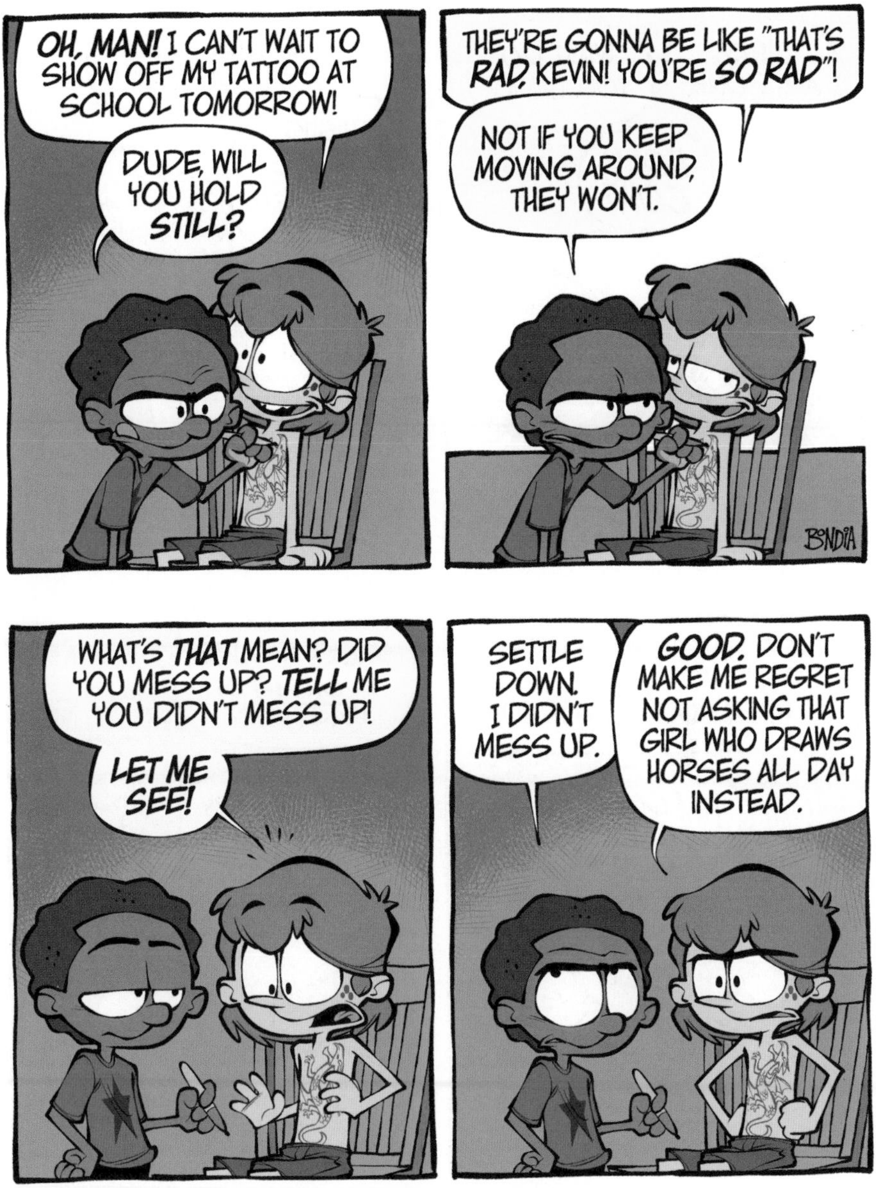
OH, MAN! I CAN'T WAIT TO SHOW OFF MY TATTOO AT SCHOOL TOMORROW!
DUDE, WILL YOU HOLD STILL?
THEY'RE GONNA BE LIKE "THAT'S RAD, KEVIN! YOU'RE SO RAD"!
NOT IF YOU KEEP MOVING AROUND, THEY WON'T.
BONDIA
WHAT'S THAT MEAN? DID YOU MESS UP? TELL ME YOU DIDN'T MESS UP!
LET ME SEE!
SETTLE DOWN. I DIDN'T MESS UP.
GOOD. DON'T MAKE ME REGRET NOT ASKING THAT GIRL WHO DRAWS HORSES ALL DAY INSTEAD.

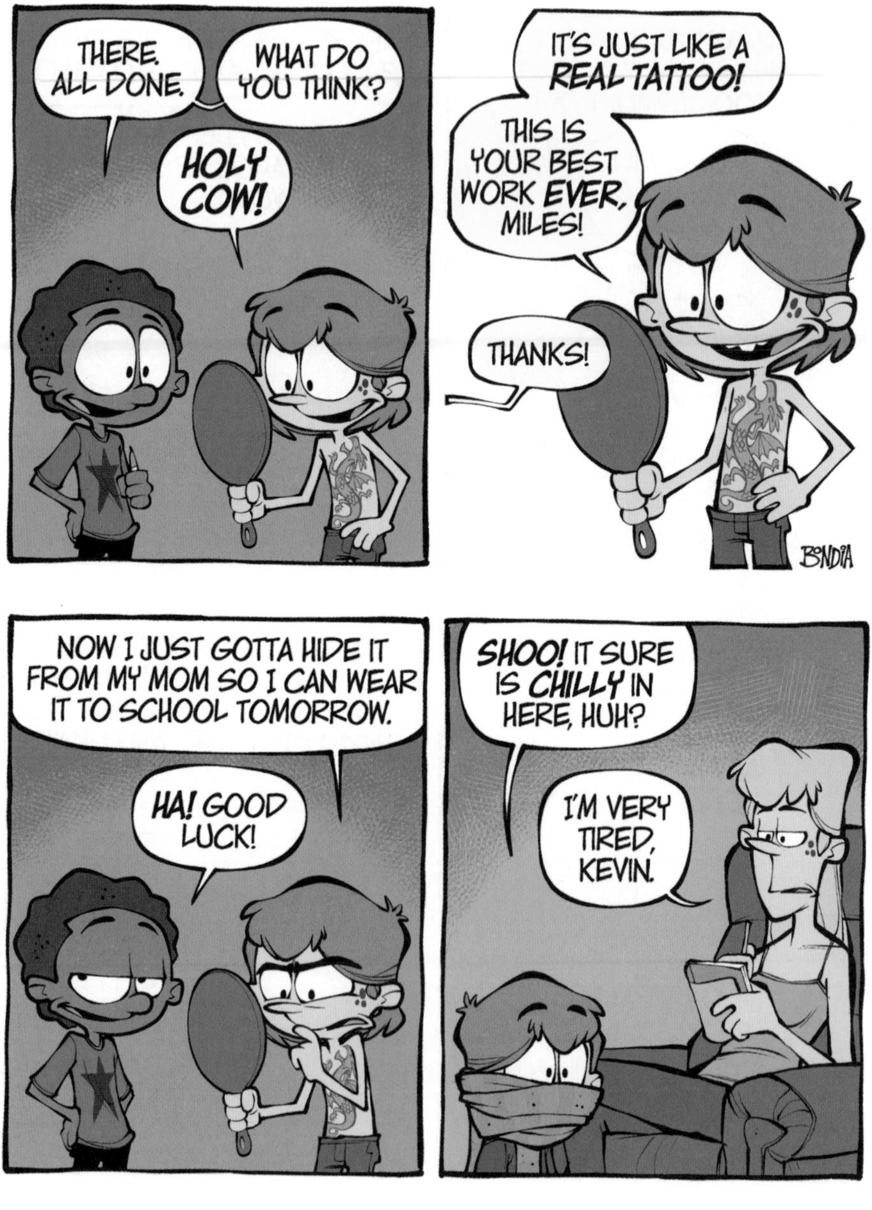
THERE. ALL DONE.
WHAT DO YOU THINK?
HOLY COW!
IT'S JUST LIKE A REAL TATTOO!
THIS IS YOUR BEST WORK EVER, MILES!
THANKS!
BONDIA
NOW I JUST GOTTA HIDE IT FROM MY MOM SO I CAN WEAR IT TO SCHOOL TOMORROW.
HA! GOOD LUCK!
SHOO! IT SURE IS CHILLY IN HERE, HUH?
I'M VERY TIRED, KEVIN.

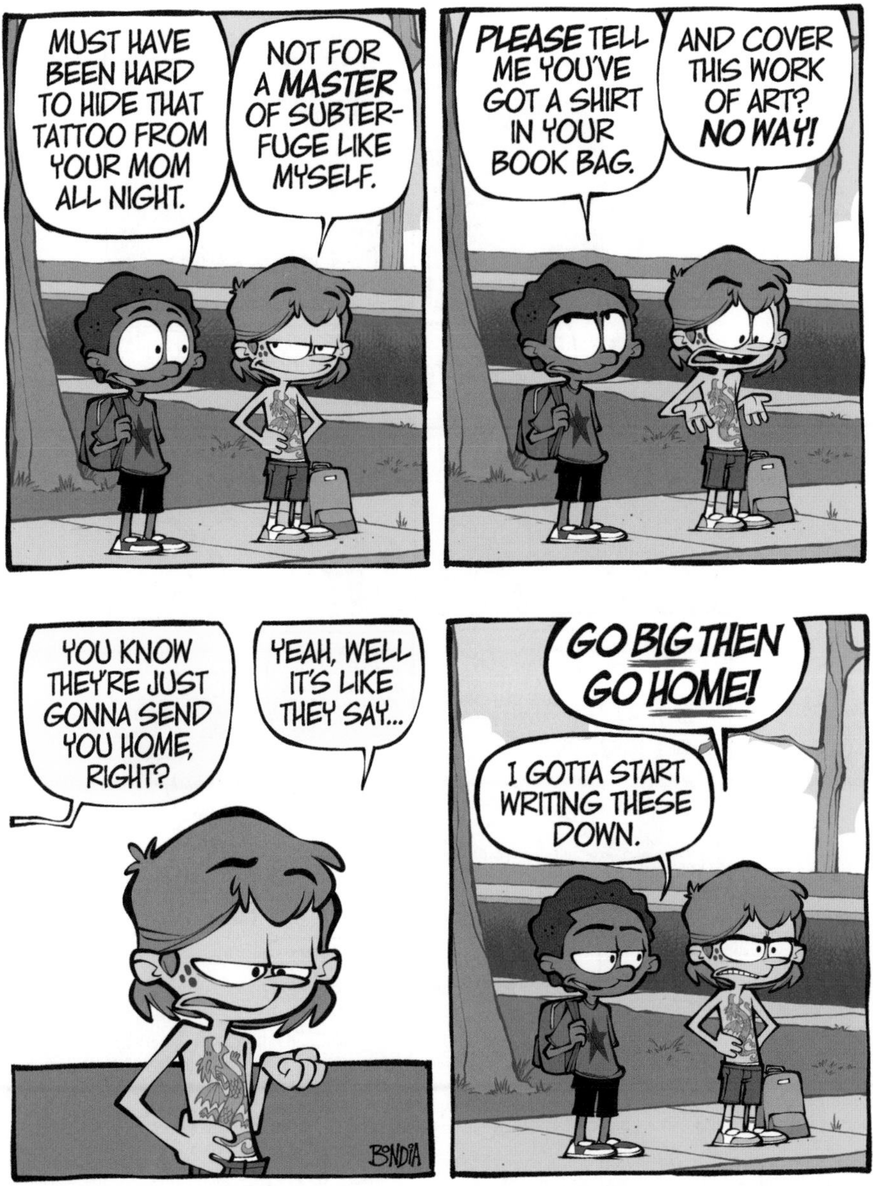
MUST HAVE BEEN HARD TO HIDE THAT TATTOO FROM YOUR MOM ALL NIGHT.
NOT FOR A **MASTER** OF SUBTERFUGE LIKE MYSELF.
PLEASE TELL ME YOU'VE GOT A SHIRT IN YOUR BOOK BAG.
AND COVER THIS WORK OF ART? **NO WAY!**
YOU KNOW THEY'RE JUST GONNA SEND YOU HOME, RIGHT?
YEAH, WELL IT'S LIKE THEY SAY...
BONDIA
GO BIG THEN GO HOME!
I GOTTA START WRITING THESE DOWN.

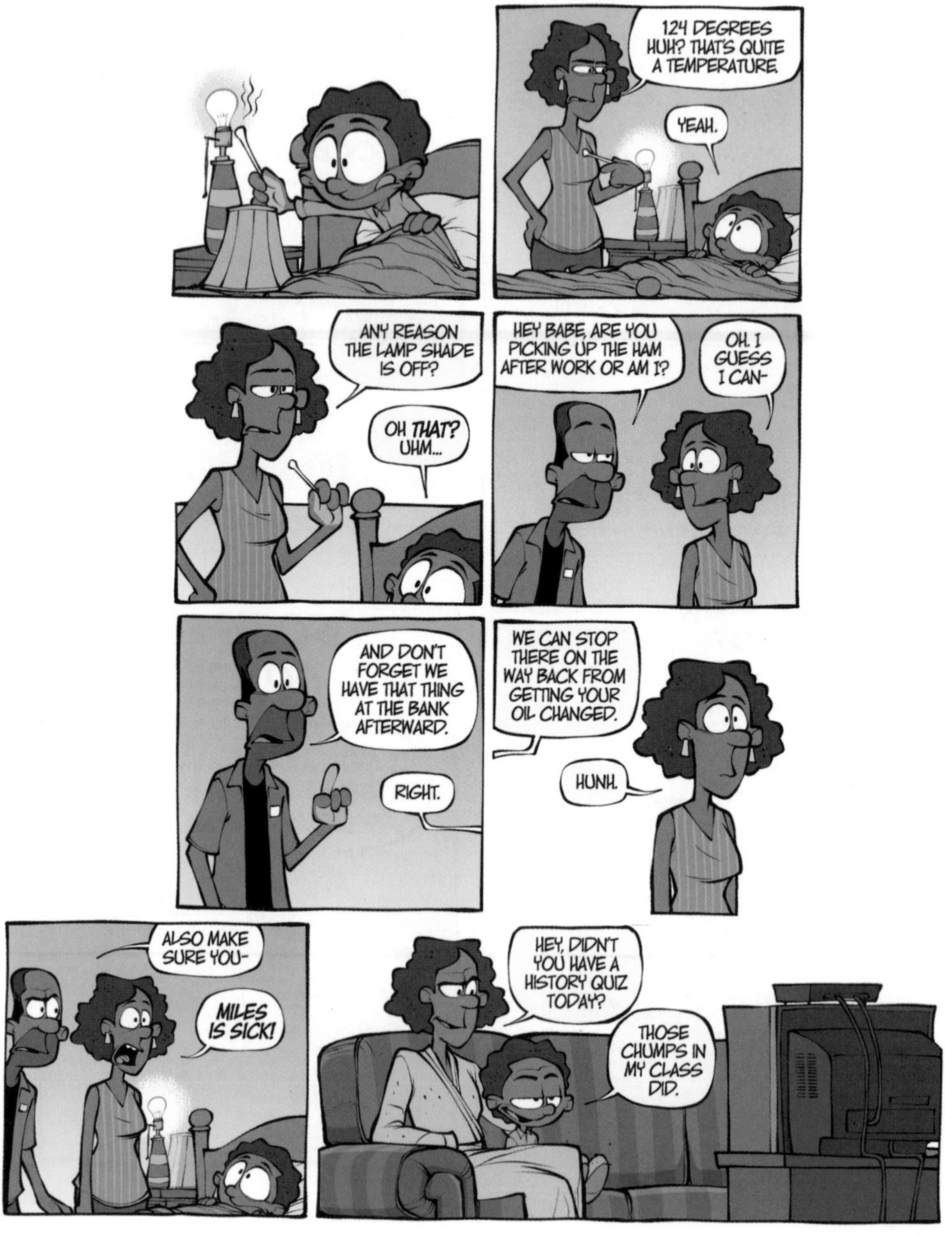
124 DEGREES HUH? THAT'S QUITE A TEMPERATURE.
YEAH.
ANY REASON THE LAMP SHADE IS OFF?
OH THAT? UHM...
HEY BABE, ARE YOU PICKING UP THE HAM AFTER WORK OR AM I?
OH. I GUESS I CAN-
AND DON'T FORGET WE HAVE THAT THING AT THE BANK AFTERWARD.
RIGHT.
WE CAN STOP THERE ON THE WAY BACK FROM GETTING YOUR OIL CHANGED.
HUNH.
ALSO MAKE SURE YOU-
MILES IS SICK!
HEY, DIDN'T YOU HAVE A HISTORY QUIZ TODAY?
THOSE CHUMPS IN MY CLASS DID.

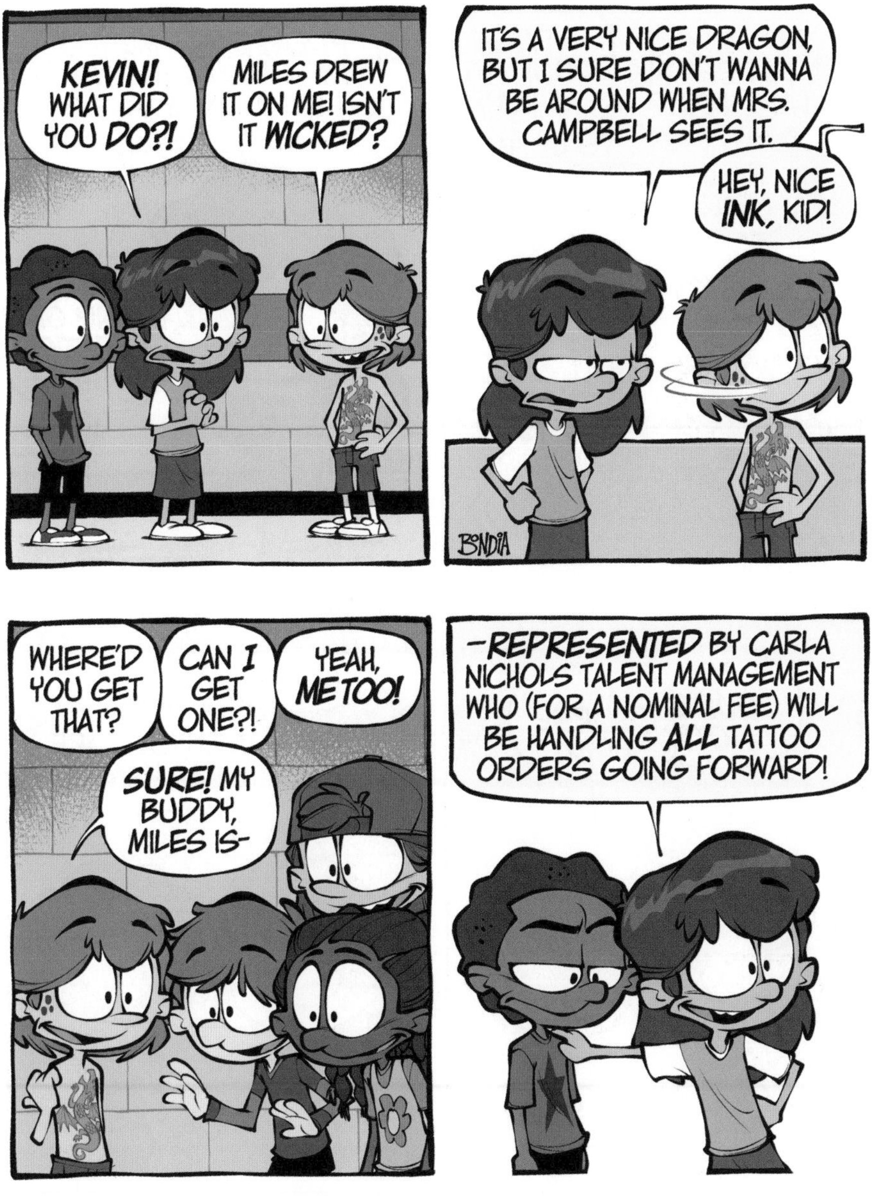
KEVIN! WHAT DID YOU DO?!
MILES DREW IT ON ME! ISN'T IT WICKED?
IT'S A VERY NICE DRAGON, BUT I SURE DON'T WANNA BE AROUND WHEN MRS. CAMPBELL SEES IT.
HEY, NICE INK, KID!
BONDIA
WHERE'D YOU GET THAT?
CAN I GET ONE?!
YEAH, ME TOO!
SURE! MY BUDDY, MILES IS-
–REPRESENTED BY CARLA NICHOLS TALENT MANAGEMENT WHO (FOR A NOMINAL FEE) WILL BE HANDLING ALL TATTOO ORDERS GOING FORWARD!

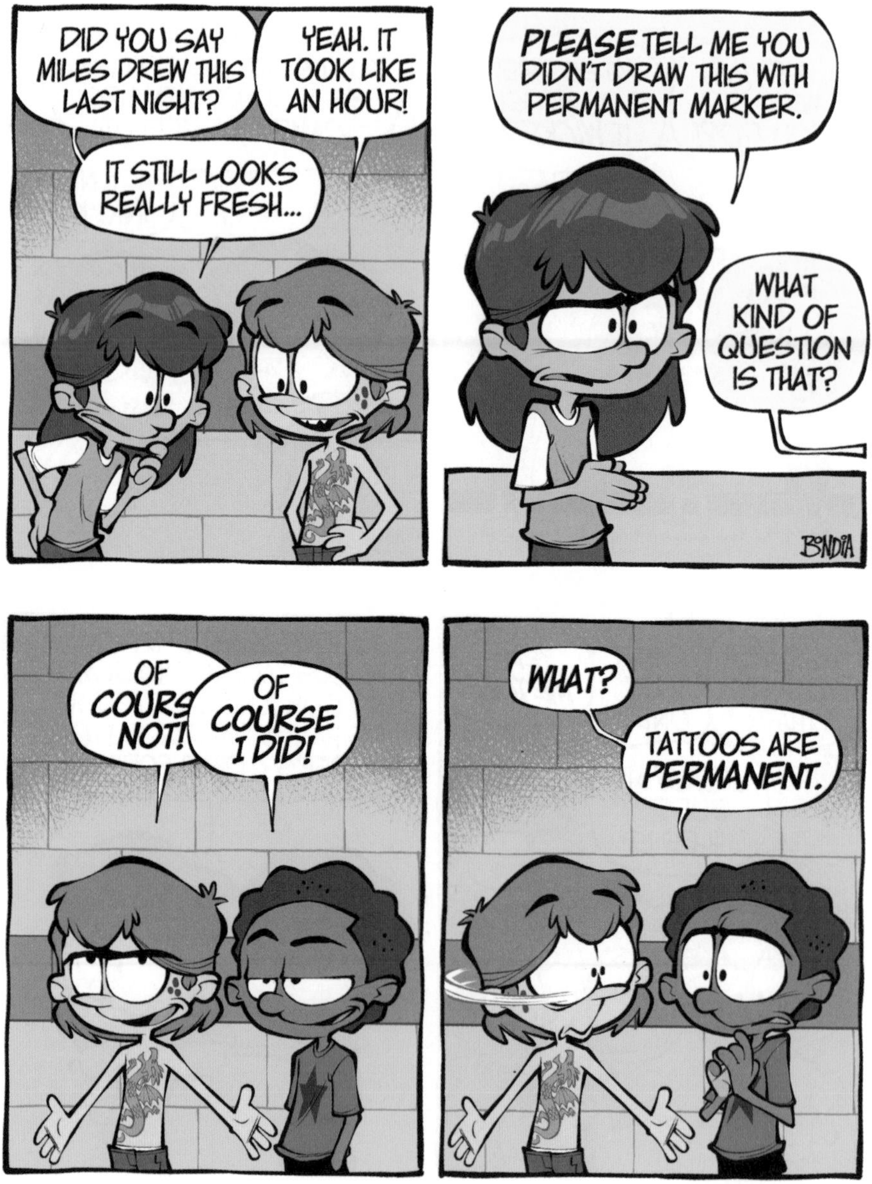
DID YOU SAY MILES DREW THIS LAST NIGHT?
YEAH. IT TOOK LIKE AN HOUR!
IT STILL LOOKS REALLY FRESH...
PLEASE TELL ME YOU DIDN'T DRAW THIS WITH PERMANENT MARKER.
WHAT KIND OF QUESTION IS THAT?
BONDIA
OF COURSE NOT!
OF COURSE I DID!
WHAT?
TATTOOS ARE PERMANENT.

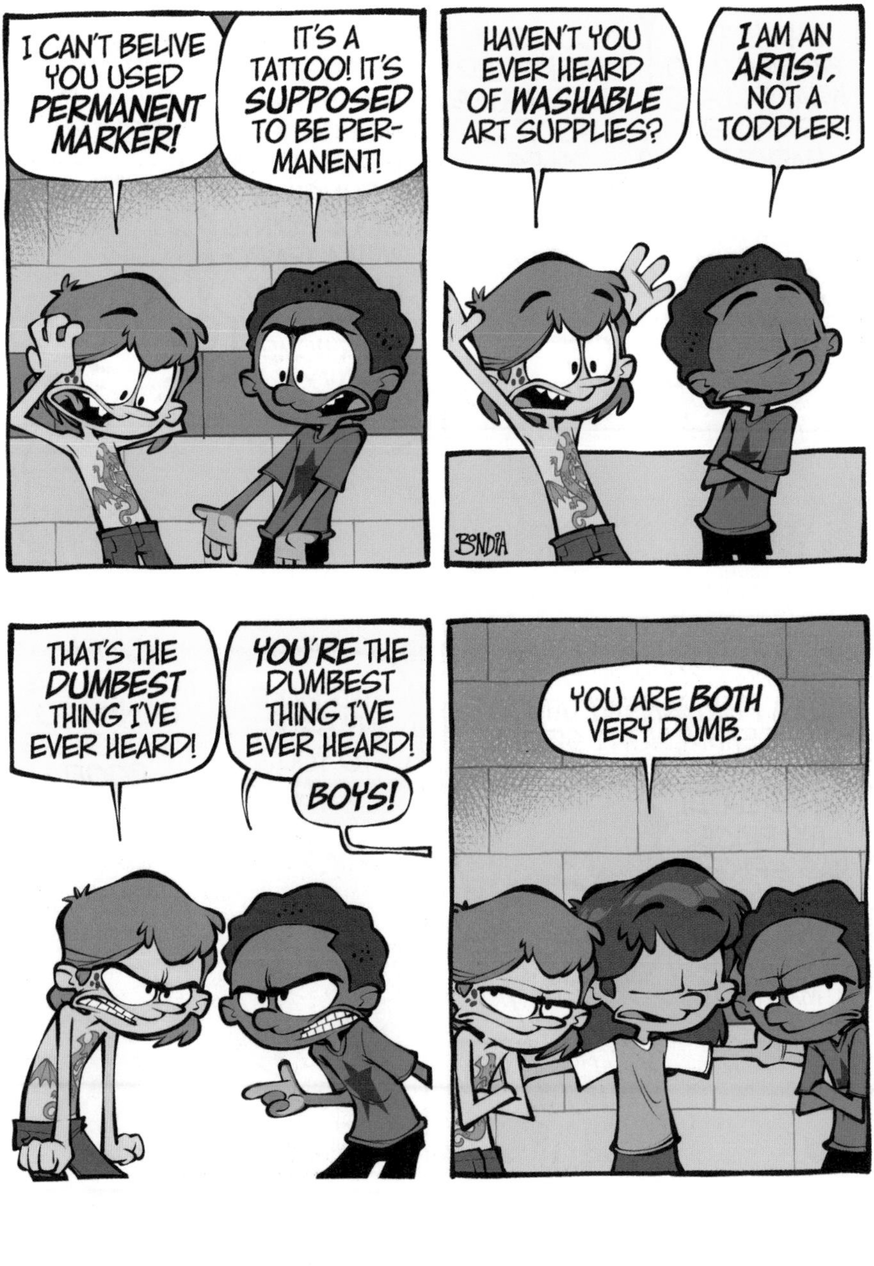
I CAN'T BELIVE YOU USED PERMANENT MARKER!
IT'S A TATTOO! IT'S SUPPOSED TO BE PER-MANENT!
HAVEN'T YOU EVER HEARD OF WASHABLE ART SUPPLIES?
I AM AN ARTIST, NOT A TODDLER!
BONDIA
THAT'S THE DUMBEST THING I'VE EVER HEARD!
YOU'RE THE DUMBEST THING I'VE EVER HEARD!
BOYS!
YOU ARE BOTH VERY DUMB.

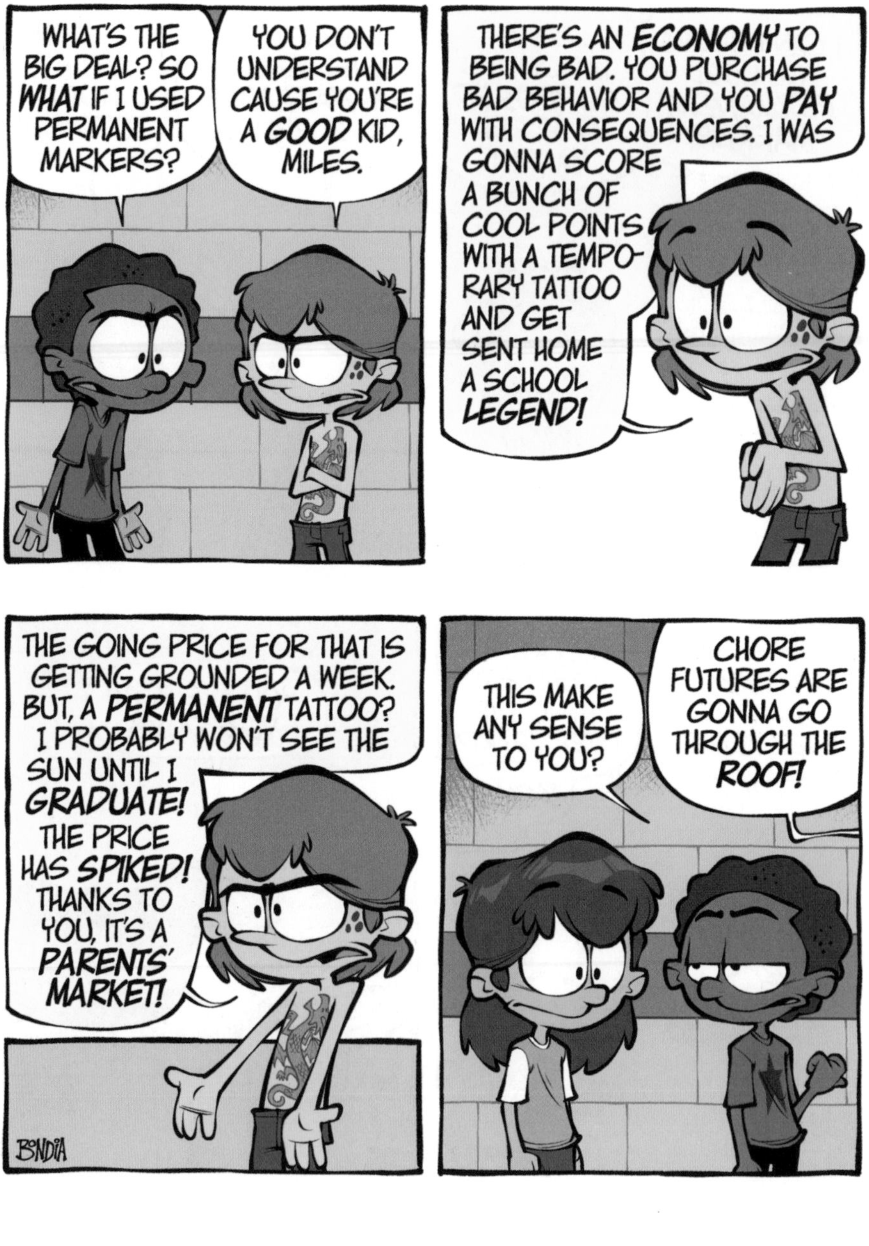
WHAT'S THE BIG DEAL? SO WHAT IF I USED PERMANENT MARKERS?
YOU DON'T UNDERSTAND CAUSE YOU'RE A GOOD KID, MILES.
THERE'S AN ECONOMY TO BEING BAD. YOU PURCHASE BAD BEHAVIOR AND YOU PAY WITH CONSEQUENCES. I WAS GONNA SCORE A BUNCH OF COOL POINTS WITH A TEMPORARY TATTOO AND GET SENT HOME A SCHOOL LEGEND!
THE GOING PRICE FOR THAT IS GETTING GROUNDED A WEEK. BUT, A PERMANENT TATTOO? I PROBABLY WON'T SEE THE SUN UNTIL I GRADUATE! THE PRICE HAS SPIKED! THANKS TO YOU, IT'S A PARENTS' MARKET!
BONDIA
THIS MAKE ANY SENSE TO YOU?
CHORE FUTURES ARE GONNA GO THROUGH THE ROOF!

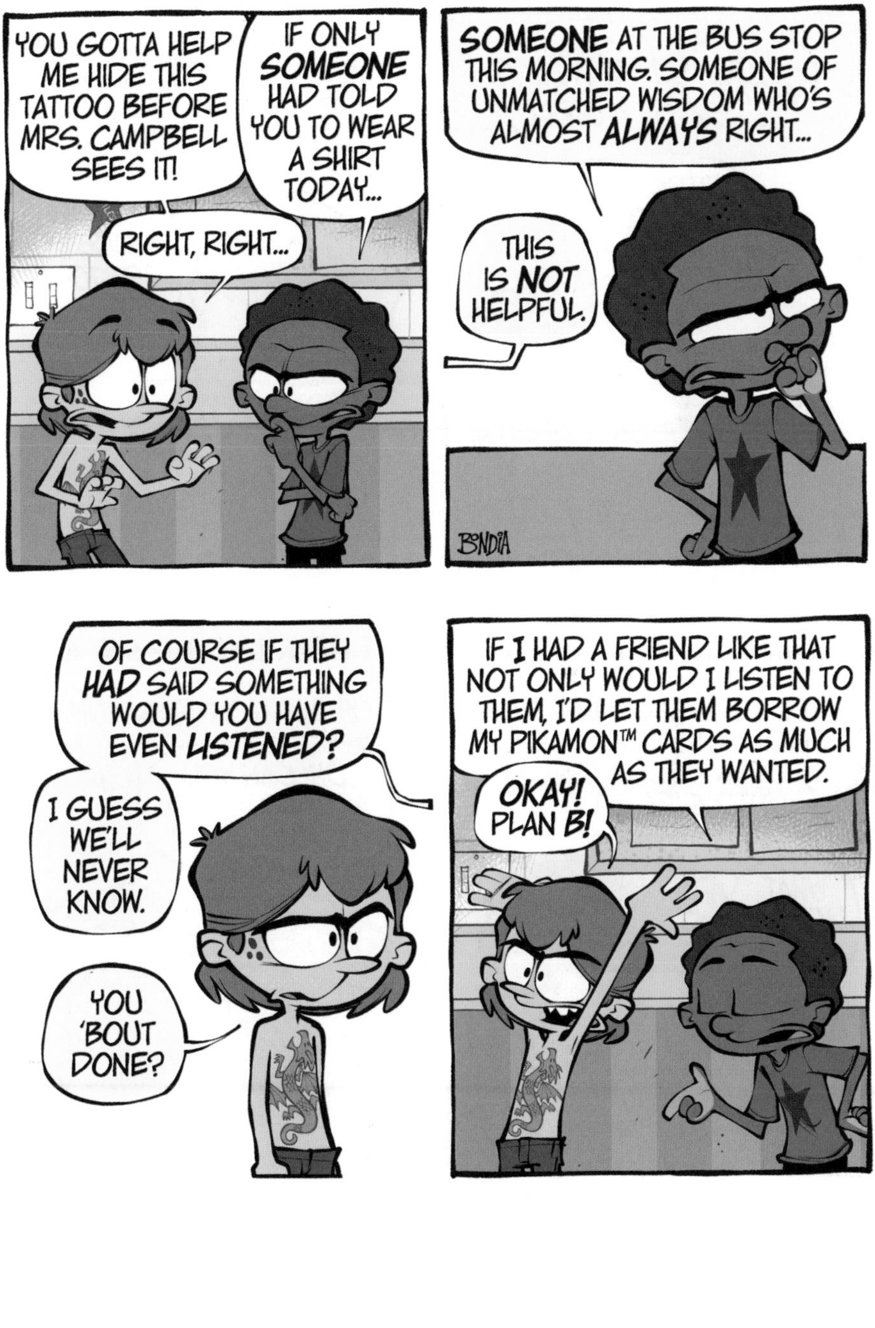
YOU GOTTA HELP ME HIDE THIS TATTOO BEFORE MRS. CAMPBELL SEES IT!
IF ONLY SOMEONE HAD TOLD YOU TO WEAR A SHIRT TODAY...
RIGHT, RIGHT...
SOMEONE AT THE BUS STOP THIS MORNING. SOMEONE OF UNMATCHED WISDOM WHO'S ALMOST ALWAYS RIGHT...
THIS IS NOT HELPFUL.
OF COURSE IF THEY HAD SAID SOMETHING WOULD YOU HAVE EVEN LISTENED?
I GUESS WE'LL NEVER KNOW.
YOU 'BOUT DONE?
IF I HAD A FRIEND LIKE THAT NOT ONLY WOULD I LISTEN TO THEM, I'D LET THEM BORROW MY PIKAMON™ CARDS AS MUCH AS THEY WANTED.
OKAY! PLAN B!

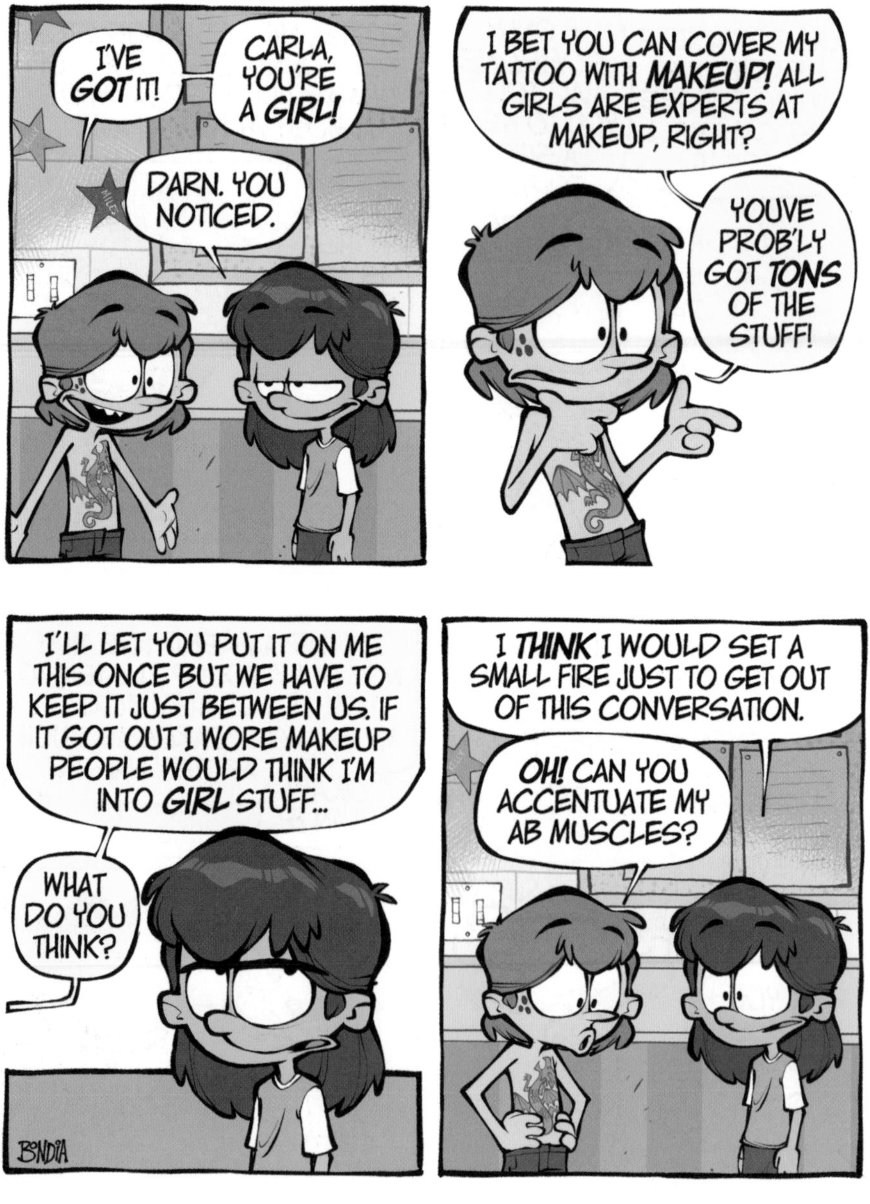
I'VE GOT IT!
CARLA, YOU'RE A GIRL!
DARN. YOU NOTICED.
I BET YOU CAN COVER MY TATTOO WITH MAKEUP! ALL GIRLS ARE EXPERTS AT MAKEUP, RIGHT?
YOUVE PROB'LY GOT TONS OF THE STUFF!
I'LL LET YOU PUT IT ON ME THIS ONCE BUT WE HAVE TO KEEP IT JUST BETWEEN US. IF IT GOT OUT I WORE MAKEUP PEOPLE WOULD THINK I'M INTO GIRL STUFF...
WHAT DO YOU THINK?
BONDIA
I THINK I WOULD SET A SMALL FIRE JUST TO GET OUT OF THIS CONVERSATION.
OH! CAN YOU ACCENTUATE MY AB MUSCLES?

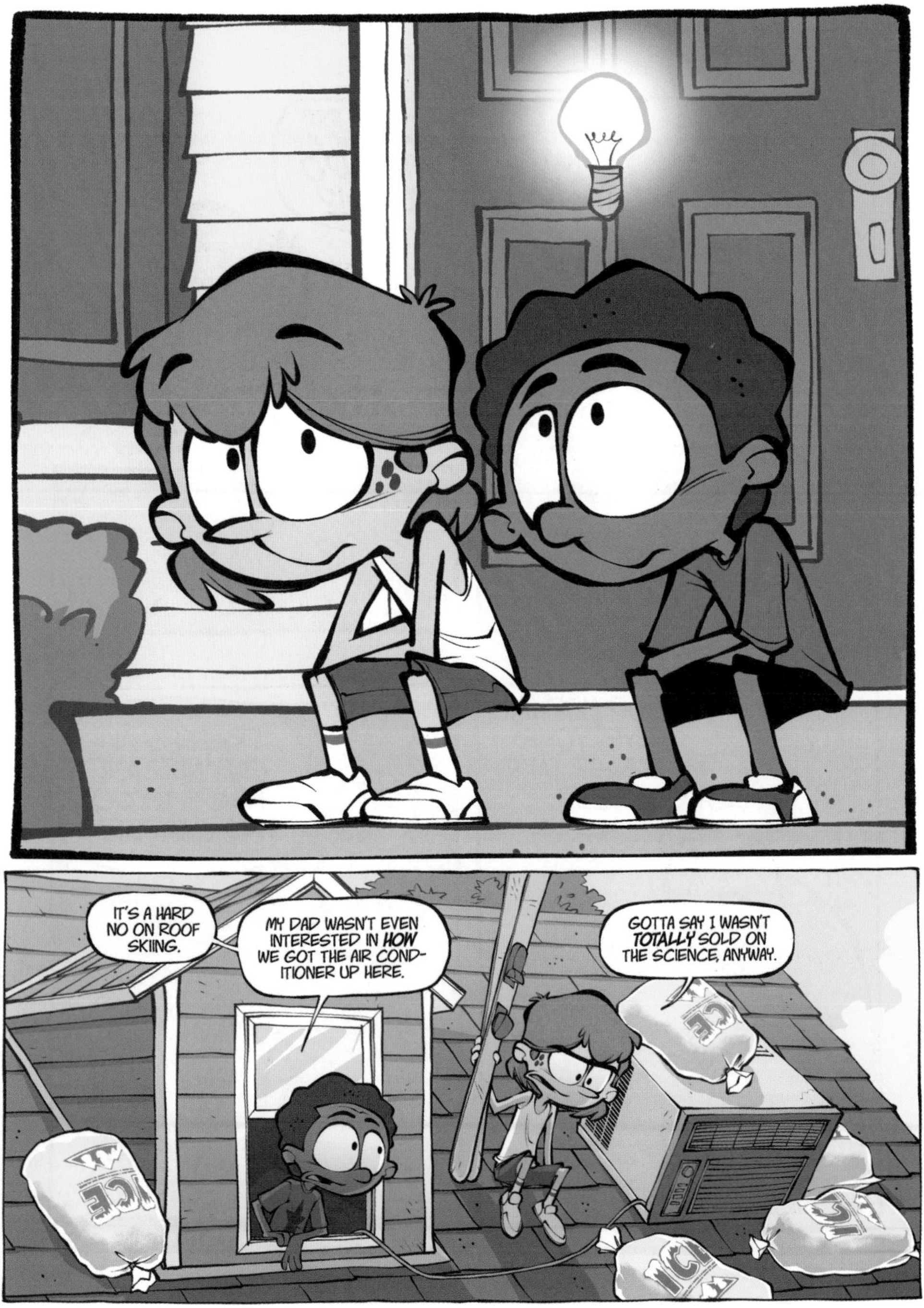
IT'S A HARD NO ON ROOF SKIING.
MY DAD WASN'T EVEN INTERESTED IN *HOW* WE GOT THE AIR CONDITIONER UP HERE.
GOTTA SAY I WASN'T *TOTALLY* SOLD ON THE SCIENCE, ANYWAY.

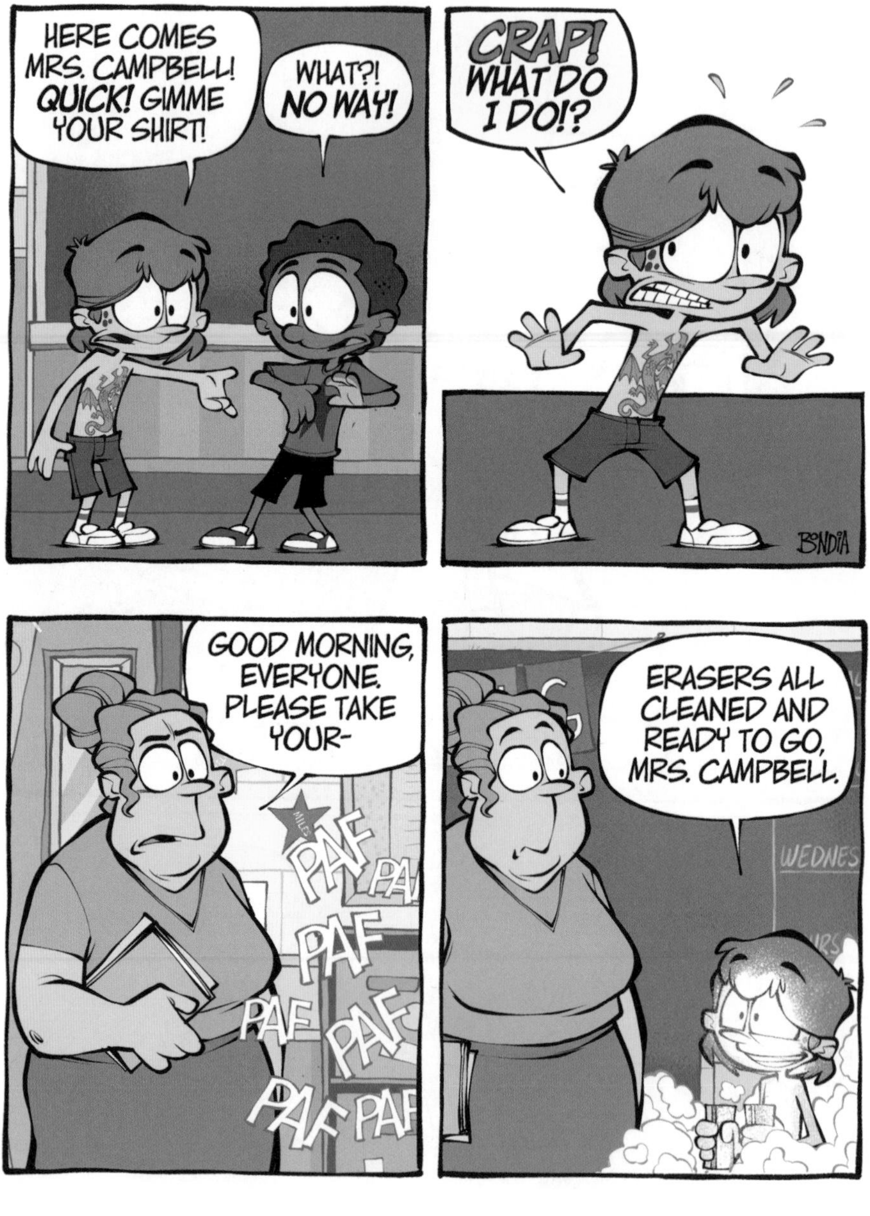
HERE COMES MRS. CAMPBELL! QUICK! GIMME YOUR SHIRT!
WHAT?! NO WAY!
CRAP! WHAT DO I DO!?
GOOD MORNING, EVERYONE. PLEASE TAKE YOUR-
PAF
PAF
PAF
PAF
PAF
ERASERS ALL CLEANED AND READY TO GO, MRS. CAMPBELL.

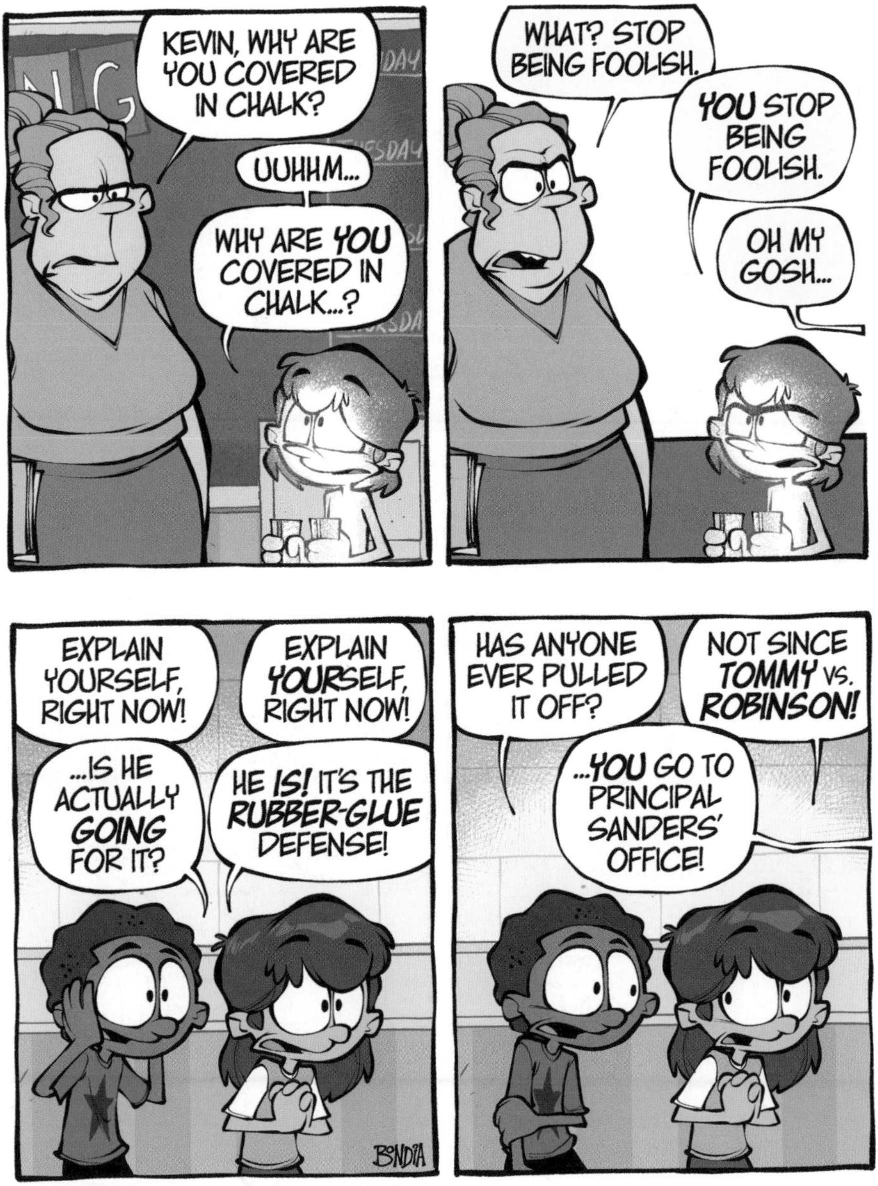
KEVIN, WHY ARE YOU COVERED IN CHALK?
UUHHM...
WHY ARE *YOU* COVERED IN CHALK...?
WHAT? STOP BEING FOOLISH.
YOU STOP BEING FOOLISH.
OH MY GOSH...
EXPLAIN YOURSELF, RIGHT NOW!
EXPLAIN *YOURSELF*, RIGHT NOW!
...IS HE ACTUALLY *GOING* FOR IT?
HE *IS!* IT'S THE *RUBBER-GLUE* DEFENSE!
BONDIA
HAS ANYONE EVER PULLED IT OFF?
NOT SINCE *TOMMY* VS. *ROBINSON!*
...*YOU* GO TO PRINCIPAL SANDERS' OFFICE!

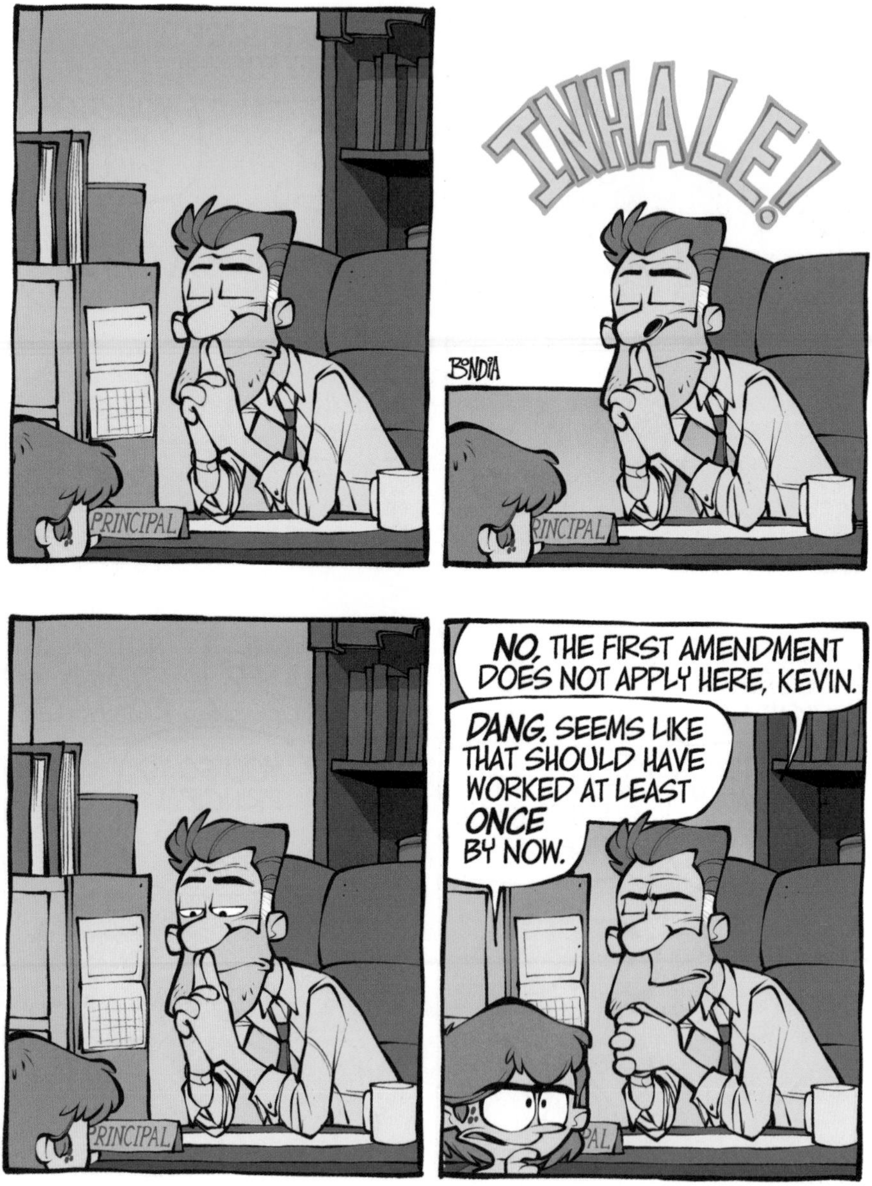
PRINCIPAL
INHALE!
BONDIA
RINCIPAL
PRINCIPAL
NO, THE FIRST AMENDMENT DOES NOT APPLY HERE, KEVIN.
DANG. SEEMS LIKE THAT SHOULD HAVE WORKED AT LEAST ONCE BY NOW.

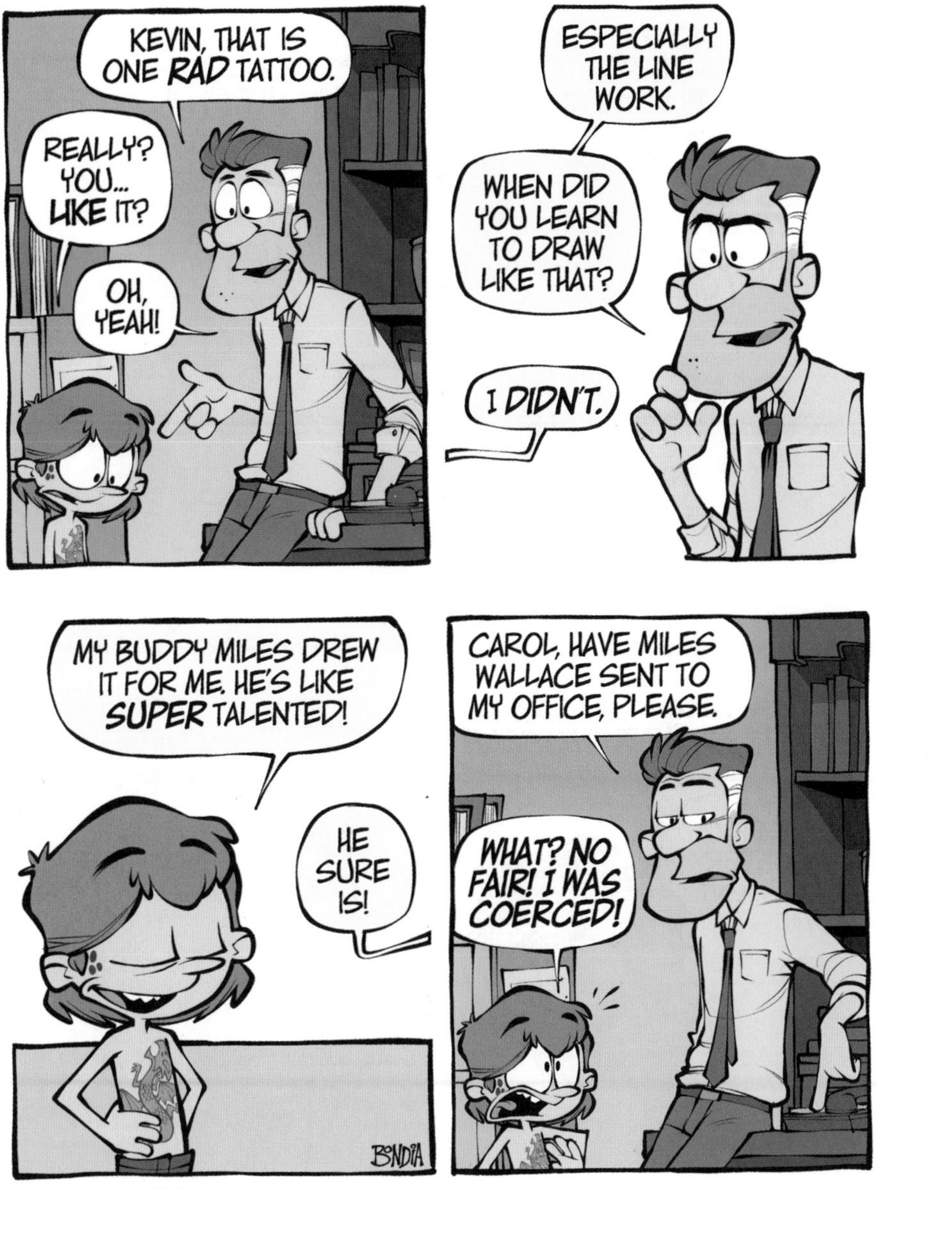
KEVIN, THAT IS ONE **RAD** TATTOO.
REALLY? YOU... **LIKE** IT?
OH, YEAH!
ESPECIALLY THE LINE WORK.
WHEN DID YOU LEARN TO DRAW LIKE THAT?
I **DIDN'T.**
MY BUDDY MILES DREW IT FOR ME. HE'S LIKE **SUPER** TALENTED!
HE SURE IS!
BONDIA
CAROL, HAVE MILES WALLACE SENT TO MY OFFICE, PLEASE.
WHAT? NO FAIR! I WAS COERCED!

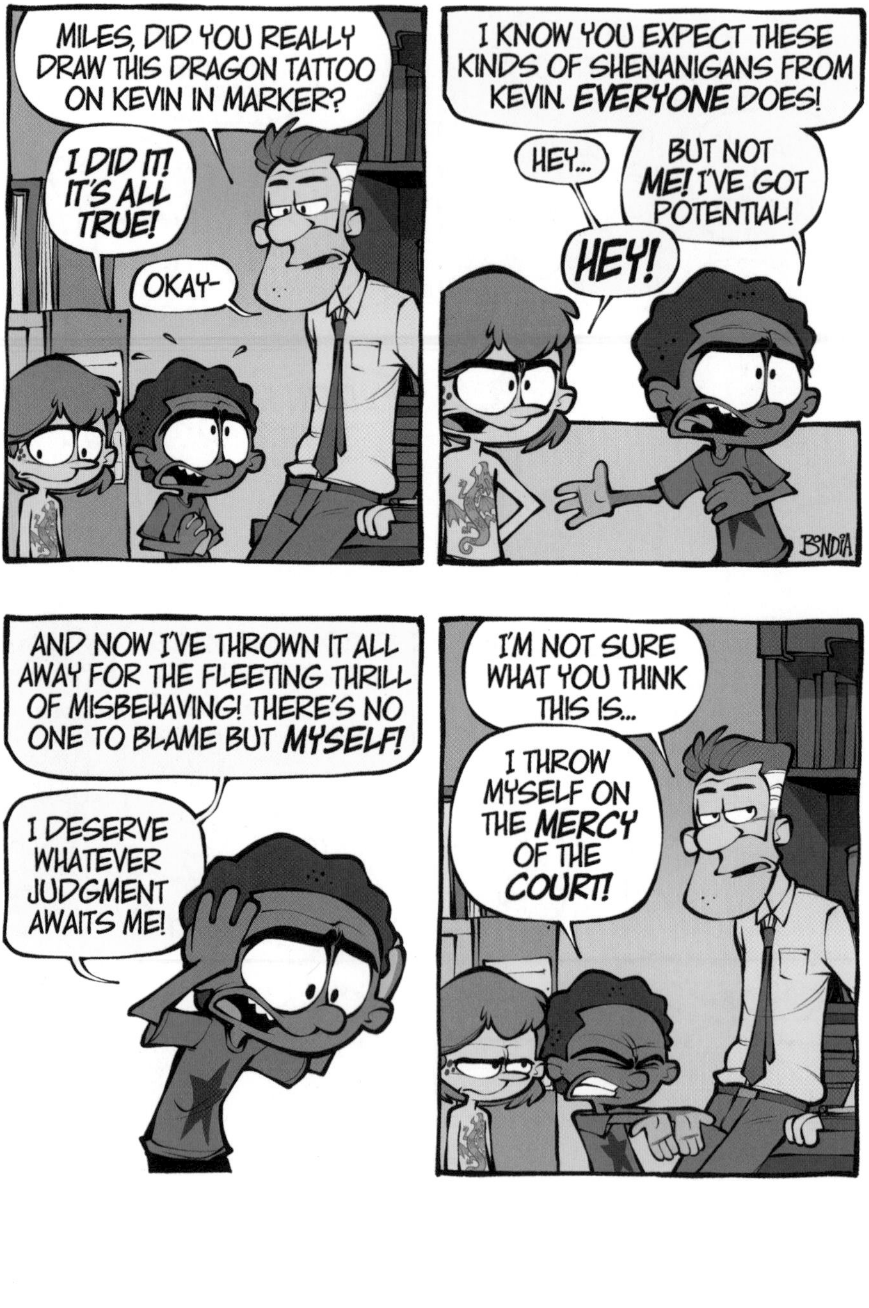
MILES, DID YOU REALLY DRAW THIS DRAGON TATTOO ON KEVIN IN MARKER?
I DID IT! IT'S ALL TRUE!
OKAY-
I KNOW YOU EXPECT THESE KINDS OF SHENANIGANS FROM KEVIN. EVERYONE DOES!
HEY...
BUT NOT ME! I'VE GOT POTENTIAL!
HEY!
BONDIA
AND NOW I'VE THROWN IT ALL AWAY FOR THE FLEETING THRILL OF MISBEHAVING! THERE'S NO ONE TO BLAME BUT MYSELF!
I DESERVE WHATEVER JUDGMENT AWAITS ME!
I'M NOT SURE WHAT YOU THINK THIS IS...
I THROW MYSELF ON THE MERCY OF THE COURT!

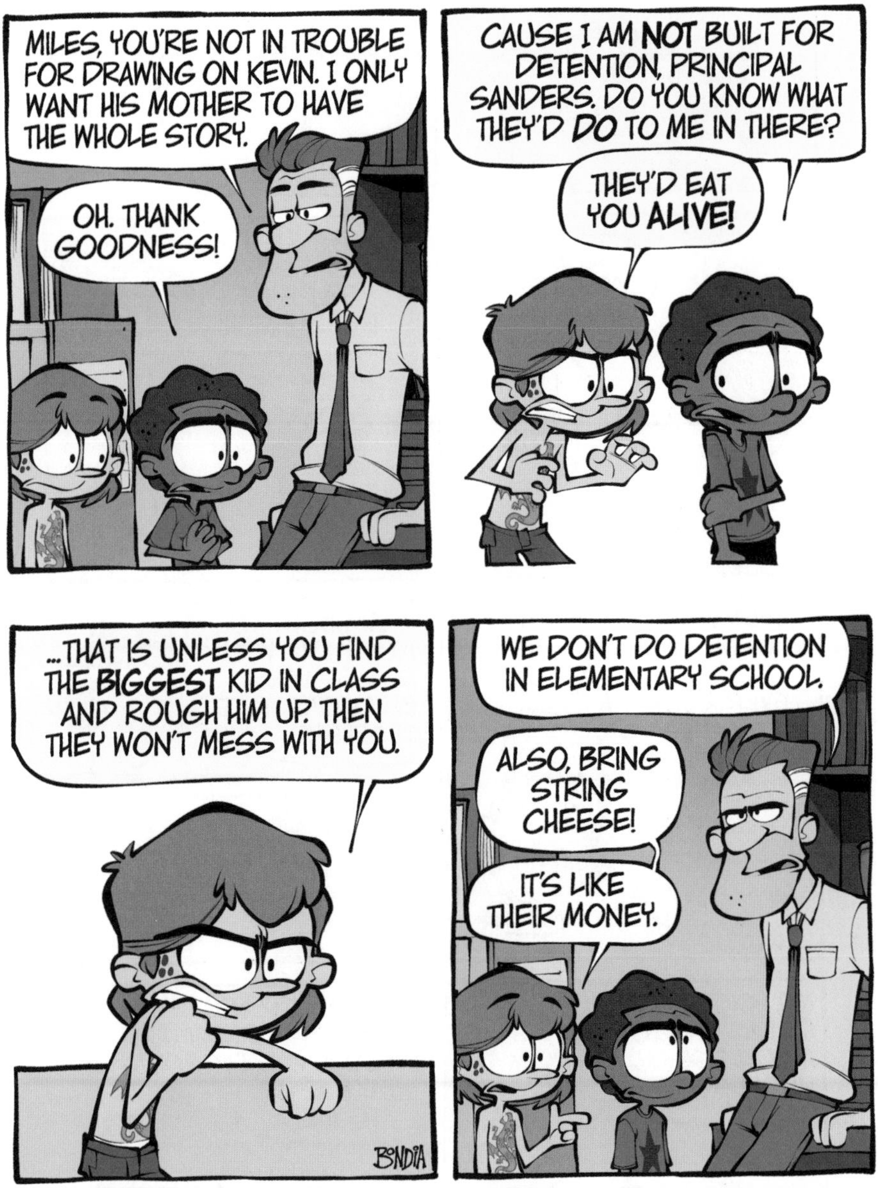
MILES, YOU'RE NOT IN TROUBLE FOR DRAWING ON KEVIN. I ONLY WANT HIS MOTHER TO HAVE THE WHOLE STORY.
OH. THANK GOODNESS!
CAUSE I AM NOT BUILT FOR DETENTION, PRINCIPAL SANDERS. DO YOU KNOW WHAT THEY'D DO TO ME IN THERE?
THEY'D EAT YOU ALIVE!
...THAT IS UNLESS YOU FIND THE BIGGEST KID IN CLASS AND ROUGH HIM UP. THEN THEY WON'T MESS WITH YOU.
BONDIA
WE DON'T DO DETENTION IN ELEMENTARY SCHOOL.
ALSO, BRING STRING CHEESE!
IT'S LIKE THEIR MONEY.

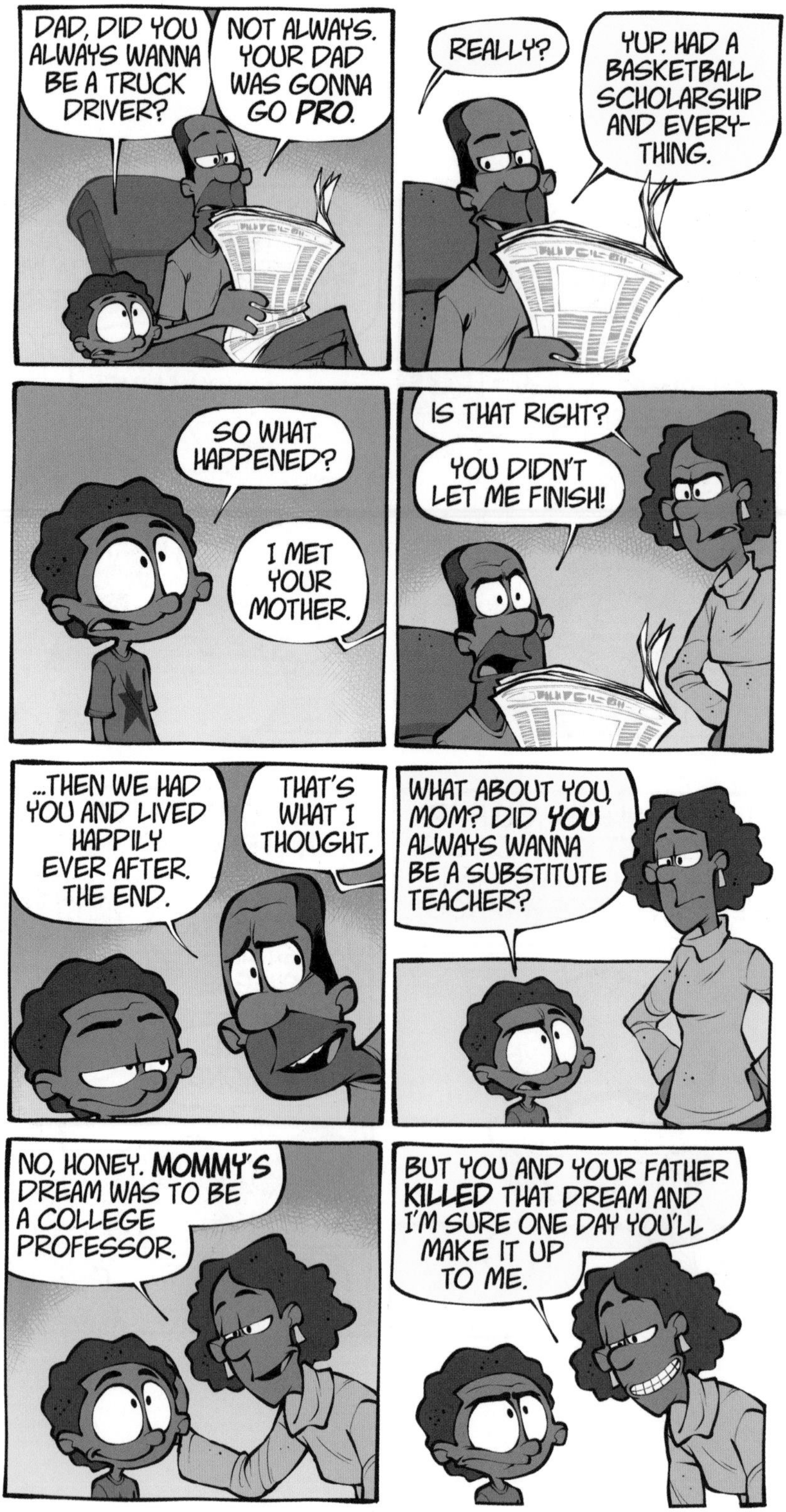
DAD, DID YOU ALWAYS WANNA BE A TRUCK DRIVER?
NOT ALWAYS. YOUR DAD WAS GONNA GO PRO.
REALLY?
YUP. HAD A BASKETBALL SCHOLARSHIP AND EVERY-THING.
SO WHAT HAPPENED?
I MET YOUR MOTHER.
IS THAT RIGHT?
YOU DIDN'T LET ME FINISH!
...THEN WE HAD YOU AND LIVED HAPPILY EVER AFTER. THE END.
THAT'S WHAT I THOUGHT.
WHAT ABOUT YOU, MOM? DID YOU ALWAYS WANNA BE A SUBSTITUTE TEACHER?
NO, HONEY. MOMMY'S DREAM WAS TO BE A COLLEGE PROFESSOR.
BUT YOU AND YOUR FATHER KILLED THAT DREAM AND I'M SURE ONE DAY YOU'LL MAKE IT UP TO ME.

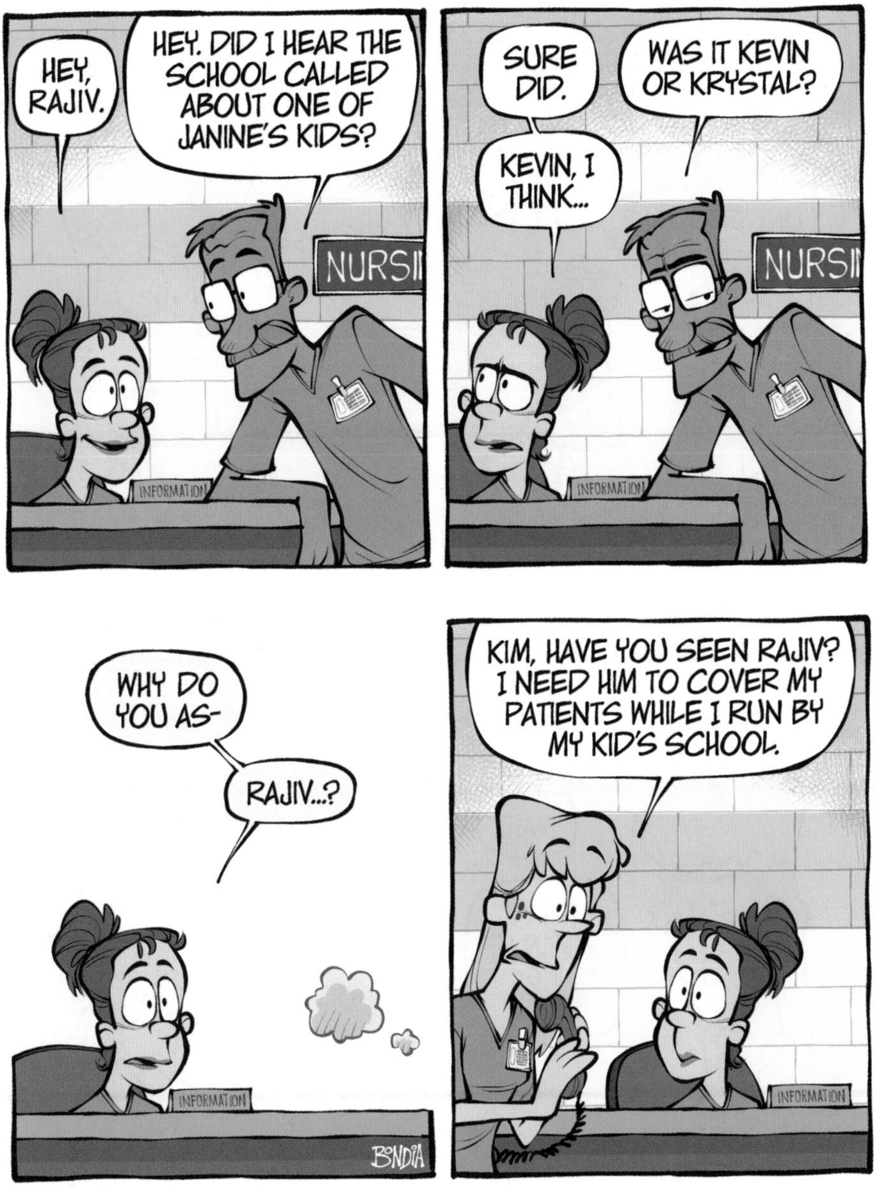
HEY, RAJIV.
HEY. DID I HEAR THE SCHOOL CALLED ABOUT ONE OF JANINE'S KIDS?
NURSI
INFORMATION
SURE DID.
KEVIN, I THINK...
WAS IT KEVIN OR KRYSTAL?
NURSI
INFORMATION
WHY DO YOU AS-
RAJIV...?
INFORMATION
BONDIA
KIM, HAVE YOU SEEN RAJIV? I NEED HIM TO COVER MY PATIENTS WHILE I RUN BY MY KID'S SCHOOL.
INFORMATION

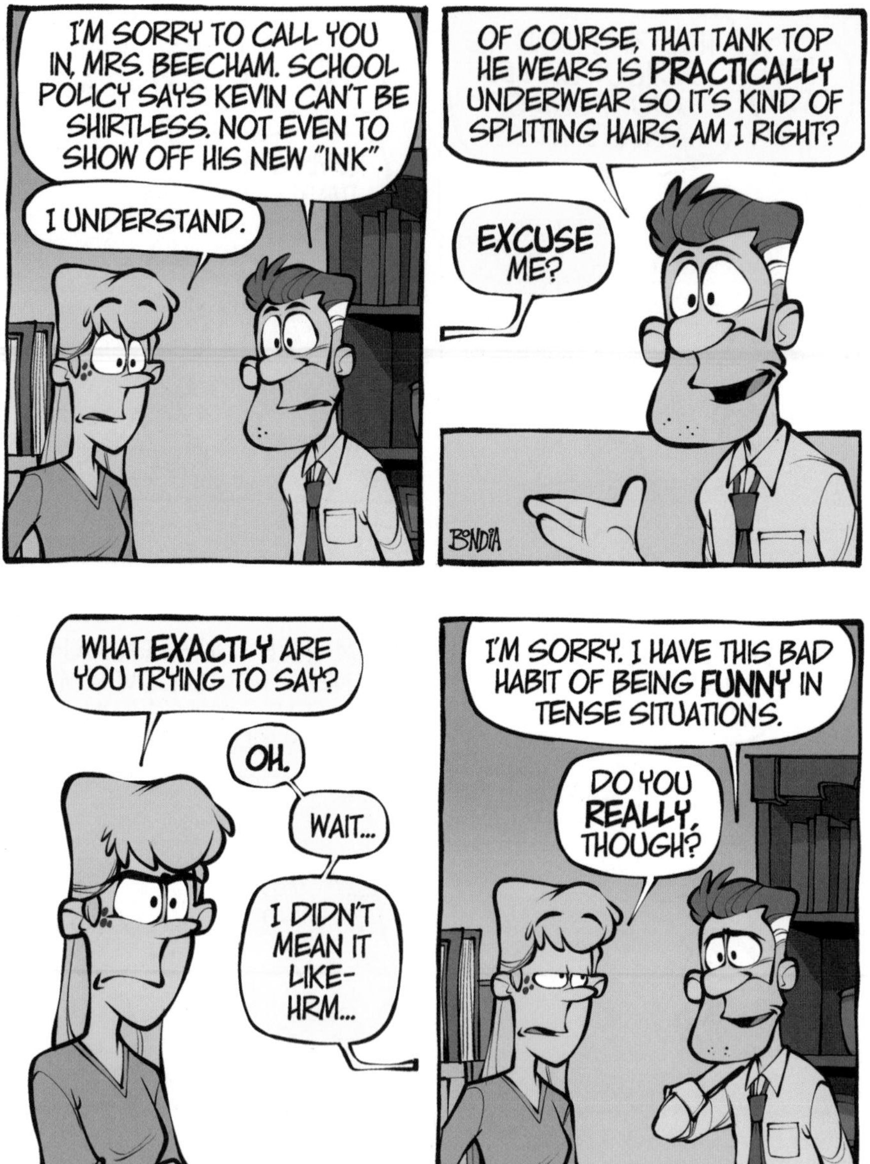
I'M SORRY TO CALL YOU IN, MRS. BEECHAM. SCHOOL POLICY SAYS KEVIN CAN'T BE SHIRTLESS. NOT EVEN TO SHOW OFF HIS NEW "INK".
I UNDERSTAND.
OF COURSE, THAT TANK TOP HE WEARS IS **PRACTICALLY** UNDERWEAR SO IT'S KIND OF SPLITTING HAIRS, AM I RIGHT?
EXCUSE ME?
BONDIA
WHAT **EXACTLY** ARE YOU TRYING TO SAY?
OH.
WAIT...
I DIDN'T MEAN IT LIKE- HRM...
I'M SORRY. I HAVE THIS BAD HABIT OF BEING **FUNNY** IN TENSE SITUATIONS.
DO YOU **REALLY**, THOUGH?

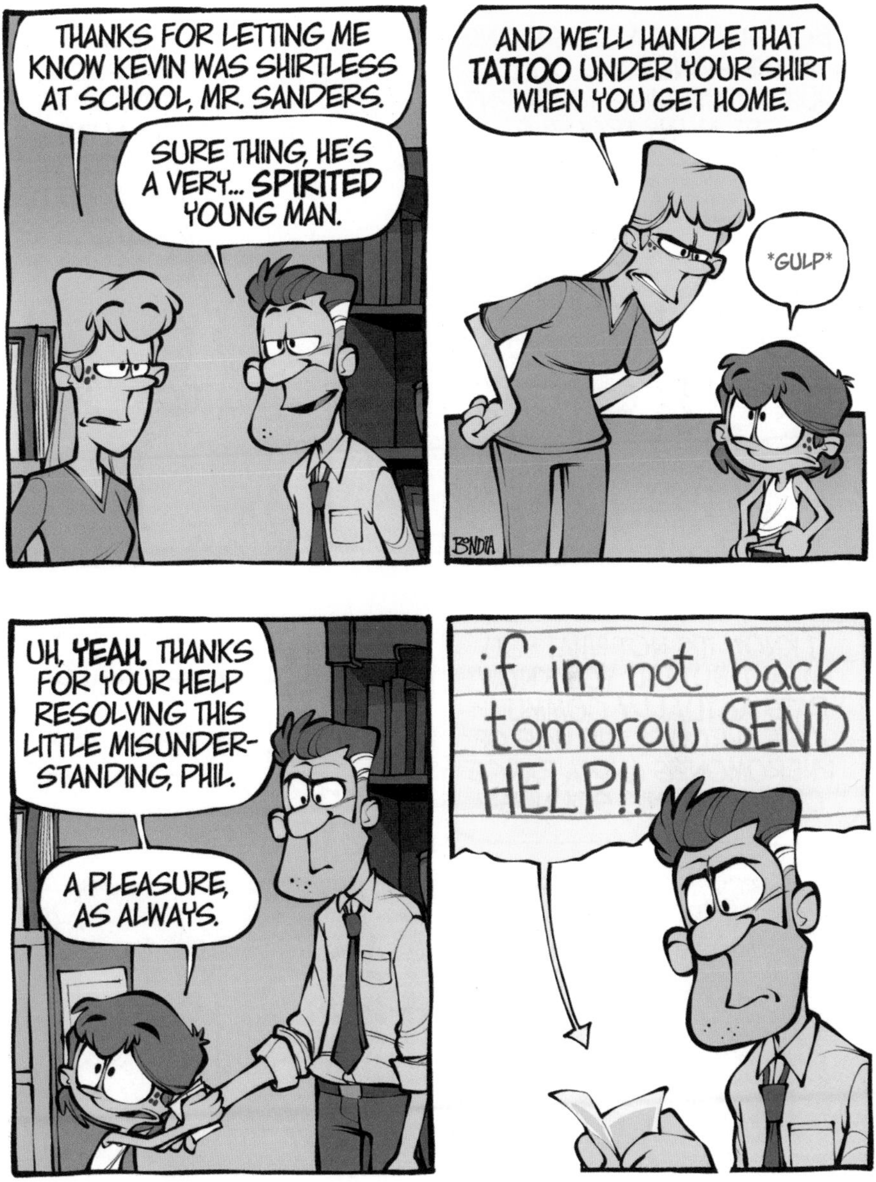
THANKS FOR LETTING ME KNOW KEVIN WAS SHIRTLESS AT SCHOOL, MR. SANDERS.
SURE THING, HE'S A VERY... SPIRITED YOUNG MAN.
AND WE'LL HANDLE THAT TATTOO UNDER YOUR SHIRT WHEN YOU GET HOME.
GULP
BONDIA
UH, YEAH. THANKS FOR YOUR HELP RESOLVING THIS LITTLE MISUNDERSTANDING, PHIL.
A PLEASURE, AS ALWAYS.
if im not back tomorow SEND HELP!!

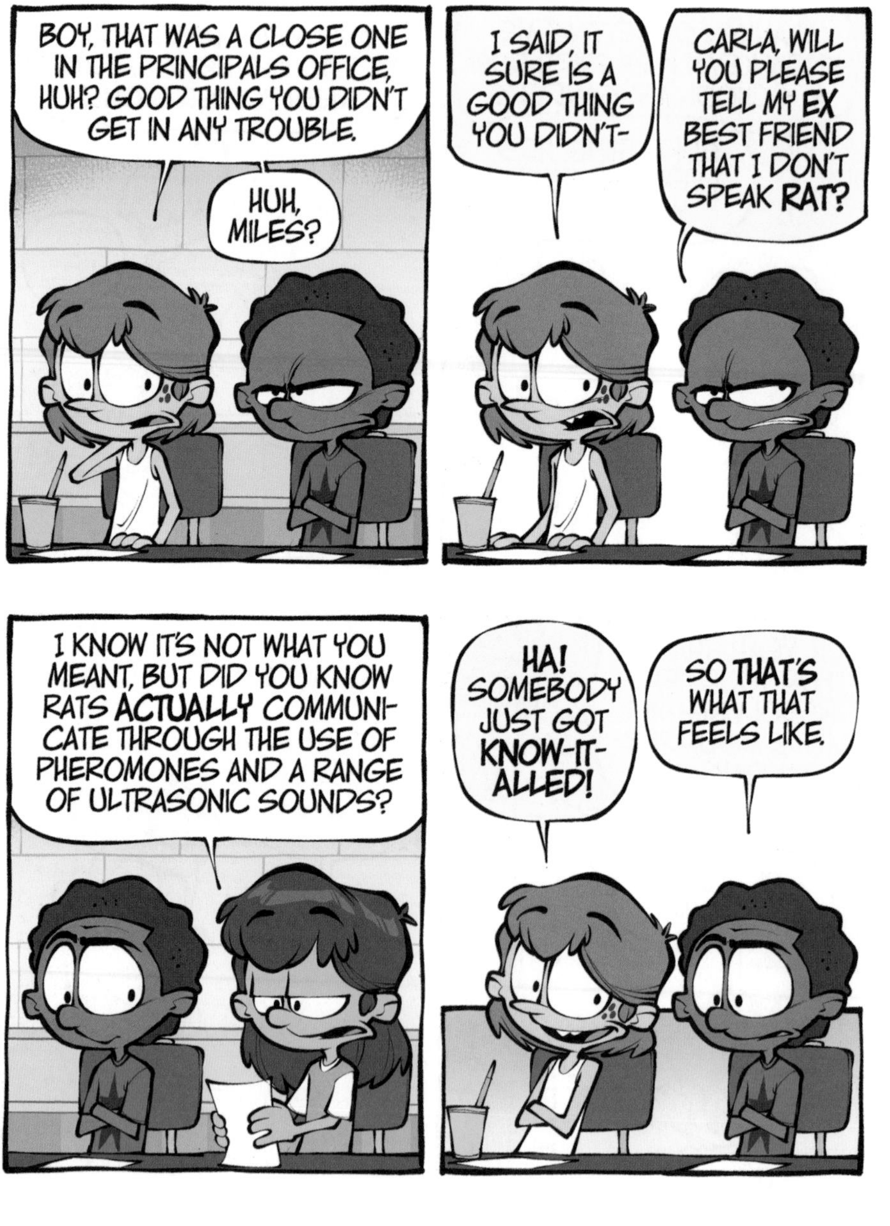
BOY, THAT WAS A CLOSE ONE IN THE PRINCIPALS OFFICE, HUH? GOOD THING YOU DIDN'T GET IN ANY TROUBLE.
HUH, MILES?
I SAID, IT SURE IS A GOOD THING YOU DIDN'T-
CARLA, WILL YOU PLEASE TELL MY **EX** BEST FRIEND THAT I DON'T SPEAK **RAT?**
I KNOW IT'S NOT WHAT YOU MEANT, BUT DID YOU KNOW RATS **ACTUALLY** COMMUNI-CATE THROUGH THE USE OF PHEROMONES AND A RANGE OF ULTRASONIC SOUNDS?
HA! SOMEBODY JUST GOT **KNOW-IT-ALLED!**
SO **THAT'S** WHAT THAT FEELS LIKE.

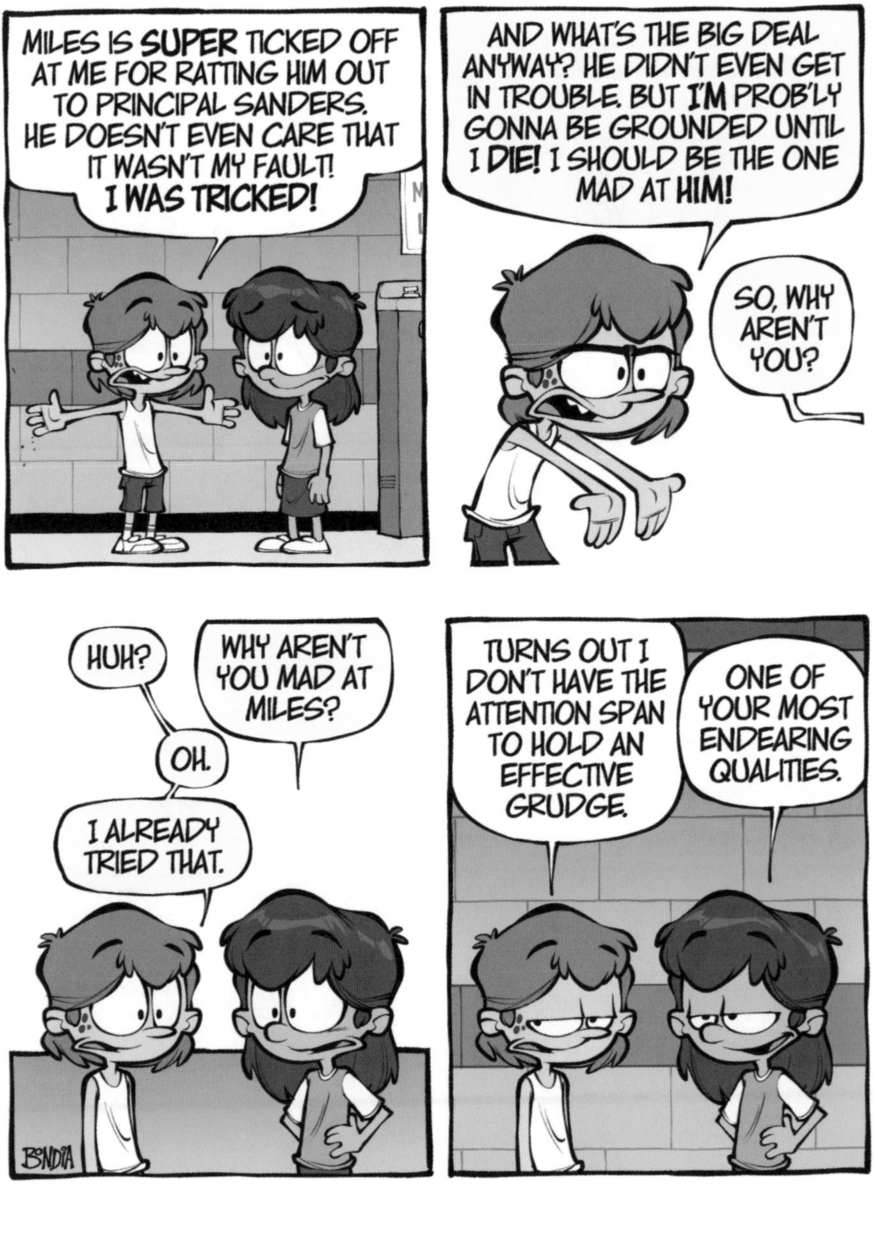
MILES IS SUPER TICKED OFF AT ME FOR RATTING HIM OUT TO PRINCIPAL SANDERS. HE DOESN'T EVEN CARE THAT IT WASN'T MY FAULT! I WAS TRICKED!
AND WHAT'S THE BIG DEAL ANYWAY? HE DIDN'T EVEN GET IN TROUBLE. BUT I'M PROB'LY GONNA BE GROUNDED UNTIL I DIE! I SHOULD BE THE ONE MAD AT HIM!
SO, WHY AREN'T YOU?
HUH?
WHY AREN'T YOU MAD AT MILES?
OH.
I ALREADY TRIED THAT.
BONDIA
TURNS OUT I DON'T HAVE THE ATTENTION SPAN TO HOLD AN EFFECTIVE GRUDGE.
ONE OF YOUR MOST ENDEARING QUALITIES.

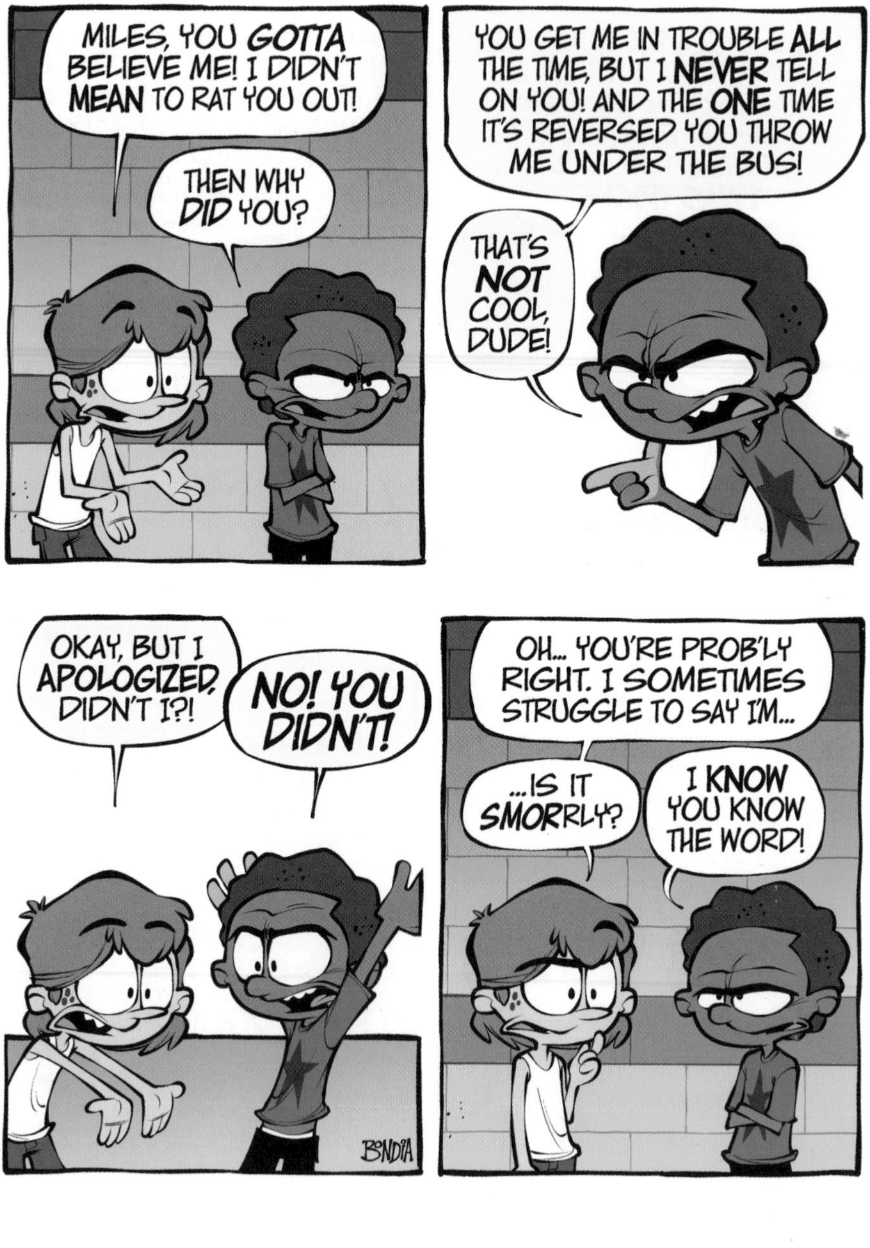
MILES, YOU GOTTA BELIEVE ME! I DIDN'T MEAN TO RAT YOU OUT!
THEN WHY DID YOU?
YOU GET ME IN TROUBLE ALL THE TIME, BUT I NEVER TELL ON YOU! AND THE ONE TIME IT'S REVERSED YOU THROW ME UNDER THE BUS!
THAT'S NOT COOL, DUDE!
OKAY, BUT I APOLOGIZED, DIDN'T I?!
NO! YOU DIDN'T!
BONDIA
OH... YOU'RE PROB'LY RIGHT. I SOMETIMES STRUGGLE TO SAY I'M...
...IS IT SMORRLY?
I KNOW YOU KNOW THE WORD!

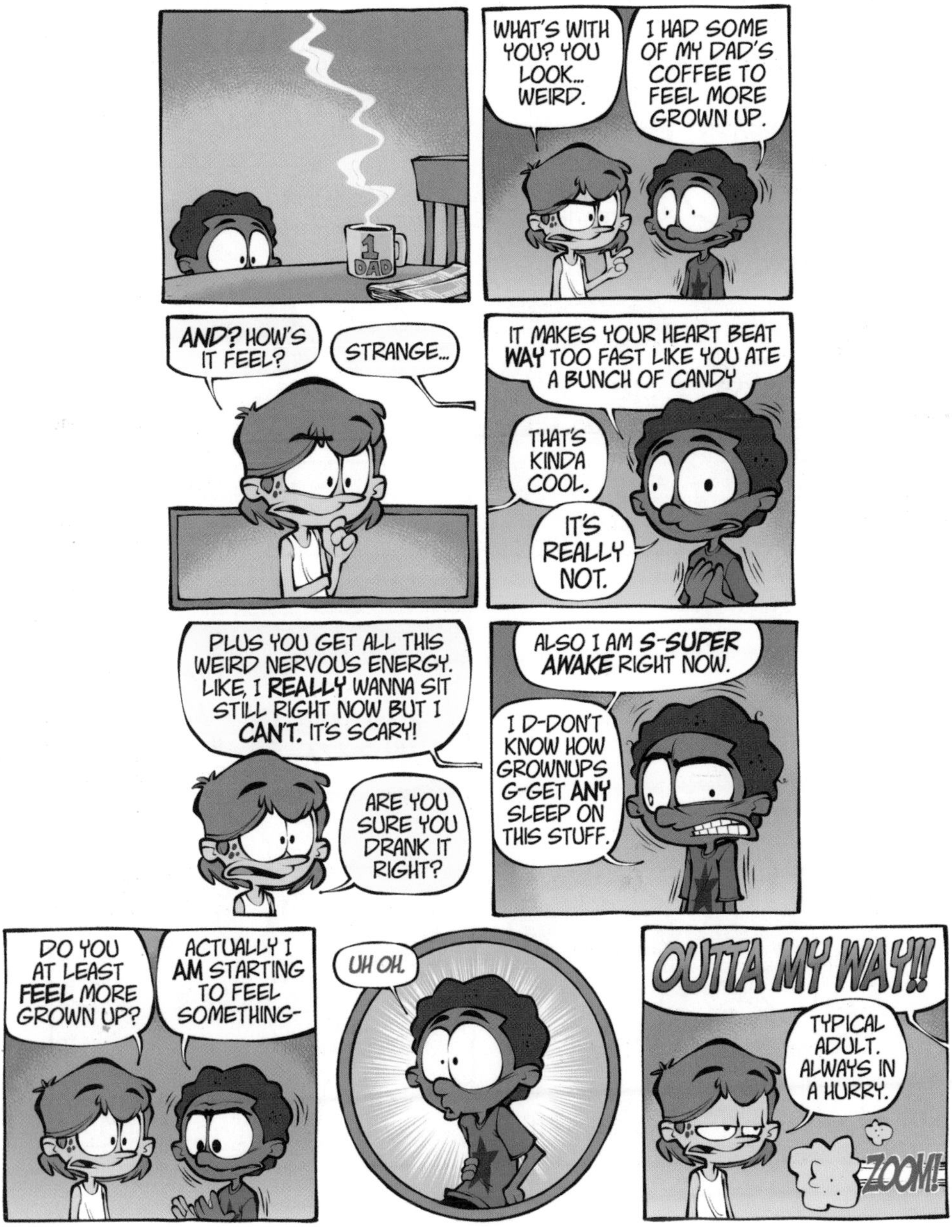
WHAT'S WITH YOU? YOU LOOK... WEIRD.
I HAD SOME OF MY DAD'S COFFEE TO FEEL MORE GROWN UP.
AND? HOW'S IT FEEL?
STRANGE...
IT MAKES YOUR HEART BEAT WAY TOO FAST LIKE YOU ATE A BUNCH OF CANDY
THAT'S KINDA COOL.
IT'S REALLY NOT.
PLUS YOU GET ALL THIS WEIRD NERVOUS ENERGY. LIKE, I REALLY WANNA SIT STILL RIGHT NOW BUT I CAN'T. IT'S SCARY!
ARE YOU SURE YOU DRANK IT RIGHT?
ALSO I AM S-SUPER AWAKE RIGHT NOW.
I D-DON'T KNOW HOW GROWNUPS G-GET ANY SLEEP ON THIS STUFF.
DO YOU AT LEAST FEEL MORE GROWN UP?
ACTUALLY I AM STARTING TO FEEL SOMETHING-
UH OH.
OUTTA MY WAY!!
TYPICAL ADULT. ALWAYS IN A HURRY.
ZOOM!

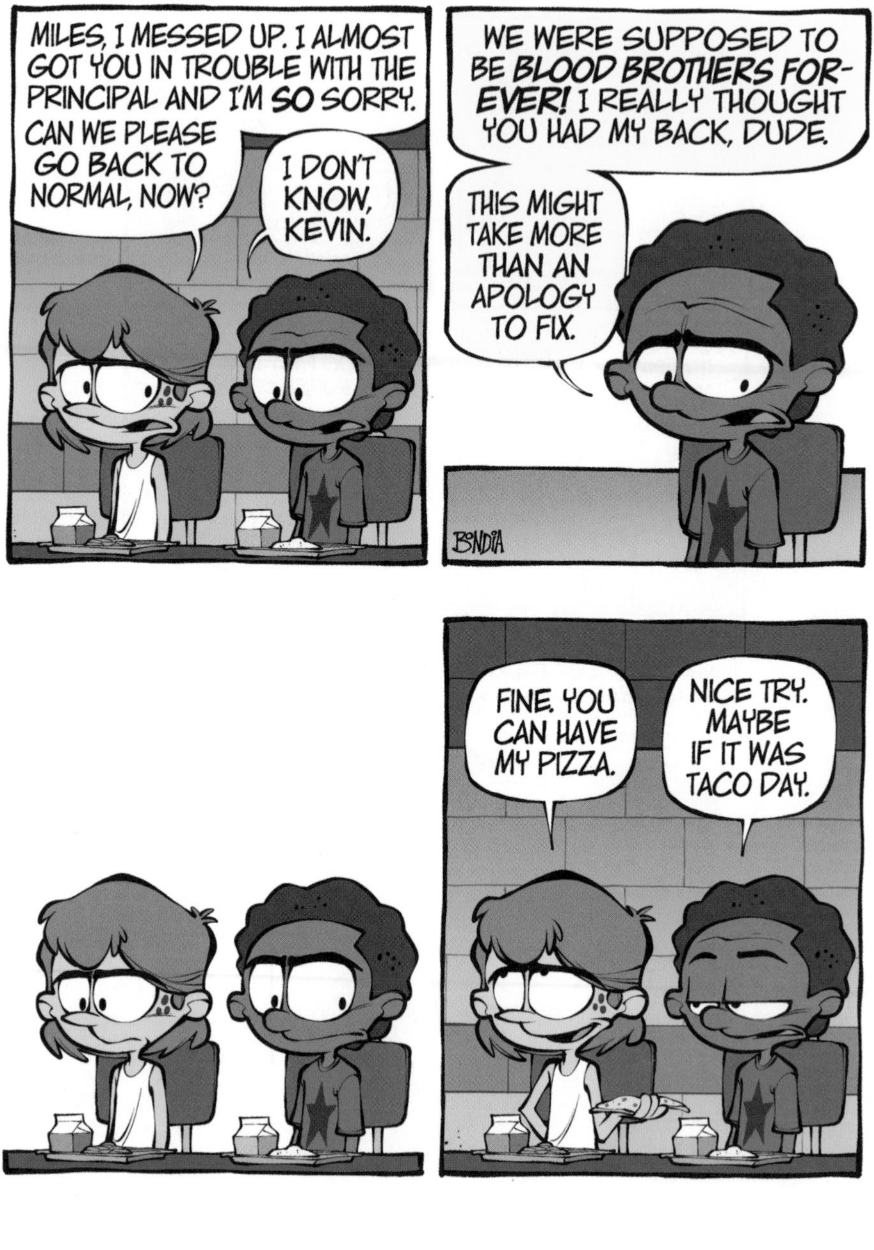
MILES, I MESSED UP. I ALMOST GOT YOU IN TROUBLE WITH THE PRINCIPAL AND I'M **SO** SORRY.
CAN WE PLEASE GO BACK TO NORMAL, NOW?
I DON'T KNOW, KEVIN.
WE WERE SUPPOSED TO BE ***BLOOD BROTHERS FOREVER!*** I REALLY THOUGHT YOU HAD MY BACK, DUDE.
THIS MIGHT TAKE MORE THAN AN APOLOGY TO FIX.
BONDIA
FINE. YOU CAN HAVE MY PIZZA.
NICE TRY. MAYBE IF IT WAS TACO DAY.

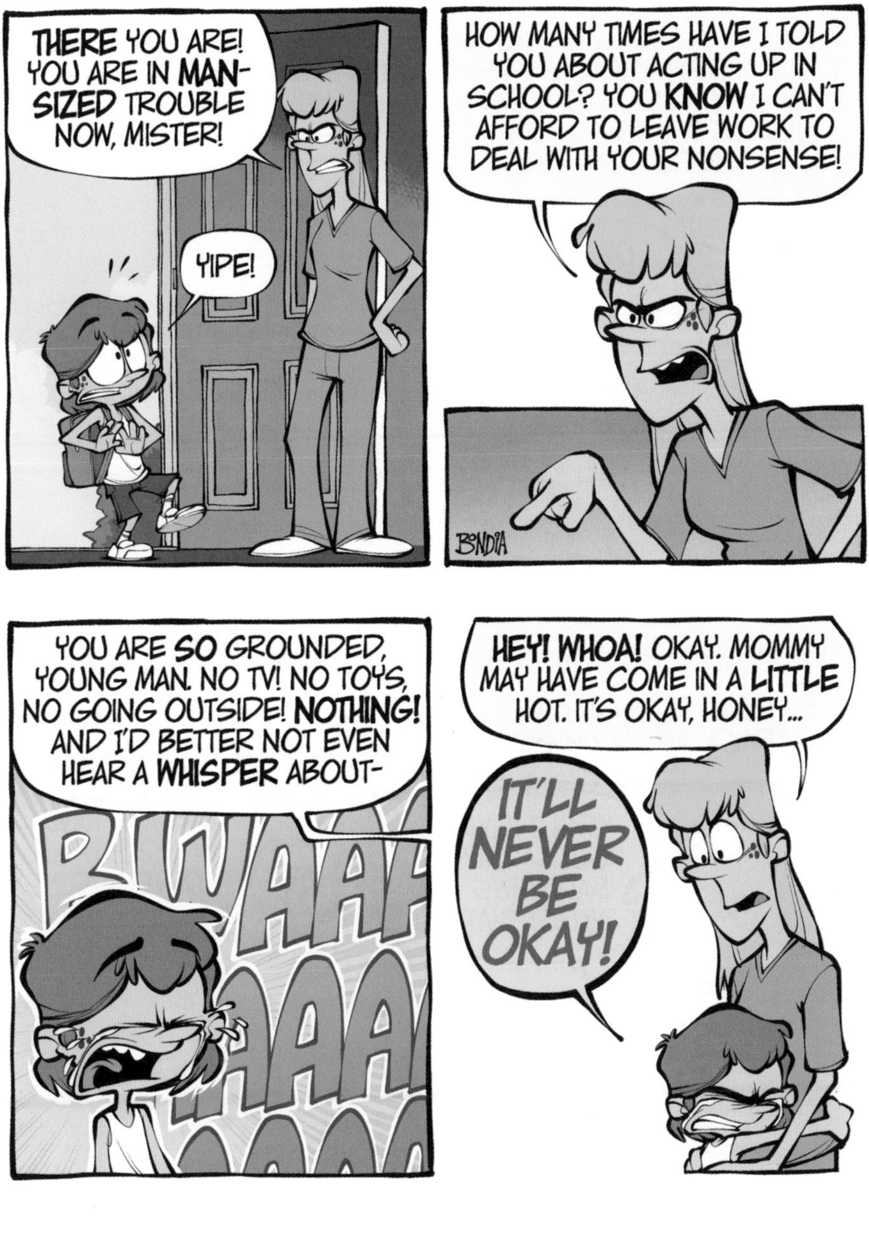
THERE YOU ARE! YOU ARE IN MAN-SIZED TROUBLE NOW, MISTER!
YIPE!
HOW MANY TIMES HAVE I TOLD YOU ABOUT ACTING UP IN SCHOOL? YOU KNOW I CAN'T AFFORD TO LEAVE WORK TO DEAL WITH YOUR NONSENSE!
YOU ARE SO GROUNDED, YOUNG MAN. NO TV! NO TOYS, NO GOING OUTSIDE! NOTHING! AND I'D BETTER NOT EVEN HEAR A WHISPER ABOUT-
HEY! WHOA! OKAY. MOMMY MAY HAVE COME IN A LITTLE HOT. IT'S OKAY, HONEY...
IT'LL NEVER BE OKAY!

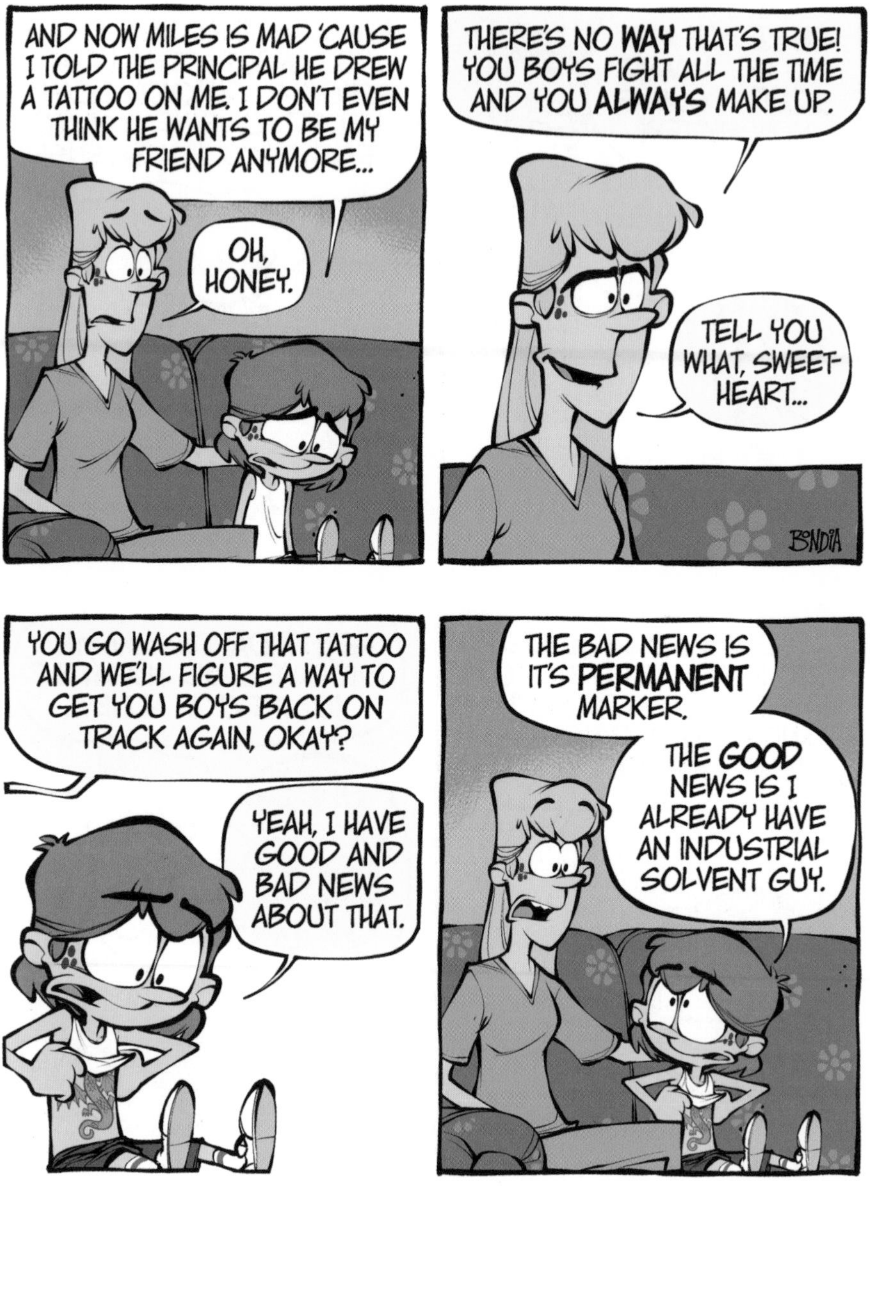
AND NOW MILES IS MAD 'CAUSE I TOLD THE PRINCIPAL HE DREW A TATTOO ON ME. I DON'T EVEN THINK HE WANTS TO BE MY FRIEND ANYMORE...
OH, HONEY.
THERE'S NO WAY THAT'S TRUE! YOU BOYS FIGHT ALL THE TIME AND YOU ALWAYS MAKE UP.
TELL YOU WHAT, SWEET-HEART...
BONDIA
YOU GO WASH OFF THAT TATTOO AND WE'LL FIGURE A WAY TO GET YOU BOYS BACK ON TRACK AGAIN, OKAY?
YEAH, I HAVE GOOD AND BAD NEWS ABOUT THAT.
THE BAD NEWS IS IT'S PERMANENT MARKER.
THE GOOD NEWS IS I ALREADY HAVE AN INDUSTRIAL SOLVENT GUY.

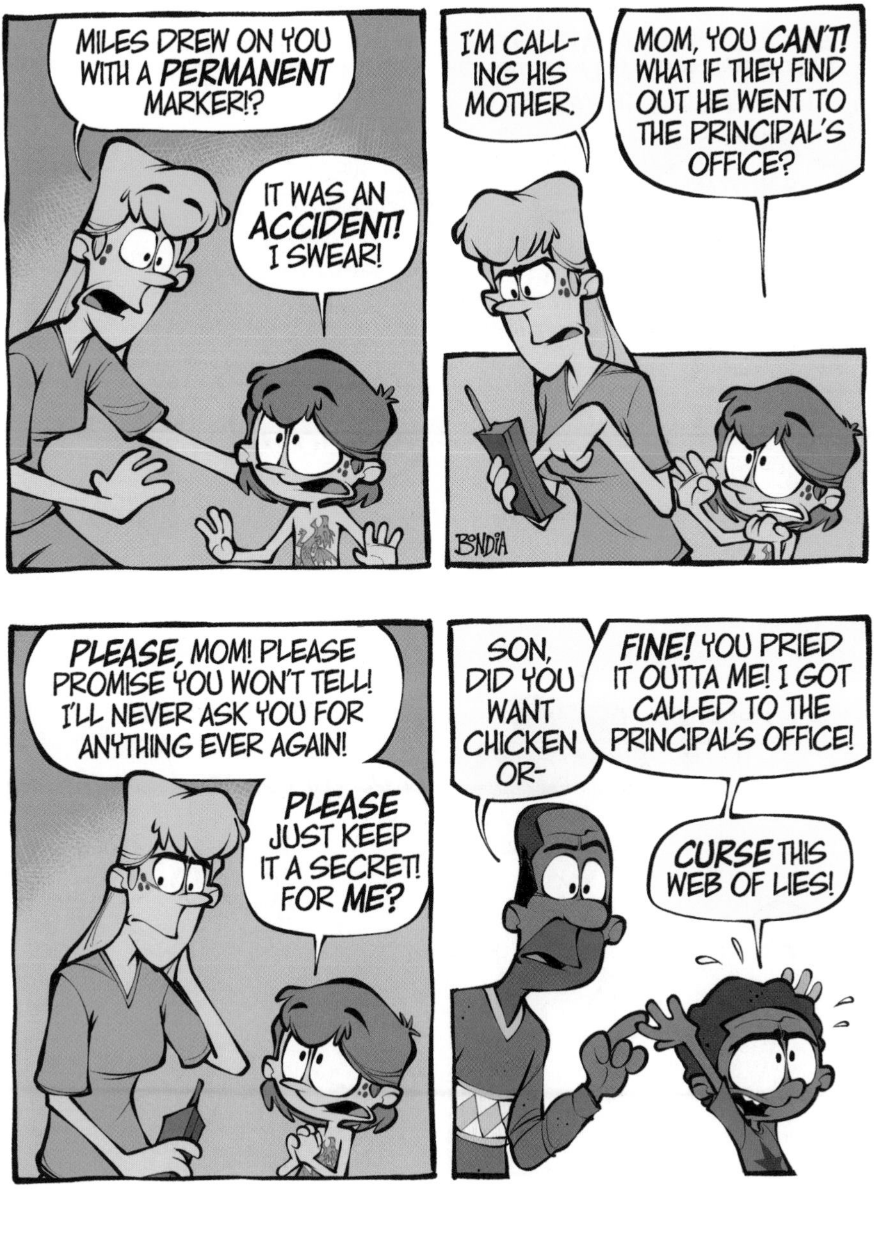
MILES DREW ON YOU WITH A PERMANENT MARKER!?
IT WAS AN ACCIDENT! I SWEAR!
I'M CALL-ING HIS MOTHER.
MOM, YOU CAN'T! WHAT IF THEY FIND OUT HE WENT TO THE PRINCIPAL'S OFFICE?
BONDIA
PLEASE, MOM! PLEASE PROMISE YOU WON'T TELL! I'LL NEVER ASK YOU FOR ANYTHING EVER AGAIN!
PLEASE JUST KEEP IT A SECRET! FOR ME?
SON, DID YOU WANT CHICKEN OR-
FINE! YOU PRIED IT OUTTA ME! I GOT CALLED TO THE PRINCIPAL'S OFFICE!
CURSE THIS WEB OF LIES!

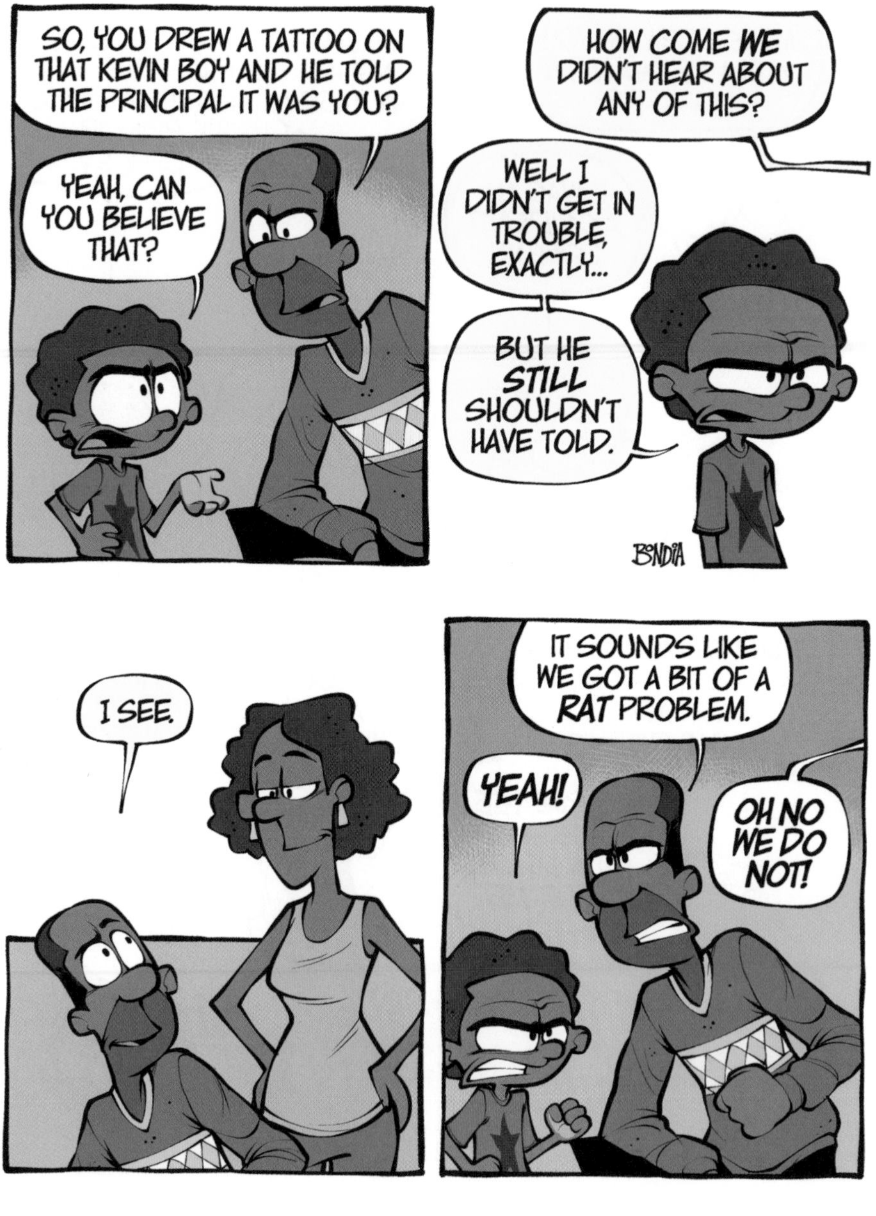
SO, YOU DREW A TATTOO ON THAT KEVIN BOY AND HE TOLD THE PRINCIPAL IT WAS YOU?
YEAH, CAN YOU BELIEVE THAT?
HOW COME WE DIDN'T HEAR ABOUT ANY OF THIS?
WELL I DIDN'T GET IN TROUBLE, EXACTLY...
BUT HE STILL SHOULDN'T HAVE TOLD.
BONDIA
I SEE.
IT SOUNDS LIKE WE GOT A BIT OF A RAT PROBLEM.
YEAH!
OH NO WE DO NOT!

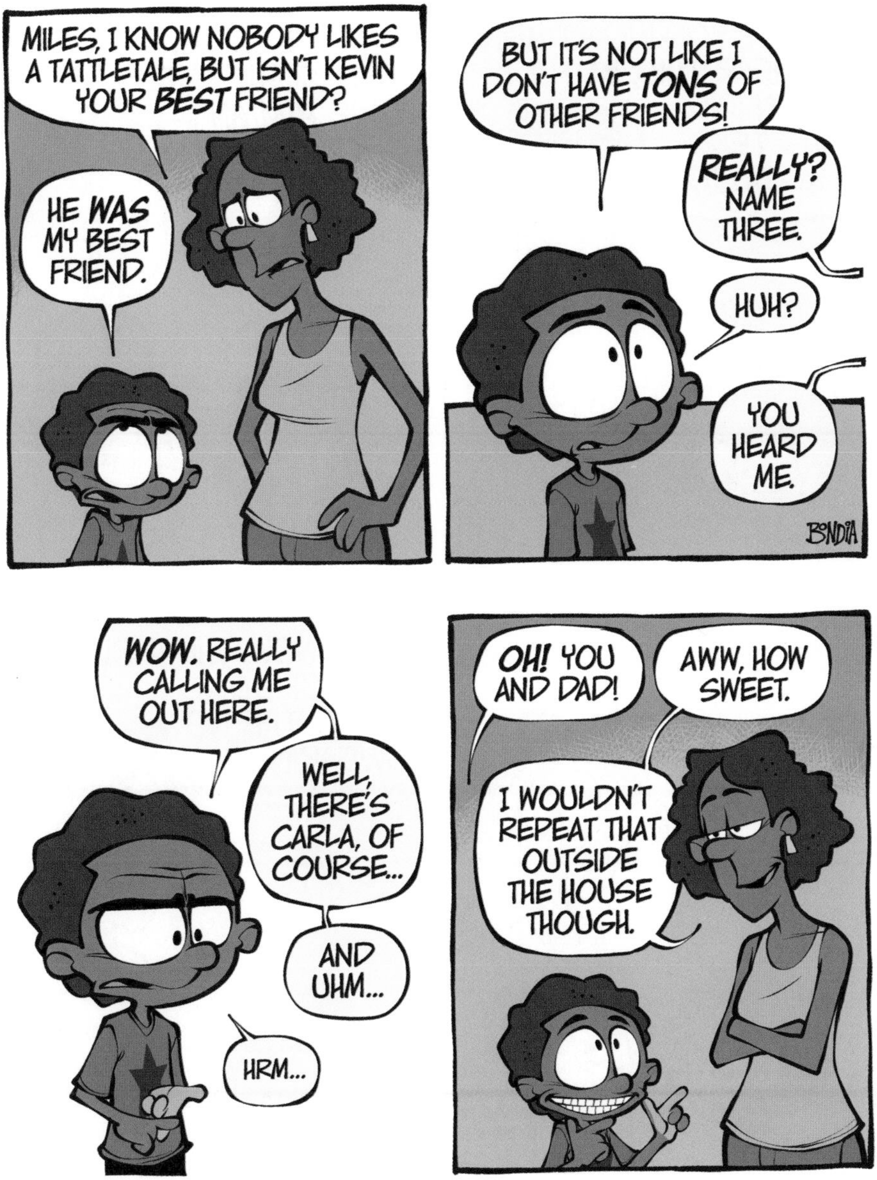
MILES, I KNOW NOBODY LIKES A TATTLETALE, BUT ISN'T KEVIN YOUR **BEST** FRIEND?
HE **WAS** MY BEST FRIEND.
BUT IT'S NOT LIKE I DON'T HAVE **TONS** OF OTHER FRIENDS!
REALLY? NAME THREE.
HUH?
YOU HEARD ME.
BONDIA
WOW. REALLY CALLING ME OUT HERE.
WELL, THERE'S CARLA, OF COURSE...
AND UHM...
HRM...
OH! YOU AND DAD!
AWW, HOW SWEET.
I WOULDN'T REPEAT THAT OUTSIDE THE HOUSE THOUGH.

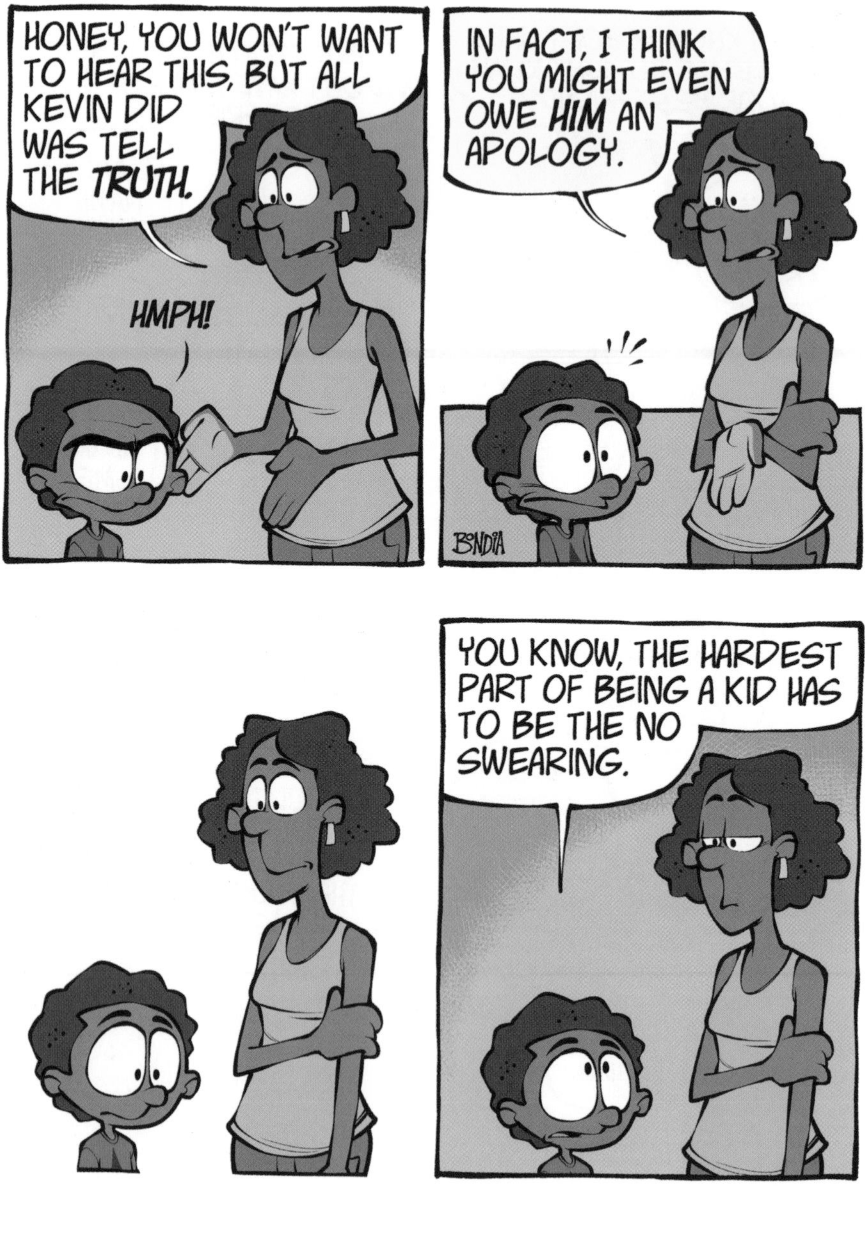
HONEY, YOU WON'T WANT TO HEAR THIS, BUT ALL KEVIN DID WAS TELL THE TRUTH.
HMPH!
IN FACT, I THINK YOU MIGHT EVEN OWE HIM AN APOLOGY.
BONDIA
YOU KNOW, THE HARDEST PART OF BEING A KID HAS TO BE THE NO SWEARING.

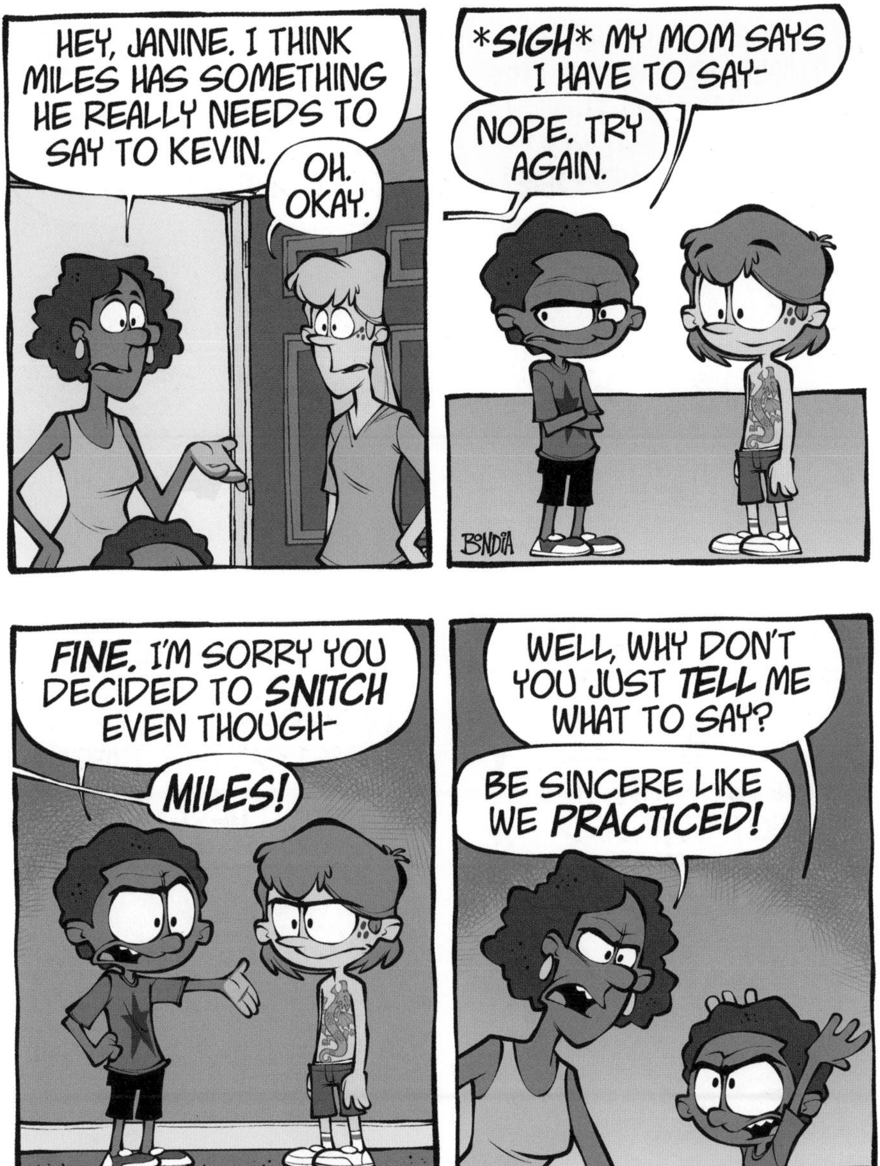
HEY, JANINE. I THINK MILES HAS SOMETHING HE REALLY NEEDS TO SAY TO KEVIN.
OH. OKAY.
SIGH MY MOM SAYS I HAVE TO SAY-
NOPE. TRY AGAIN.
BONDIA
FINE. I'M SORRY YOU DECIDED TO SNITCH EVEN THOUGH-
MILES!
WELL, WHY DON'T YOU JUST TELL ME WHAT TO SAY?
BE SINCERE LIKE WE PRACTICED!

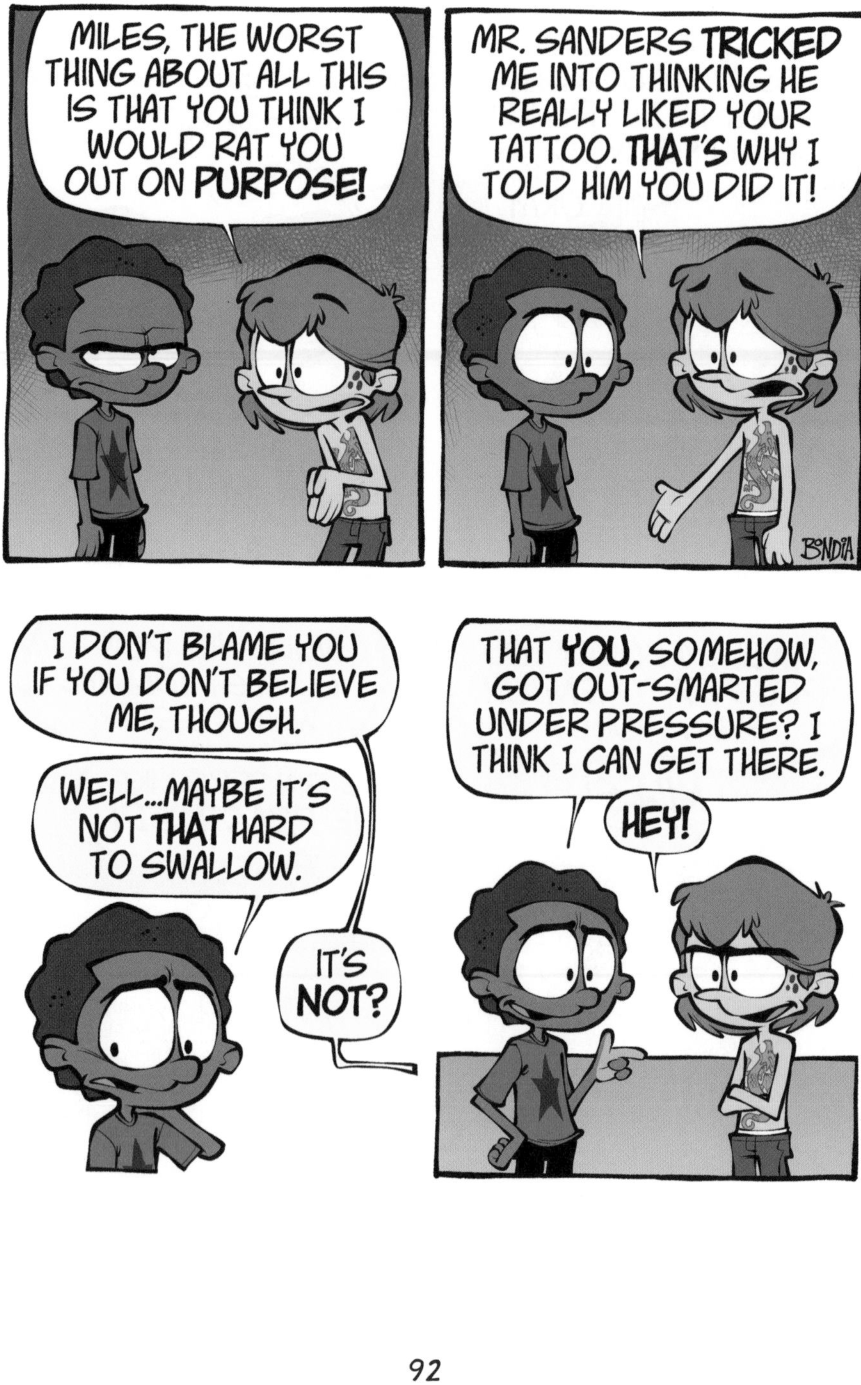
MILES, THE WORST THING ABOUT ALL THIS IS THAT YOU THINK I WOULD RAT YOU OUT ON **PURPOSE!**
MR. SANDERS **TRICKED** ME INTO THINKING HE REALLY LIKED YOUR TATTOO. **THAT'S** WHY I TOLD HIM YOU DID IT!
BONDIA
I DON'T BLAME YOU IF YOU DON'T BELIEVE ME, THOUGH.
WELL...MAYBE IT'S NOT **THAT** HARD TO SWALLOW.
IT'S **NOT?**
THAT **YOU**, SOMEHOW, GOT OUT-SMARTED UNDER PRESSURE? I THINK I CAN GET THERE.
HEY!

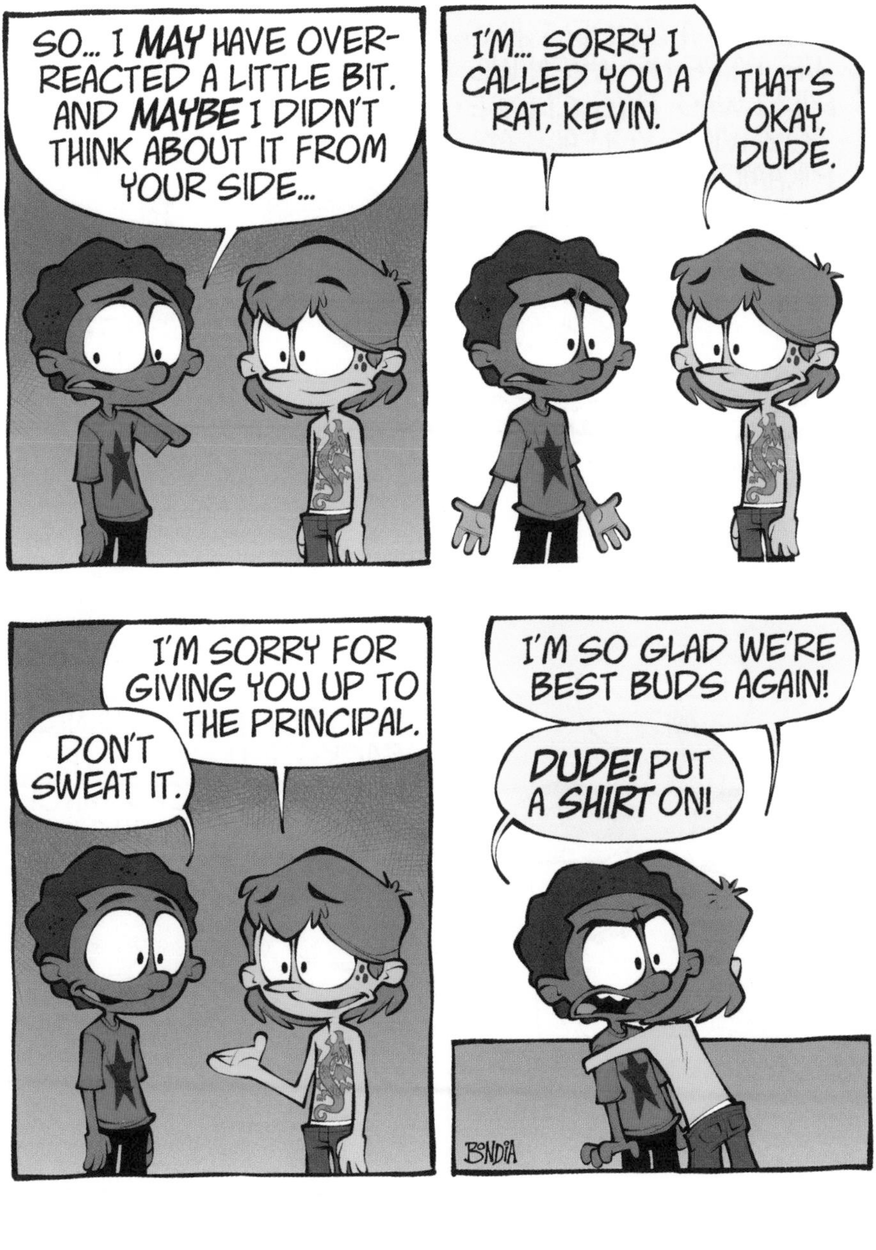
SO... I **MAY** HAVE OVER-REACTED A LITTLE BIT. AND **MAYBE** I DIDN'T THINK ABOUT IT FROM YOUR SIDE...
I'M... SORRY I CALLED YOU A RAT, KEVIN.
THAT'S OKAY, DUDE.
I'M SORRY FOR GIVING YOU UP TO THE PRINCIPAL.
DON'T SWEAT IT.
I'M SO GLAD WE'RE BEST BUDS AGAIN!
DUDE! PUT A **SHIRT** ON!
BONDIA

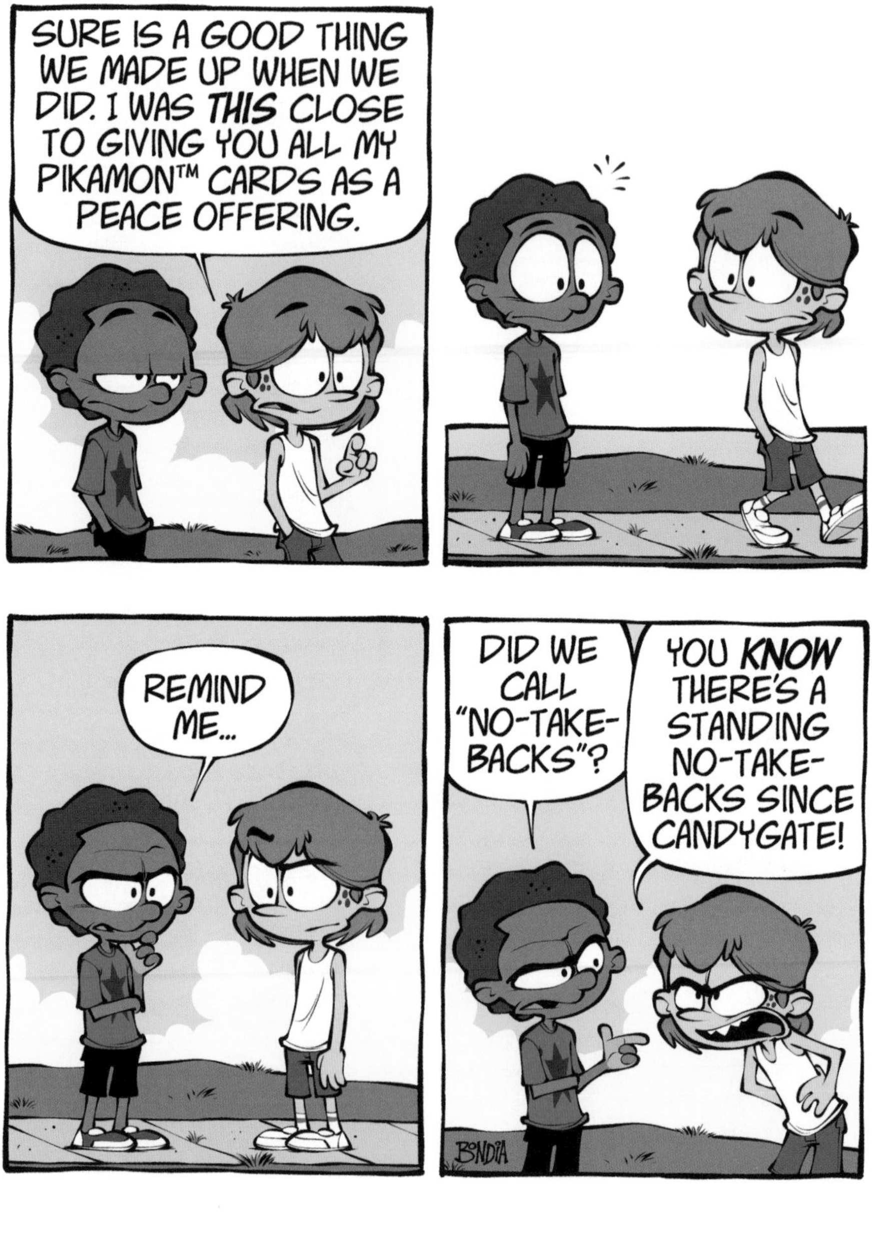
SURE IS A GOOD THING WE MADE UP WHEN WE DID. I WAS THIS CLOSE TO GIVING YOU ALL MY PIKAMON™ CARDS AS A PEACE OFFERING.
REMIND ME...
DID WE CALL "NO-TAKE-BACKS"?
YOU KNOW THERE'S A STANDING NO-TAKE-BACKS SINCE CANDYGATE!
BONDIA

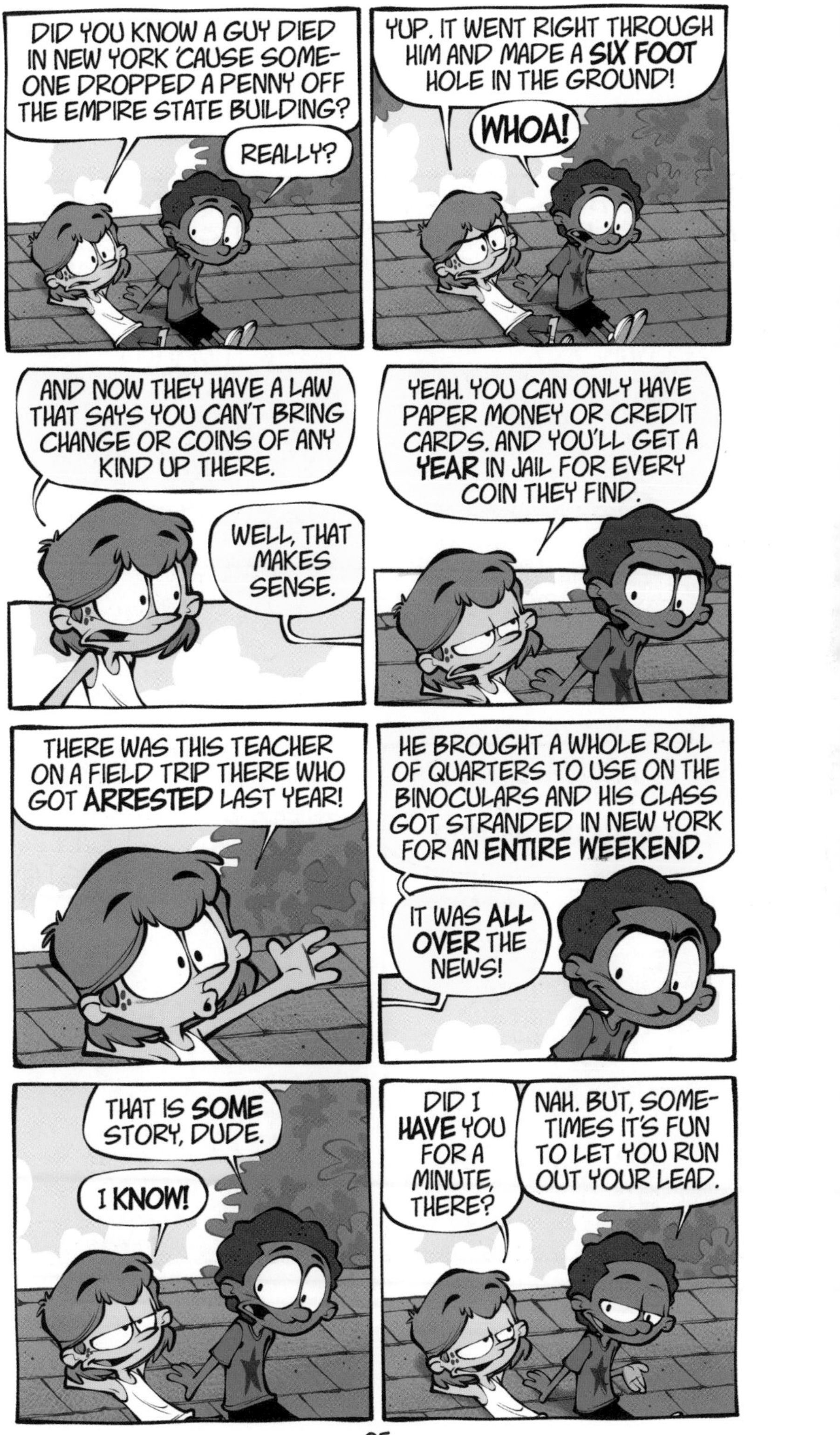
DID YOU KNOW A GUY DIED IN NEW YORK 'CAUSE SOME-ONE DROPPED A PENNY OFF THE EMPIRE STATE BUILDING?
REALLY?
YUP. IT WENT RIGHT THROUGH HIM AND MADE A SIX FOOT HOLE IN THE GROUND!
WHOA!
AND NOW THEY HAVE A LAW THAT SAYS YOU CAN'T BRING CHANGE OR COINS OF ANY KIND UP THERE.
WELL, THAT MAKES SENSE.
YEAH. YOU CAN ONLY HAVE PAPER MONEY OR CREDIT CARDS. AND YOU'LL GET A YEAR IN JAIL FOR EVERY COIN THEY FIND.
THERE WAS THIS TEACHER ON A FIELD TRIP THERE WHO GOT ARRESTED LAST YEAR!
HE BROUGHT A WHOLE ROLL OF QUARTERS TO USE ON THE BINOCULARS AND HIS CLASS GOT STRANDED IN NEW YORK FOR AN ENTIRE WEEKEND.
IT WAS ALL OVER THE NEWS!
THAT IS SOME STORY, DUDE.
I KNOW!
DID I HAVE YOU FOR A MINUTE, THERE?
NAH. BUT, SOME-TIMES IT'S FUN TO LET YOU RUN OUT YOUR LEAD.

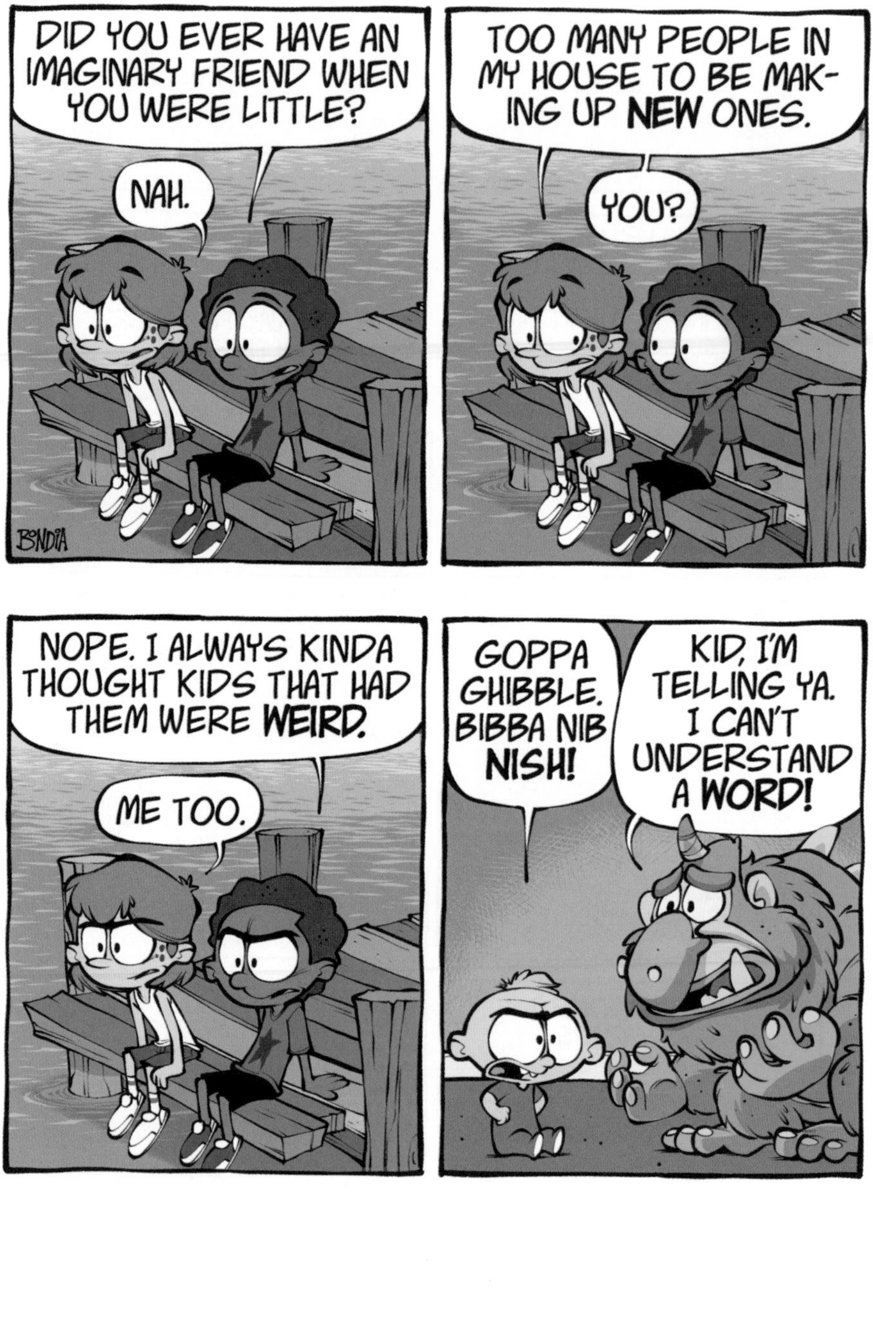
DID YOU EVER HAVE AN IMAGINARY FRIEND WHEN YOU WERE LITTLE?
NAH.
BONDIA
TOO MANY PEOPLE IN MY HOUSE TO BE MAKING UP NEW ONES.
YOU?
NOPE. I ALWAYS KINDA THOUGHT KIDS THAT HAD THEM WERE WEIRD.
ME TOO.
GOPPA GHIBBLE. BIBBA NIB NISH!
KID, I'M TELLING YA. I CAN'T UNDERSTAND A WORD!

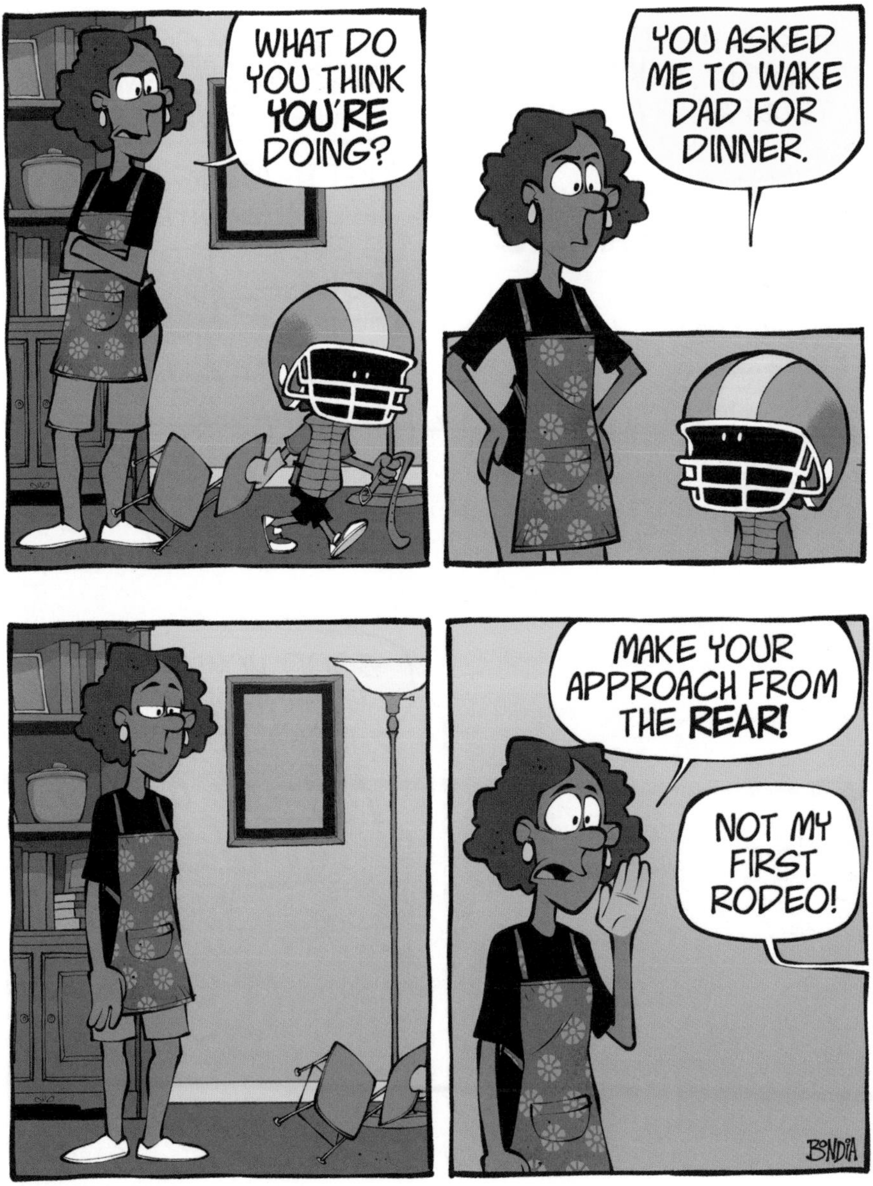
WHAT DO YOU THINK **YOU'RE** DOING?
YOU ASKED ME TO WAKE DAD FOR DINNER.
MAKE YOUR APPROACH FROM THE **REAR!**
NOT MY FIRST RODEO!
BONDIA

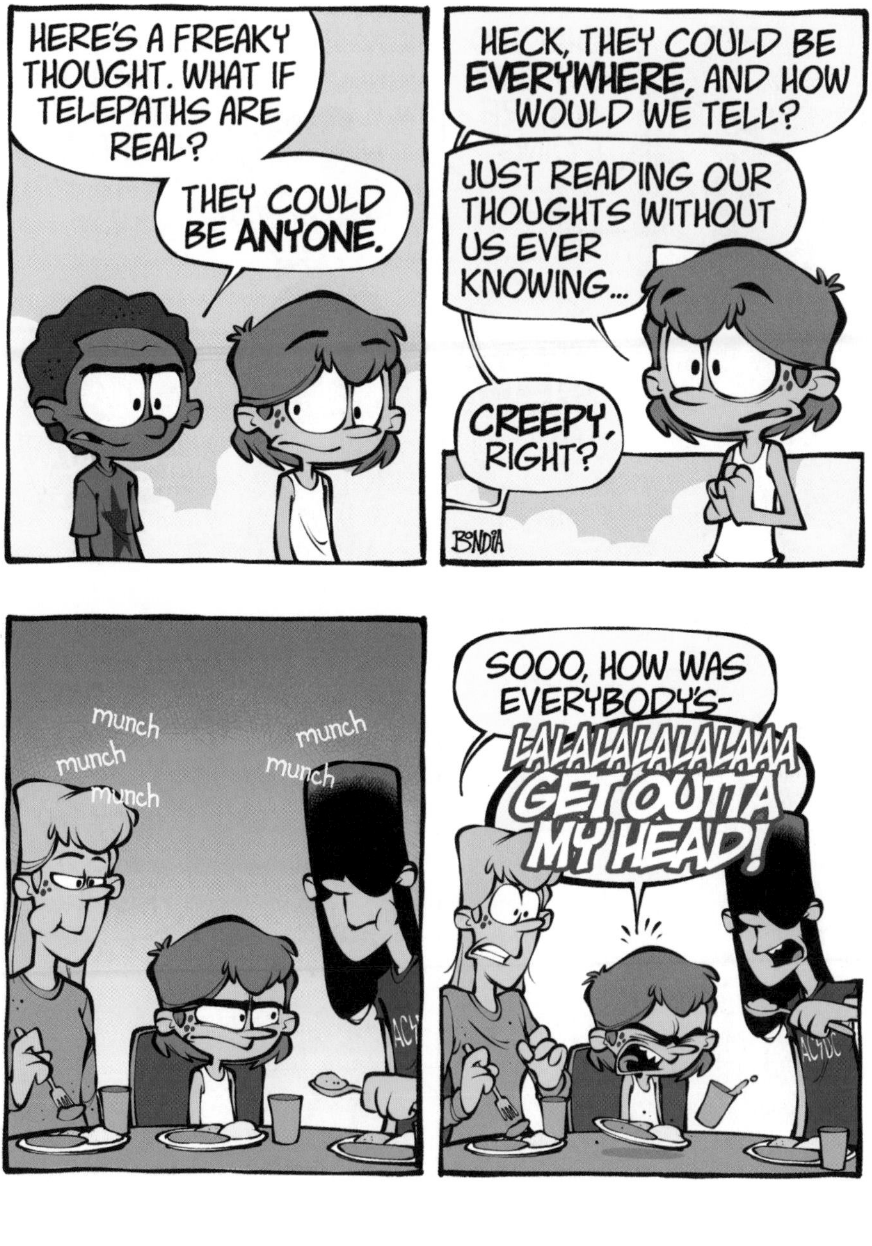
HERE'S A FREAKY THOUGHT. WHAT IF TELEPATHS ARE REAL?
THEY COULD BE **ANYONE.**
HECK, THEY COULD BE **EVERYWHERE,** AND HOW WOULD WE TELL?
JUST READING OUR THOUGHTS WITHOUT US EVER KNOWING...
CREEPY, RIGHT?
BONDIA
munch
munch
munch
munch
munch
SOOO, HOW WAS EVERYBODY'S-
LALALALALALAAA GET OUTTA MY HEAD!

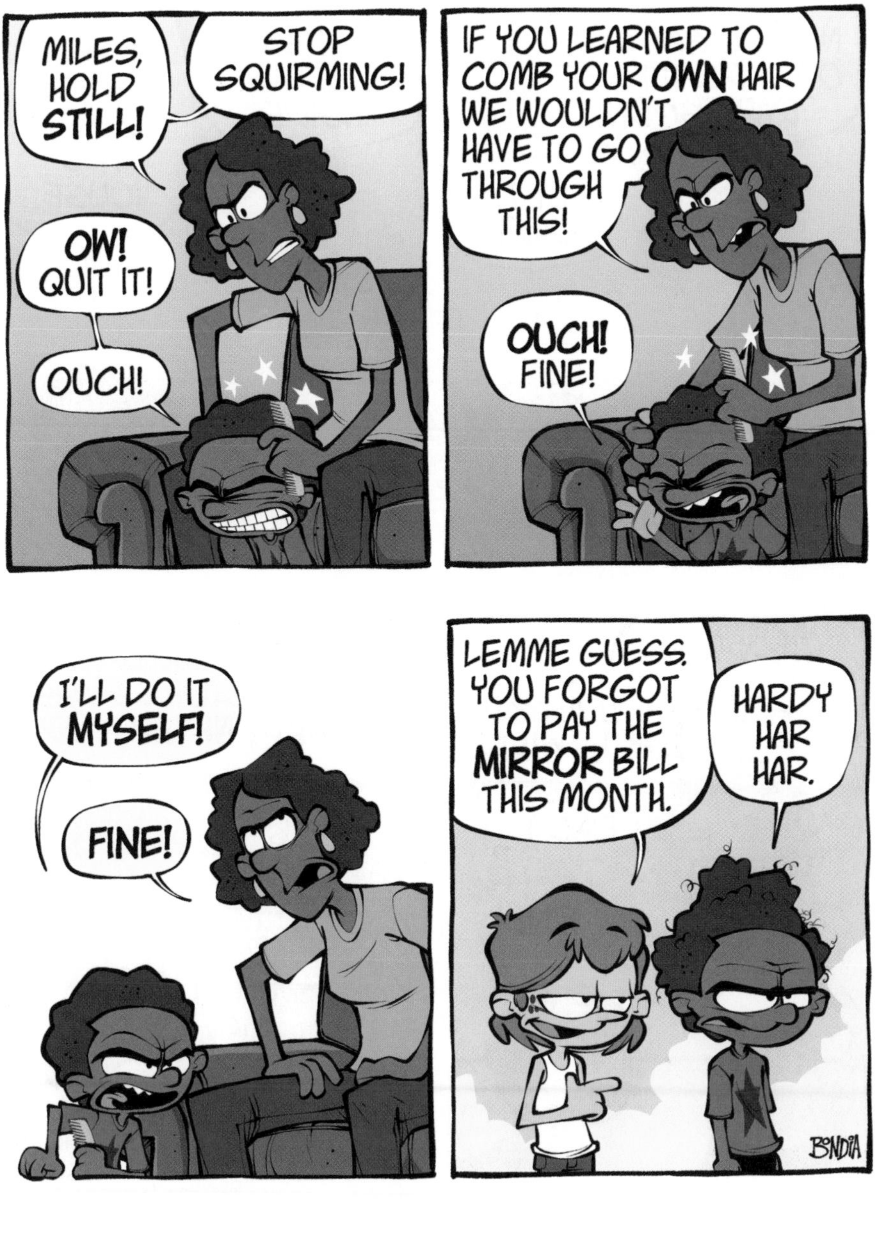
MILES, HOLD STILL!
STOP SQUIRMING!
OW! QUIT IT!
OUCH!
IF YOU LEARNED TO COMB YOUR OWN HAIR WE WOULDN'T HAVE TO GO THROUGH THIS!
OUCH! FINE!
I'LL DO IT MYSELF!
FINE!
LEMME GUESS. YOU FORGOT TO PAY THE MIRROR BILL THIS MONTH.
HARDY HAR HAR.
BONDIA

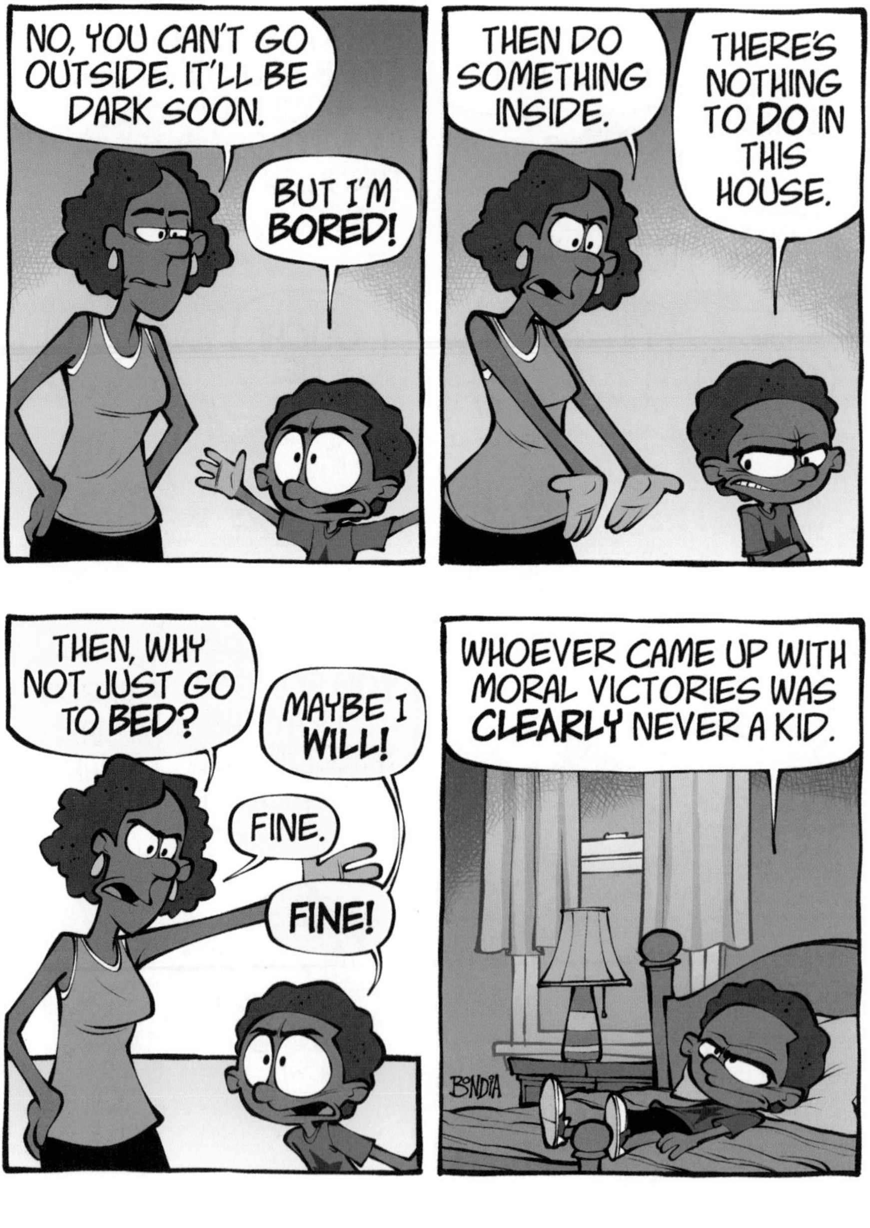
NO, YOU CAN'T GO OUTSIDE. IT'LL BE DARK SOON.
BUT I'M **BORED!**
THEN DO SOMETHING INSIDE.
THERE'S NOTHING TO **DO** IN THIS HOUSE.
THEN, WHY NOT JUST GO TO **BED?**
MAYBE I **WILL!**
FINE.
FINE!
WHOEVER CAME UP WITH MORAL VICTORIES WAS **CLEARLY** NEVER A KID.
BONDIA

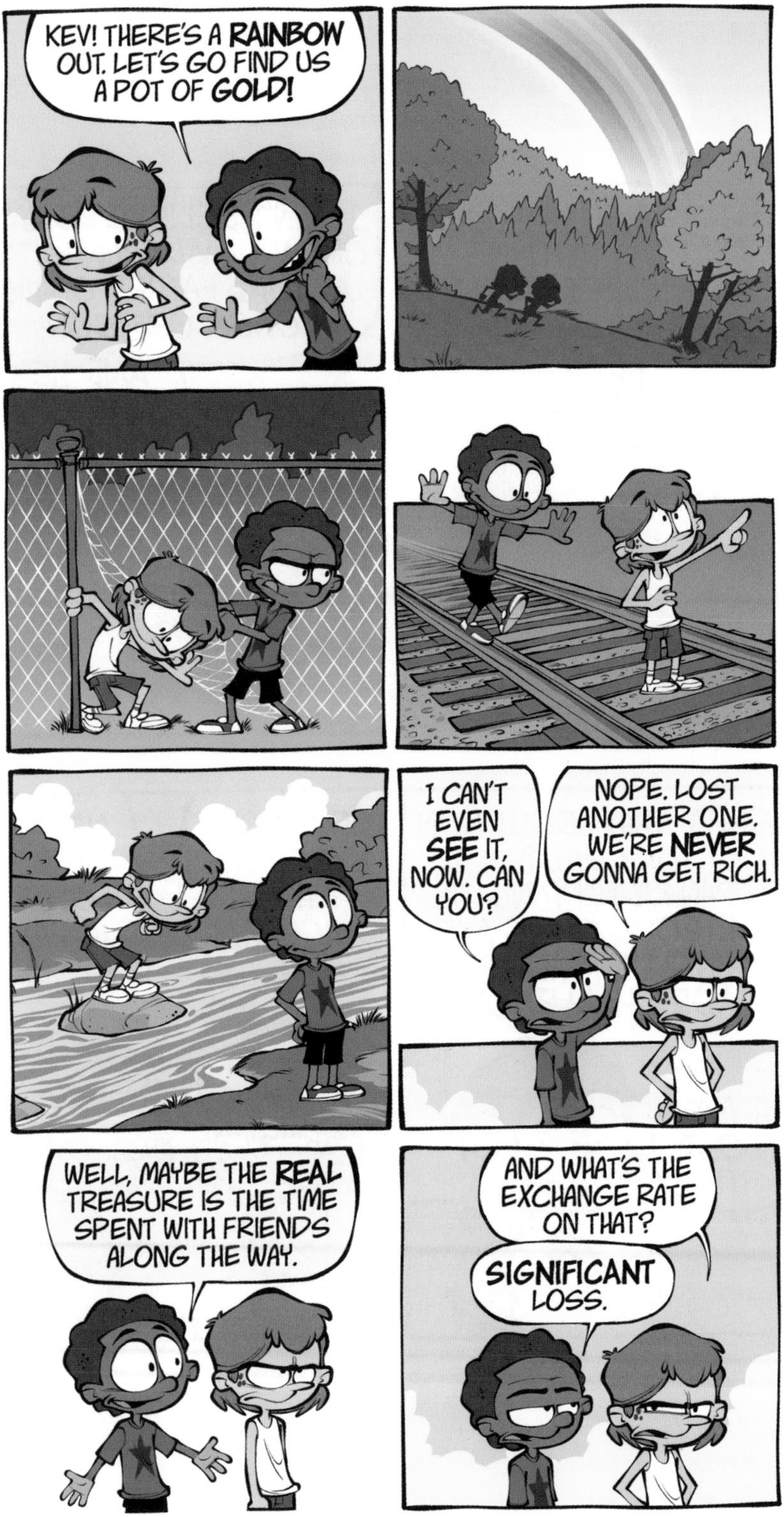
KEV! THERE'S A RAINBOW OUT. LET'S GO FIND US A POT OF GOLD!
I CAN'T EVEN SEE IT, NOW. CAN YOU?
NOPE. LOST ANOTHER ONE. WE'RE NEVER GONNA GET RICH.
WELL, MAYBE THE REAL TREASURE IS THE TIME SPENT WITH FRIENDS ALONG THE WAY.
AND WHAT'S THE EXCHANGE RATE ON THAT?
SIGNIFICANT LOSS.

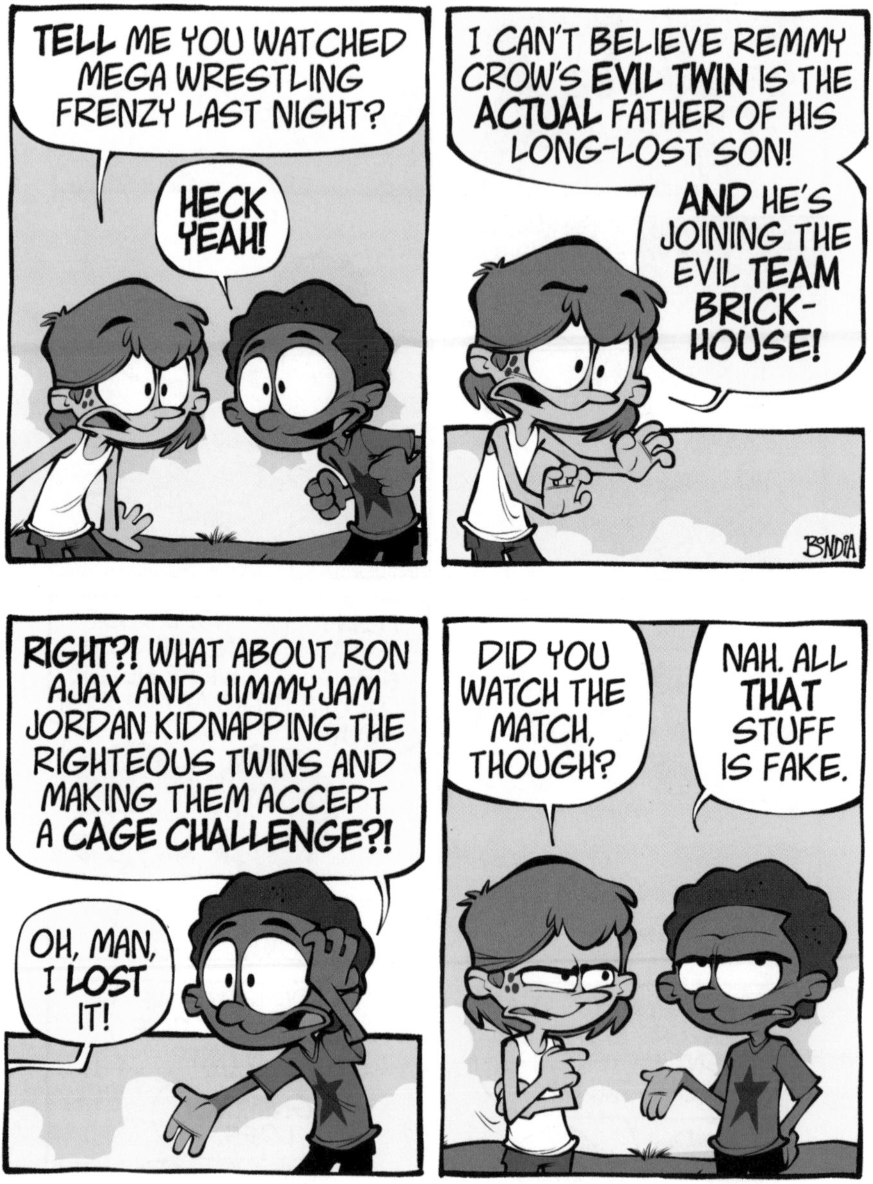
TELL ME YOU WATCHED MEGA WRESTLING FRENZY LAST NIGHT?
HECK YEAH!
I CAN'T BELIEVE REMMY CROW'S EVIL TWIN IS THE ACTUAL FATHER OF HIS LONG-LOST SON!
AND HE'S JOINING THE EVIL TEAM BRICK-HOUSE!
BONDIA
RIGHT?! WHAT ABOUT RON AJAX AND JIMMYJAM JORDAN KIDNAPPING THE RIGHTEOUS TWINS AND MAKING THEM ACCEPT A CAGE CHALLENGE?!
OH, MAN, I LOST IT!
DID YOU WATCH THE MATCH, THOUGH?
NAH. ALL THAT STUFF IS FAKE.

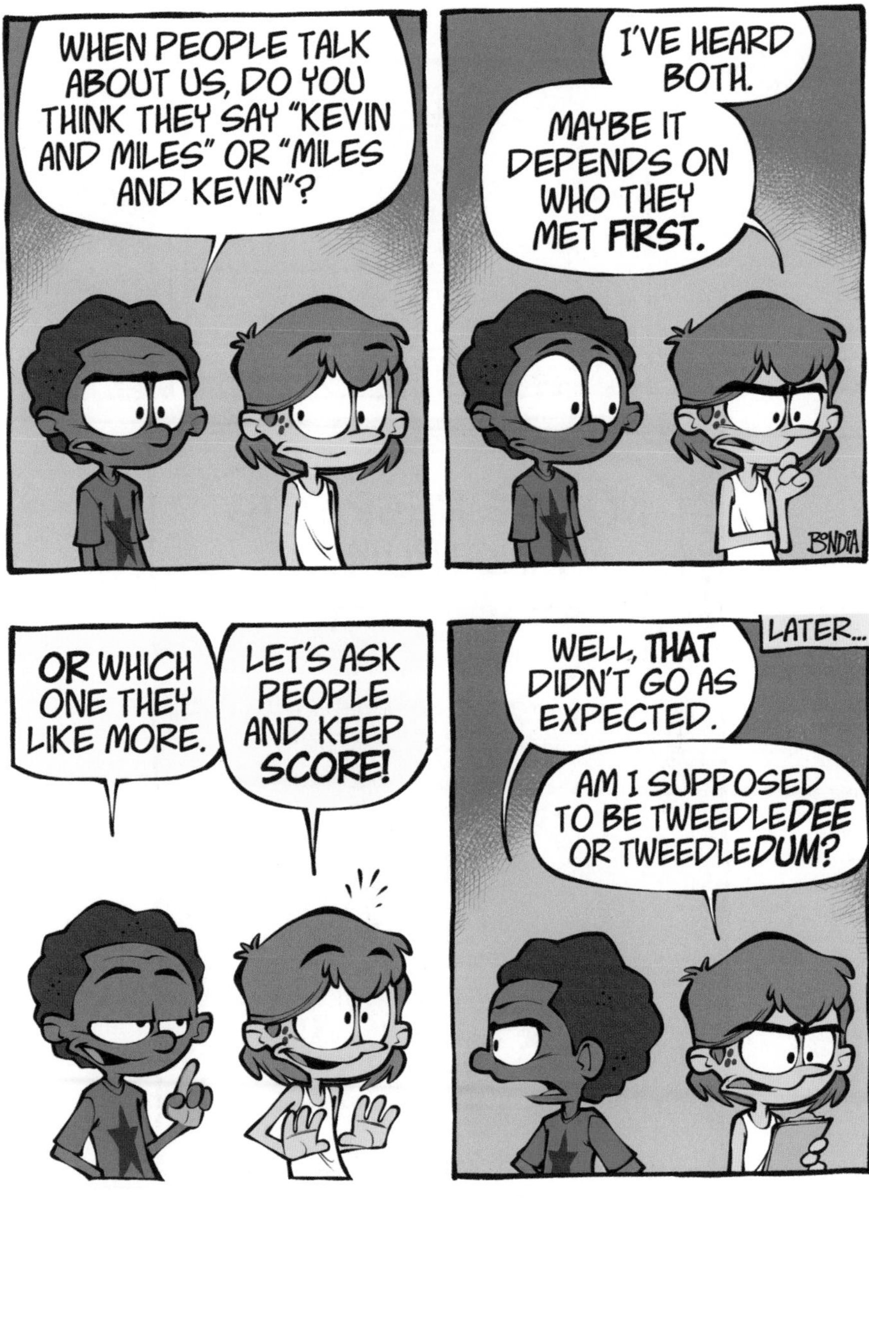
WHEN PEOPLE TALK ABOUT US, DO YOU THINK THEY SAY "KEVIN AND MILES" OR "MILES AND KEVIN"?
I'VE HEARD BOTH.
MAYBE IT DEPENDS ON WHO THEY MET **FIRST.**
BONDIA
OR WHICH ONE THEY LIKE MORE.
LET'S ASK PEOPLE AND KEEP **SCORE!**
LATER...
WELL, **THAT** DIDN'T GO AS EXPECTED.
AM I SUPPOSED TO BE TWEEDLE**DEE** OR TWEEDLE**DUM**?

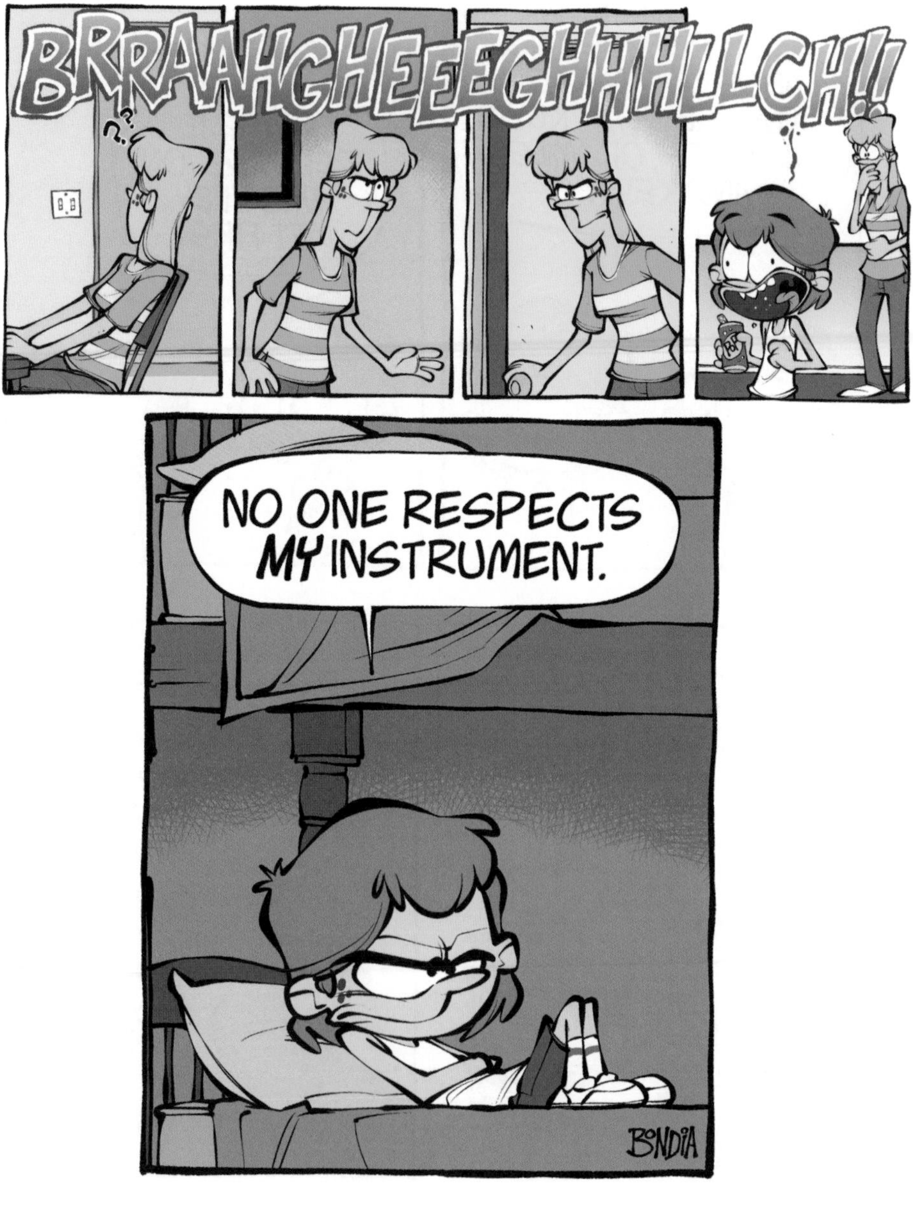
BRRAAHGHEEEEGHHHLLCH!!
NO ONE RESPECTS MY INSTRUMENT.
BONDIA

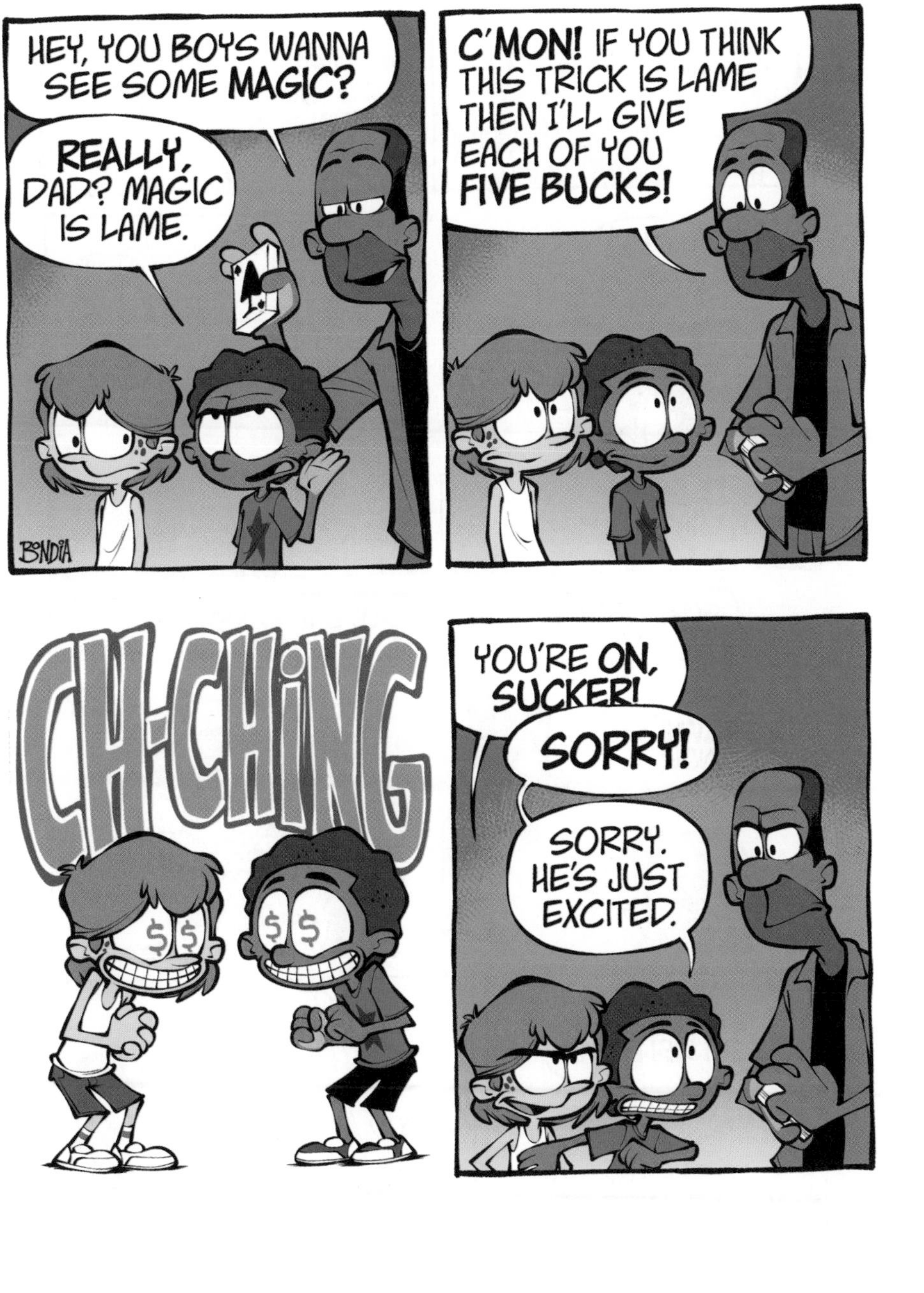
HEY, YOU BOYS WANNA SEE SOME **MAGIC?**
REALLY, DAD? MAGIC IS LAME.
BONDIA
C'MON! IF YOU THINK THIS TRICK IS LAME THEN I'LL GIVE EACH OF YOU **FIVE BUCKS!**
CH-CHING
YOU'RE **ON, SUCKER!**
SORRY!
SORRY. HE'S JUST EXCITED.

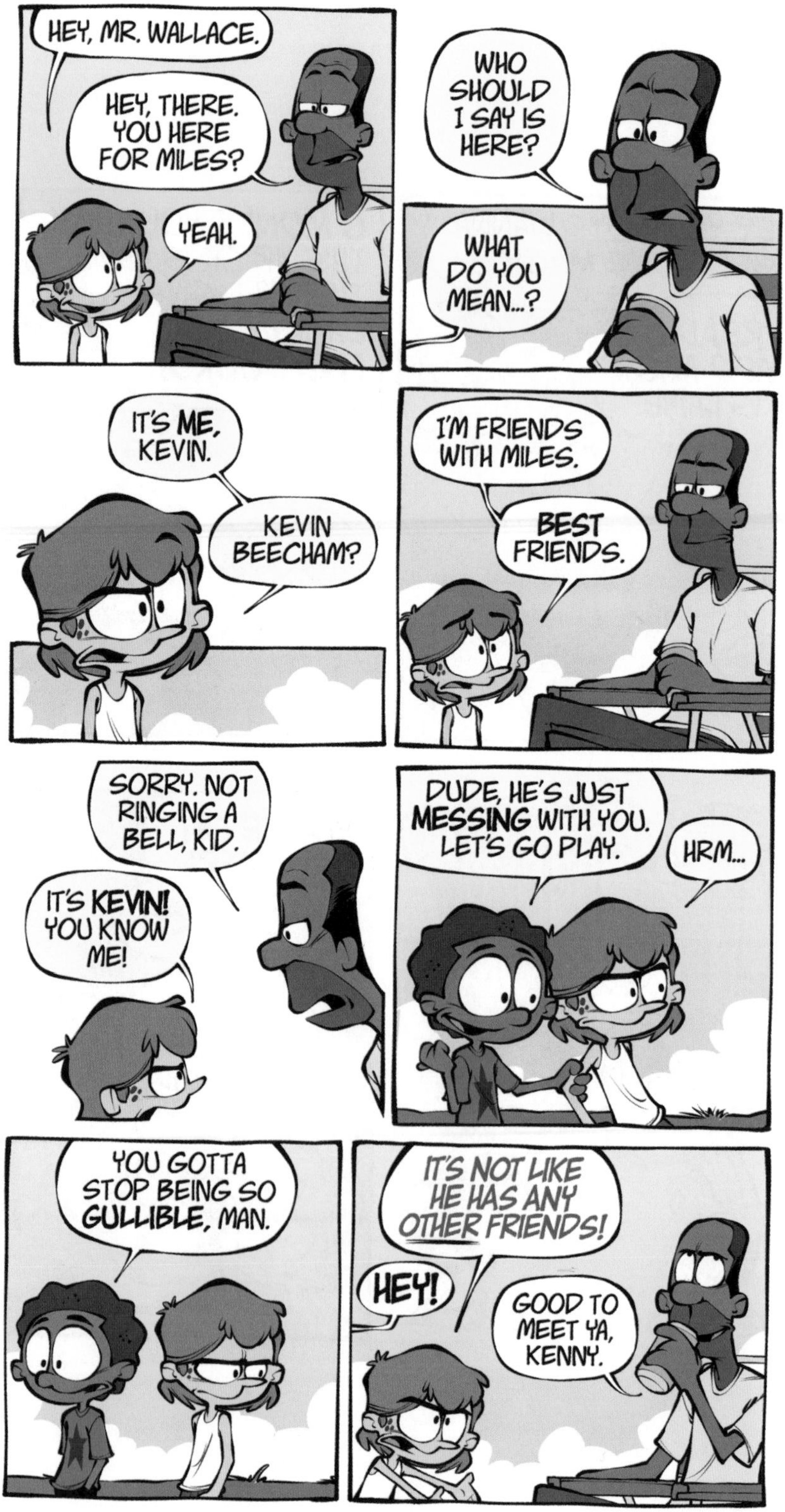
HEY, MR. WALLACE.
HEY, THERE. YOU HERE FOR MILES?
YEAH.
WHO SHOULD I SAY IS HERE?
WHAT DO YOU MEAN...?
IT'S **ME,** KEVIN.
KEVIN BEECHAM?
I'M FRIENDS WITH MILES.
BEST FRIENDS.
SORRY. NOT RINGING A BELL, KID.
IT'S **KEVIN!** YOU KNOW ME!
DUDE, HE'S JUST **MESSING** WITH YOU. LET'S GO PLAY.
HRM...
YOU GOTTA STOP BEING SO **GULLIBLE,** MAN.
IT'S NOT LIKE HE HAS ANY OTHER FRIENDS!
HEY!
GOOD TO MEET YA, KENNY.

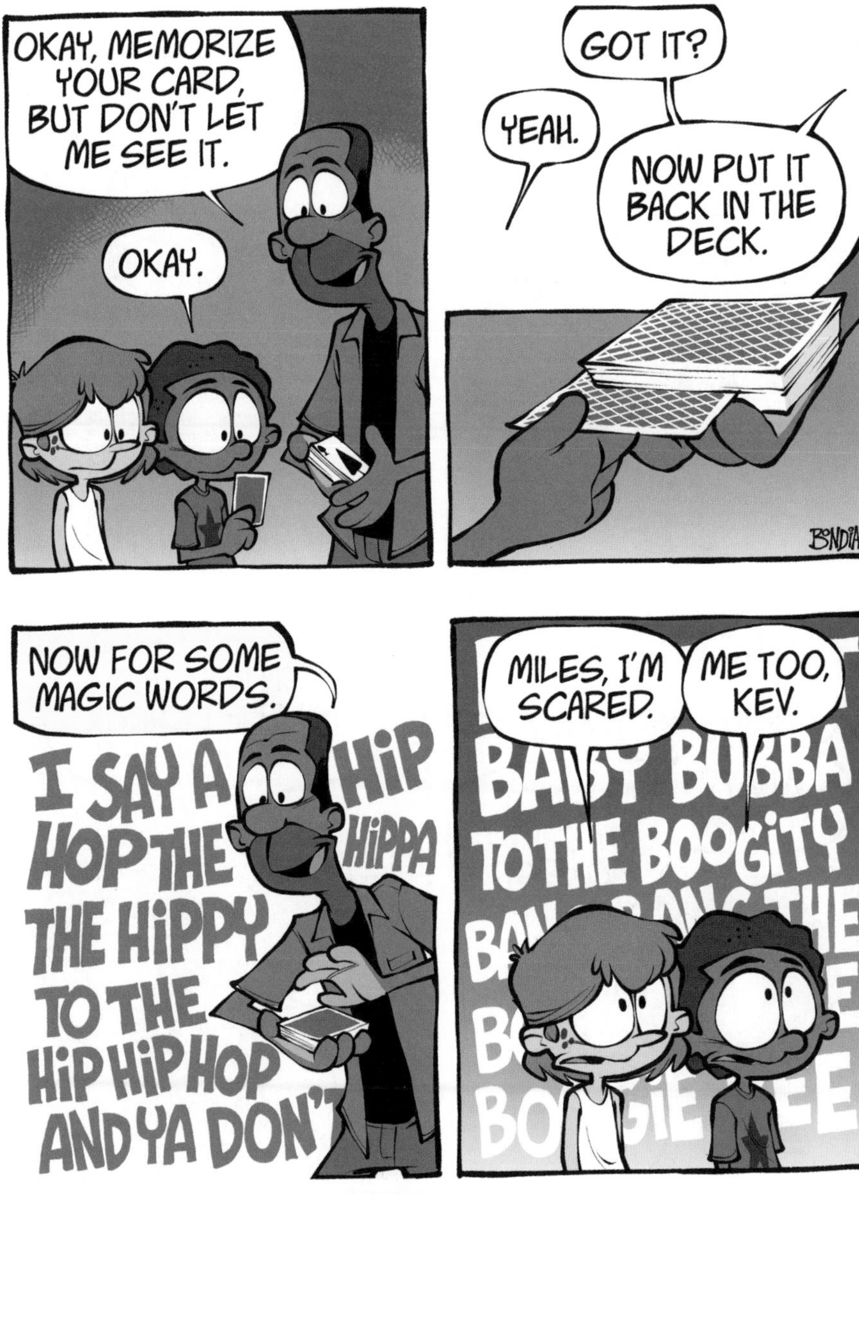
OKAY, MEMORIZE YOUR CARD, BUT DON'T LET ME SEE IT.
OKAY.
GOT IT?
YEAH.
NOW PUT IT BACK IN THE DECK.
BONDIA
NOW FOR SOME MAGIC WORDS.
I SAY A HIP HOP THE HIPPA THE HIPPY TO THE HIP HIP HOP AND YA DON'T
MILES, I'M SCARED.
ME TOO, KEV.
BABY BUBBA TO THE BOOGITY

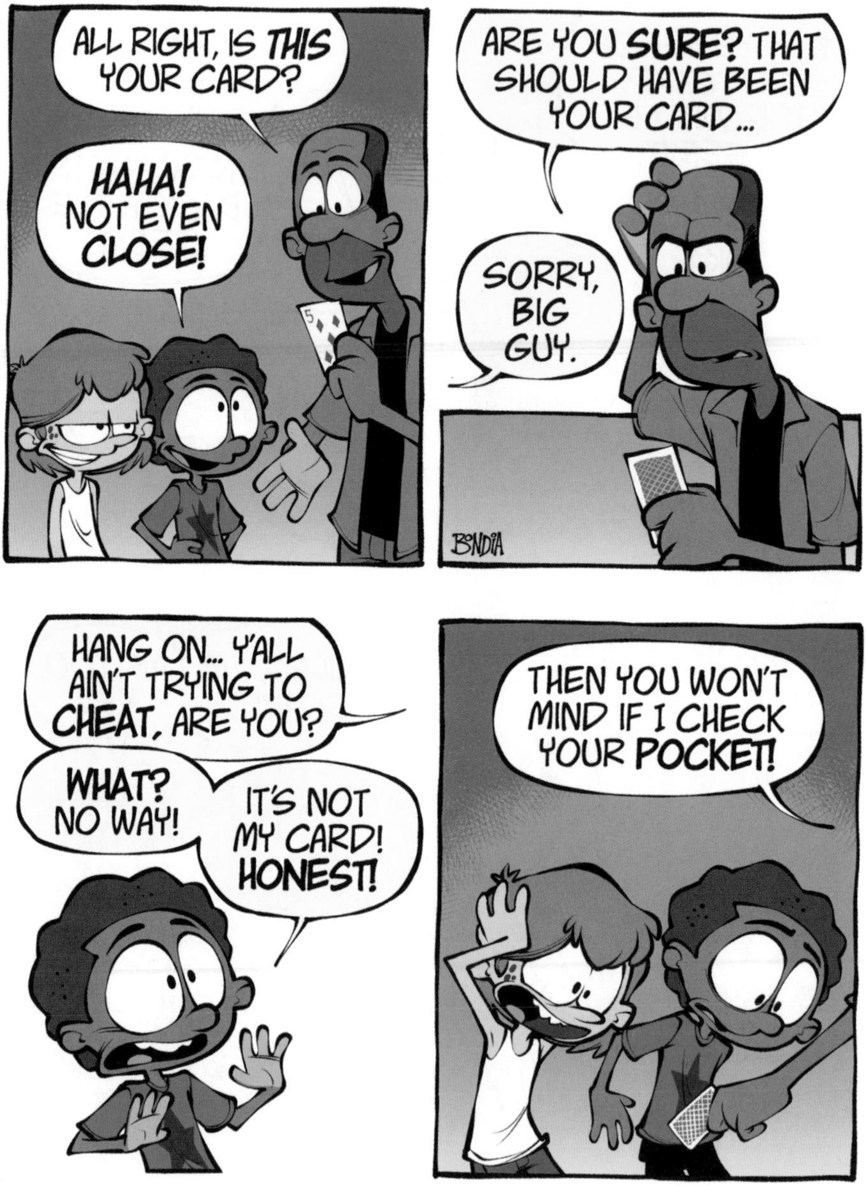
ALL RIGHT, IS THIS YOUR CARD?
HAHA! NOT EVEN CLOSE!
5
ARE YOU SURE? THAT SHOULD HAVE BEEN YOUR CARD...
SORRY, BIG GUY.
BONDIA
HANG ON... Y'ALL AIN'T TRYING TO CHEAT, ARE YOU?
WHAT? NO WAY!
IT'S NOT MY CARD! HONEST!
THEN YOU WON'T MIND IF I CHECK YOUR POCKET!

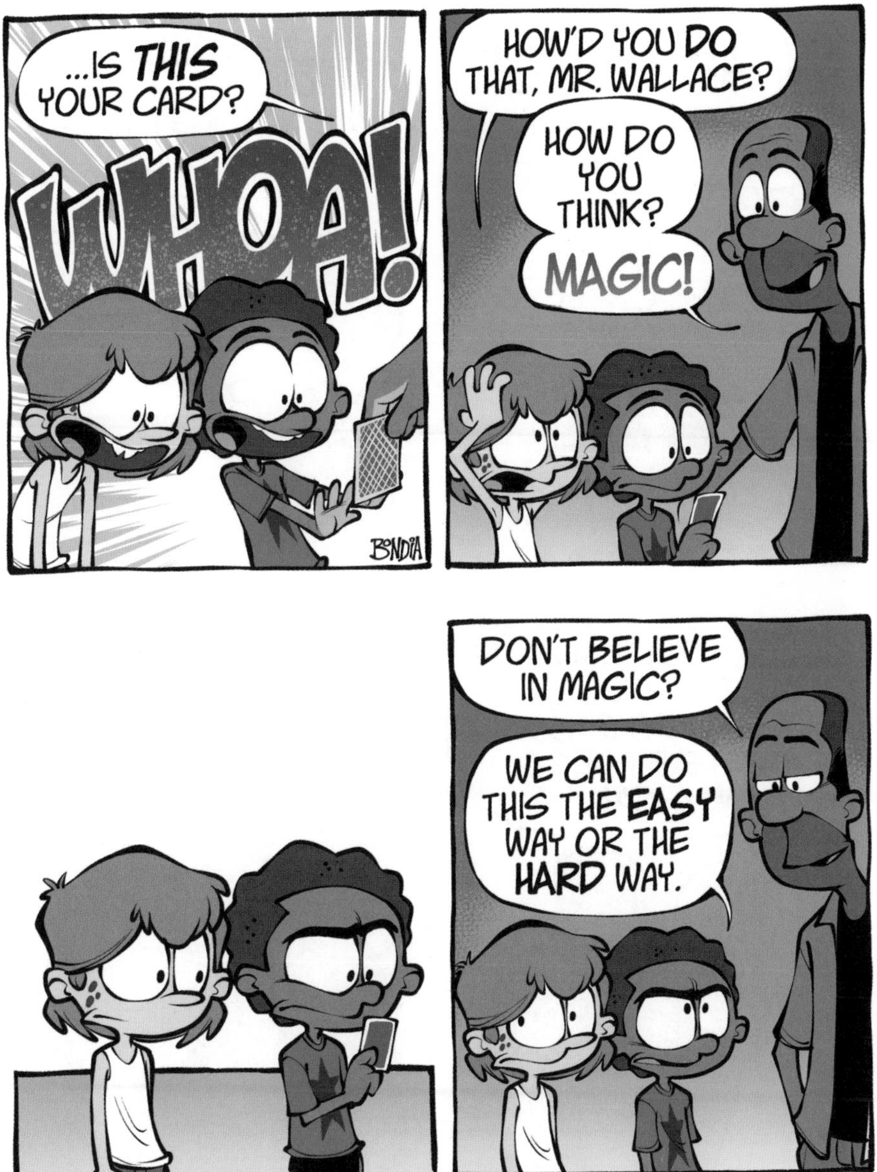
...IS THIS YOUR CARD?
WHOA!
BONDIA
HOW'D YOU DO THAT, MR. WALLACE?
HOW DO YOU THINK?
MAGIC!
DON'T BELIEVE IN MAGIC?
WE CAN DO THIS THE EASY WAY OR THE HARD WAY.

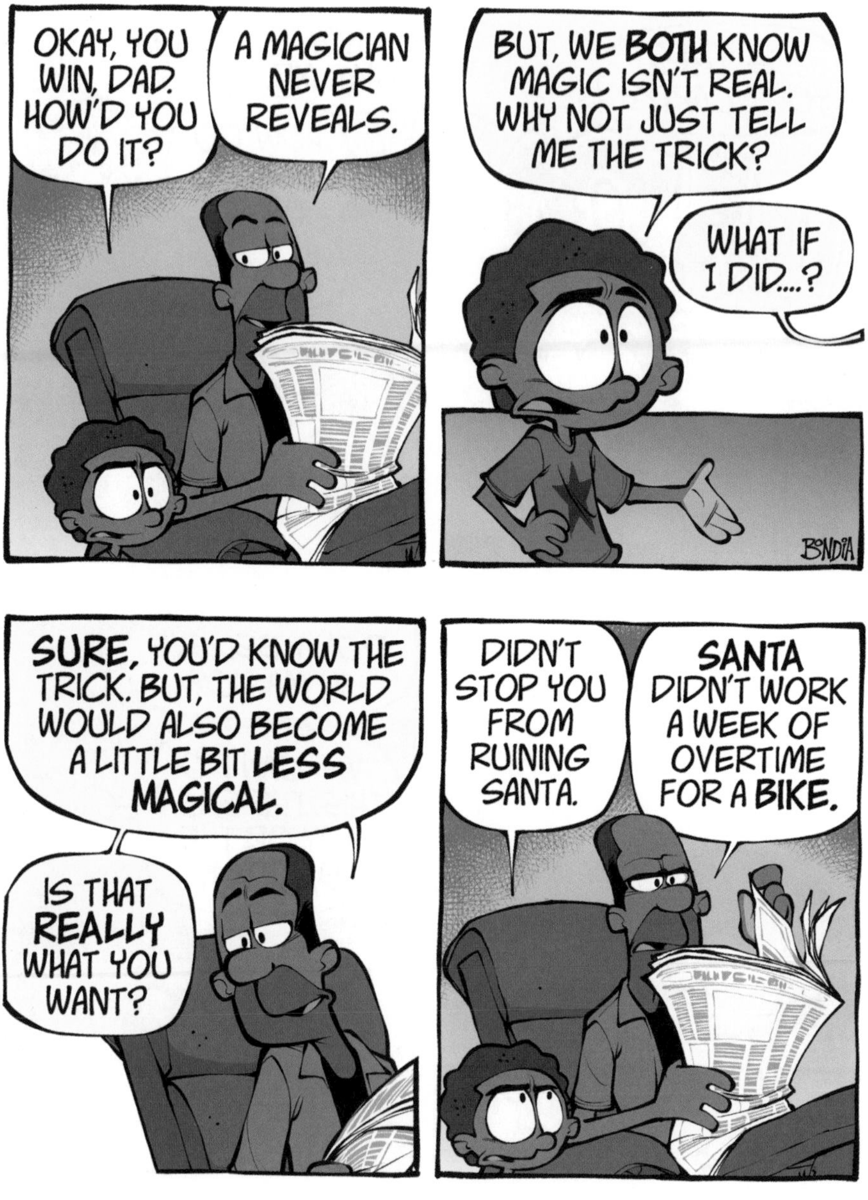
OKAY, YOU WIN, DAD. HOW'D YOU DO IT?
A MAGICIAN NEVER REVEALS.
BUT, WE BOTH KNOW MAGIC ISN'T REAL. WHY NOT JUST TELL ME THE TRICK?
WHAT IF I DID...?
BONDIA
SURE, YOU'D KNOW THE TRICK. BUT, THE WORLD WOULD ALSO BECOME A LITTLE BIT LESS MAGICAL.
IS THAT REALLY WHAT YOU WANT?
DIDN'T STOP YOU FROM RUINING SANTA.
SANTA DIDN'T WORK A WEEK OF OVERTIME FOR A BIKE.

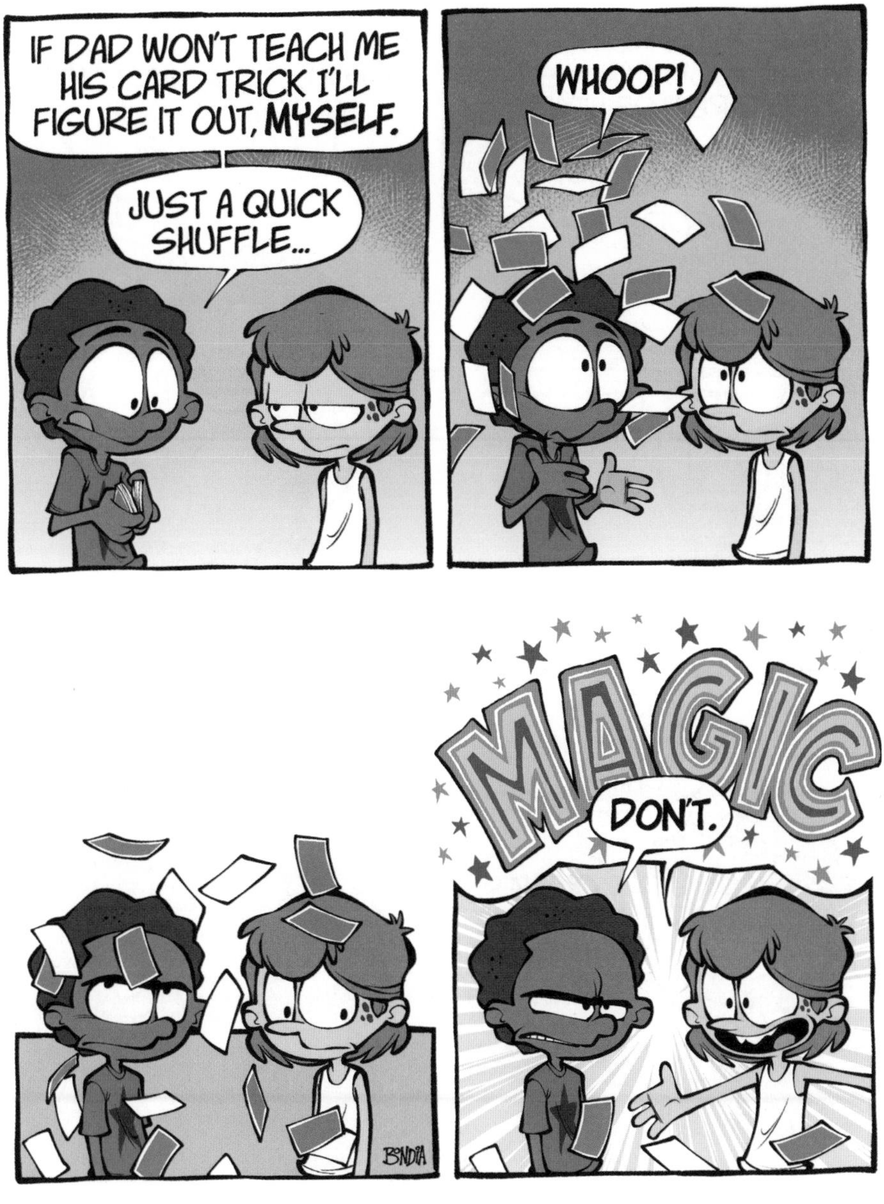
IF DAD WON'T TEACH ME HIS CARD TRICK I'LL FIGURE IT OUT, **MYSELF.**
JUST A QUICK SHUFFLE...
WHOOP!
MAGIC
DON'T.
BONDIA

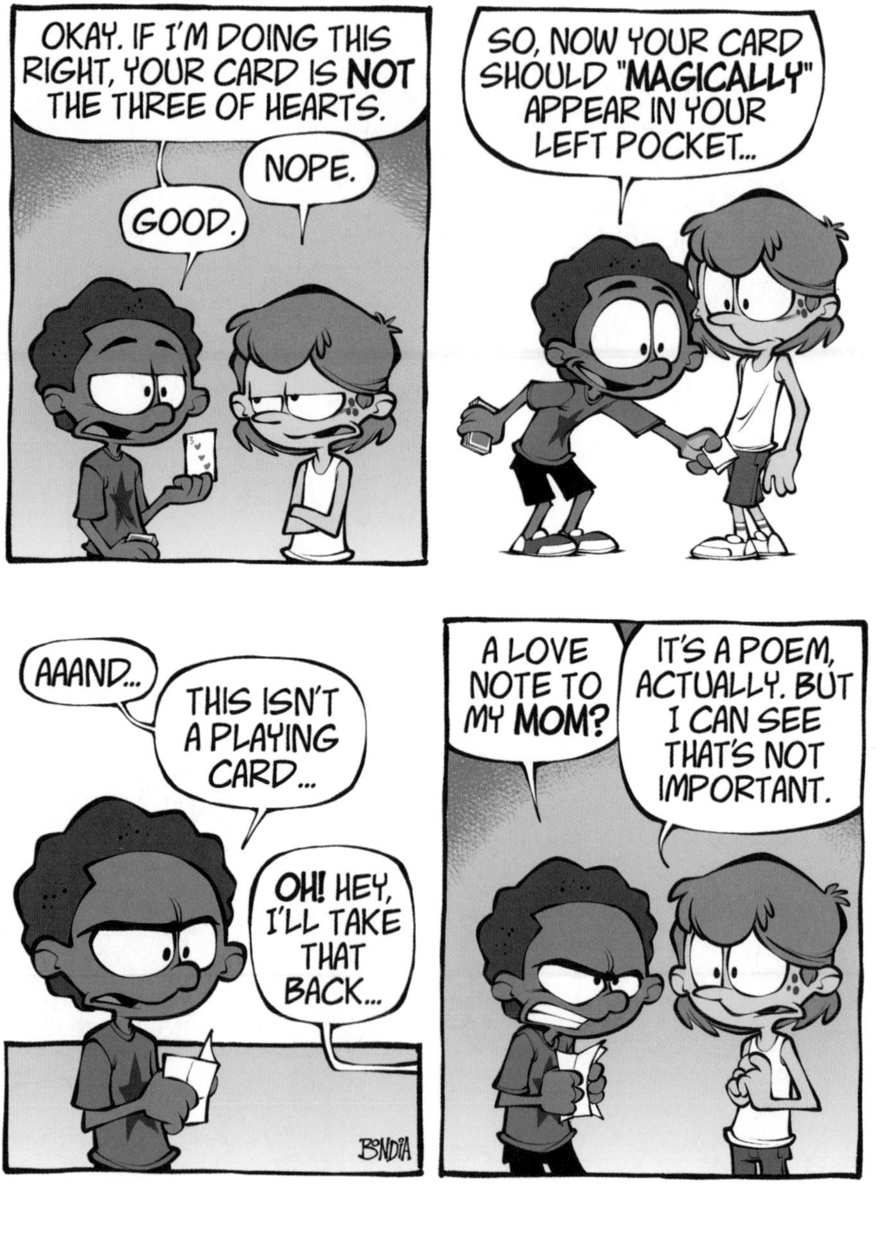

OKAY. IF I'M DOING THIS RIGHT, YOUR CARD IS **NOT** THE THREE OF HEARTS.
NOPE.
GOOD.
SO, NOW YOUR CARD SHOULD "**MAGICALLY**" APPEAR IN YOUR LEFT POCKET...
AAAND...
THIS ISN'T A PLAYING CARD...
OH! HEY, I'LL TAKE THAT BACK...
BONDIA
A LOVE NOTE TO MY **MOM?**
IT'S A POEM, ACTUALLY. BUT I CAN SEE THAT'S NOT IMPORTANT.

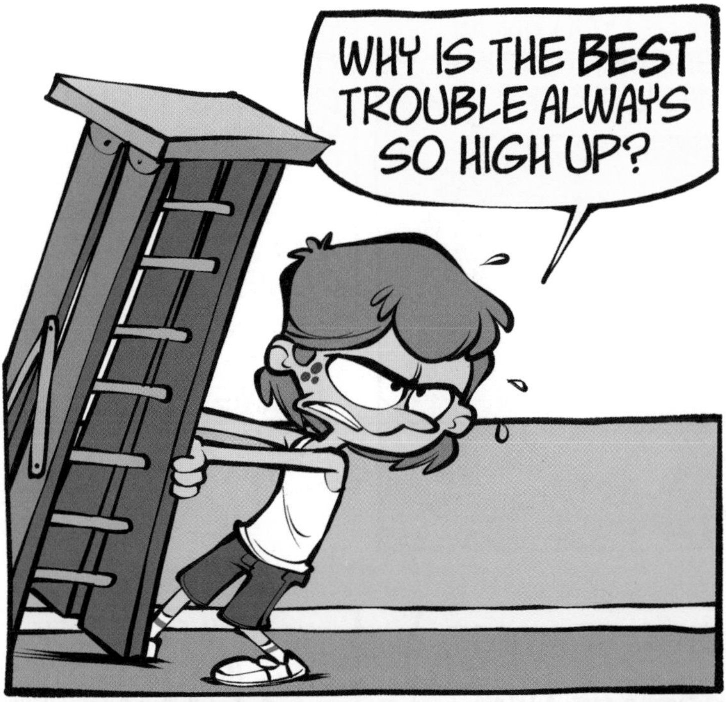
WHY IS THE BEST TROUBLE ALWAYS SO HIGH UP?

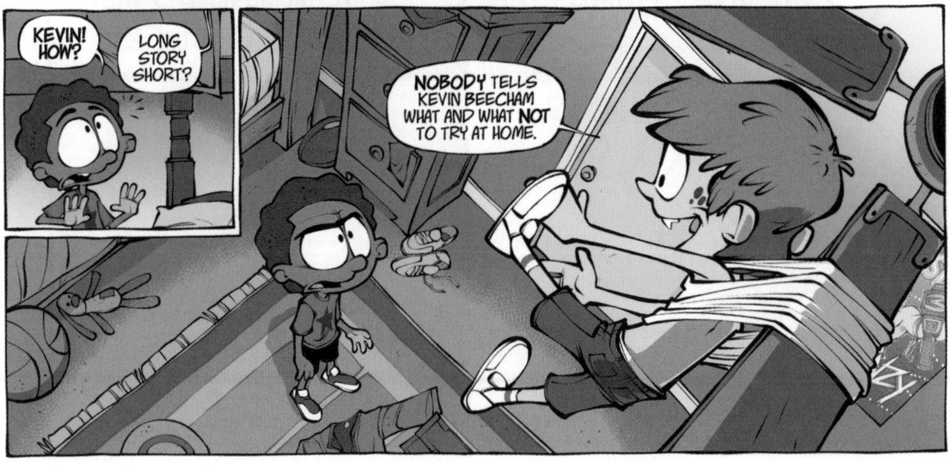
KEVIN! HOW?
LONG STORY SHORT?
NOBODY TELLS KEVIN BEECHAM WHAT AND WHAT NOT TO TRY AT HOME.

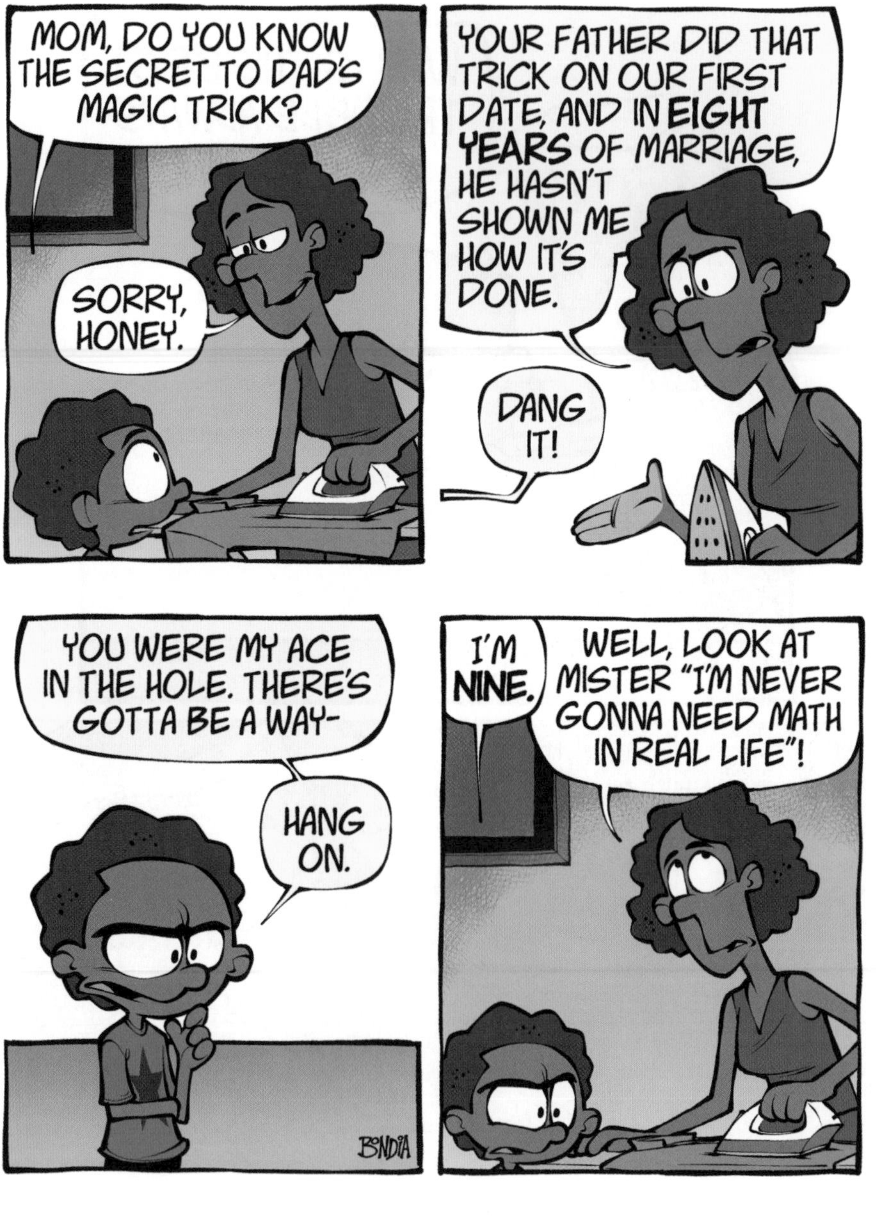
MOM, DO YOU KNOW THE SECRET TO DAD'S MAGIC TRICK?
SORRY, HONEY.
YOUR FATHER DID THAT TRICK ON OUR FIRST DATE, AND IN **EIGHT YEARS** OF MARRIAGE, HE HASN'T SHOWN ME HOW IT'S DONE.
DANG IT!
YOU WERE MY ACE IN THE HOLE. THERE'S GOTTA BE A WAY-
HANG ON.
BONDIA
I'M **NINE.**
WELL, LOOK AT MISTER "I'M NEVER GONNA NEED MATH IN REAL LIFE"!

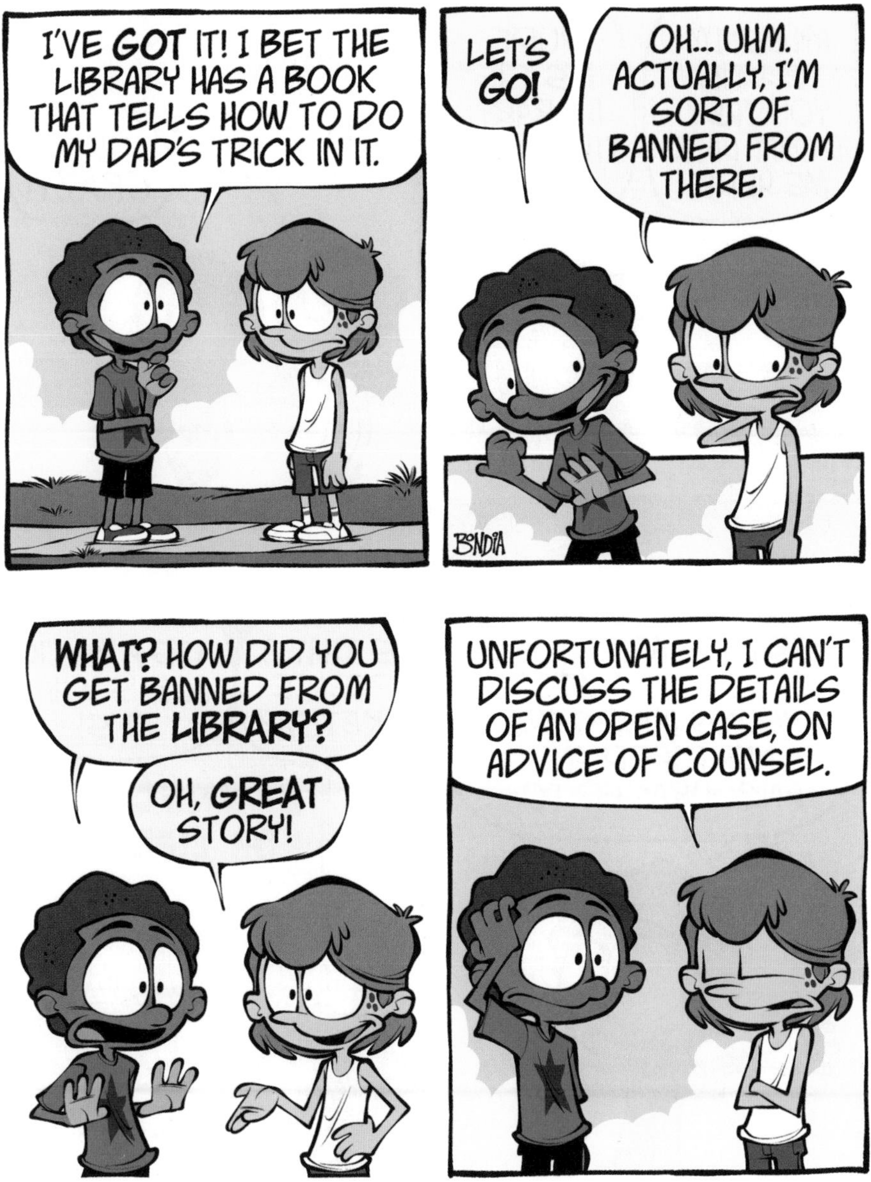
I'VE **GOT** IT! I BET THE LIBRARY HAS A BOOK THAT TELLS HOW TO DO MY DAD'S TRICK IN IT.
LET'S **GO!**
OH... UHM. ACTUALLY, I'M SORT OF BANNED FROM THERE.
BONDIA
WHAT? HOW DID YOU GET BANNED FROM THE **LIBRARY?**
OH, **GREAT** STORY!
UNFORTUNATELY, I CAN'T DISCUSS THE DETAILS OF AN OPEN CASE, ON ADVICE OF COUNSEL.

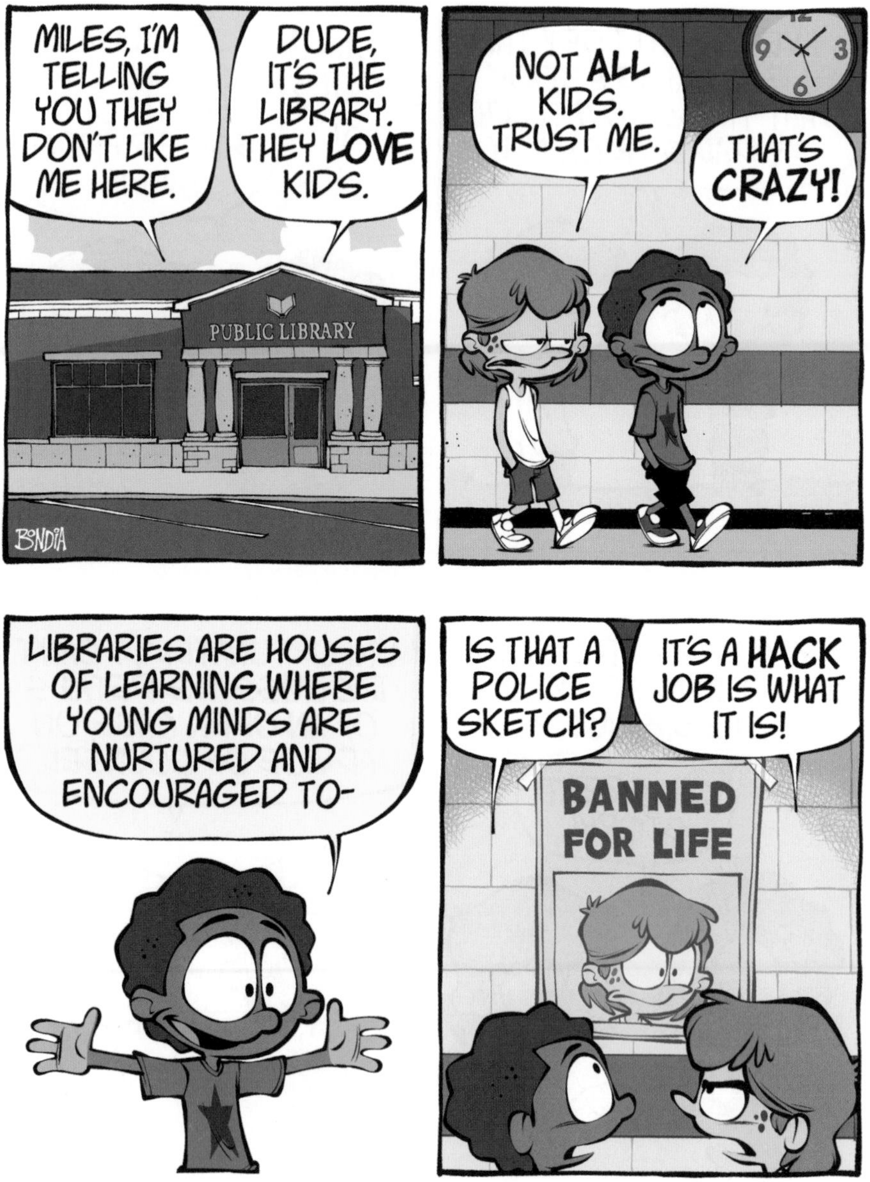
MILES, I'M TELLING YOU THEY DON'T LIKE ME HERE.
DUDE, IT'S THE LIBRARY. THEY **LOVE** KIDS.
PUBLIC LIBRARY
BONDIA
NOT **ALL** KIDS. TRUST ME.
THAT'S **CRAZY!**
LIBRARIES ARE HOUSES OF LEARNING WHERE YOUNG MINDS ARE NURTURED AND ENCOURAGED TO-
IS THAT A POLICE SKETCH?
IT'S A **HACK** JOB IS WHAT IT IS!
BANNED FOR LIFE

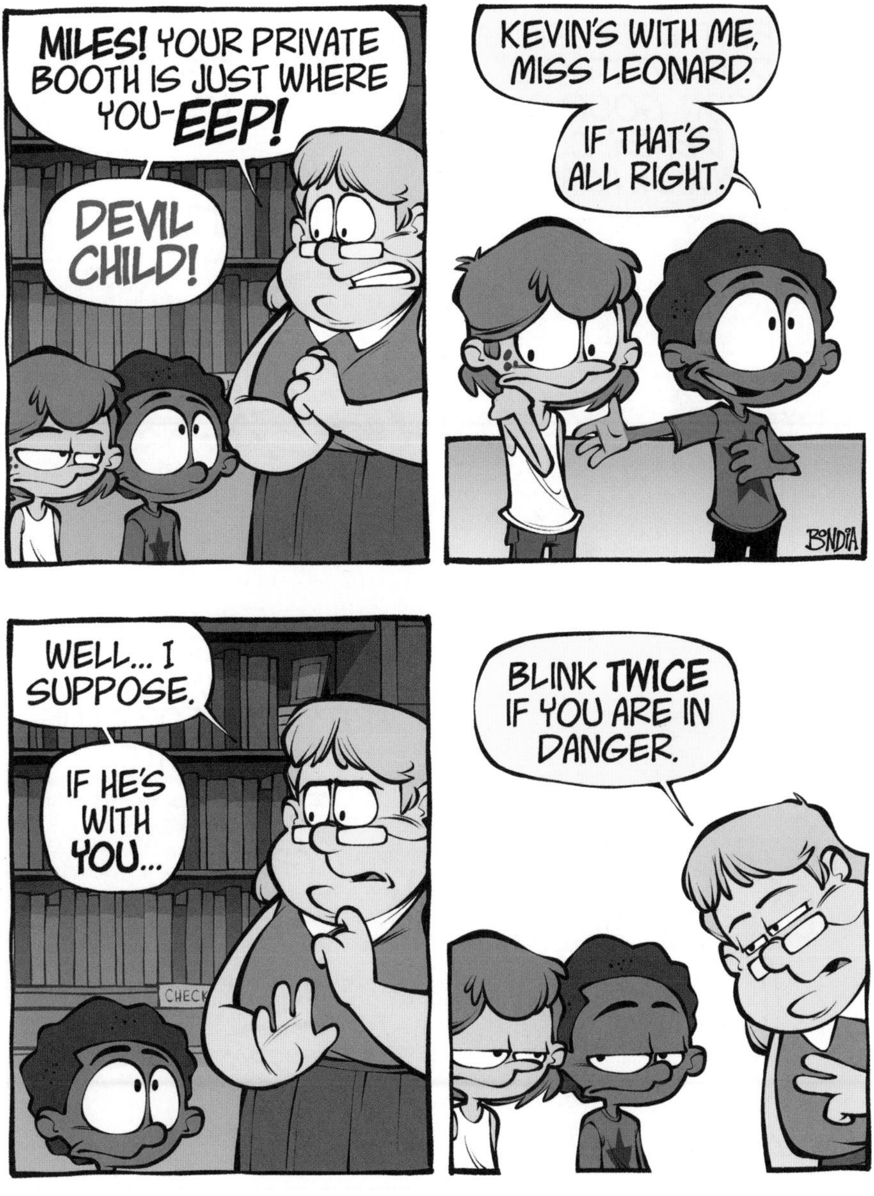
MILES! YOUR PRIVATE BOOTH IS JUST WHERE YOU-EEP!
DEVIL CHILD!
KEVIN'S WITH ME, MISS LEONARD.
IF THAT'S ALL RIGHT.
BONDIA
WELL... I SUPPOSE.
IF HE'S WITH YOU...
CHECK
BLINK TWICE IF YOU ARE IN DANGER.

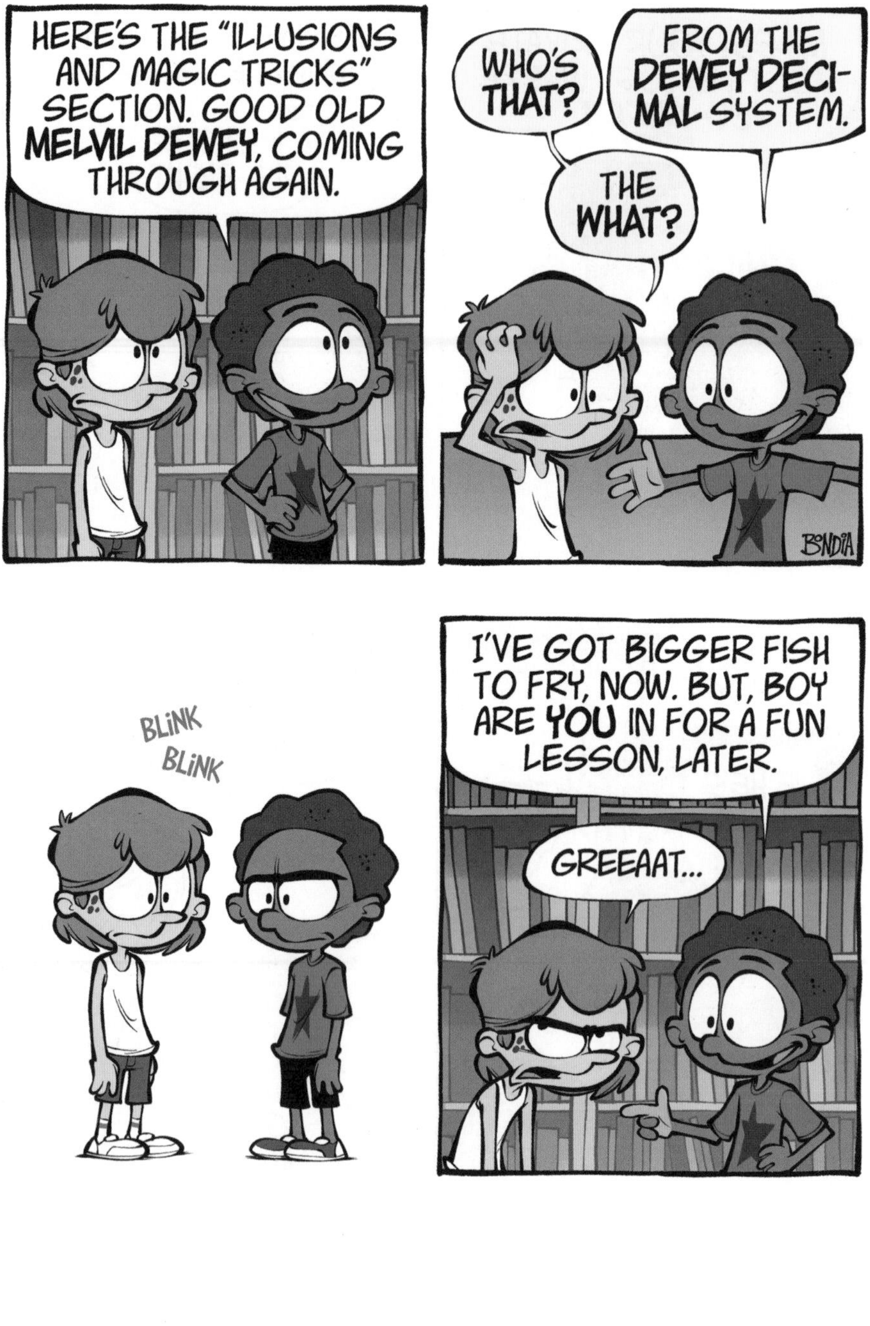
HERE'S THE "ILLUSIONS AND MAGIC TRICKS" SECTION. GOOD OLD MELVIL DEWEY, COMING THROUGH AGAIN.
WHO'S THAT?
THE WHAT?
FROM THE DEWEY DECIMAL SYSTEM.
BONDIA
BLINK
BLINK
I'VE GOT BIGGER FISH TO FRY, NOW. BUT, BOY ARE YOU IN FOR A FUN LESSON, LATER.
GREEAAT...

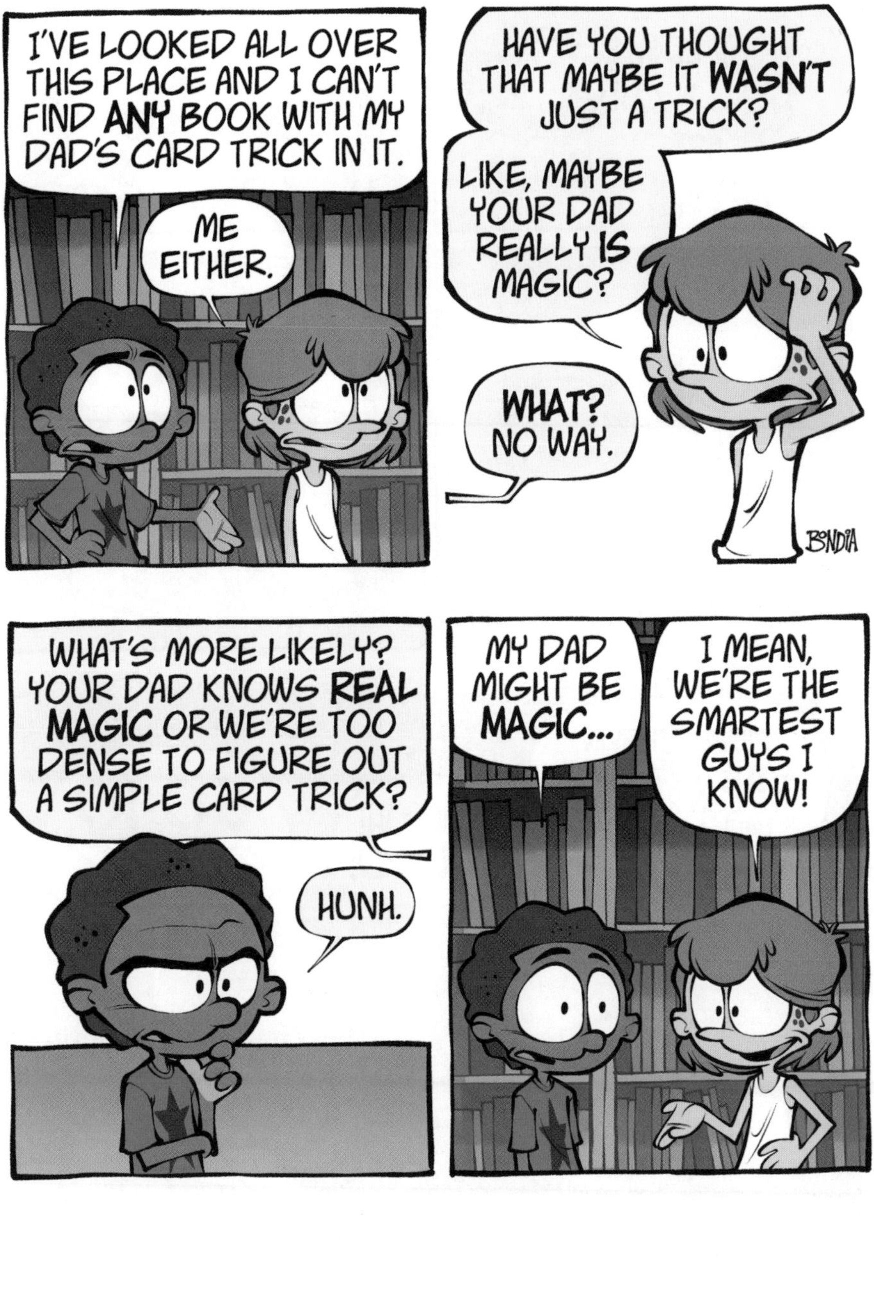
I'VE LOOKED ALL OVER THIS PLACE AND I CAN'T FIND **ANY** BOOK WITH MY DAD'S CARD TRICK IN IT.
ME EITHER.
HAVE YOU THOUGHT THAT MAYBE IT **WASN'T** JUST A TRICK?
LIKE, MAYBE YOUR DAD REALLY **IS** MAGIC?
WHAT? NO WAY.
BONDIA
WHAT'S MORE LIKELY? YOUR DAD KNOWS **REAL MAGIC** OR WE'RE TOO DENSE TO FIGURE OUT A SIMPLE CARD TRICK?
HUNH.
MY DAD MIGHT BE **MAGIC...**
I MEAN, WE'RE THE SMARTEST GUYS I KNOW!

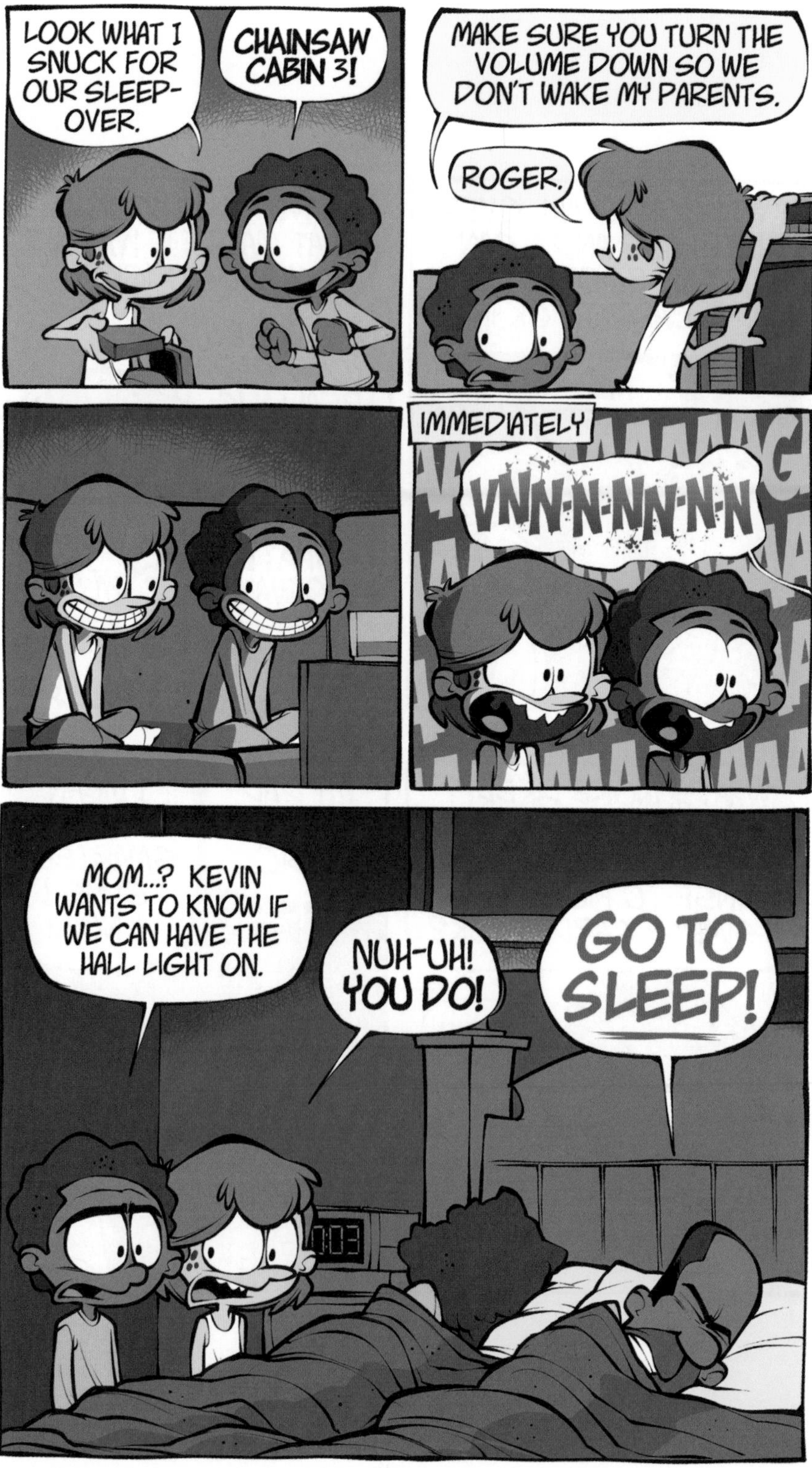

LOOK WHAT I SNUCK FOR OUR SLEEP-OVER.
CHAINSAW CABIN 3!
MAKE SURE YOU TURN THE VOLUME DOWN SO WE DON'T WAKE MY PARENTS.
ROGER.
IMMEDIATELY
VNN-N-NN-N-N
MOM...? KEVIN WANTS TO KNOW IF WE CAN HAVE THE HALL LIGHT ON.
NUH-UH! YOU DO!
GO TO SLEEP!

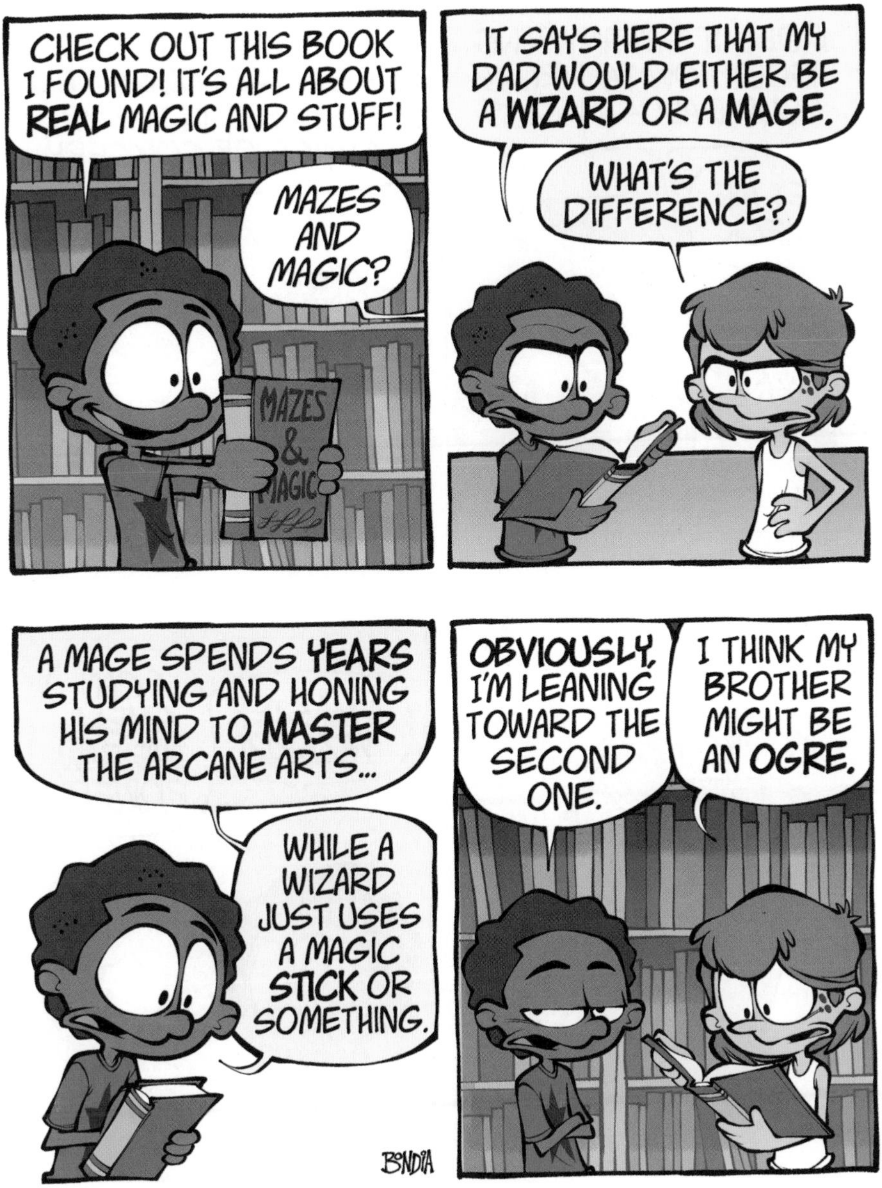
CHECK OUT THIS BOOK I FOUND! IT'S ALL ABOUT REAL MAGIC AND STUFF!
MAZES AND MAGIC?
MAZES & MAGIC
IT SAYS HERE THAT MY DAD WOULD EITHER BE A WIZARD OR A MAGE.
WHAT'S THE DIFFERENCE?
A MAGE SPENDS YEARS STUDYING AND HONING HIS MIND TO MASTER THE ARCANE ARTS...
WHILE A WIZARD JUST USES A MAGIC STICK OR SOMETHING.
BONDIA
OBVIOUSLY, I'M LEANING TOWARD THE SECOND ONE.
I THINK MY BROTHER MIGHT BE AN OGRE.

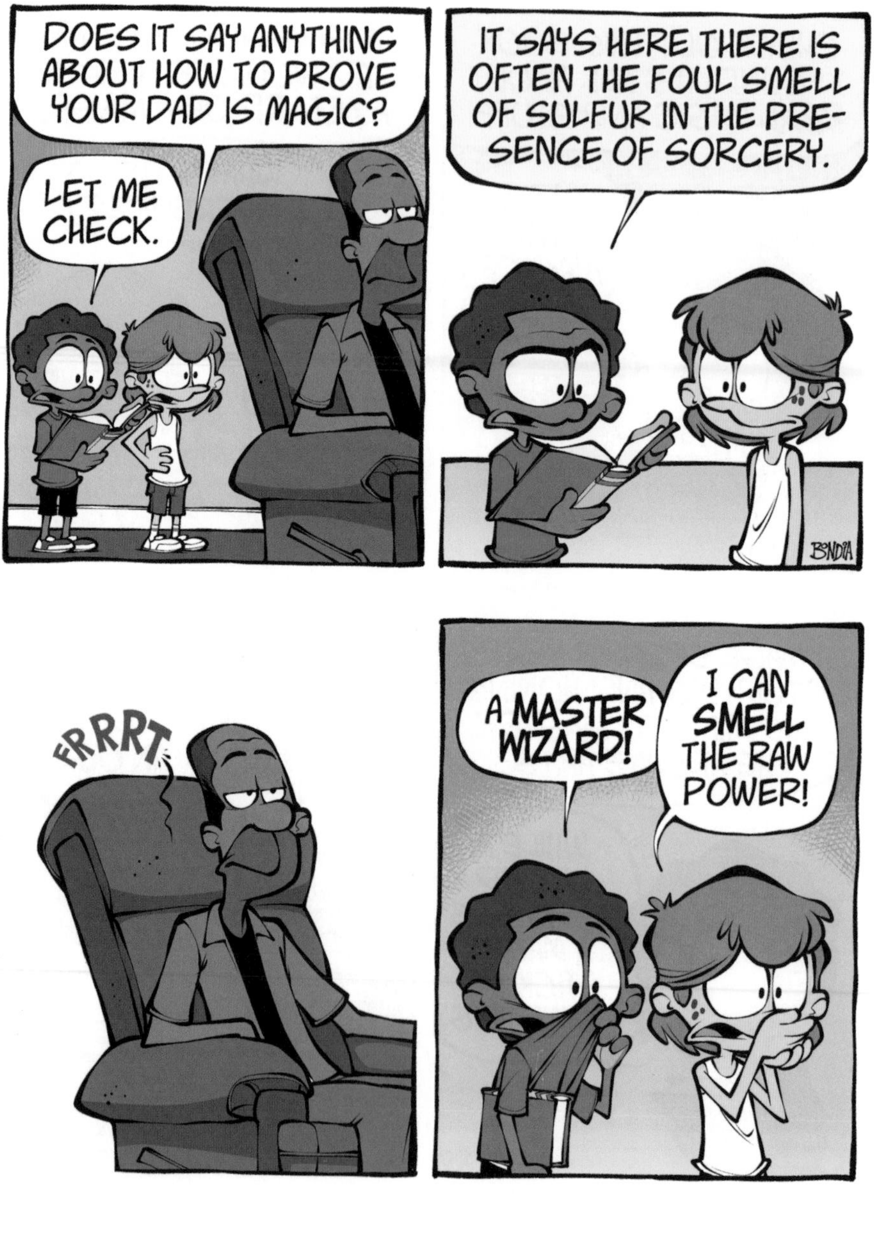
DOES IT SAY ANYTHING ABOUT HOW TO PROVE YOUR DAD IS MAGIC?
LET ME CHECK.
IT SAYS HERE THERE IS OFTEN THE FOUL SMELL OF SULFUR IN THE PRE- SENCE OF SORCERY.
BONDIA
FRRRT
A **MASTER WIZARD!**
I CAN **SMELL** THE RAW POWER!

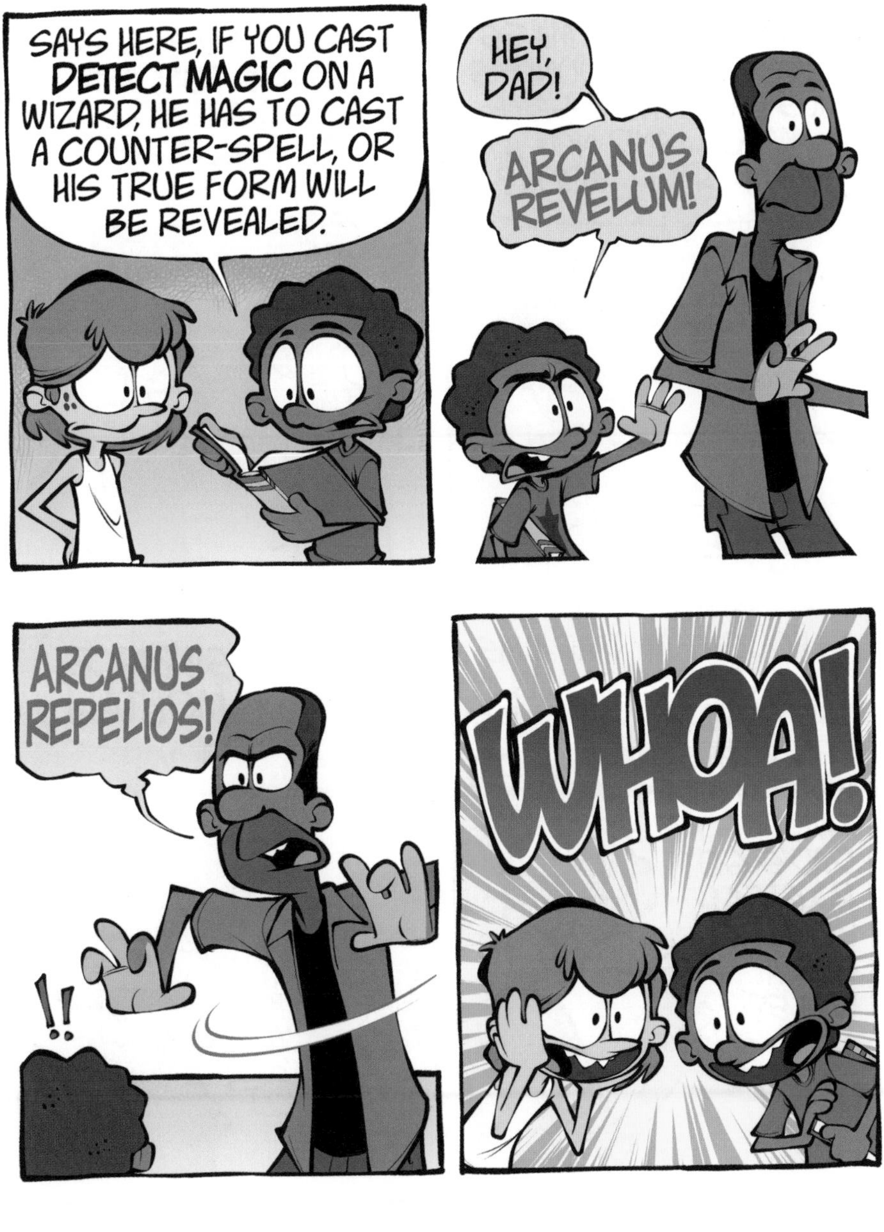
SAYS HERE, IF YOU CAST DETECT MAGIC ON A WIZARD, HE HAS TO CAST A COUNTER-SPELL, OR HIS TRUE FORM WILL BE REVEALED.
HEY, DAD!
ARCANUS REVELUM!
ARCANUS REPELIOS!
!!
WHOA!

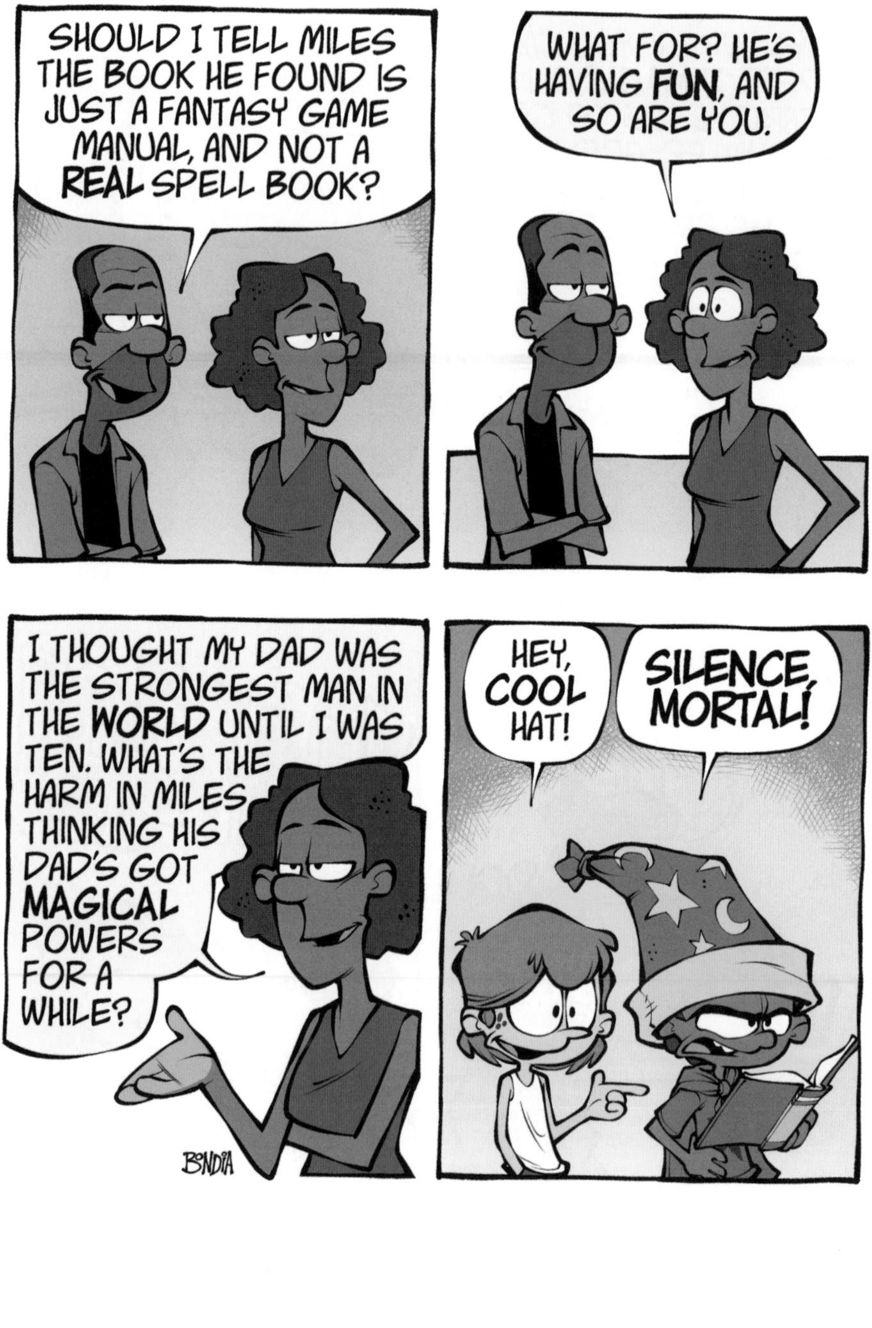
SHOULD I TELL MILES THE BOOK HE FOUND IS JUST A FANTASY GAME MANUAL, AND NOT A REAL SPELL BOOK?
WHAT FOR? HE'S HAVING FUN, AND SO ARE YOU.
I THOUGHT MY DAD WAS THE STRONGEST MAN IN THE WORLD UNTIL I WAS TEN. WHAT'S THE HARM IN MILES THINKING HIS DAD'S GOT MAGICAL POWERS FOR A WHILE?
BONDIA
HEY, COOL HAT!
SILENCE, MORTAL!

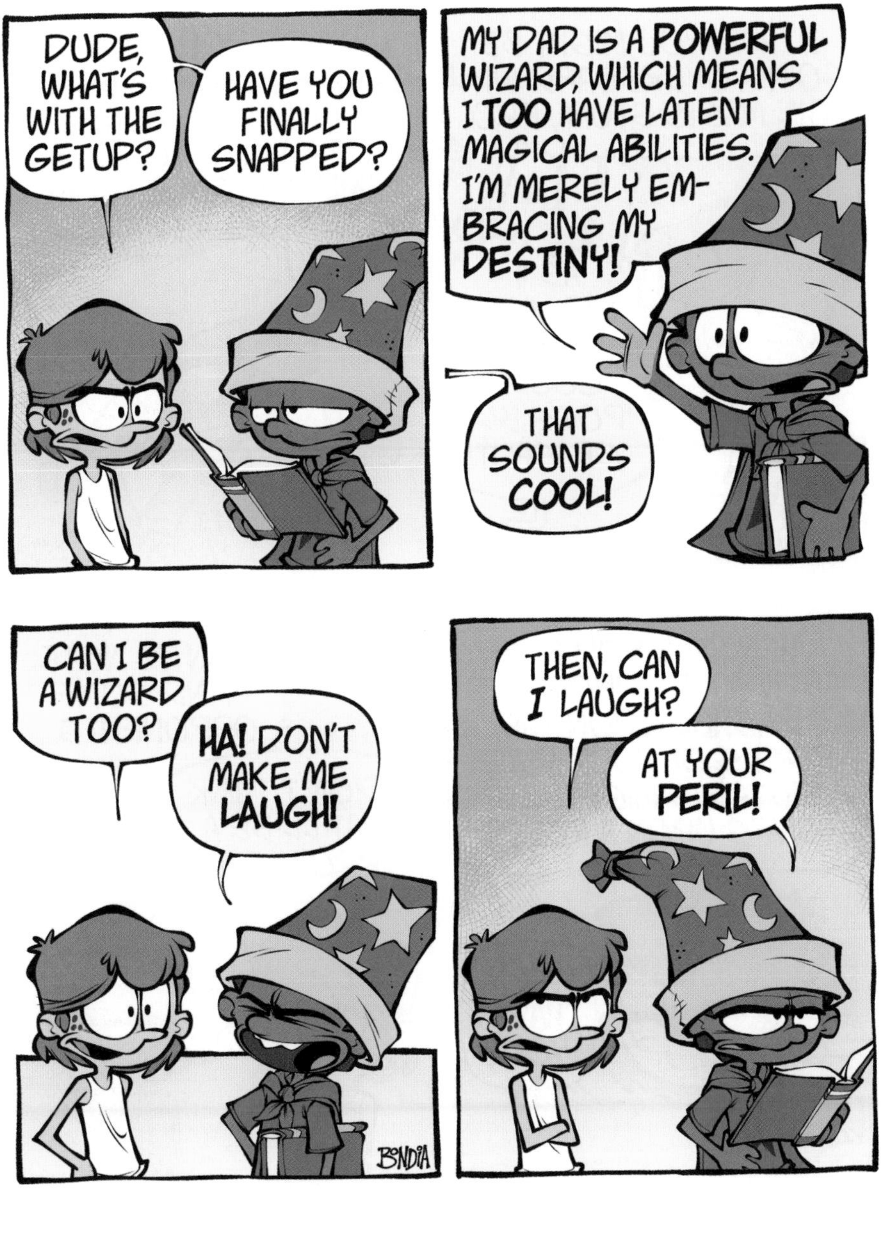
DUDE, WHAT'S WITH THE GETUP?
HAVE YOU FINALLY SNAPPED?
MY DAD IS A **POWERFUL** WIZARD, WHICH MEANS I **TOO** HAVE LATENT MAGICAL ABILITIES. I'M MERELY EMBRACING MY **DESTINY!**
THAT SOUNDS **COOL!**
CAN I BE A WIZARD TOO?
HA! DON'T MAKE ME **LAUGH!**
BONDIA
THEN, CAN *I* LAUGH?
AT YOUR **PERIL!**

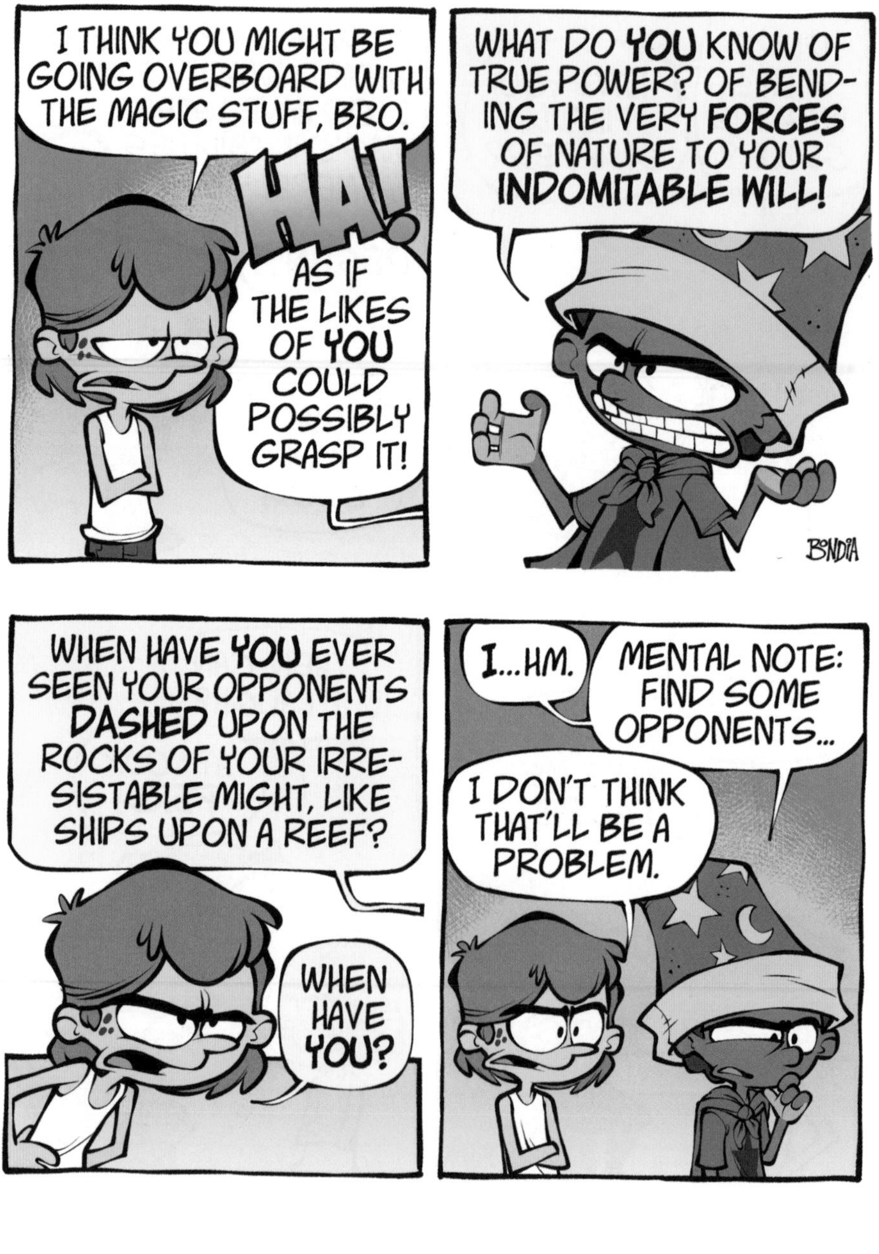

I THINK YOU MIGHT BE GOING OVERBOARD WITH THE MAGIC STUFF, BRO.
HA!
AS IF THE LIKES OF YOU COULD POSSIBLY GRASP IT!
WHAT DO YOU KNOW OF TRUE POWER? OF BENDING THE VERY FORCES OF NATURE TO YOUR INDOMITABLE WILL!
BONDIA
WHEN HAVE YOU EVER SEEN YOUR OPPONENTS DASHED UPON THE ROCKS OF YOUR IRRESISTABLE MIGHT, LIKE SHIPS UPON A REEF?
WHEN HAVE YOU?
I...HM.
MENTAL NOTE: FIND SOME OPPONENTS...
I DON'T THINK THAT'LL BE A PROBLEM.

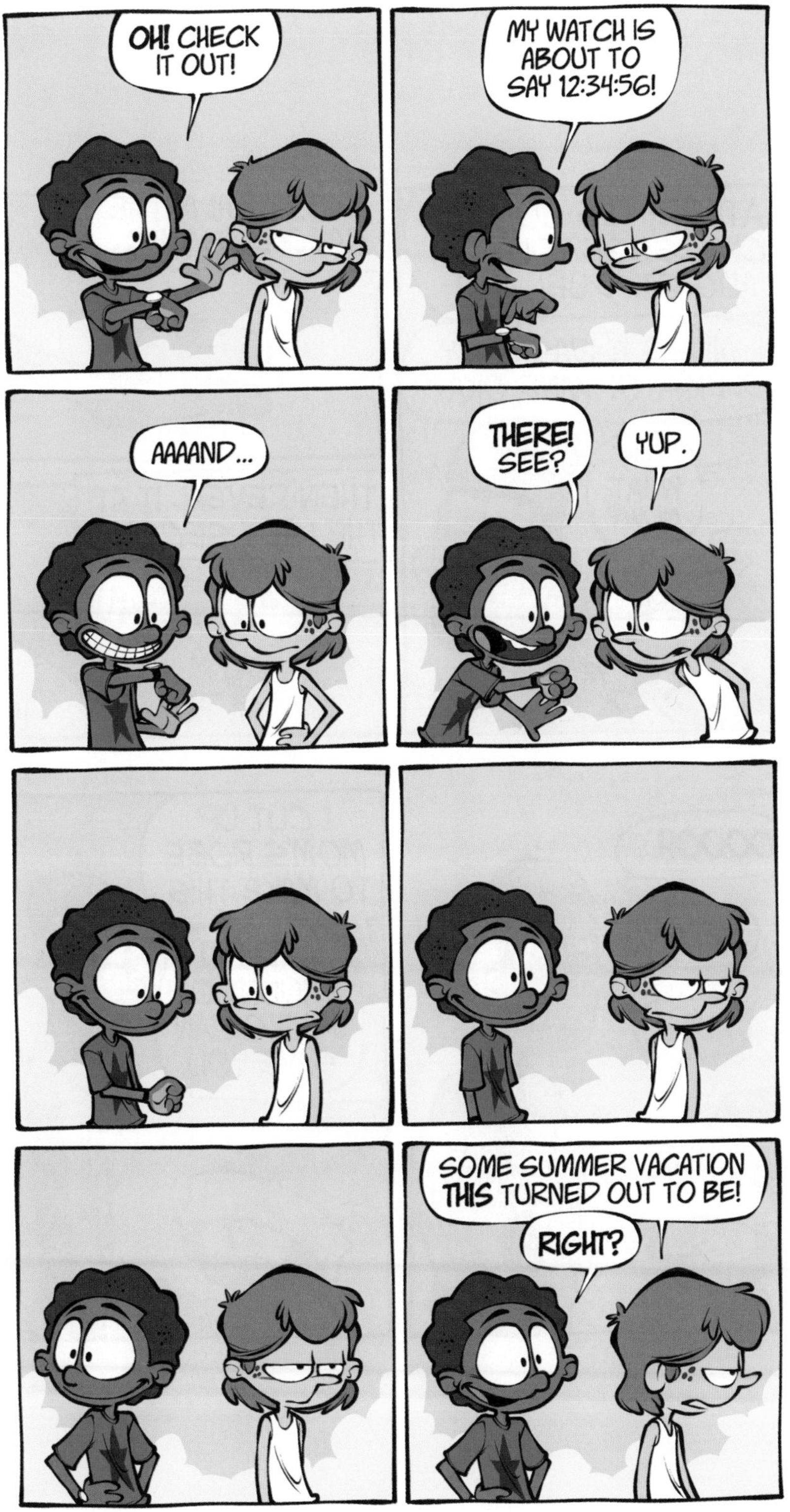
OH! CHECK IT OUT!
MY WATCH IS ABOUT TO SAY 12:34:56!
AAAAND...
THERE! SEE?
YUP.
SOME SUMMER VACATION THIS TURNED OUT TO BE!
RIGHT?

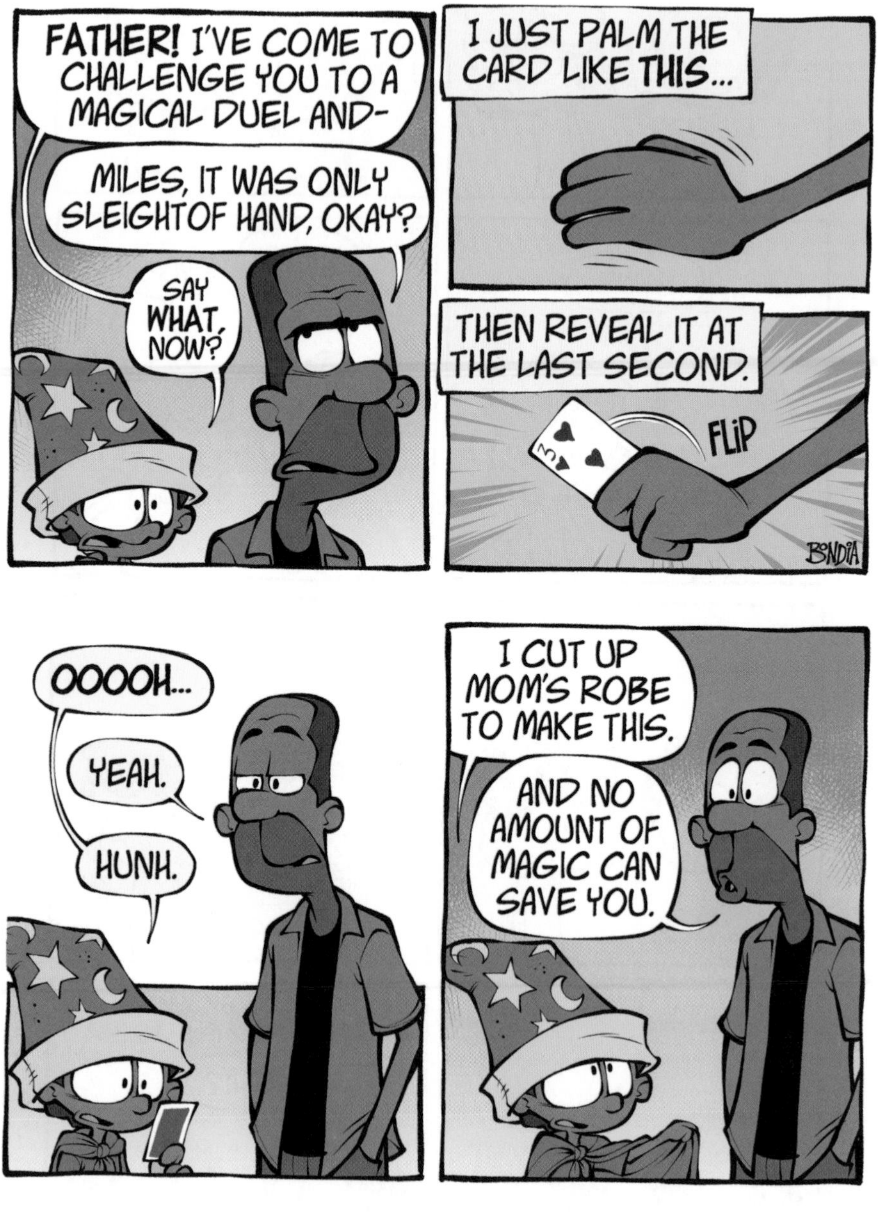
FATHER! I'VE COME TO CHALLENGE YOU TO A MAGICAL DUEL AND-
MILES, IT WAS ONLY SLEIGHTOF HAND, OKAY?
SAY WHAT, NOW?
I JUST PALM THE CARD LIKE THIS...
THEN REVEAL IT AT THE LAST SECOND.
FLIP
BONDIA
OOOOH...
YEAH.
HUNH.
I CUT UP MOM'S ROBE TO MAKE THIS.
AND NO AMOUNT OF MAGIC CAN SAVE YOU.

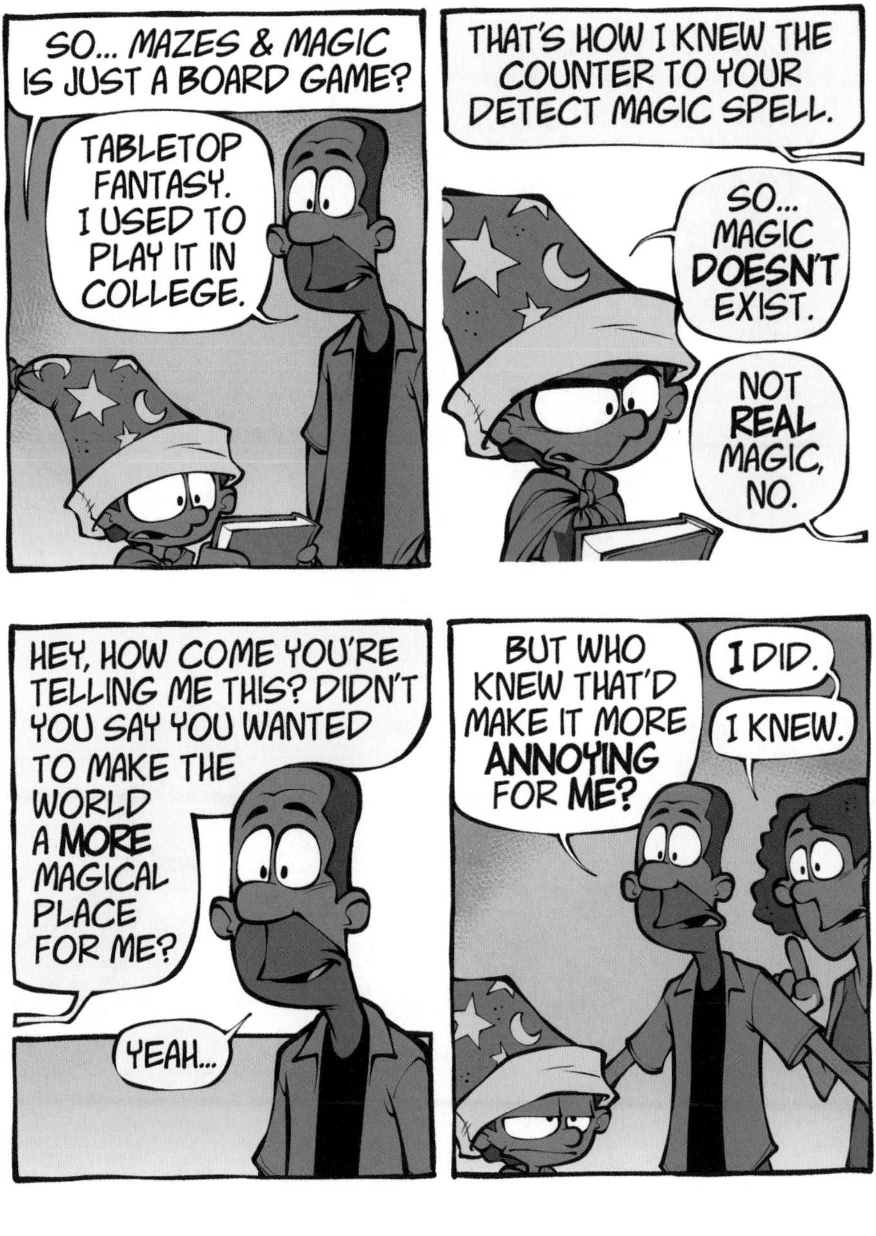
SO... MAZES & MAGIC IS JUST A BOARD GAME?
TABLETOP FANTASY. I USED TO PLAY IT IN COLLEGE.
THAT'S HOW I KNEW THE COUNTER TO YOUR DETECT MAGIC SPELL.
SO... MAGIC DOESN'T EXIST.
NOT REAL MAGIC, NO.
HEY, HOW COME YOU'RE TELLING ME THIS? DIDN'T YOU SAY YOU WANTED TO MAKE THE WORLD A MORE MAGICAL PLACE FOR ME?
YEAH...
BUT WHO KNEW THAT'D MAKE IT MORE ANNOYING FOR ME?
I DID.
I KNEW.

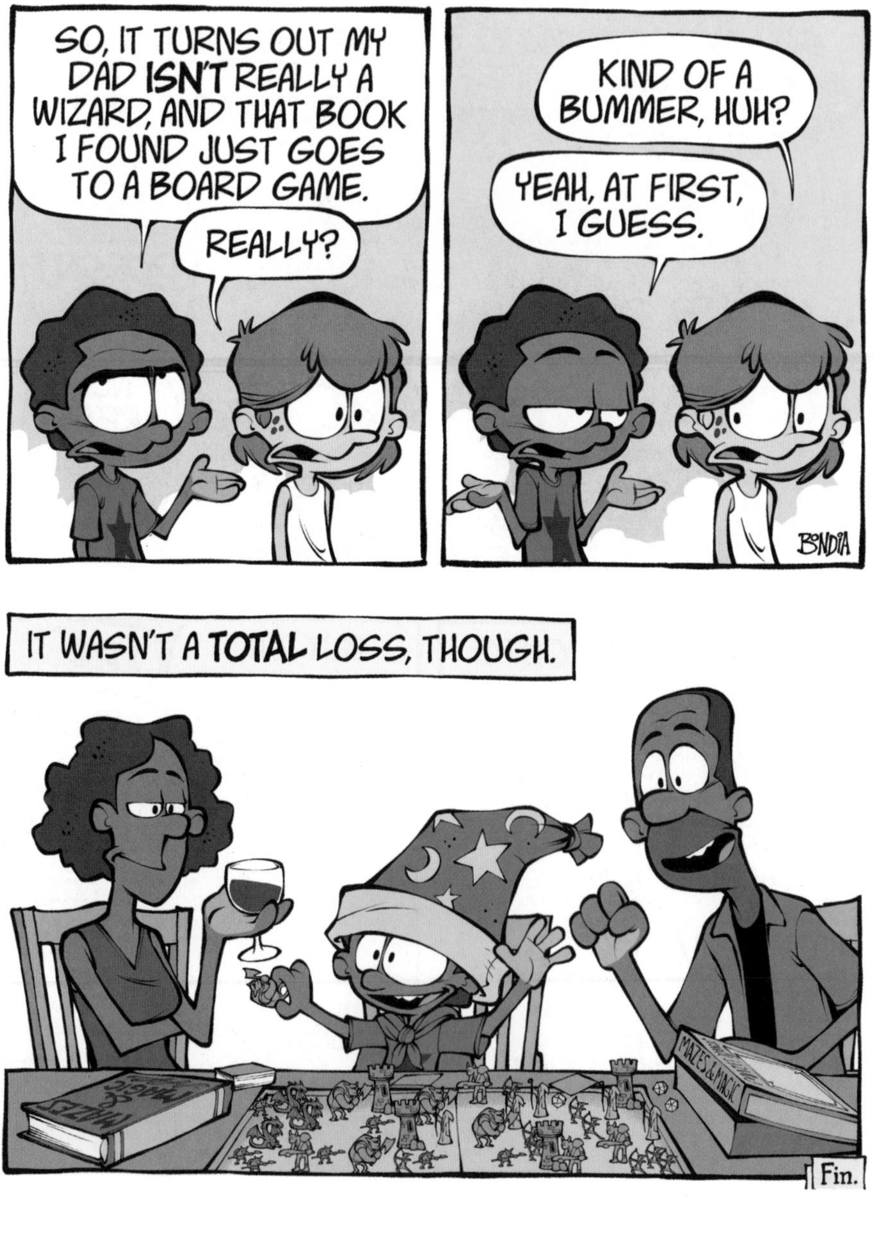
SO, IT TURNS OUT MY DAD **ISN'T** REALLY A WIZARD, AND THAT BOOK I FOUND JUST GOES TO A BOARD GAME.
REALLY?
KIND OF A BUMMER, HUH?
YEAH, AT FIRST, I GUESS.
BONDIA
IT WASN'T A **TOTAL** LOSS, THOUGH.
MAZES & MAGIC
Fin.

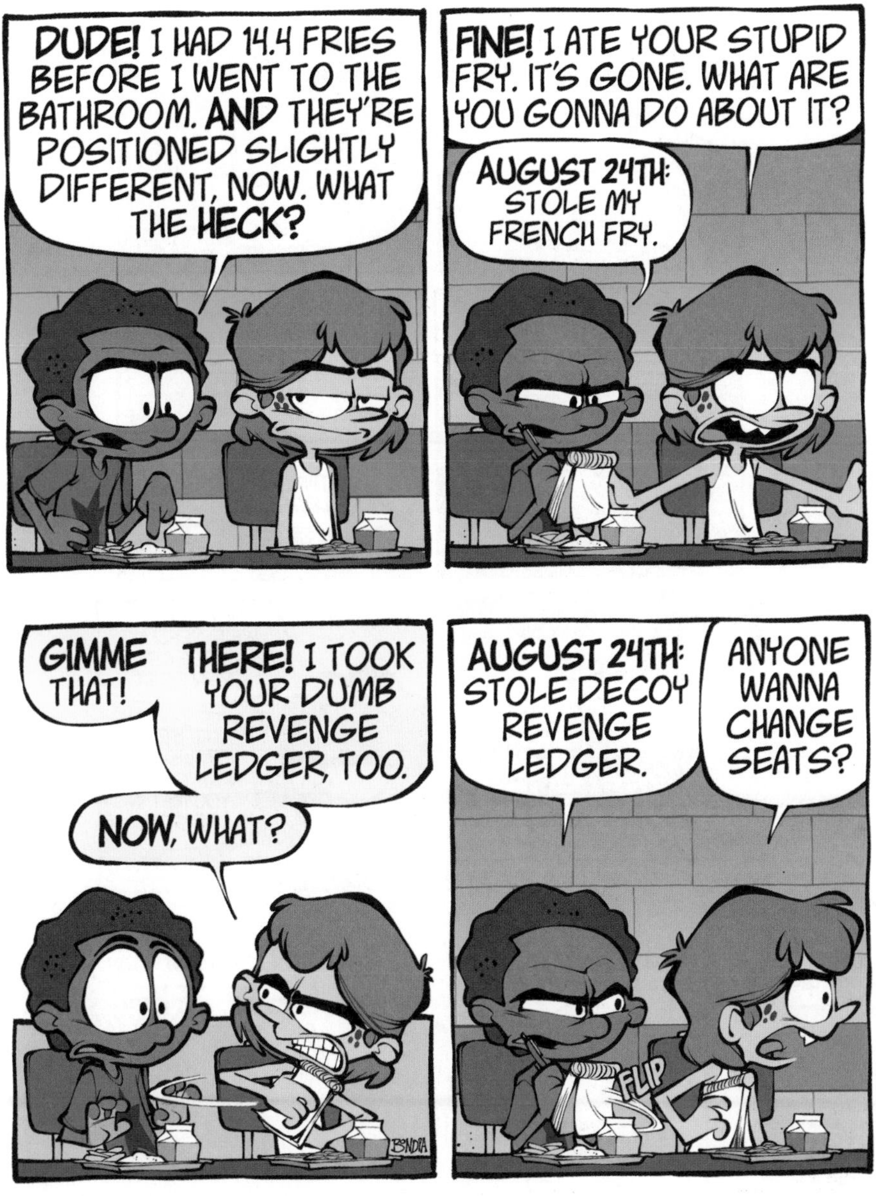
DUDE! I HAD 14.4 FRIES BEFORE I WENT TO THE BATHROOM. AND THEY'RE POSITIONED SLIGHTLY DIFFERENT, NOW. WHAT THE HECK?
FINE! I ATE YOUR STUPID FRY. IT'S GONE. WHAT ARE YOU GONNA DO ABOUT IT?
AUGUST 24TH: STOLE MY FRENCH FRY.
GIMME THAT!
THERE! I TOOK YOUR DUMB REVENGE LEDGER, TOO.
NOW, WHAT?
BONDIA
AUGUST 24TH: STOLE DECOY REVENGE LEDGER.
ANYONE WANNA CHANGE SEATS?
FLIP

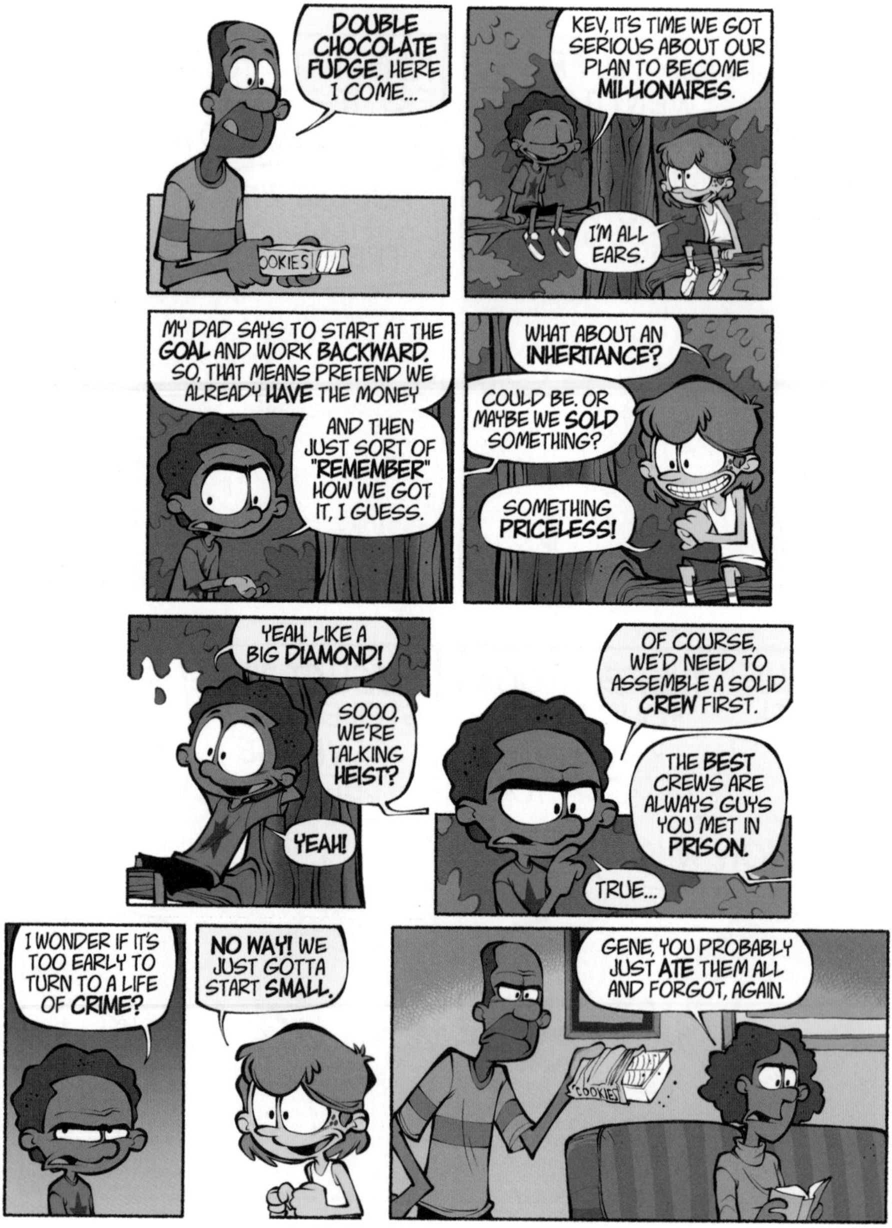

DOUBLE CHOCOLATE FUDGE, HERE I COME...
COOKIES
KEV, IT'S TIME WE GOT SERIOUS ABOUT OUR PLAN TO BECOME MILLIONAIRES.
I'M ALL EARS.
MY DAD SAYS TO START AT THE GOAL AND WORK BACKWARD. SO, THAT MEANS PRETEND WE ALREADY HAVE THE MONEY
AND THEN JUST SORT OF "REMEMBER" HOW WE GOT IT, I GUESS.
WHAT ABOUT AN INHERITANCE?
COULD BE. OR MAYBE WE SOLD SOMETHING?
SOMETHING PRICELESS!
YEAH. LIKE A BIG DIAMOND!
SOOO, WE'RE TALKING HEIST?
YEAH!
OF COURSE, WE'D NEED TO ASSEMBLE A SOLID CREW FIRST.
THE BEST CREWS ARE ALWAYS GUYS YOU MET IN PRISON.
TRUE...
I WONDER IF IT'S TOO EARLY TO TURN TO A LIFE OF CRIME?
NO WAY! WE JUST GOTTA START SMALL.
GENE, YOU PROBABLY JUST ATE THEM ALL AND FORGOT, AGAIN.
COOKIES

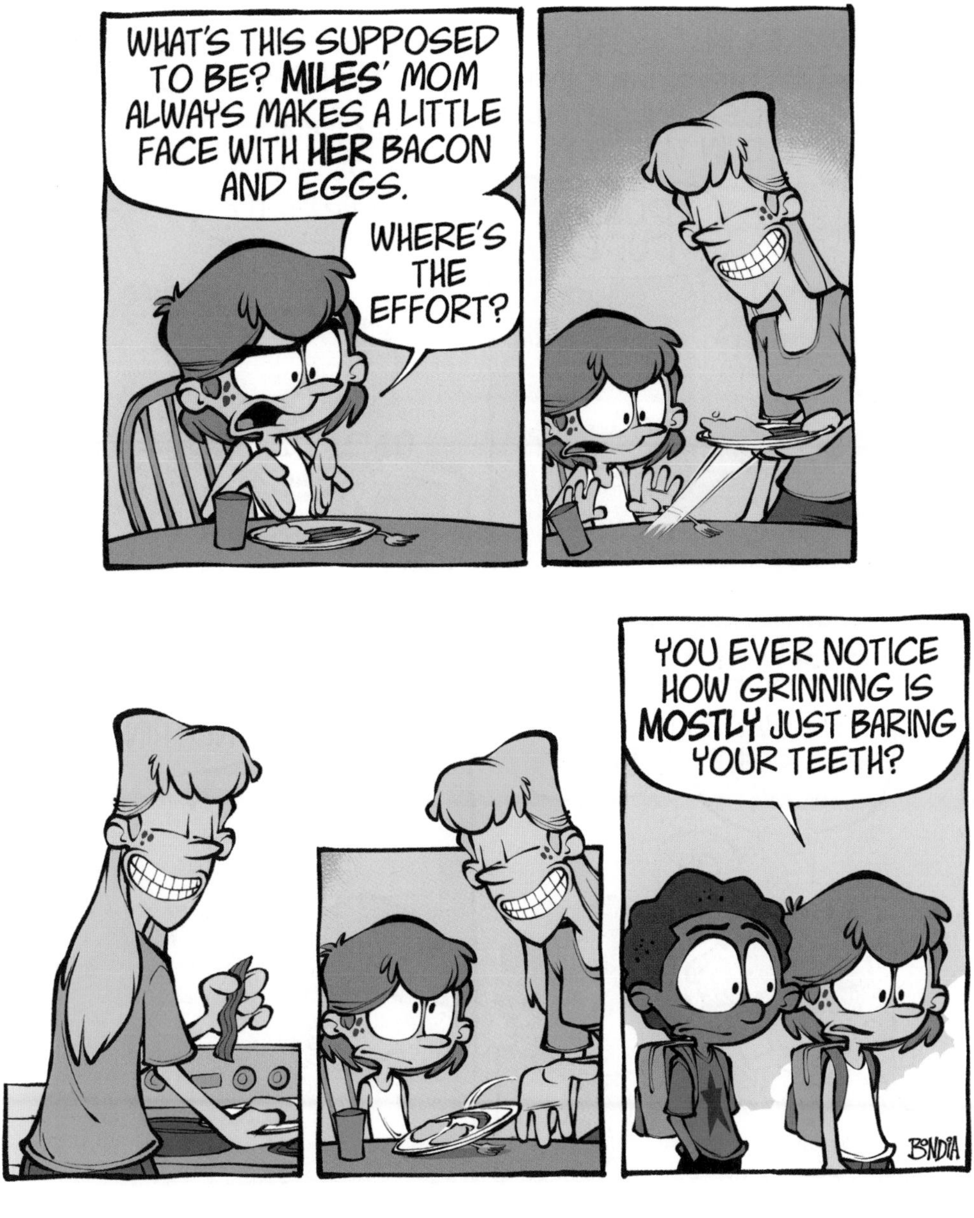
WHAT'S THIS SUPPOSED TO BE? MILES' MOM ALWAYS MAKES A LITTLE FACE WITH HER BACON AND EGGS.
WHERE'S THE EFFORT?
YOU EVER NOTICE HOW GRINNING IS MOSTLY JUST BARING YOUR TEETH?
BONDIA

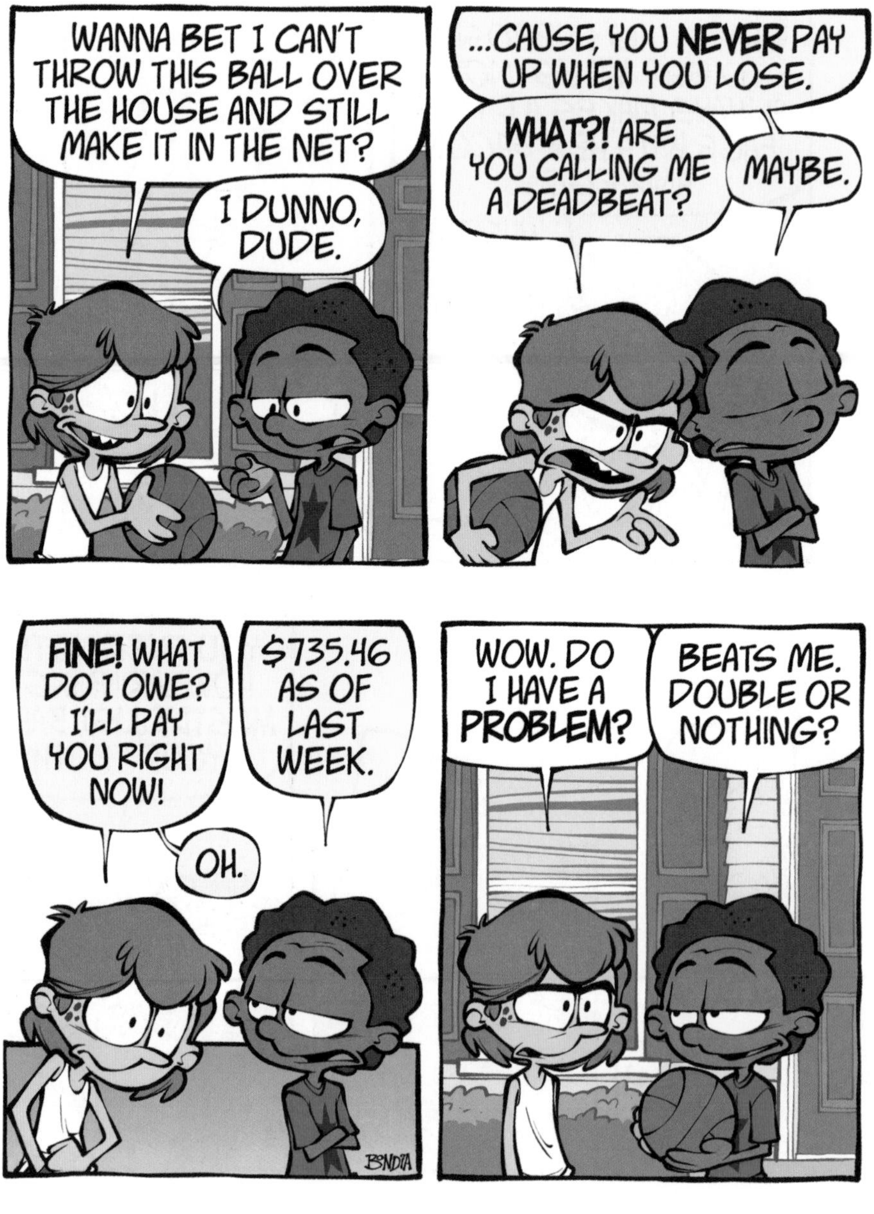
WANNA BET I CAN'T THROW THIS BALL OVER THE HOUSE AND STILL MAKE IT IN THE NET?
I DUNNO, DUDE.
...CAUSE, YOU NEVER PAY UP WHEN YOU LOSE.
WHAT?! ARE YOU CALLING ME A DEADBEAT?
MAYBE.
FINE! WHAT DO I OWE? I'LL PAY YOU RIGHT NOW!
$735.46 AS OF LAST WEEK.
OH.
BONDIA
WOW. DO I HAVE A PROBLEM?
BEATS ME. DOUBLE OR NOTHING?

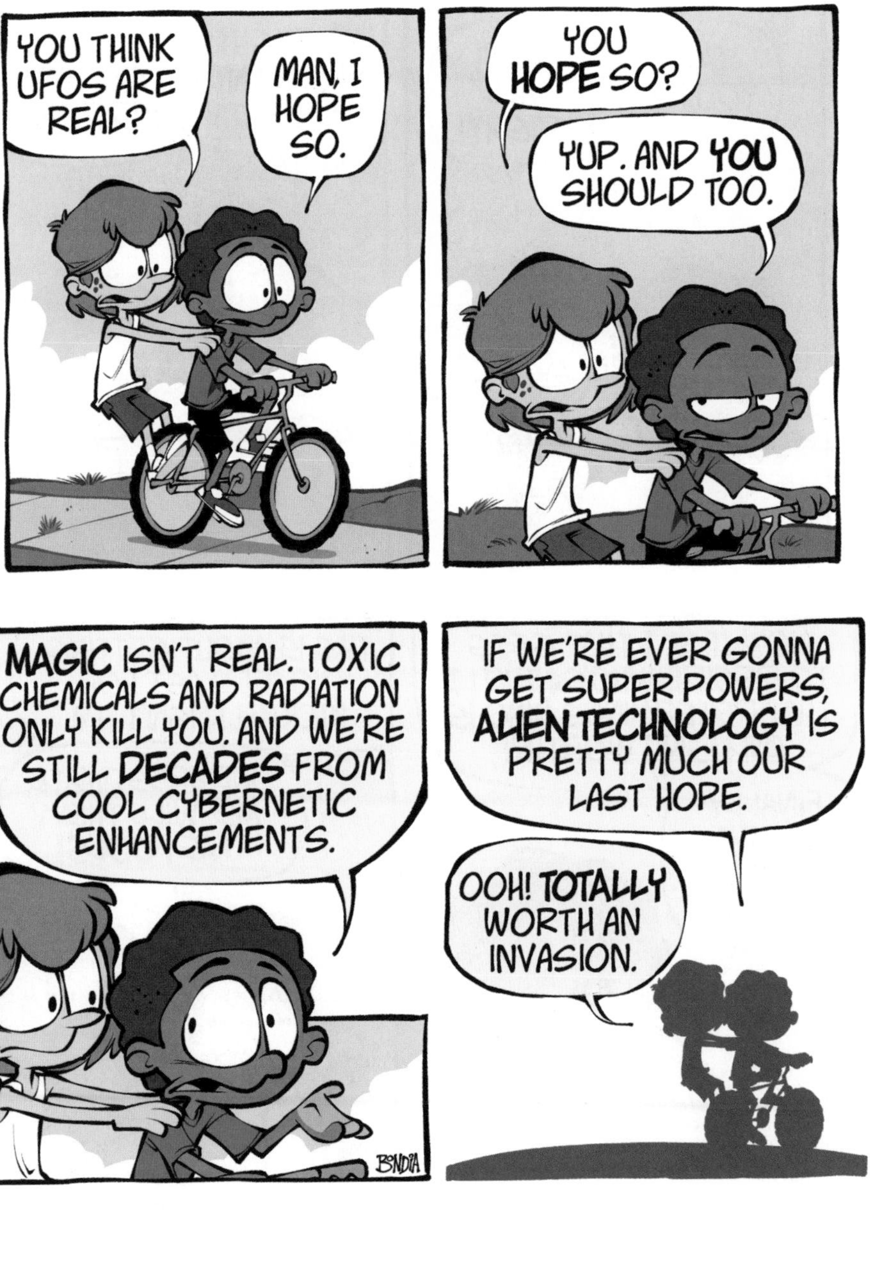
YOU THINK UFOS ARE REAL?
MAN, I HOPE SO.
YOU **HOPE** SO?
YUP. AND **YOU** SHOULD TOO.
MAGIC ISN'T REAL. TOXIC CHEMICALS AND RADIATION ONLY KILL YOU. AND WE'RE STILL **DECADES** FROM COOL CYBERNETIC ENHANCEMENTS.
IF WE'RE EVER GONNA GET SUPER POWERS, **ALIEN TECHNOLOGY** IS PRETTY MUCH OUR LAST HOPE.
OOH! **TOTALLY** WORTH AN INVASION.
BONDIA

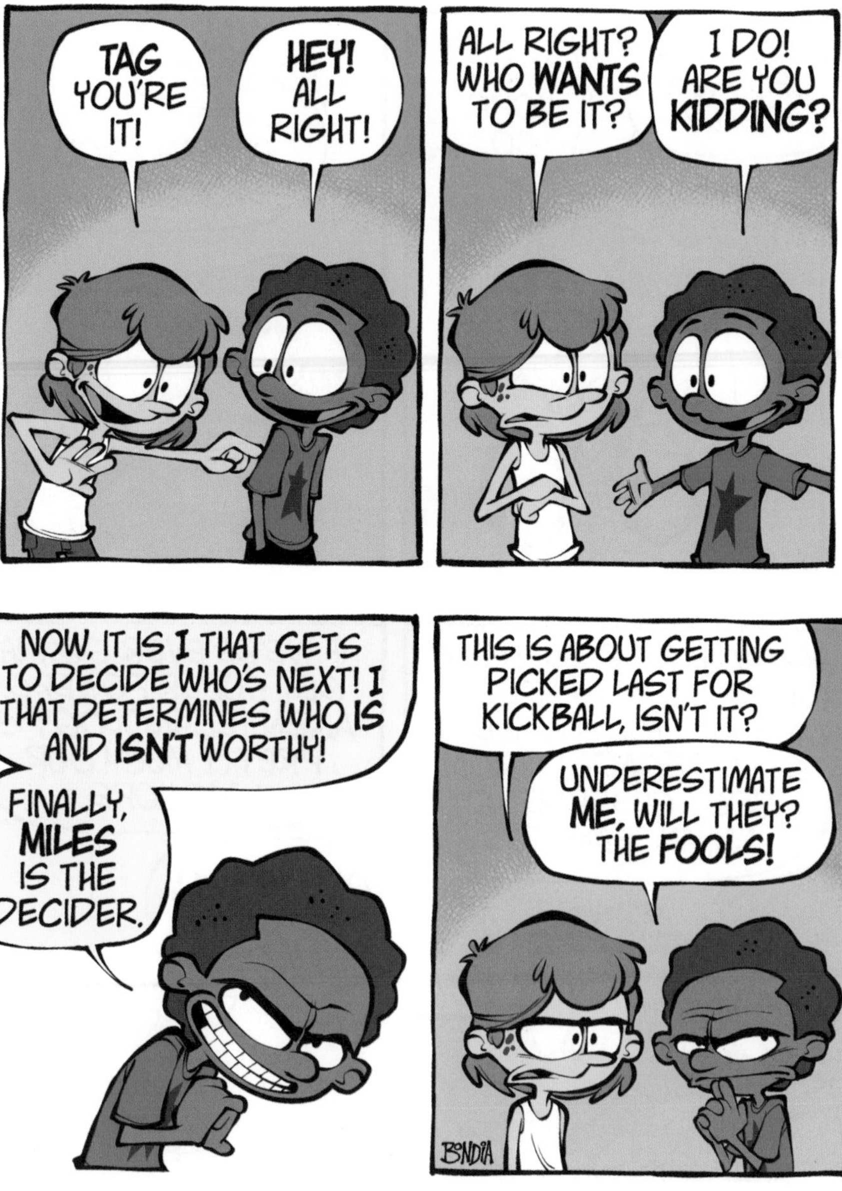
TAG YOU'RE IT!
HEY! ALL RIGHT!
ALL RIGHT? WHO WANTS TO BE IT?
I DO! ARE YOU KIDDING?
NOW, IT IS I THAT GETS TO DECIDE WHO'S NEXT! I THAT DETERMINES WHO IS AND ISN'T WORTHY!
FINALLY, MILES IS THE DECIDER.
THIS IS ABOUT GETTING PICKED LAST FOR KICKBALL, ISN'T IT?
UNDERESTIMATE ME, WILL THEY? THE FOOLS!
BONDIA

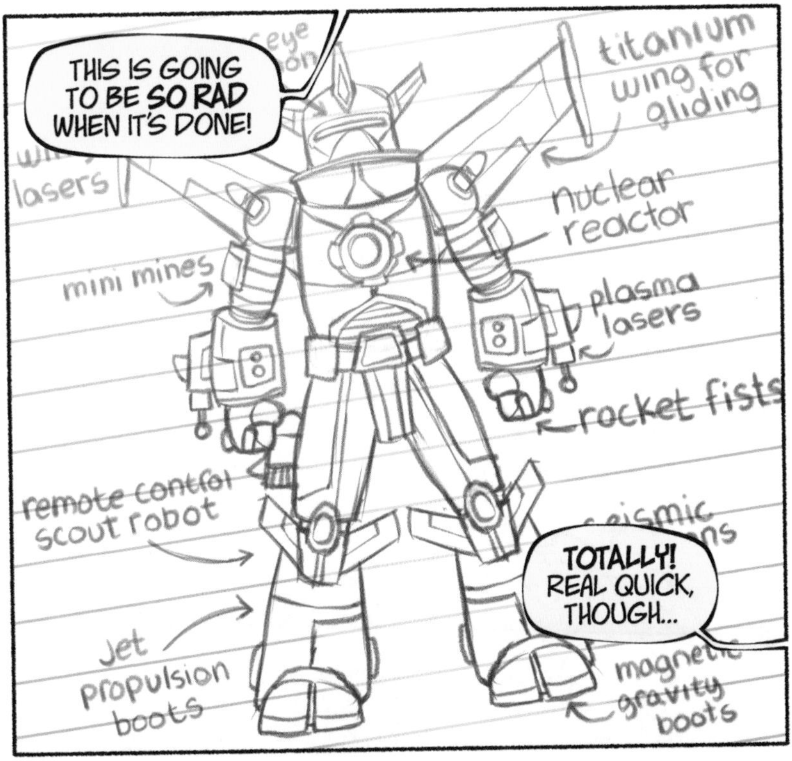
THIS IS GOING TO BE **SO RAD** WHEN IT'S DONE!
titanium wing for gliding
lasers
nuclear reactor
mini mines
plasma lasers
rocket fists
remote control scout robot
Jet propulsion boots
magnetic gravity boots
TOTALLY! REAL QUICK, THOUGH...

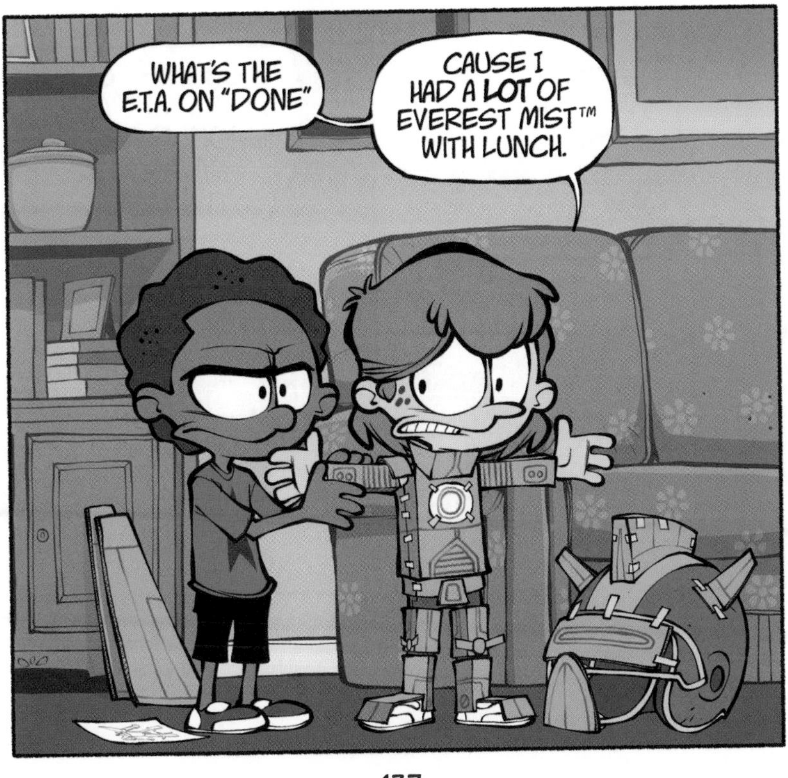
WHAT'S THE E.T.A. ON "DONE"
CAUSE I HAD A **LOT** OF EVEREST MIST™ WITH LUNCH.

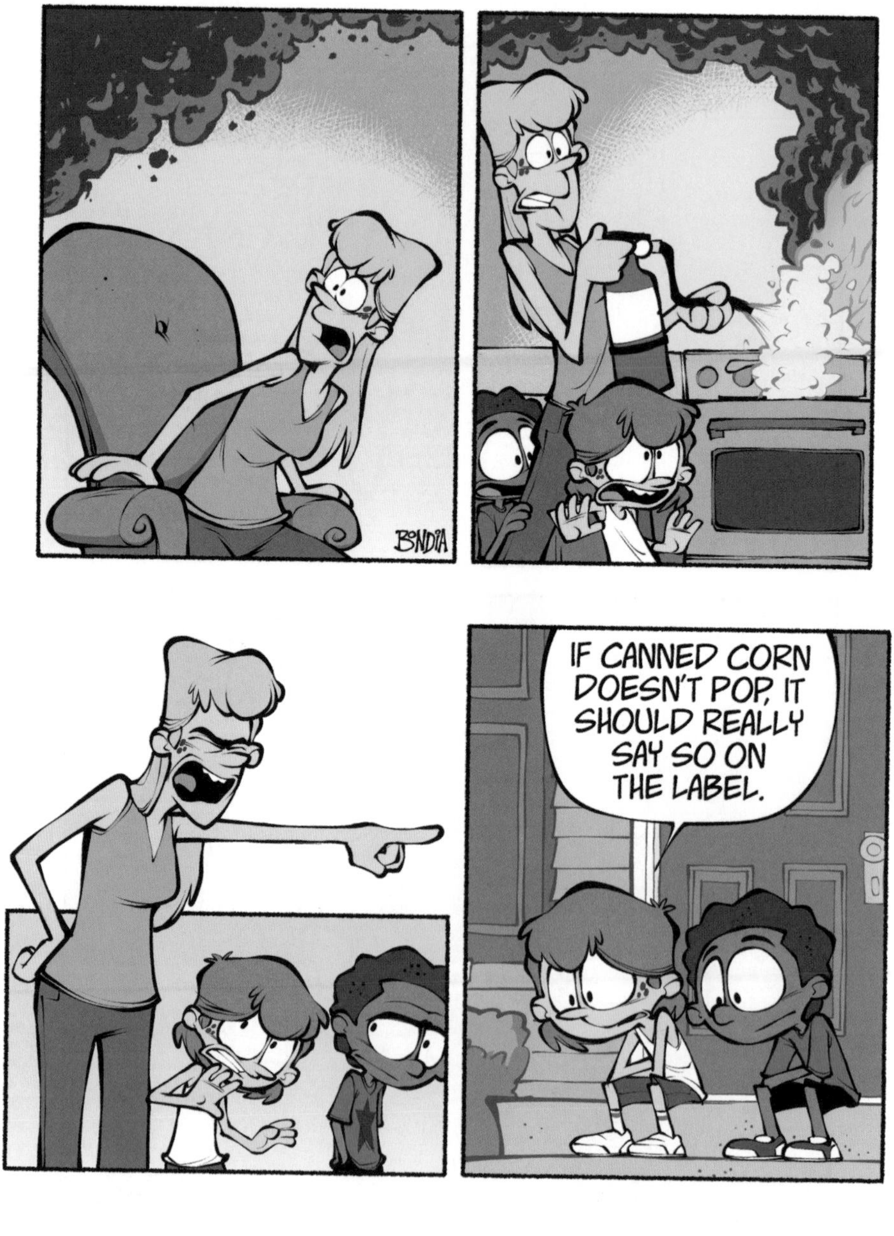
BONDIA
IF CANNED CORN DOESN'T POP, IT SHOULD REALLY SAY SO ON THE LABEL.

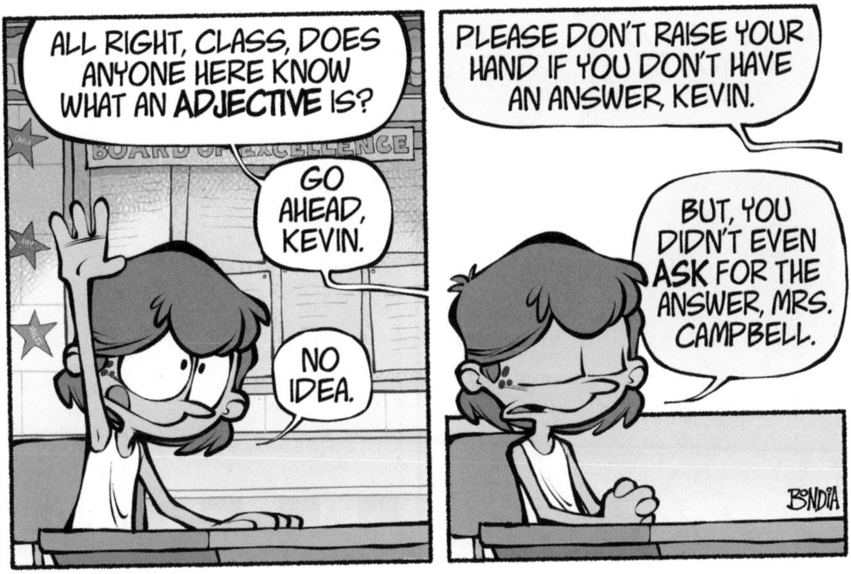
ALL RIGHT, CLASS, DOES ANYONE HERE KNOW WHAT AN **ADJECTIVE** IS?
GO AHEAD, KEVIN.
NO IDEA.
PLEASE DON'T RAISE YOUR HAND IF YOU DON'T HAVE AN ANSWER, KEVIN.
BUT, YOU DIDN'T EVEN **ASK** FOR THE ANSWER, MRS. CAMPBELL.
BONDIA

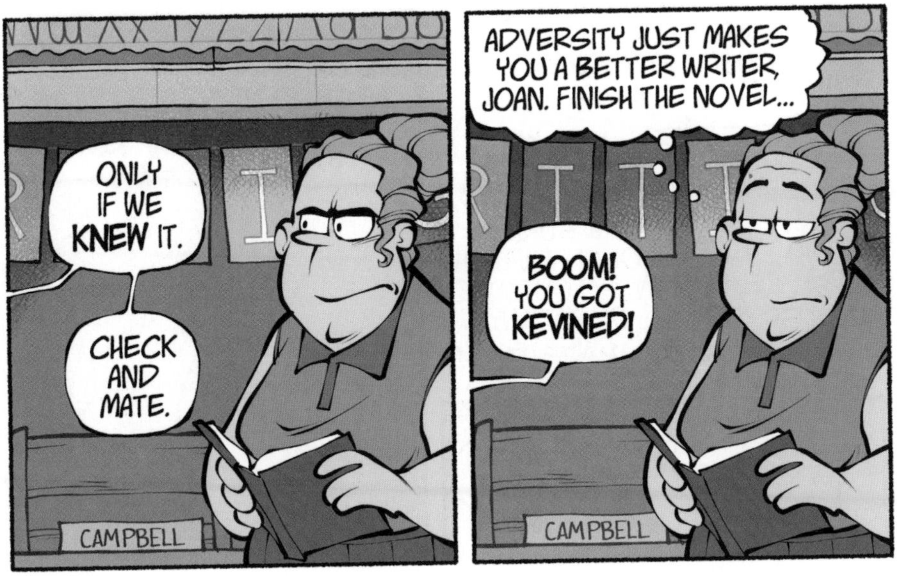
ONLY IF WE **KNEW** IT.
CHECK AND MATE.
CAMPBELL
ADVERSITY JUST MAKES YOU A BETTER WRITER, JOAN. FINISH THE NOVEL...
BOOM! YOU GOT **KEVINED!**
CAMPBELL

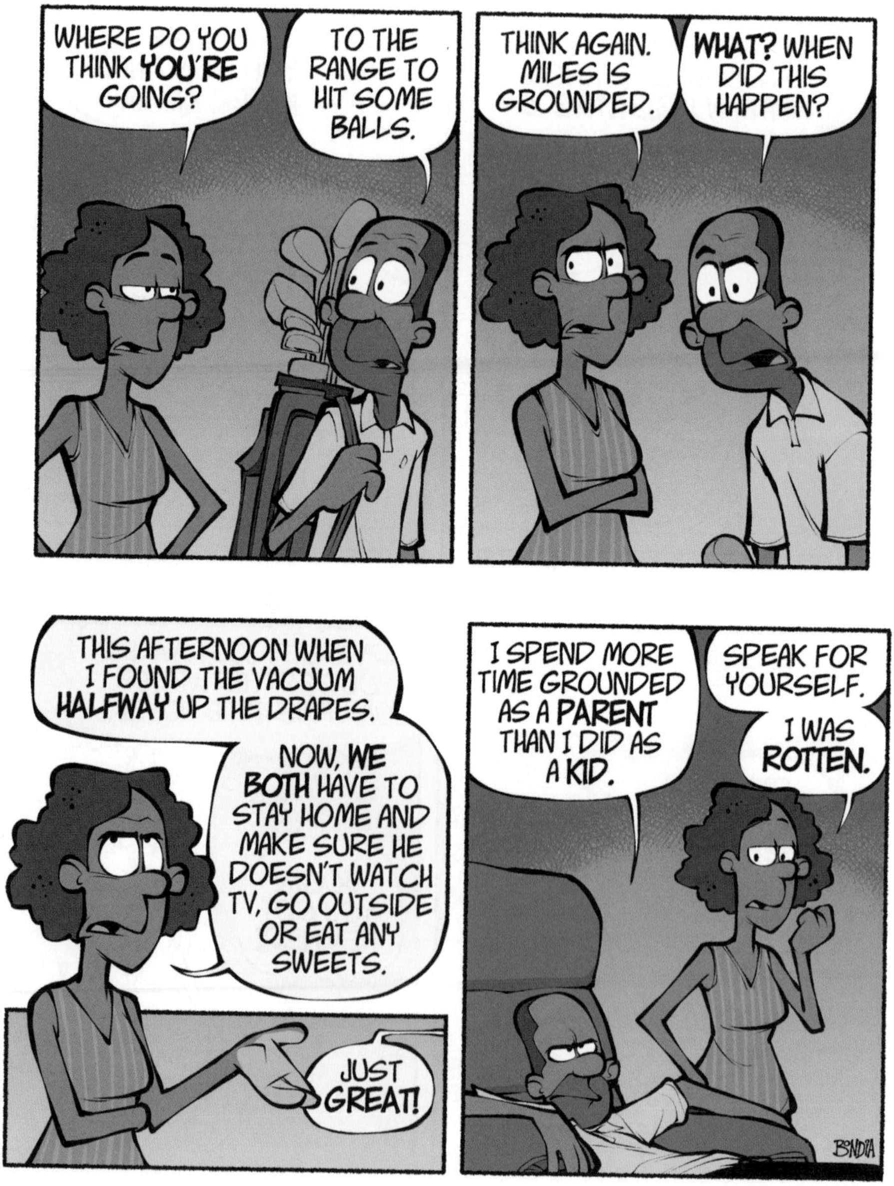
WHERE DO YOU THINK **YOU'RE** GOING?
TO THE RANGE TO HIT SOME BALLS.
THINK AGAIN. MILES IS GROUNDED.
WHAT? WHEN DID THIS HAPPEN?
THIS AFTERNOON WHEN I FOUND THE VACUUM **HALFWAY** UP THE DRAPES.
NOW, **WE BOTH** HAVE TO STAY HOME AND MAKE SURE HE DOESN'T WATCH TV, GO OUTSIDE OR EAT ANY SWEETS.
JUST **GREAT!**
I SPEND MORE TIME GROUNDED AS A **PARENT** THAN I DID AS A **KID**.
SPEAK FOR YOURSELF.
I WAS **ROTTEN.**
BONDIA

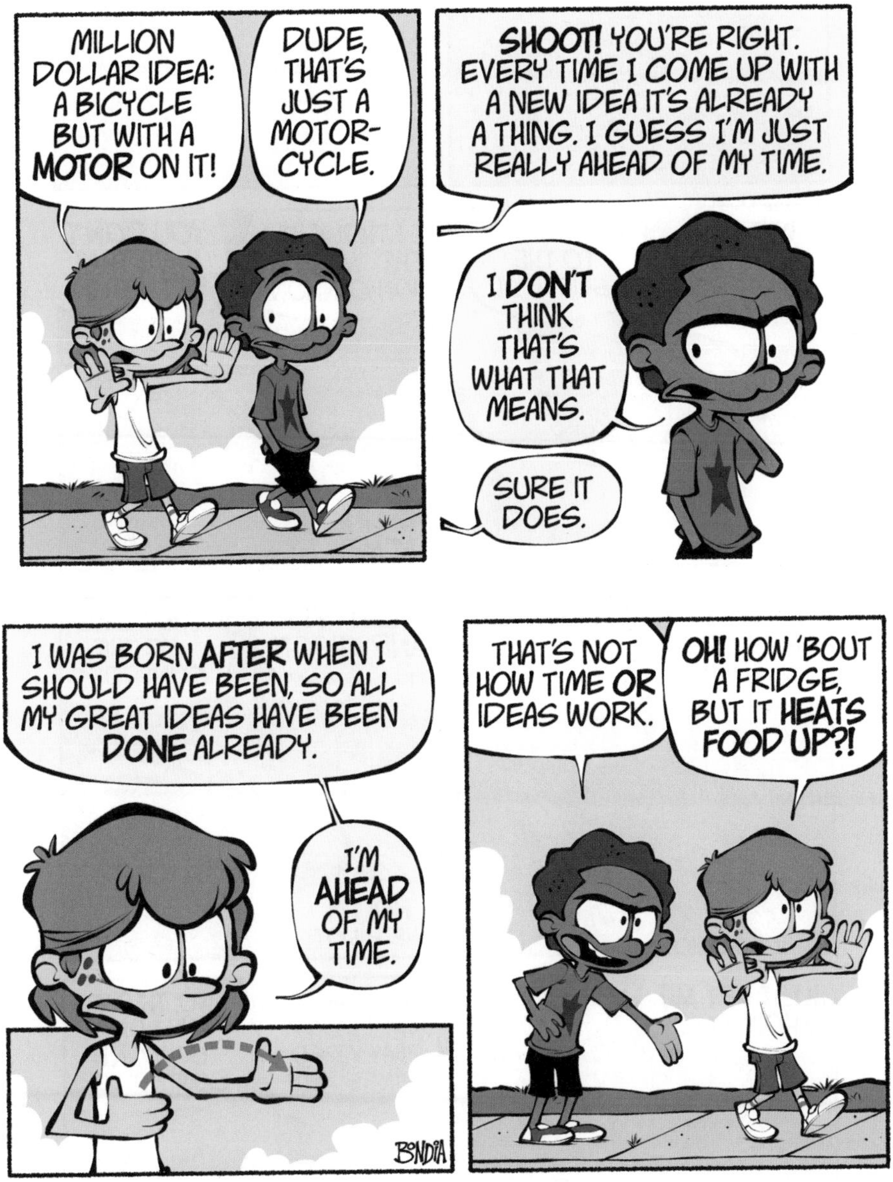
MILLION DOLLAR IDEA: A BICYCLE BUT WITH A **MOTOR** ON IT!
DUDE, THAT'S JUST A MOTOR-CYCLE.
SHOOT! YOU'RE RIGHT. EVERY TIME I COME UP WITH A NEW IDEA IT'S ALREADY A THING. I GUESS I'M JUST REALLY AHEAD OF MY TIME.
I **DON'T** THINK THAT'S WHAT THAT MEANS.
SURE IT DOES.
I WAS BORN **AFTER** WHEN I SHOULD HAVE BEEN, SO ALL MY GREAT IDEAS HAVE BEEN **DONE** ALREADY.
I'M **AHEAD** OF MY TIME.
BONDIA
THAT'S NOT HOW TIME **OR** IDEAS WORK.
OH! HOW 'BOUT A FRIDGE, BUT IT **HEATS FOOD UP?!**

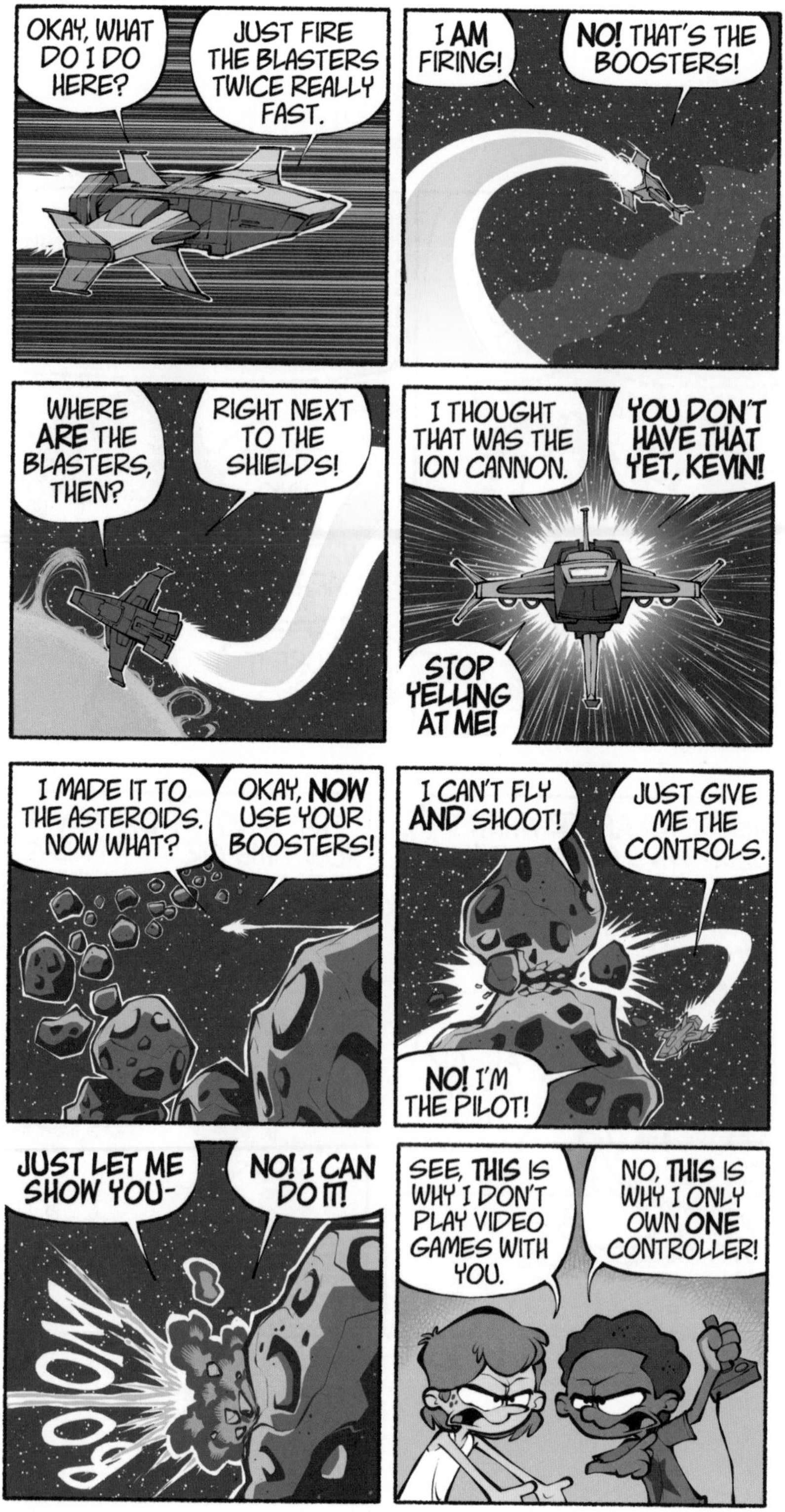
OKAY, WHAT DO I DO HERE?
JUST FIRE THE BLASTERS TWICE REALLY FAST.
I AM FIRING!
NO! THAT'S THE BOOSTERS!
WHERE ARE THE BLASTERS, THEN?
RIGHT NEXT TO THE SHIELDS!
I THOUGHT THAT WAS THE ION CANNON.
YOU DON'T HAVE THAT YET, KEVIN!
STOP YELLING AT ME!
I MADE IT TO THE ASTEROIDS. NOW WHAT?
OKAY, NOW USE YOUR BOOSTERS!
I CAN'T FLY AND SHOOT!
JUST GIVE ME THE CONTROLS.
NO! I'M THE PILOT!
JUST LET ME SHOW YOU-
NO! I CAN DO IT!
BOOOM
SEE, THIS IS WHY I DON'T PLAY VIDEO GAMES WITH YOU.
NO, THIS IS WHY I ONLY OWN ONE CONTROLLER!

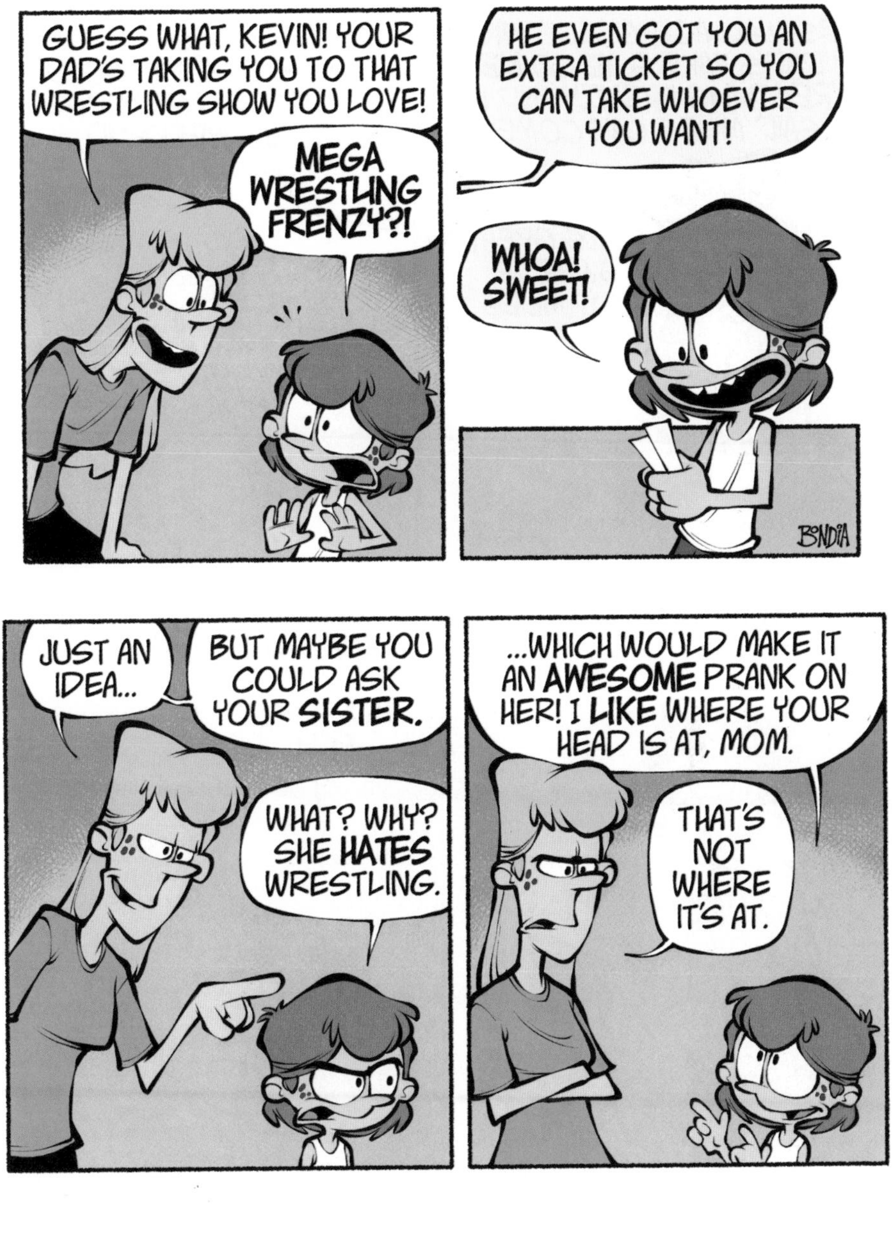
GUESS WHAT, KEVIN! YOUR DAD'S TAKING YOU TO THAT WRESTLING SHOW YOU LOVE!
MEGA WRESTLING FRENZY?!
HE EVEN GOT YOU AN EXTRA TICKET SO YOU CAN TAKE WHOEVER YOU WANT!
WHOA! SWEET!
BONDIA
JUST AN IDEA...
BUT MAYBE YOU COULD ASK YOUR SISTER.
WHAT? WHY? SHE HATES WRESTLING.
...WHICH WOULD MAKE IT AN AWESOME PRANK ON HER! I LIKE WHERE YOUR HEAD IS AT, MOM.
THAT'S NOT WHERE IT'S AT.

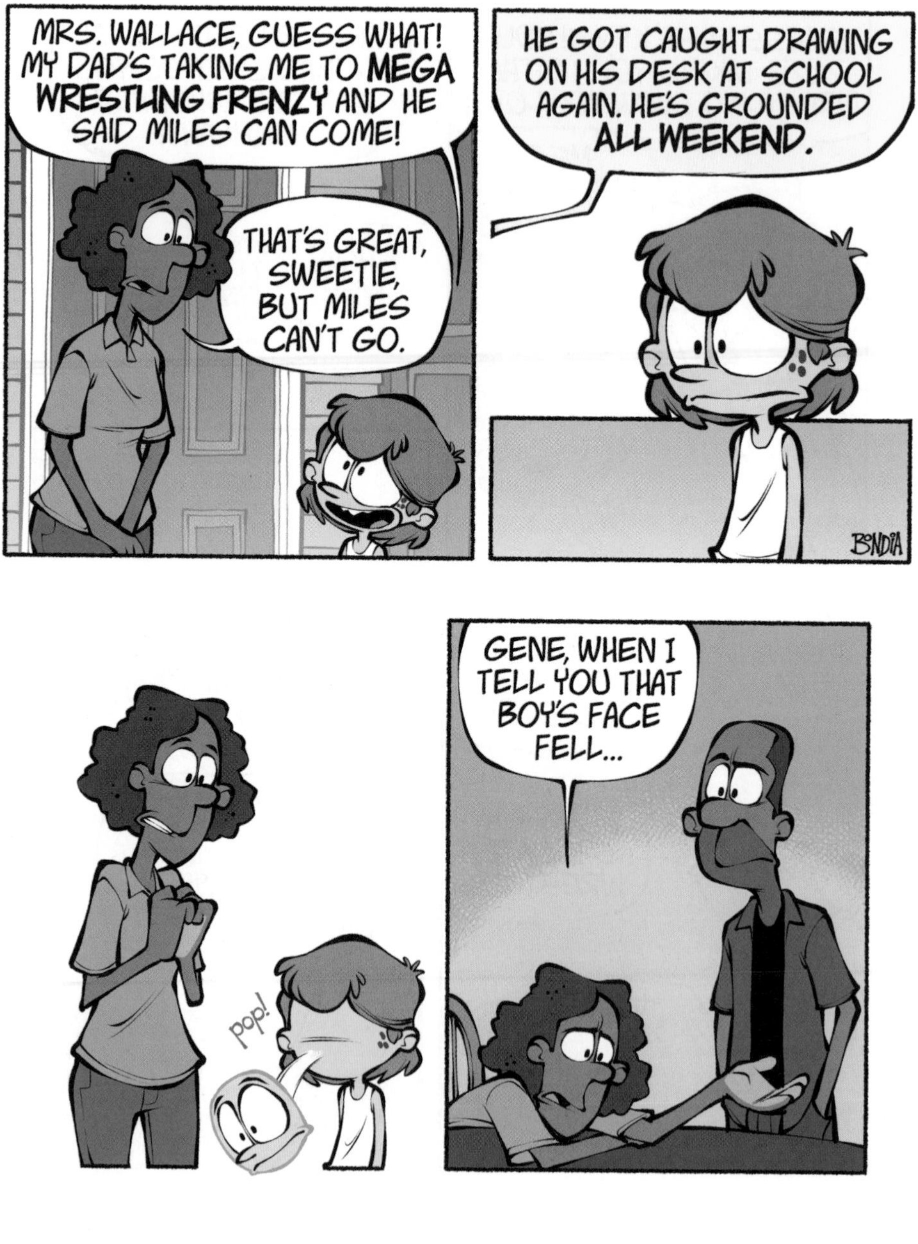
MRS. WALLACE, GUESS WHAT! MY DAD'S TAKING ME TO **MEGA WRESTLING FRENZY** AND HE SAID MILES CAN COME!
THAT'S GREAT, SWEETIE, BUT MILES CAN'T GO.
HE GOT CAUGHT DRAWING ON HIS DESK AT SCHOOL AGAIN. HE'S GROUNDED **ALL WEEKEND.**
BONDIA
pop!
GENE, WHEN I TELL YOU THAT BOY'S FACE FELL...

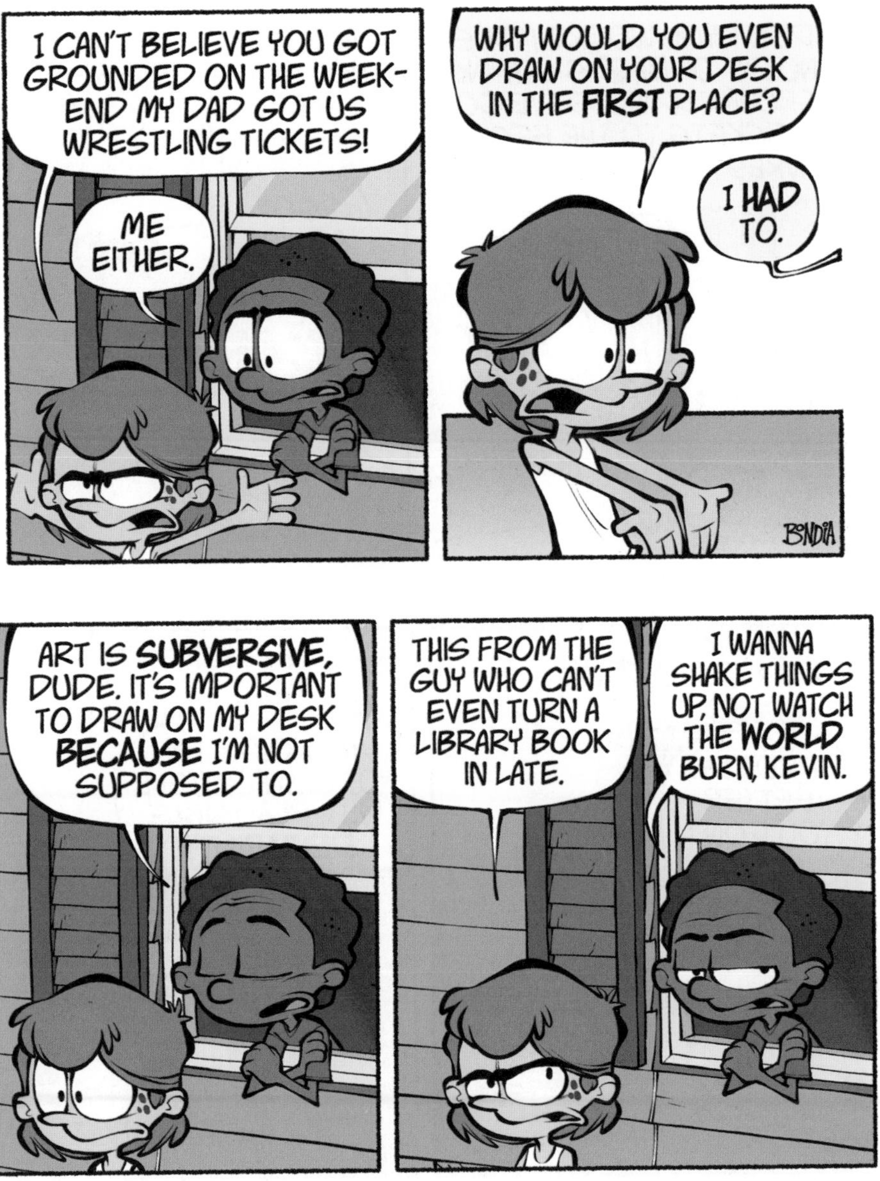
I CAN'T BELIEVE YOU GOT GROUNDED ON THE WEEK-END MY DAD GOT US WRESTLING TICKETS!
ME EITHER.
WHY WOULD YOU EVEN DRAW ON YOUR DESK IN THE **FIRST** PLACE?
I **HAD** TO.
BONDIA
ART IS **SUBVERSIVE,** DUDE. IT'S IMPORTANT TO DRAW ON MY DESK **BECAUSE** I'M NOT SUPPOSED TO.
THIS FROM THE GUY WHO CAN'T EVEN TURN A LIBRARY BOOK IN LATE.
I WANNA SHAKE THINGS UP, NOT WATCH THE **WORLD** BURN, KEVIN.

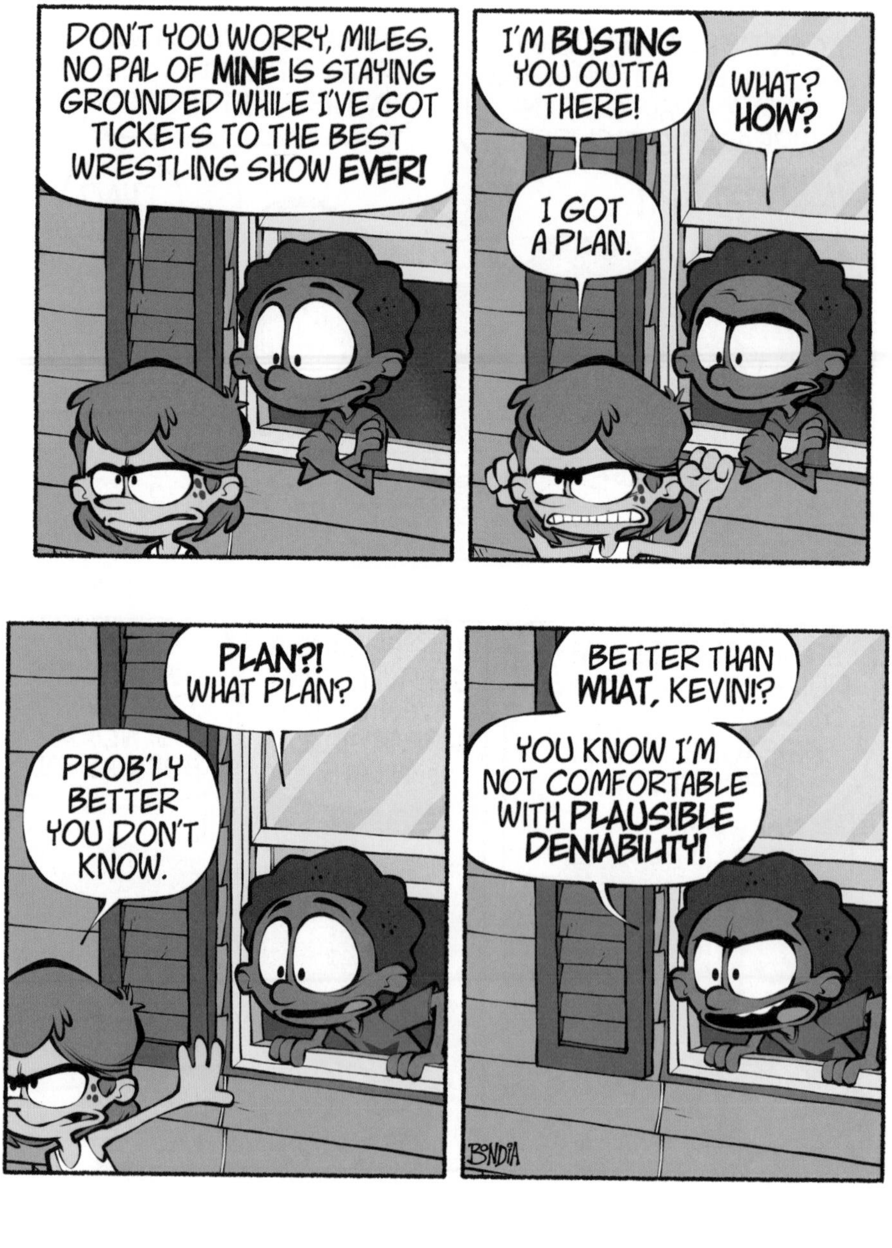
DON'T YOU WORRY, MILES. NO PAL OF **MINE** IS STAYING GROUNDED WHILE I'VE GOT TICKETS TO THE BEST WRESTLING SHOW **EVER!**
I'M **BUSTING** YOU OUTTA THERE!
I GOT A PLAN.
WHAT? **HOW?**
PLAN?! WHAT PLAN?
PROB'LY BETTER YOU DON'T KNOW.
BETTER THAN **WHAT**, KEVIN!?
YOU KNOW I'M NOT COMFORTABLE WITH **PLAUSIBLE DENIABILITY!**
BONDIA

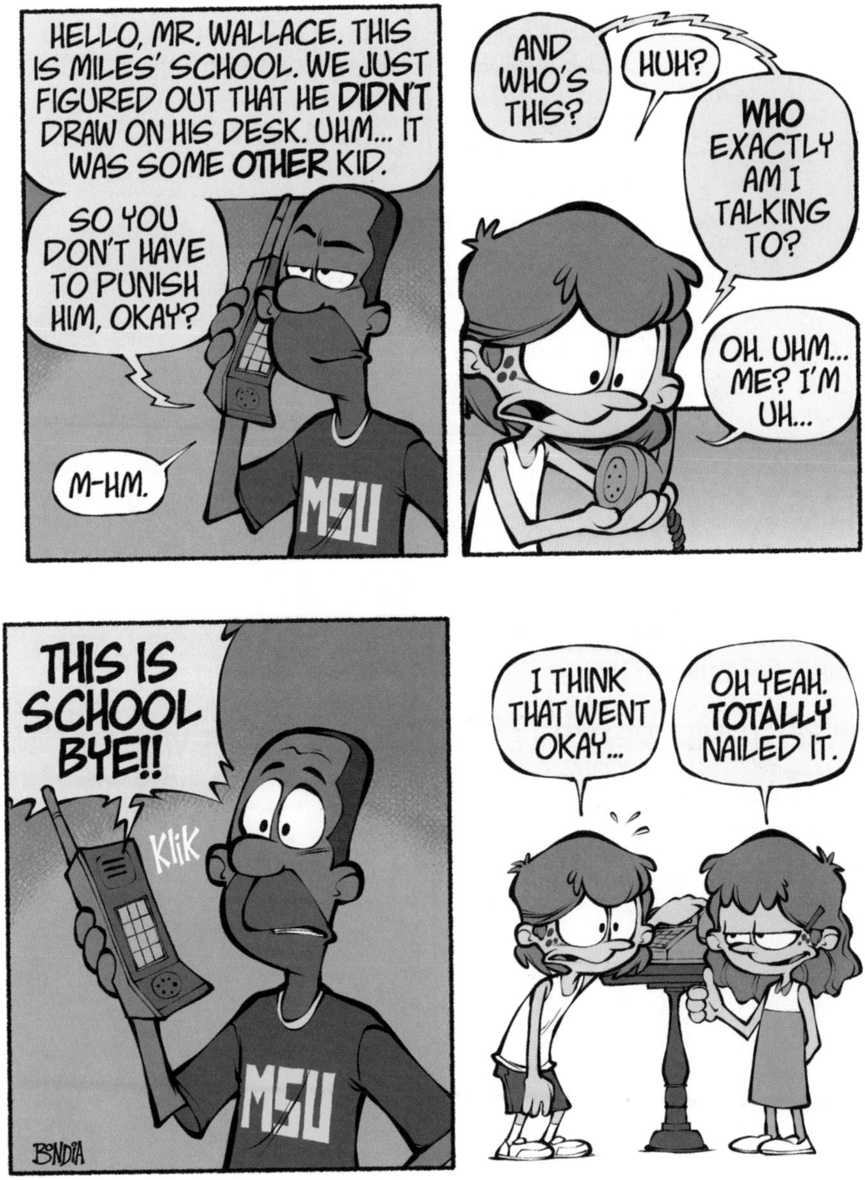
HELLO, MR. WALLACE. THIS IS MILES' SCHOOL. WE JUST FIGURED OUT THAT HE **DIDN'T** DRAW ON HIS DESK. UHM... IT WAS SOME **OTHER** KID.
SO YOU DON'T HAVE TO PUNISH HIM, OKAY?
M-HM.
AND WHO'S THIS?
HUH?
WHO EXACTLY AM I TALKING TO?
OH. UHM... ME? I'M UH...
THIS IS SCHOOL BYE!!
KLIK
I THINK THAT WENT OKAY...
OH YEAH. **TOTALLY** NAILED IT.
BONDIA

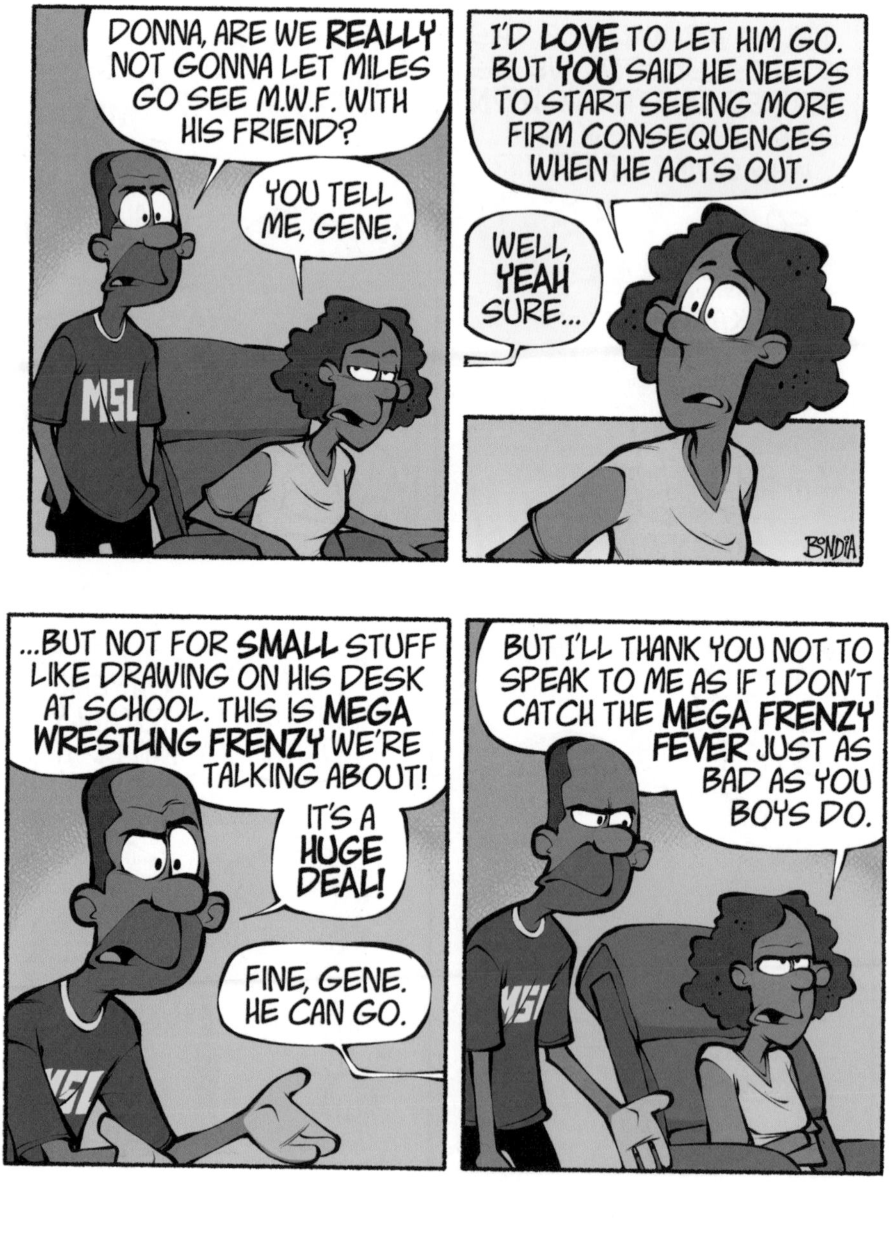
DONNA, ARE WE **REALLY** NOT GONNA LET MILES GO SEE M.W.F. WITH HIS FRIEND?
YOU TELL ME, GENE.
I'D **LOVE** TO LET HIM GO. BUT **YOU** SAID HE NEEDS TO START SEEING MORE FIRM CONSEQUENCES WHEN HE ACTS OUT.
WELL, **YEAH** SURE...
...BUT NOT FOR **SMALL** STUFF LIKE DRAWING ON HIS DESK AT SCHOOL. THIS IS **MEGA WRESTLING FRENZY** WE'RE TALKING ABOUT!
IT'S A **HUGE DEAL!**
FINE, GENE. HE CAN GO.
BUT I'LL THANK YOU NOT TO SPEAK TO ME AS IF I DON'T CATCH THE **MEGA FRENZY FEVER** JUST AS BAD AS YOU BOYS DO.

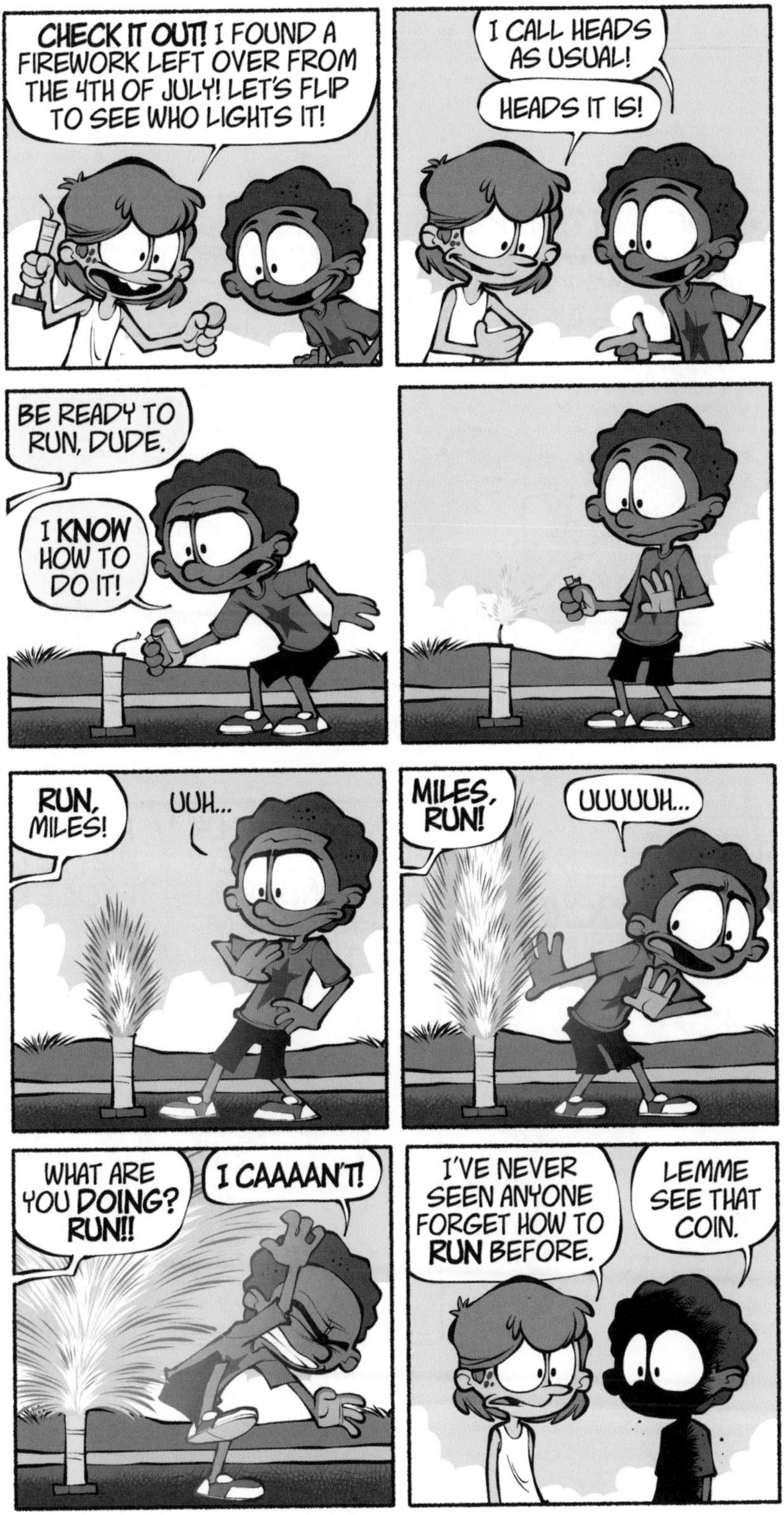
CHECK IT OUT! I FOUND A FIREWORK LEFT OVER FROM THE 4TH OF JULY! LET'S FLIP TO SEE WHO LIGHTS IT!
I CALL HEADS AS USUAL!
HEADS IT IS!
BE READY TO RUN, DUDE.
I KNOW HOW TO DO IT!
RUN, MILES!
UUH...
MILES, RUN!
UUUUUH...
WHAT ARE YOU DOING? RUN!!
I CAAAAN'T!
I'VE NEVER SEEN ANYONE FORGET HOW TO RUN BEFORE.
LEMME SEE THAT COIN.

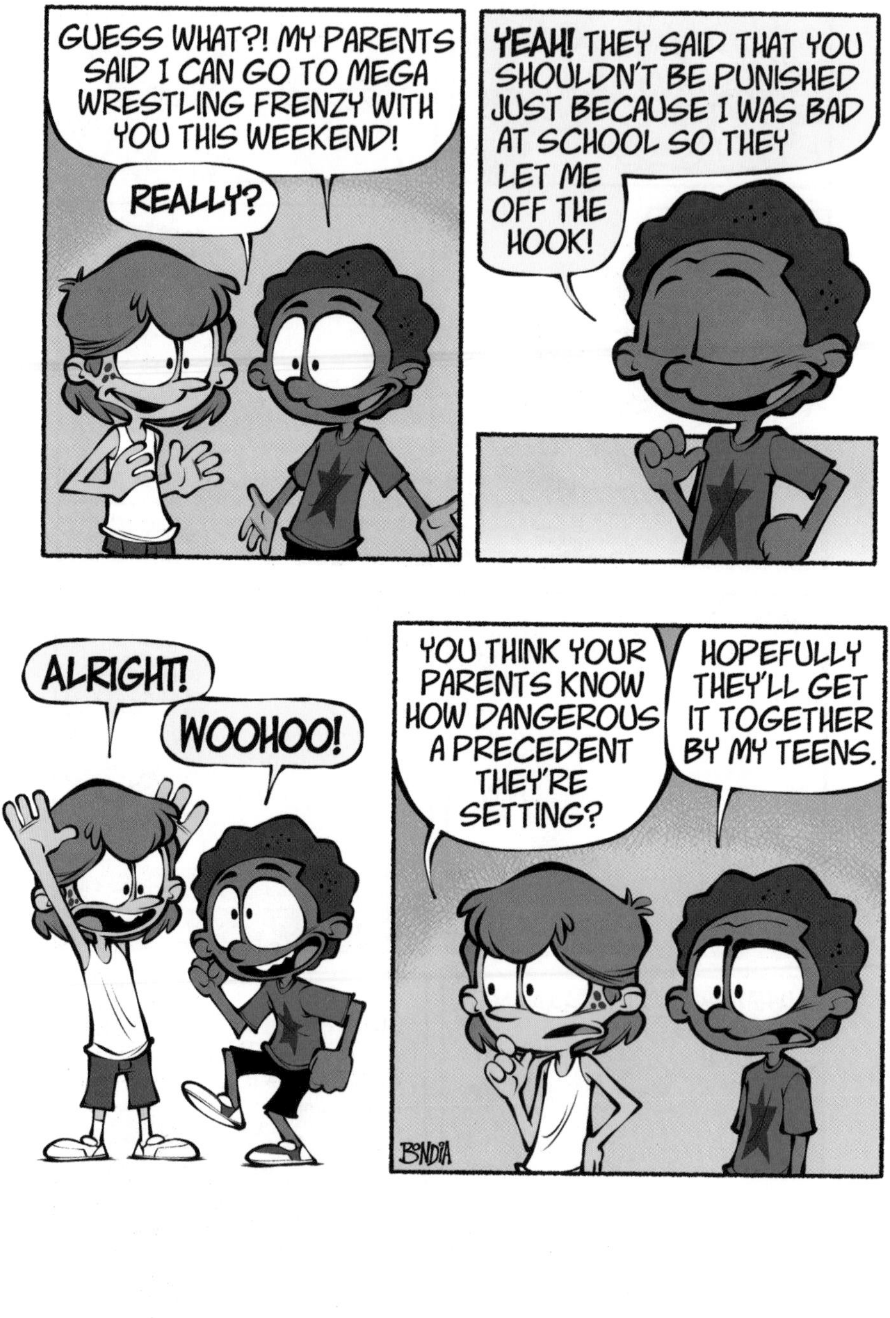
GUESS WHAT?! MY PARENTS SAID I CAN GO TO MEGA WRESTLING FRENZY WITH YOU THIS WEEKEND!
REALLY?
YEAH! THEY SAID THAT YOU SHOULDN'T BE PUNISHED JUST BECAUSE I WAS BAD AT SCHOOL SO THEY LET ME OFF THE HOOK!
ALRIGHT!
WOOHOO!
YOU THINK YOUR PARENTS KNOW HOW DANGEROUS A PRECEDENT THEY'RE SETTING?
HOPEFULLY THEY'LL GET IT TOGETHER BY MY TEENS.
BONDIA

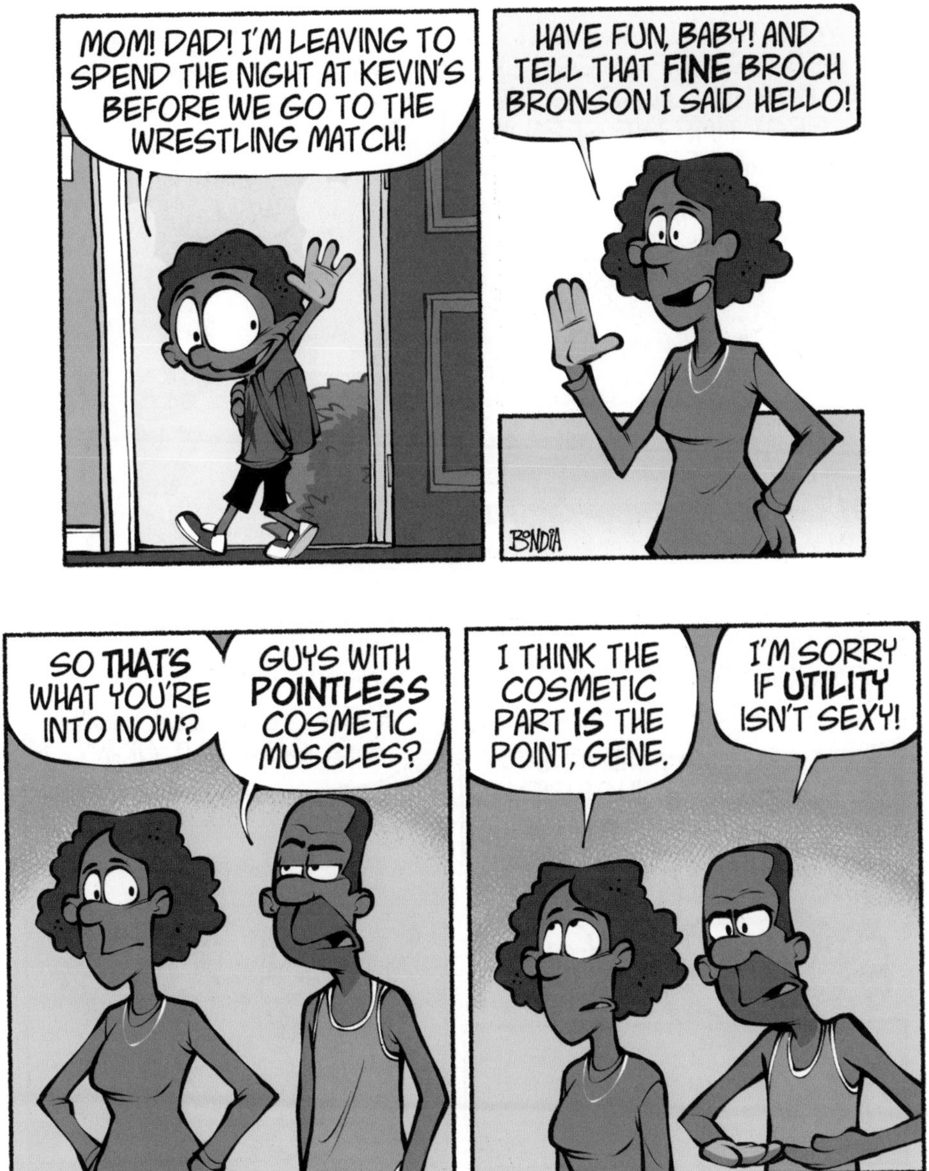
MOM! DAD! I'M LEAVING TO SPEND THE NIGHT AT KEVIN'S BEFORE WE GO TO THE WRESTLING MATCH!
HAVE FUN, BABY! AND TELL THAT **FINE** BROCH BRONSON I SAID HELLO!
BONDIA
SO **THAT'S** WHAT YOU'RE INTO NOW?
GUYS WITH **POINTLESS** COSMETIC MUSCLES?
I THINK THE COSMETIC PART **IS** THE POINT, GENE.
I'M SORRY IF **UTILITY** ISN'T SEXY!

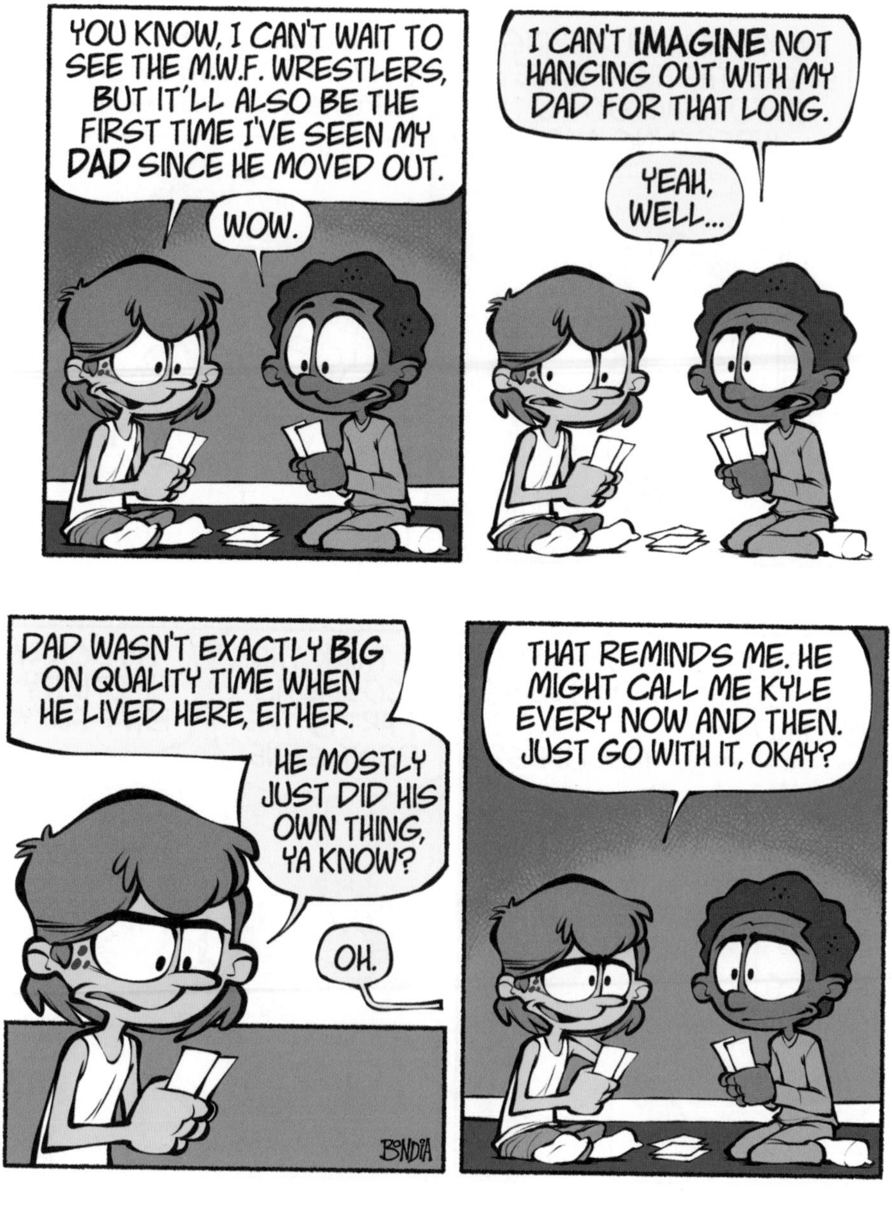
YOU KNOW, I CAN'T WAIT TO SEE THE M.W.F. WRESTLERS, BUT IT'LL ALSO BE THE FIRST TIME I'VE SEEN MY **DAD** SINCE HE MOVED OUT.
WOW.
I CAN'T **IMAGINE** NOT HANGING OUT WITH MY DAD FOR THAT LONG.
YEAH, WELL...
DAD WASN'T EXACTLY **BIG** ON QUALITY TIME WHEN HE LIVED HERE, EITHER.
HE MOSTLY JUST DID HIS OWN THING, YA KNOW?
OH.
BONDIA
THAT REMINDS ME. HE MIGHT CALL ME KYLE EVERY NOW AND THEN. JUST GO WITH IT, OKAY?

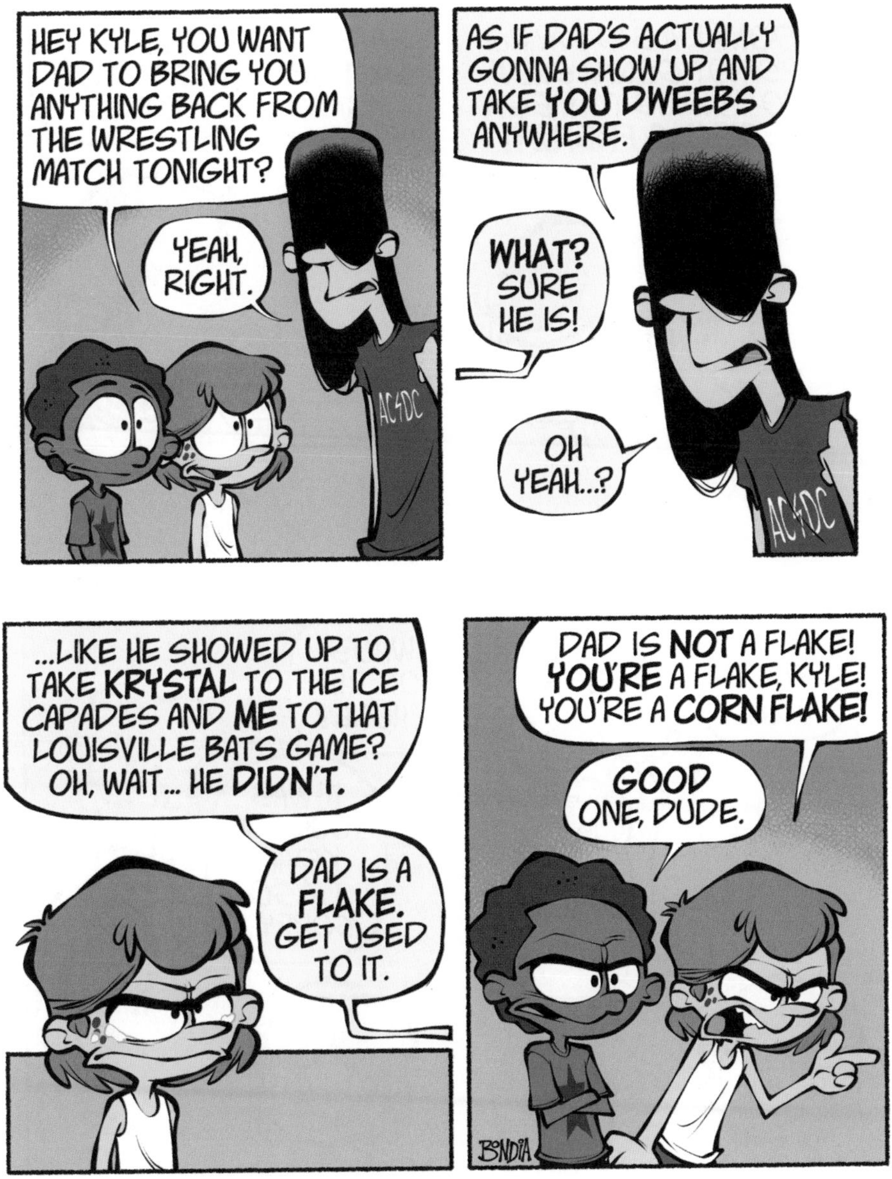
HEY KYLE, YOU WANT DAD TO BRING YOU ANYTHING BACK FROM THE WRESTLING MATCH TONIGHT?
YEAH, RIGHT.
AC/DC
AS IF DAD'S ACTUALLY GONNA SHOW UP AND TAKE YOU DWEEBS ANYWHERE.
WHAT? SURE HE IS!
OH YEAH...?
AC/DC
...LIKE HE SHOWED UP TO TAKE KRYSTAL TO THE ICE CAPADES AND ME TO THAT LOUISVILLE BATS GAME? OH, WAIT... HE DIDN'T.
DAD IS A FLAKE. GET USED TO IT.
DAD IS NOT A FLAKE! YOU'RE A FLAKE, KYLE! YOU'RE A CORN FLAKE!
GOOD ONE, DUDE.
BONDIA

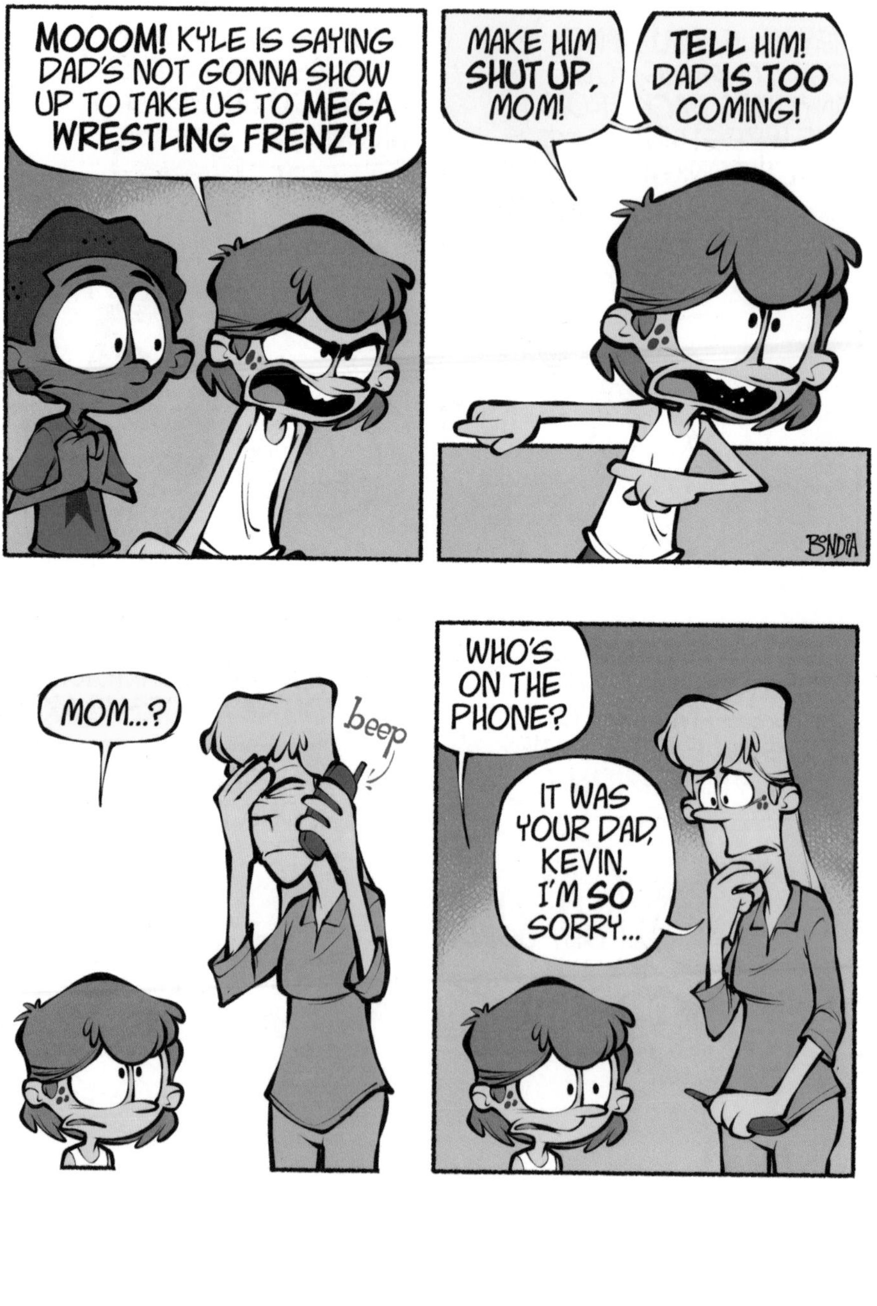
MOOOM! KYLE IS SAYING DAD'S NOT GONNA SHOW UP TO TAKE US TO **MEGA WRESTLING FRENZY!**
MAKE HIM **SHUT UP**, MOM!
TELL HIM! DAD **IS TOO** COMING!
BONDIA
MOM...?
beep
WHO'S ON THE PHONE?
IT WAS YOUR DAD, KEVIN. I'M **SO** SORRY...

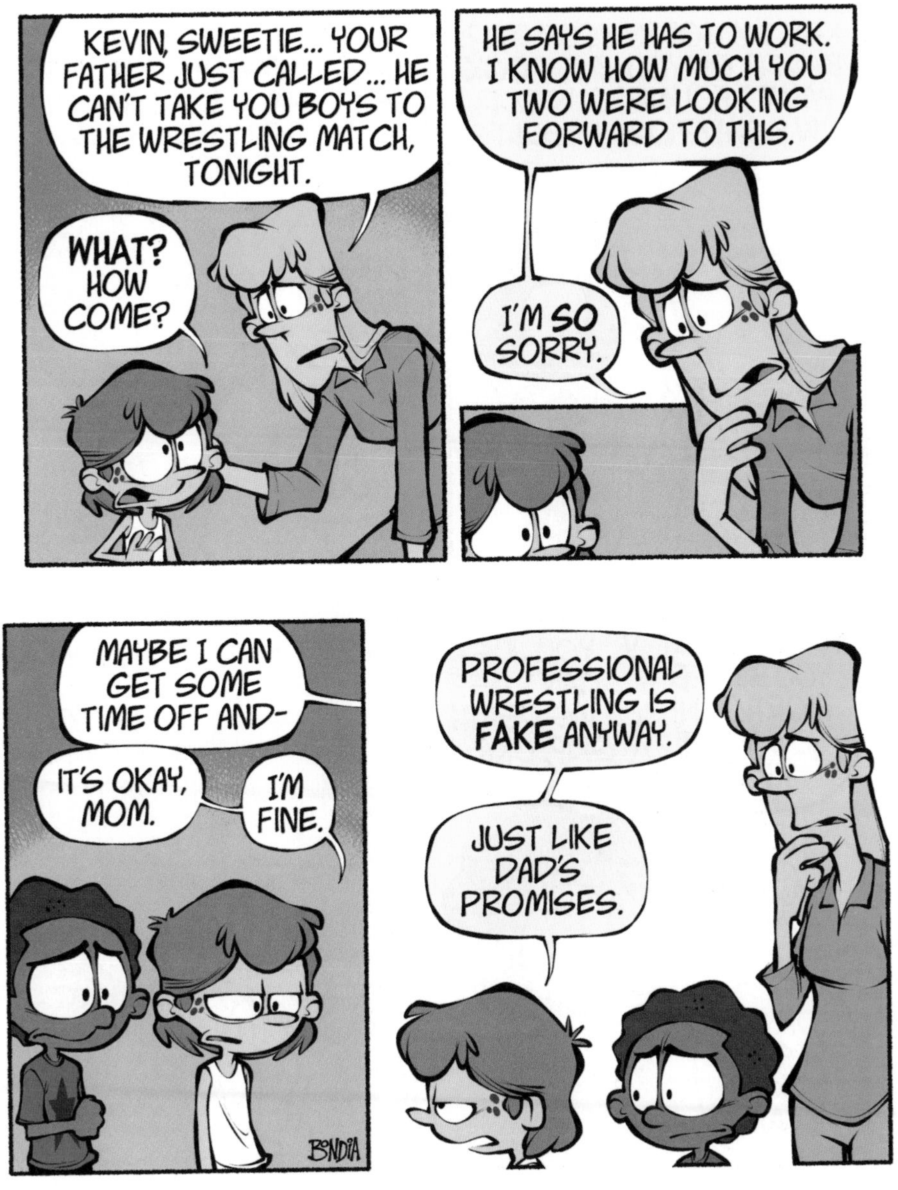
KEVIN, SWEETIE... YOUR FATHER JUST CALLED... HE CAN'T TAKE YOU BOYS TO THE WRESTLING MATCH, TONIGHT.
WHAT? HOW COME?
HE SAYS HE HAS TO WORK. I KNOW HOW MUCH YOU TWO WERE LOOKING FORWARD TO THIS.
I'M SO SORRY.
MAYBE I CAN GET SOME TIME OFF AND-
IT'S OKAY, MOM.
I'M FINE.
BONDIA
PROFESSIONAL WRESTLING IS FAKE ANYWAY.
JUST LIKE DAD'S PROMISES.

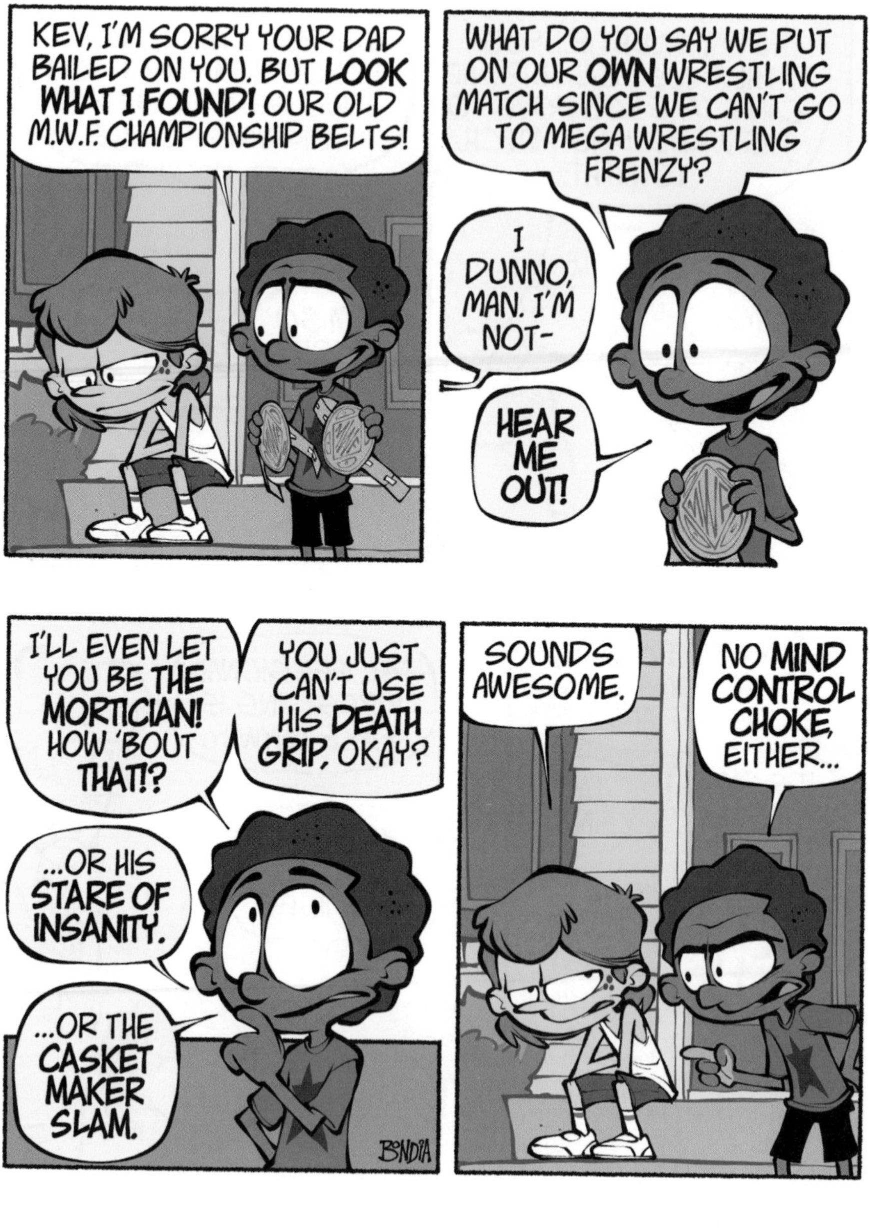
KEV, I'M SORRY YOUR DAD BAILED ON YOU. BUT LOOK WHAT I FOUND! OUR OLD M.W.F. CHAMPIONSHIP BELTS!
WHAT DO YOU SAY WE PUT ON OUR OWN WRESTLING MATCH SINCE WE CAN'T GO TO MEGA WRESTLING FRENZY?
I DUNNO, MAN. I'M NOT-
HEAR ME OUT!
I'LL EVEN LET YOU BE THE MORTICIAN! HOW 'BOUT THAT!?
YOU JUST CAN'T USE HIS DEATH GRIP, OKAY?
...OR HIS STARE OF INSANITY.
...OR THE CASKET MAKER SLAM.
BONDIA
SOUNDS AWESOME.
NO MIND CONTROL CHOKE, EITHER...

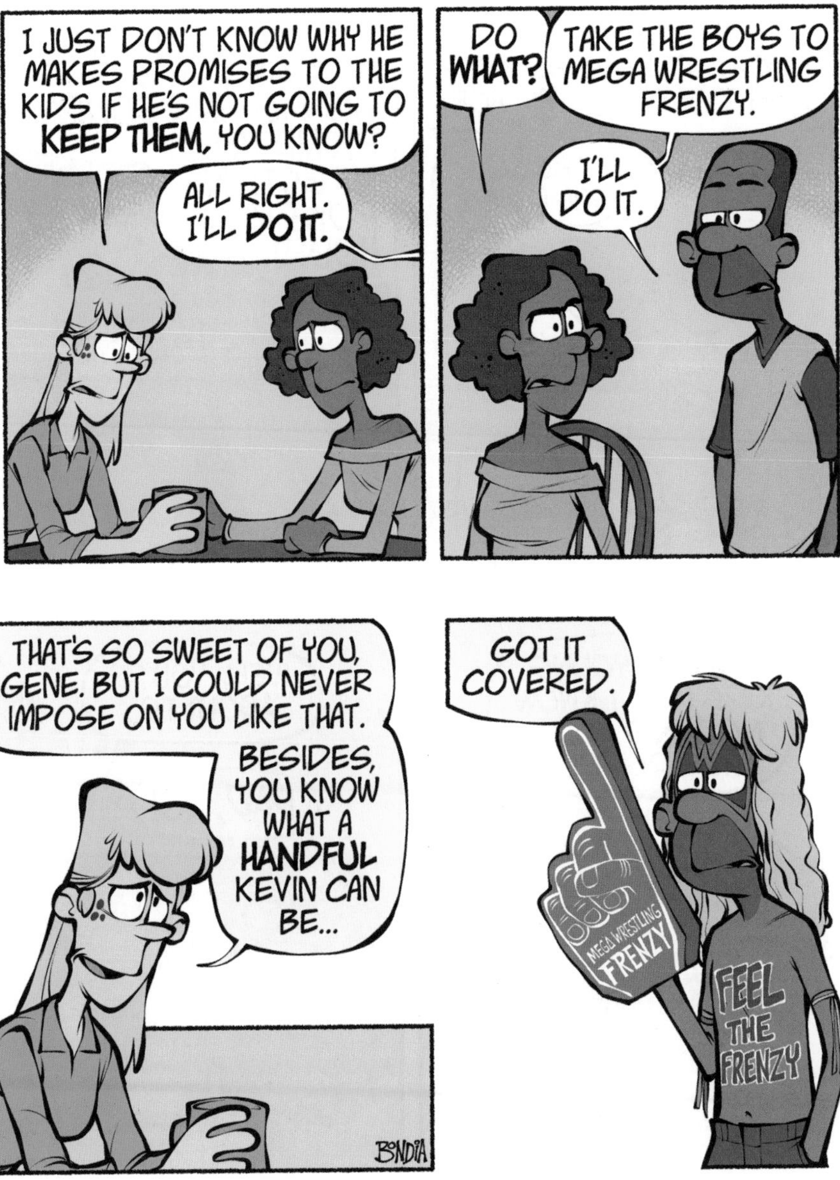
I JUST DON'T KNOW WHY HE MAKES PROMISES TO THE KIDS IF HE'S NOT GOING TO **KEEP THEM,** YOU KNOW?
ALL RIGHT. I'LL **DO IT.**
DO **WHAT?**
TAKE THE BOYS TO MEGA WRESTLING FRENZY.
I'LL DO IT.
THAT'S SO SWEET OF YOU, GENE. BUT I COULD NEVER IMPOSE ON YOU LIKE THAT.
BESIDES, YOU KNOW WHAT A **HANDFUL** KEVIN CAN BE...
BONDIA
GOT IT COVERED.
MEGA WRESTLING FRENZY
FEEL THE FRENZY

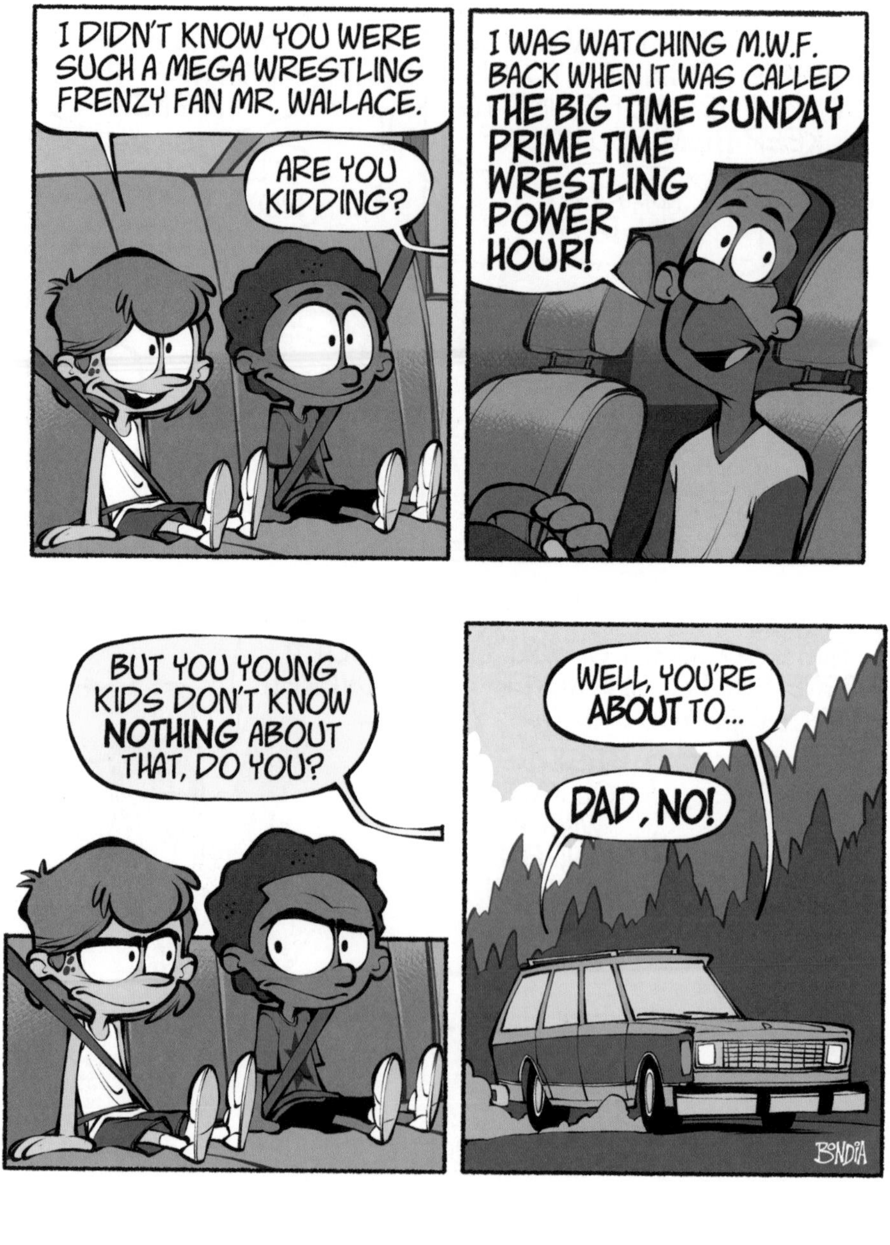
I DIDN'T KNOW YOU WERE SUCH A MEGA WRESTLING FRENZY FAN MR. WALLACE.
ARE YOU KIDDING?
I WAS WATCHING M.W.F. BACK WHEN IT WAS CALLED **THE BIG TIME SUNDAY PRIME TIME WRESTLING POWER HOUR!**
BUT YOU YOUNG KIDS DON'T KNOW **NOTHING** ABOUT THAT, DO YOU?
WELL, YOU'RE **ABOUT** TO...
DAD, NO!
BONDIA

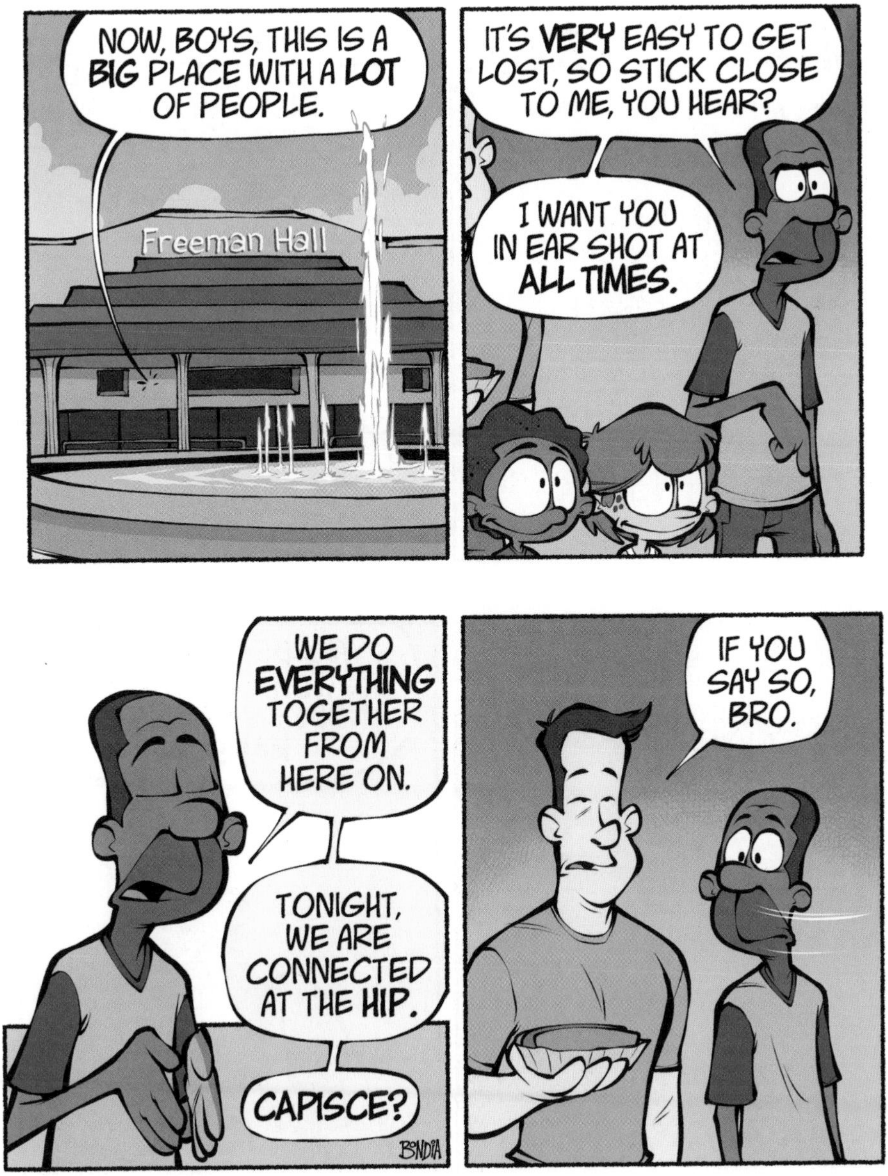
NOW, BOYS, THIS IS A **BIG** PLACE WITH A **LOT** OF PEOPLE.
Freeman Hall
IT'S **VERY** EASY TO GET LOST, SO STICK CLOSE TO ME, YOU HEAR?
I WANT YOU IN EAR SHOT AT **ALL TIMES.**
WE DO **EVERYTHING** TOGETHER FROM HERE ON.
TONIGHT, WE ARE CONNECTED AT THE **HIP**.
CAPISCE?
BONDIA
IF YOU SAY SO, BRO.

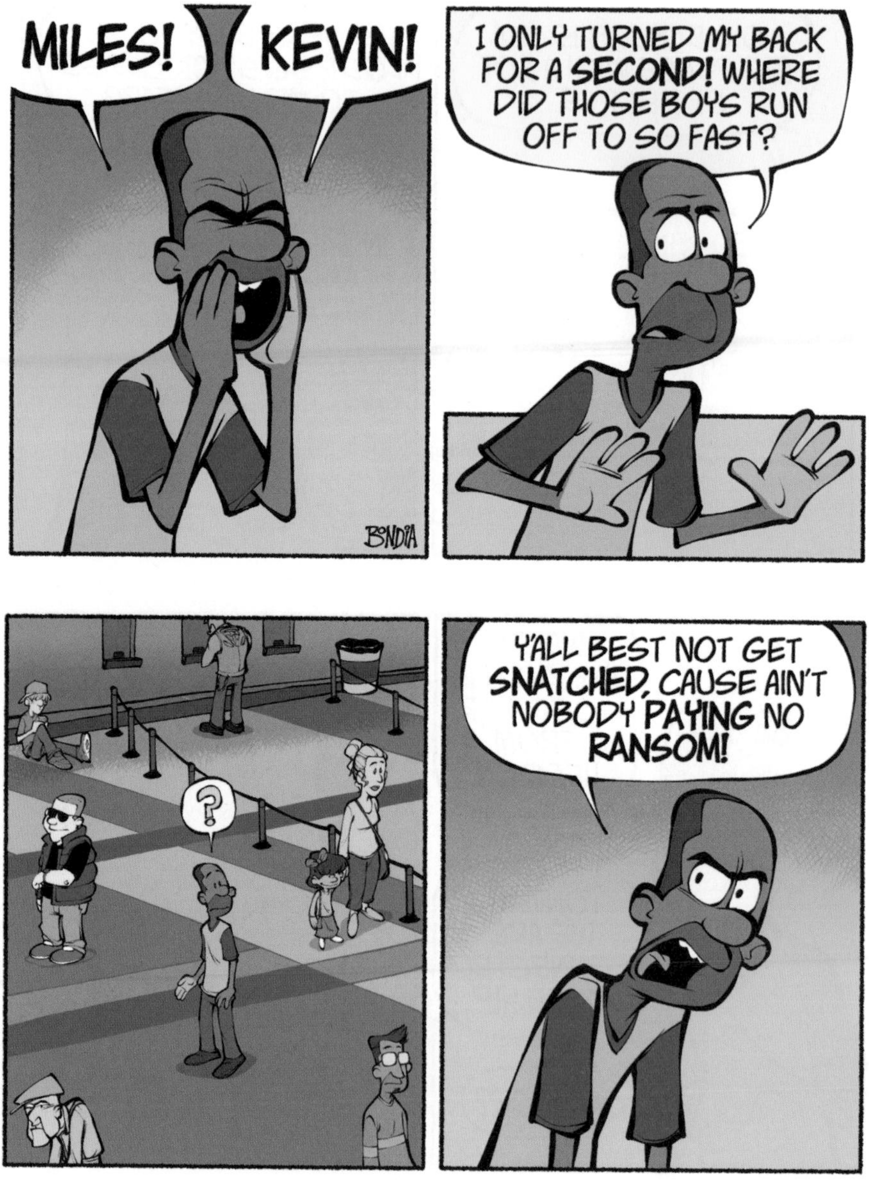
MILES!
KEVIN!
I ONLY TURNED MY BACK FOR A SECOND! WHERE DID THOSE BOYS RUN OFF TO SO FAST?
?
Y'ALL BEST NOT GET SNATCHED, CAUSE AIN'T NOBODY PAYING NO RANSOM!

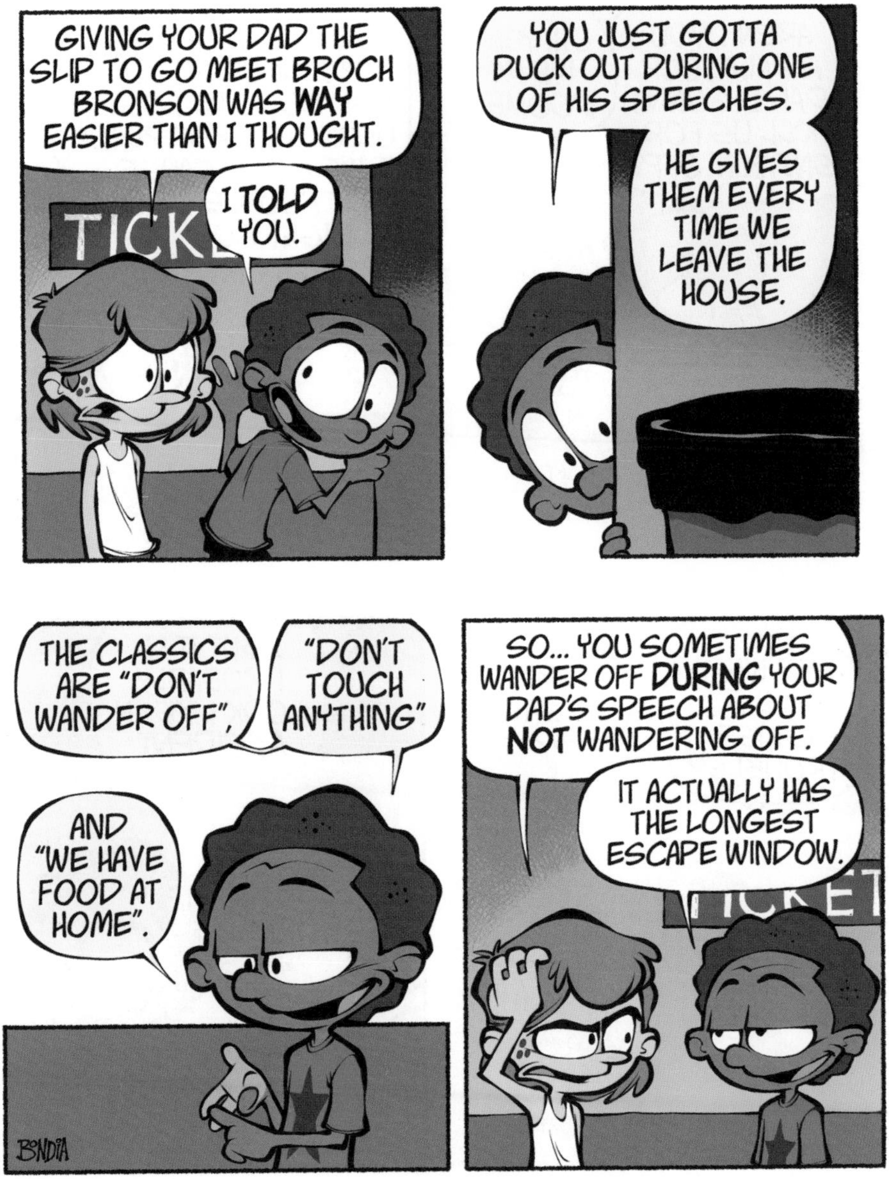
GIVING YOUR DAD THE SLIP TO GO MEET BROCH BRONSON WAS **WAY** EASIER THAN I THOUGHT.
I **TOLD** YOU.
TICK
YOU JUST GOTTA DUCK OUT DURING ONE OF HIS SPEECHES.
HE GIVES THEM EVERY TIME WE LEAVE THE HOUSE.
THE CLASSICS ARE "DON'T WANDER OFF",
"DON'T TOUCH ANYTHING"
AND "WE HAVE FOOD AT HOME".
SO... YOU SOMETIMES WANDER OFF **DURING** YOUR DAD'S SPEECH ABOUT **NOT** WANDERING OFF.
IT ACTUALLY HAS THE LONGEST ESCAPE WINDOW.
TICKET
BONDIA

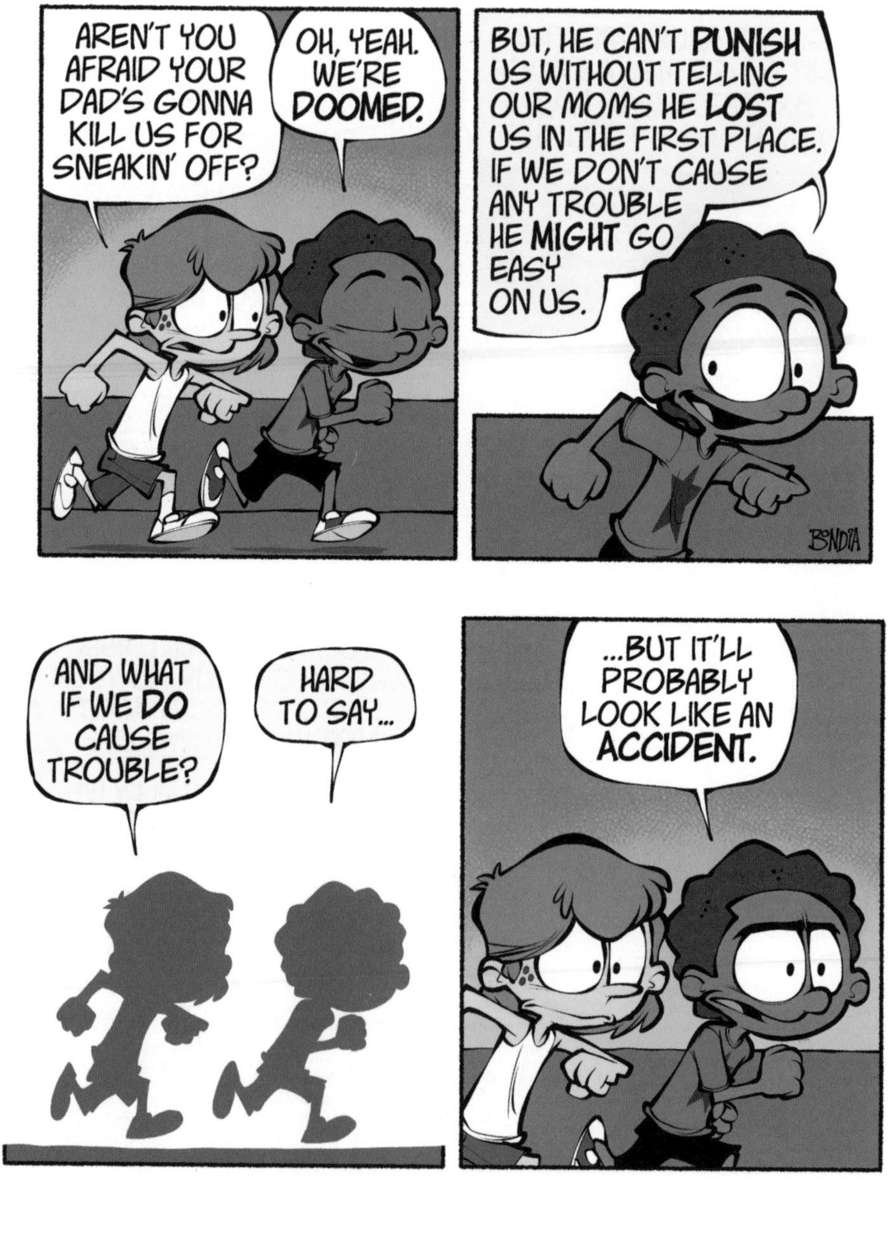
AREN'T YOU AFRAID YOUR DAD'S GONNA KILL US FOR SNEAKIN' OFF?
OH, YEAH. WE'RE DOOMED.
BUT, HE CAN'T PUNISH US WITHOUT TELLING OUR MOMS HE LOST US IN THE FIRST PLACE. IF WE DON'T CAUSE ANY TROUBLE HE MIGHT GO EASY ON US.
BONDIA
AND WHAT IF WE DO CAUSE TROUBLE?
HARD TO SAY...
...BUT IT'LL PROBABLY LOOK LIKE AN ACCIDENT.

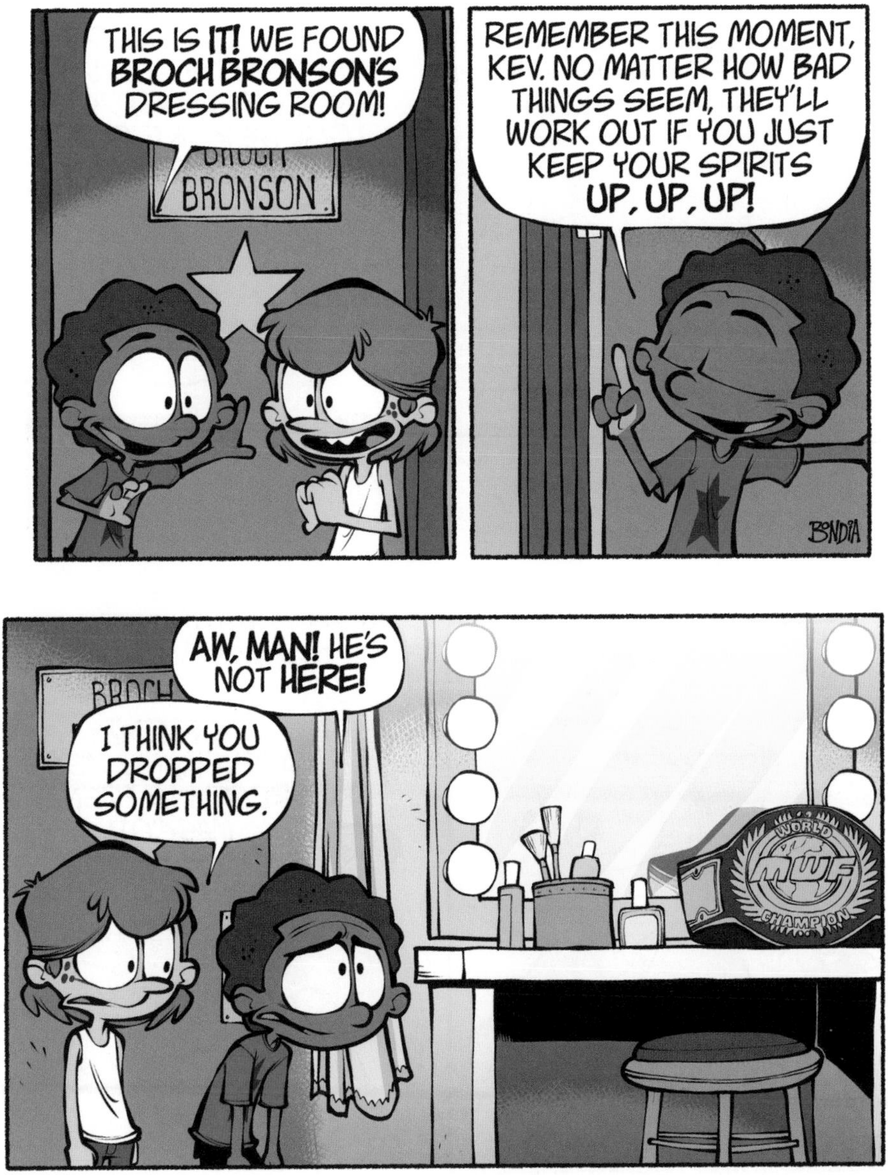
THIS IS IT! WE FOUND BROCH BRONSON'S DRESSING ROOM!
BRONSON
REMEMBER THIS MOMENT, KEV. NO MATTER HOW BAD THINGS SEEM, THEY'LL WORK OUT IF YOU JUST KEEP YOUR SPIRITS UP, UP, UP!
BONDIA
AW, MAN! HE'S NOT HERE!
I THINK YOU DROPPED SOMETHING.
WORLD
MWF
CHAMPION

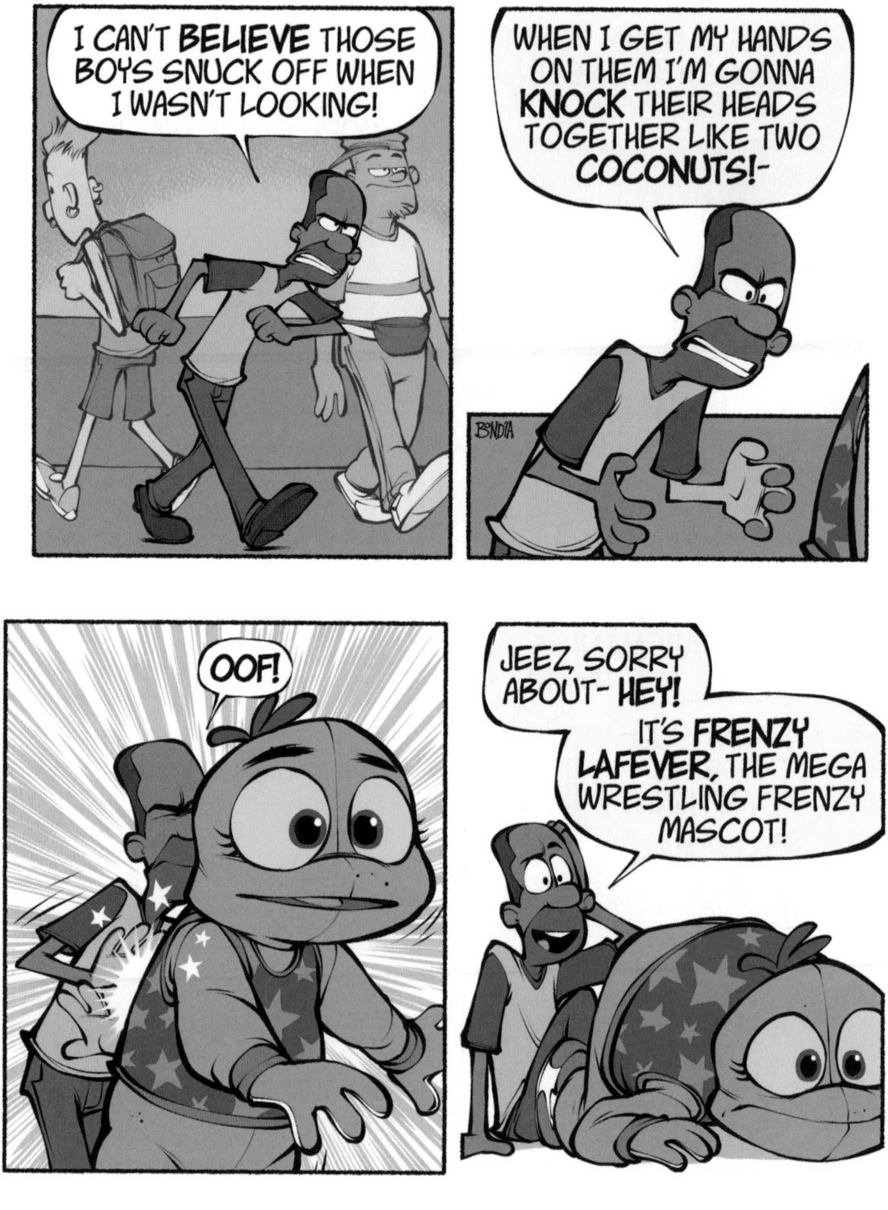
I CAN'T **BELIEVE** THOSE BOYS SNUCK OFF WHEN I WASN'T LOOKING!
WHEN I GET MY HANDS ON THEM I'M GONNA **KNOCK** THEIR HEADS TOGETHER LIKE TWO **COCONUTS!**-
BONDIA
OOF!
JEEZ, SORRY ABOUT- **HEY!**
IT'S **FRENZY LAFEVER,** THE MEGA WRESTLING FRENZY MASCOT!

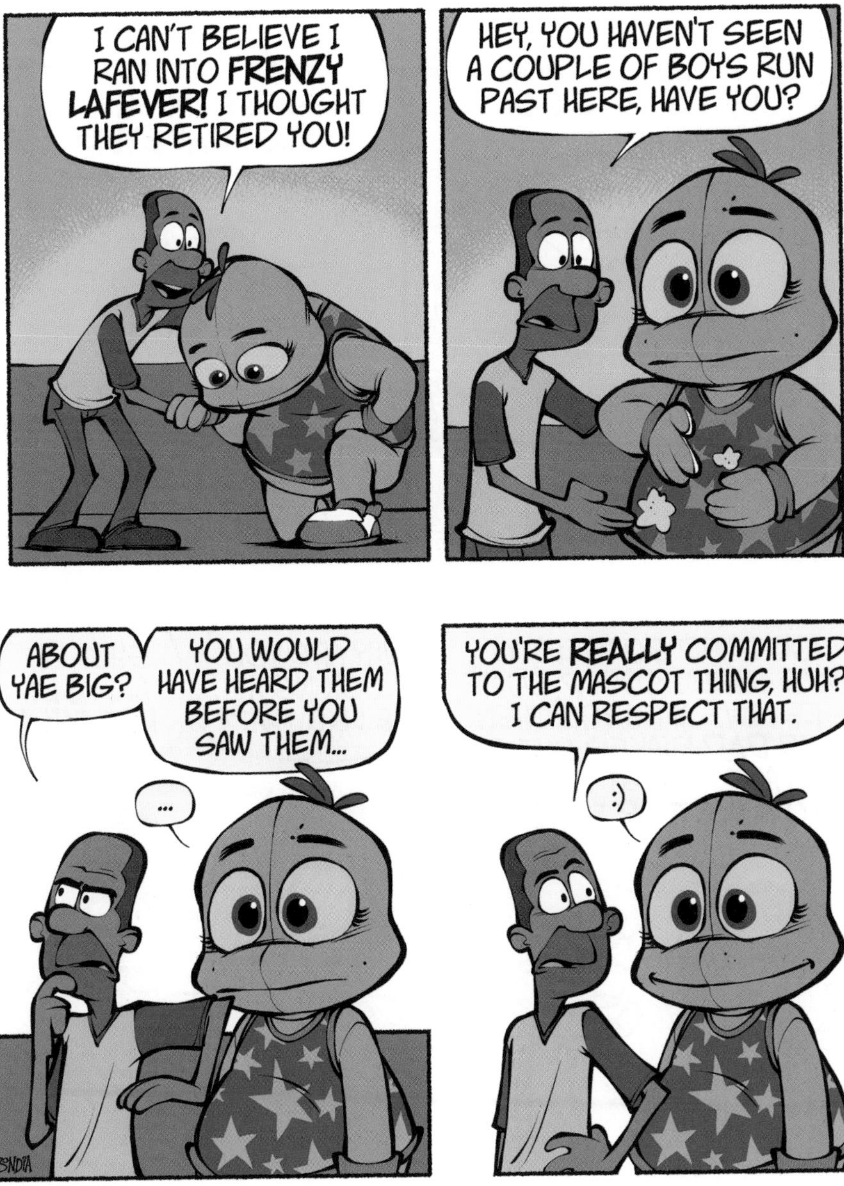

I CAN'T BELIEVE I RAN INTO FRENZY LAFEVER! I THOUGHT THEY RETIRED YOU!
HEY, YOU HAVEN'T SEEN A COUPLE OF BOYS RUN PAST HERE, HAVE YOU?
ABOUT YAE BIG?
YOU WOULD HAVE HEARD THEM BEFORE YOU SAW THEM...
...
YOU'RE REALLY COMMITTED TO THE MASCOT THING, HUH? I CAN RESPECT THAT.
:)

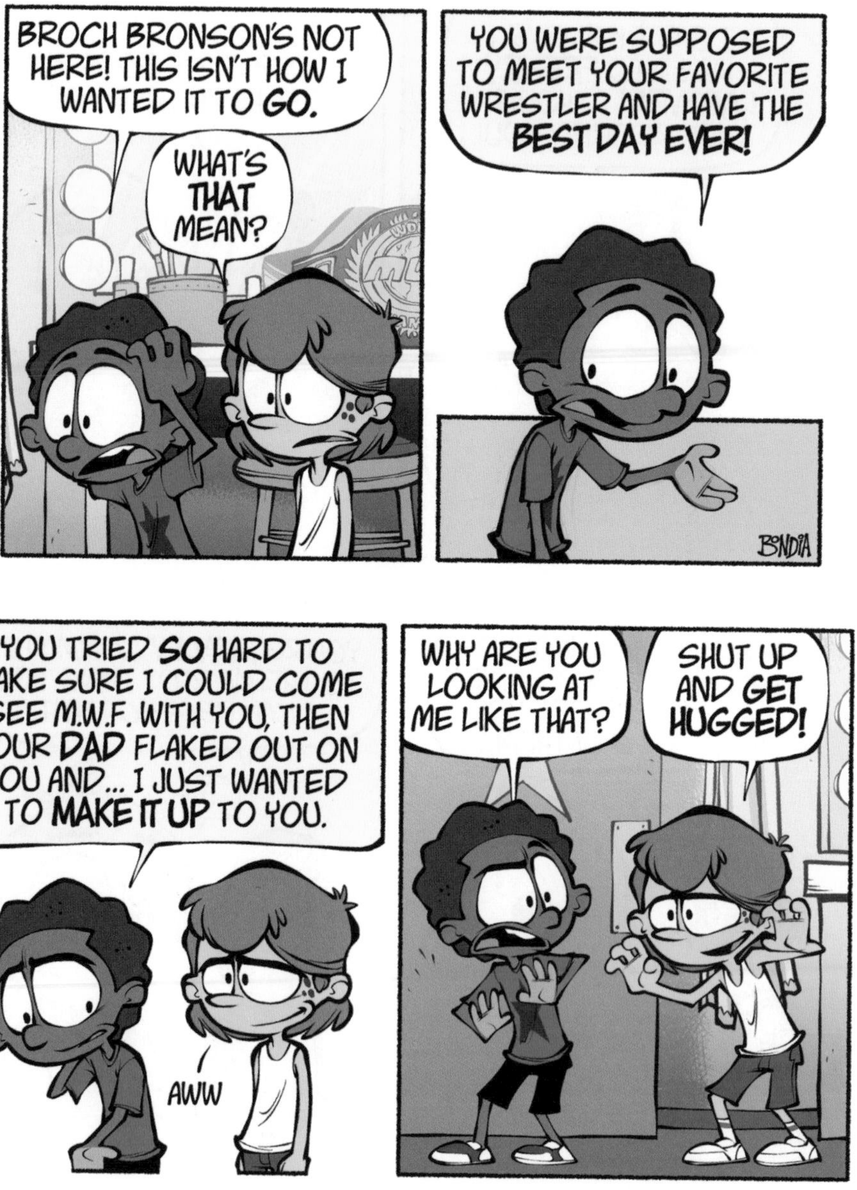
BROCH BRONSON'S NOT HERE! THIS ISN'T HOW I WANTED IT TO GO.
WHAT'S THAT MEAN?
YOU WERE SUPPOSED TO MEET YOUR FAVORITE WRESTLER AND HAVE THE BEST DAY EVER!
BONDIA
YOU TRIED SO HARD TO MAKE SURE I COULD COME SEE M.W.F. WITH YOU, THEN YOUR DAD FLAKED OUT ON YOU AND... I JUST WANTED TO MAKE IT UP TO YOU.
AWW
WHY ARE YOU LOOKING AT ME LIKE THAT?
SHUT UP AND GET HUGGED!

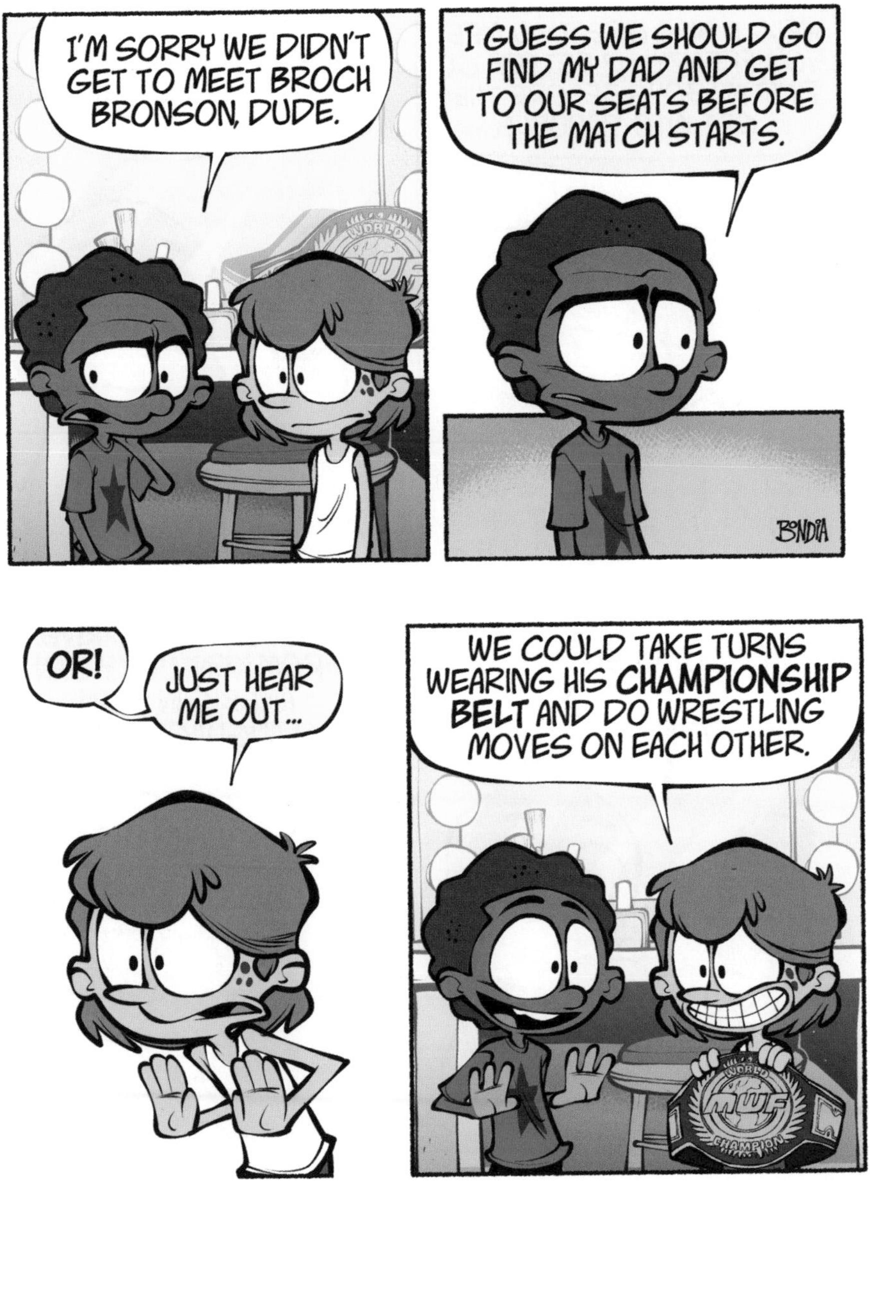
I'M SORRY WE DIDN'T GET TO MEET BROCH BRONSON, DUDE.
I GUESS WE SHOULD GO FIND MY DAD AND GET TO OUR SEATS BEFORE THE MATCH STARTS.
BONDIA
OR!
JUST HEAR ME OUT...
WE COULD TAKE TURNS WEARING HIS **CHAMPIONSHIP BELT** AND DO WRESTLING MOVES ON EACH OTHER.

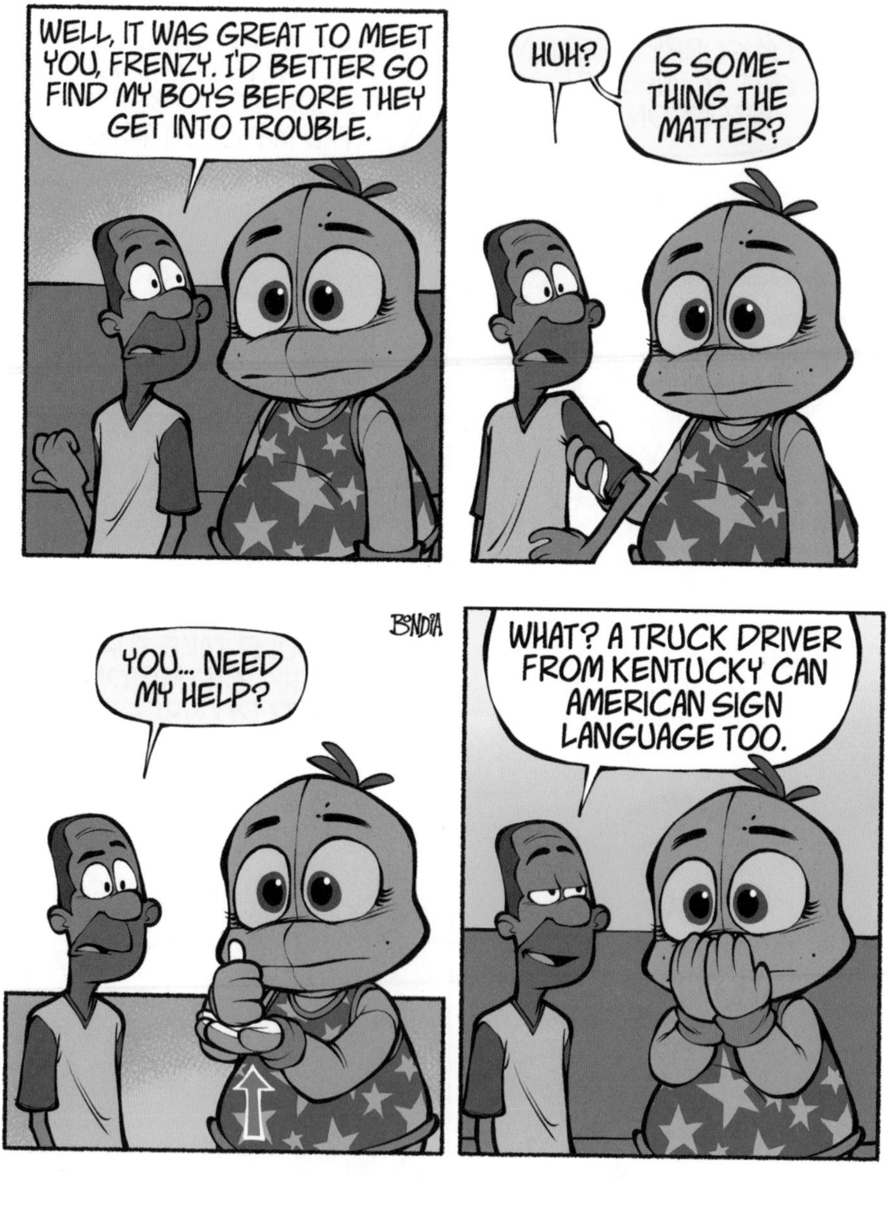
WELL, IT WAS GREAT TO MEET YOU, FRENZY. I'D BETTER GO FIND MY BOYS BEFORE THEY GET INTO TROUBLE.
HUH?
IS SOMETHING THE MATTER?
YOU... NEED MY HELP?
BONDIA
WHAT? A TRUCK DRIVER FROM KENTUCKY CAN AMERICAN SIGN LANGUAGE TOO.

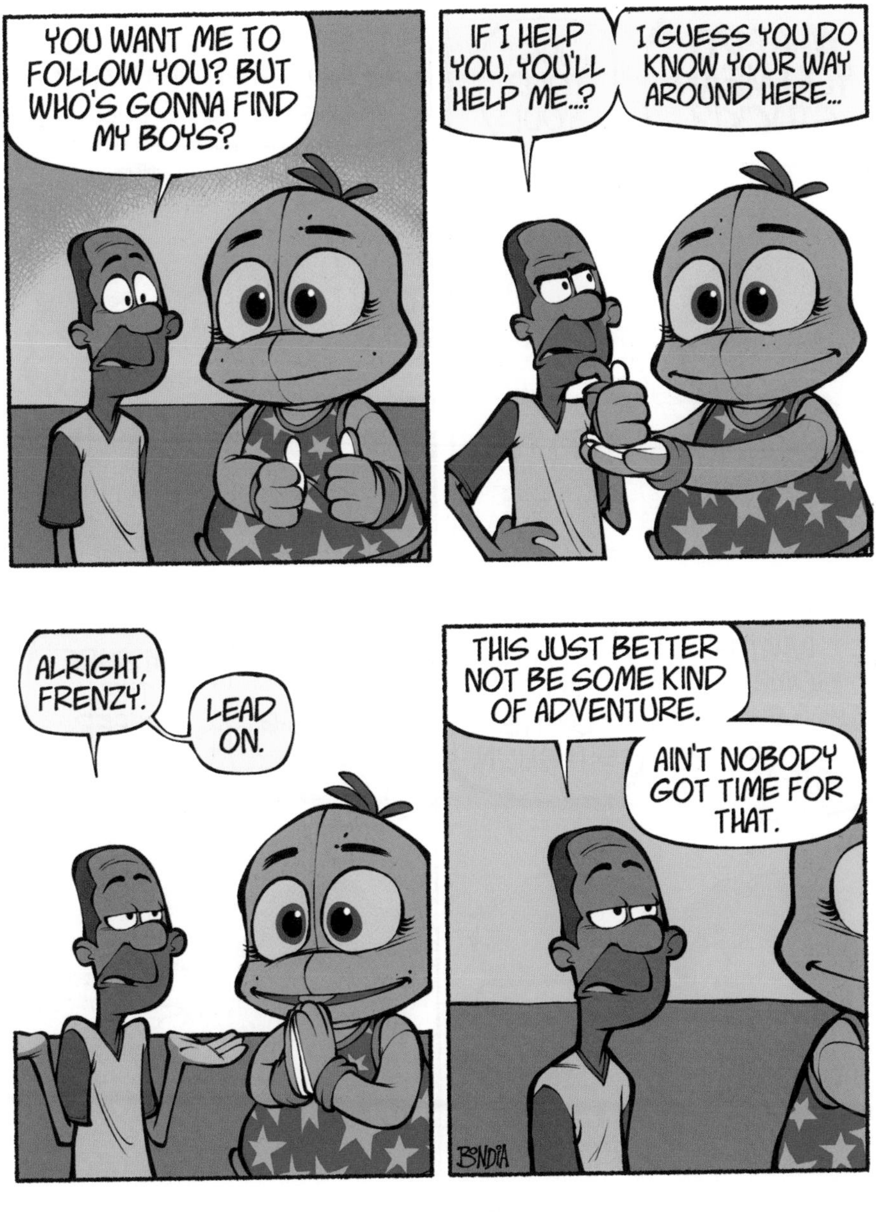
YOU WANT ME TO FOLLOW YOU? BUT WHO'S GONNA FIND MY BOYS?
IF I HELP YOU, YOU'LL HELP ME..?
I GUESS YOU DO KNOW YOUR WAY AROUND HERE...
ALRIGHT, FRENZY.
LEAD ON.
THIS JUST BETTER NOT BE SOME KIND OF ADVENTURE.
AIN'T NOBODY GOT TIME FOR THAT.
BONDIA

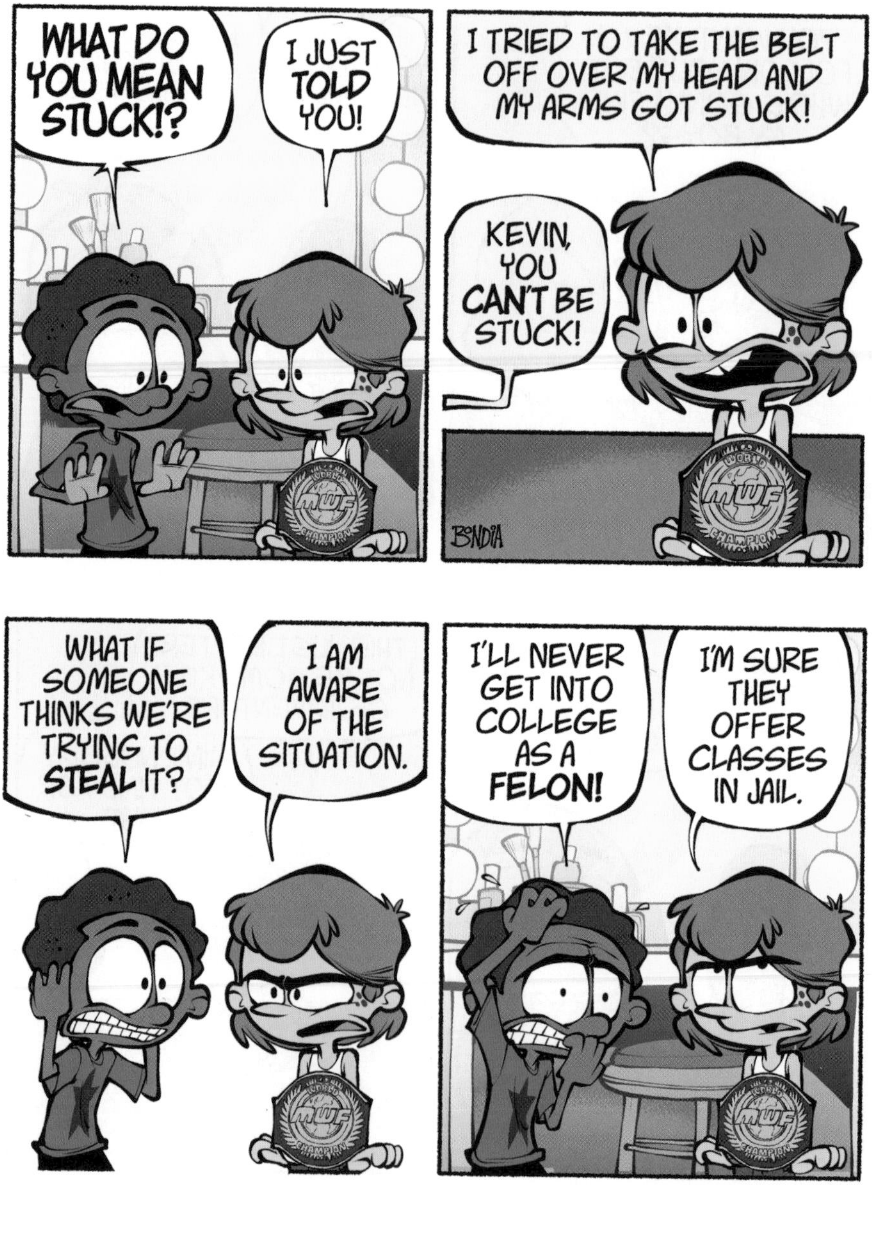
WHAT DO YOU MEAN STUCK!?
I JUST TOLD YOU!
I TRIED TO TAKE THE BELT OFF OVER MY HEAD AND MY ARMS GOT STUCK!
KEVIN, YOU CAN'T BE STUCK!
WHAT IF SOMEONE THINKS WE'RE TRYING TO STEAL IT?
I AM AWARE OF THE SITUATION.
I'LL NEVER GET INTO COLLEGE AS A FELON!
I'M SURE THEY OFFER CLASSES IN JAIL.

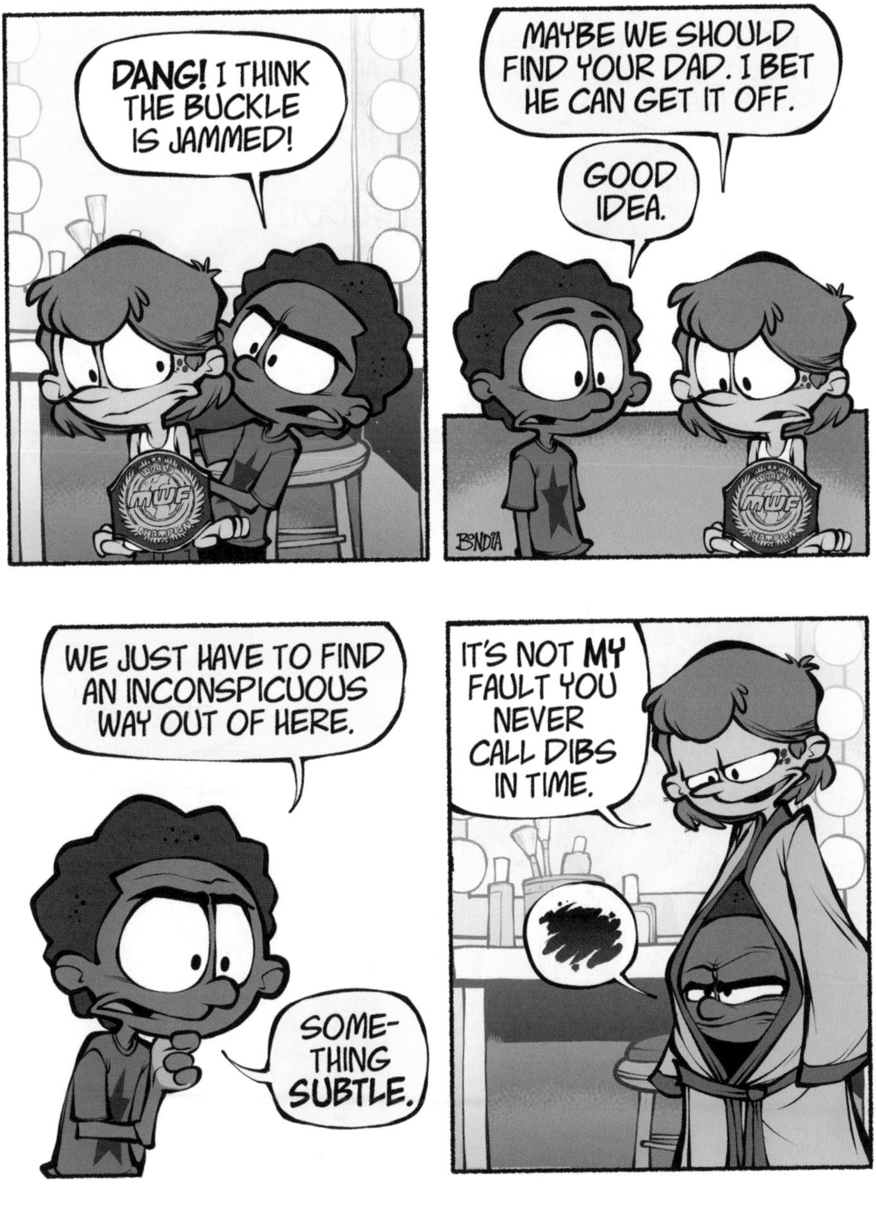
DANG! I THINK THE BUCKLE IS JAMMED!
MAYBE WE SHOULD FIND YOUR DAD. I BET HE CAN GET IT OFF.
GOOD IDEA.
WE JUST HAVE TO FIND AN INCONSPICUOUS WAY OUT OF HERE.
SOME-THING SUBTLE.
IT'S NOT MY FAULT YOU NEVER CALL DIBS IN TIME.

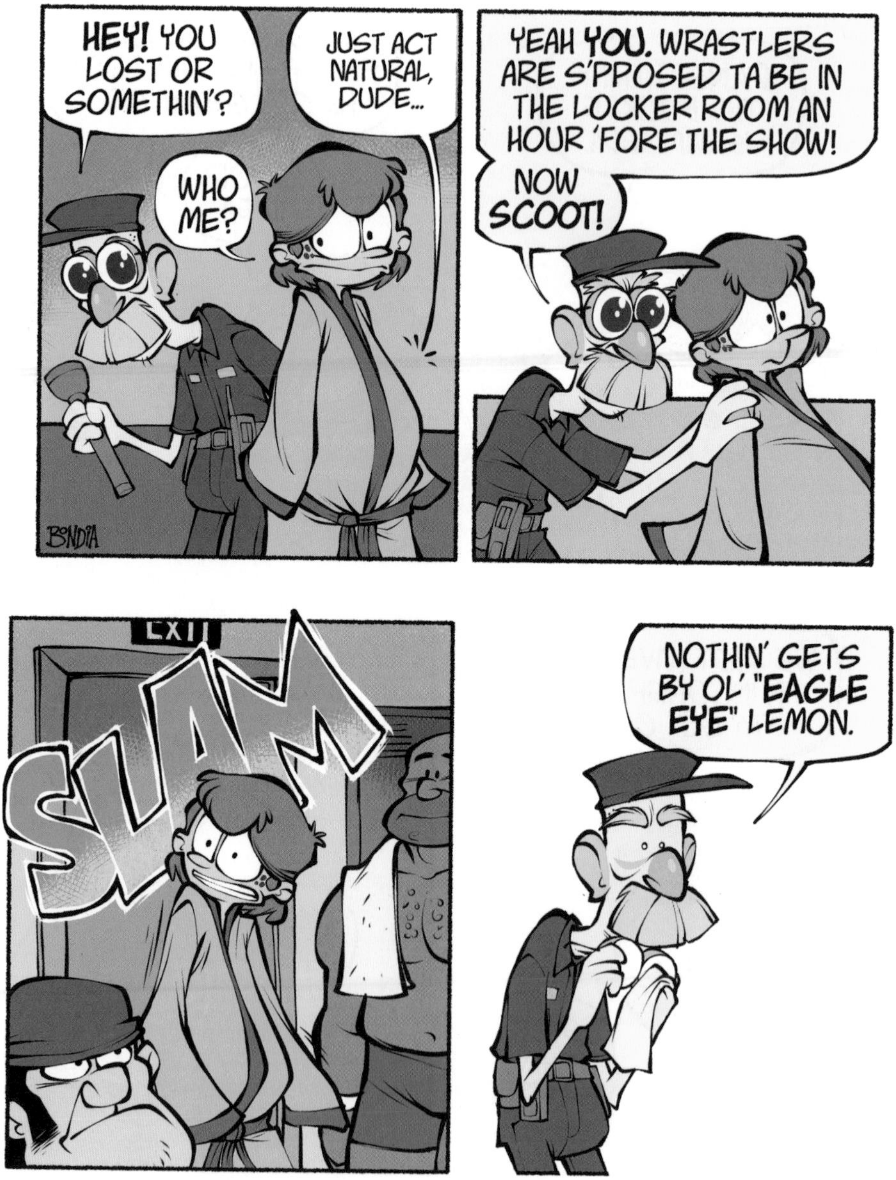
HEY! YOU LOST OR SOMETHIN'?
JUST ACT NATURAL, DUDE...
WHO ME?
YEAH YOU. WRASTLERS ARE S'PPOSED TA BE IN THE LOCKER ROOM AN HOUR 'FORE THE SHOW!
NOW SCOOT!
SLAM
NOTHIN' GETS BY OL' "EAGLE EYE" LEMON.

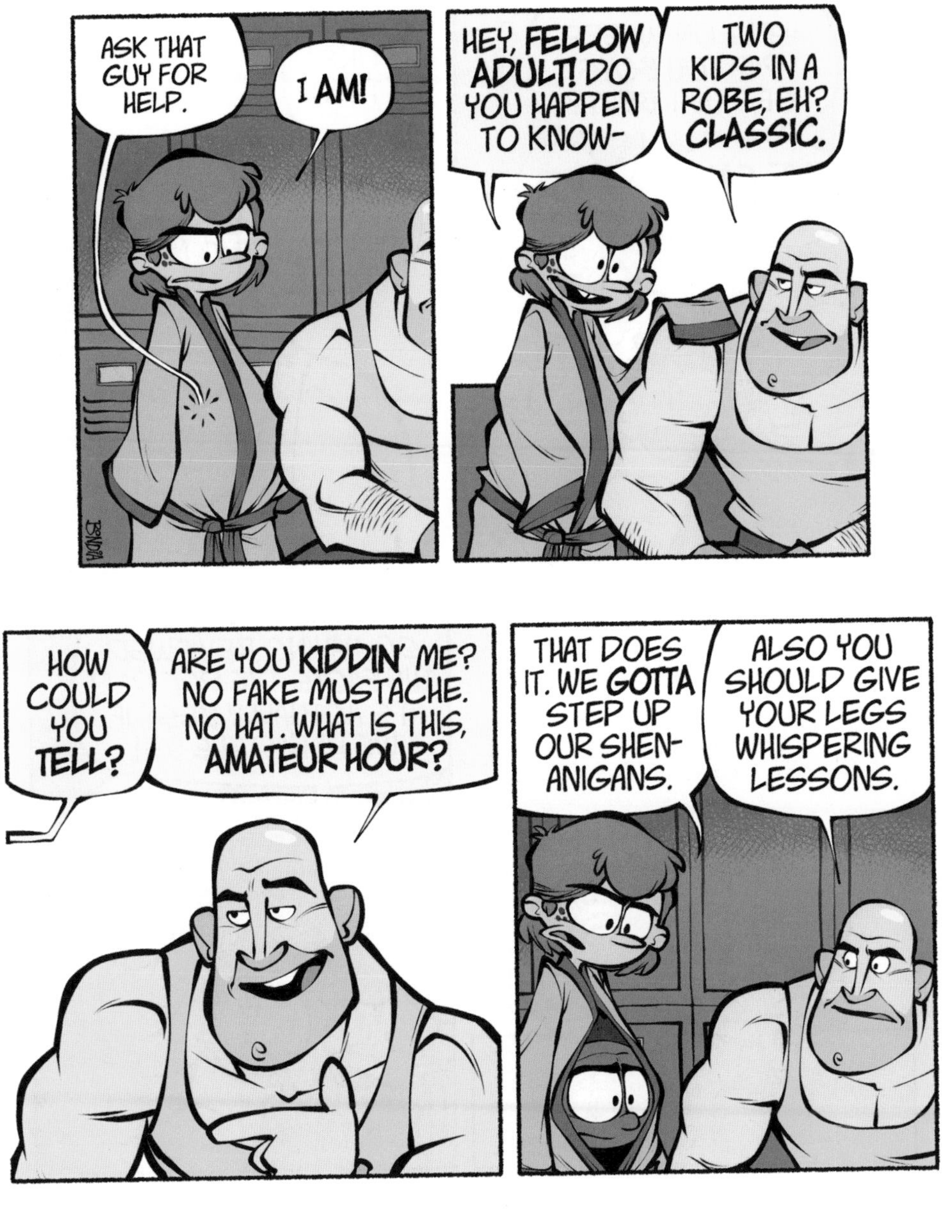
ASK THAT GUY FOR HELP.
I AM!
HEY, FELLOW ADULT! DO YOU HAPPEN TO KNOW-
TWO KIDS IN A ROBE, EH? CLASSIC.
HOW COULD YOU TELL?
ARE YOU KIDDIN' ME? NO FAKE MUSTACHE. NO HAT. WHAT IS THIS, AMATEUR HOUR?
THAT DOES IT. WE GOTTA STEP UP OUR SHEN-ANIGANS.
ALSO YOU SHOULD GIVE YOUR LEGS WHISPERING LESSONS.

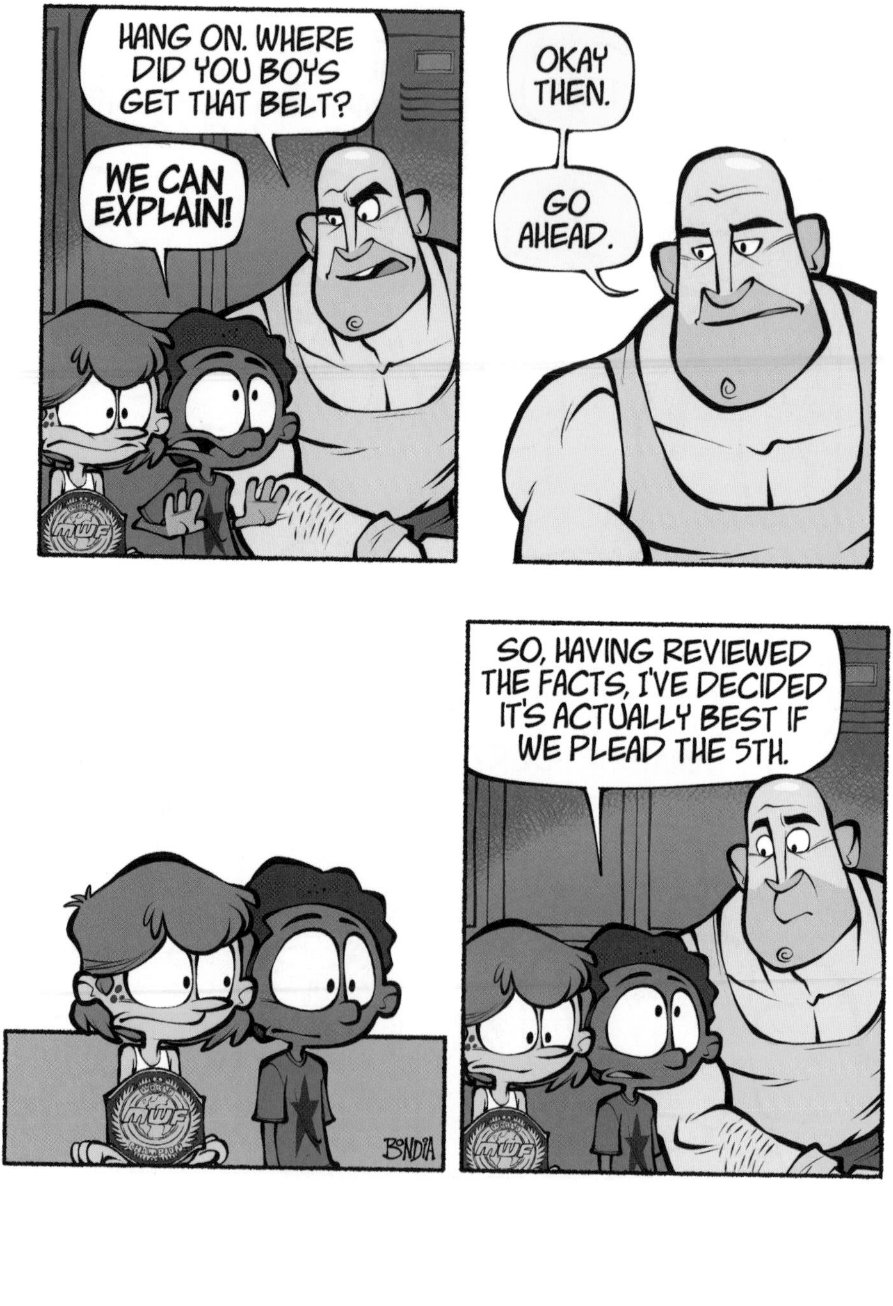
HANG ON. WHERE DID YOU BOYS GET THAT BELT?
WE CAN EXPLAIN!
OKAY THEN.
GO AHEAD.
SO, HAVING REVIEWED THE FACTS, I'VE DECIDED IT'S ACTUALLY BEST IF WE PLEAD THE 5TH.

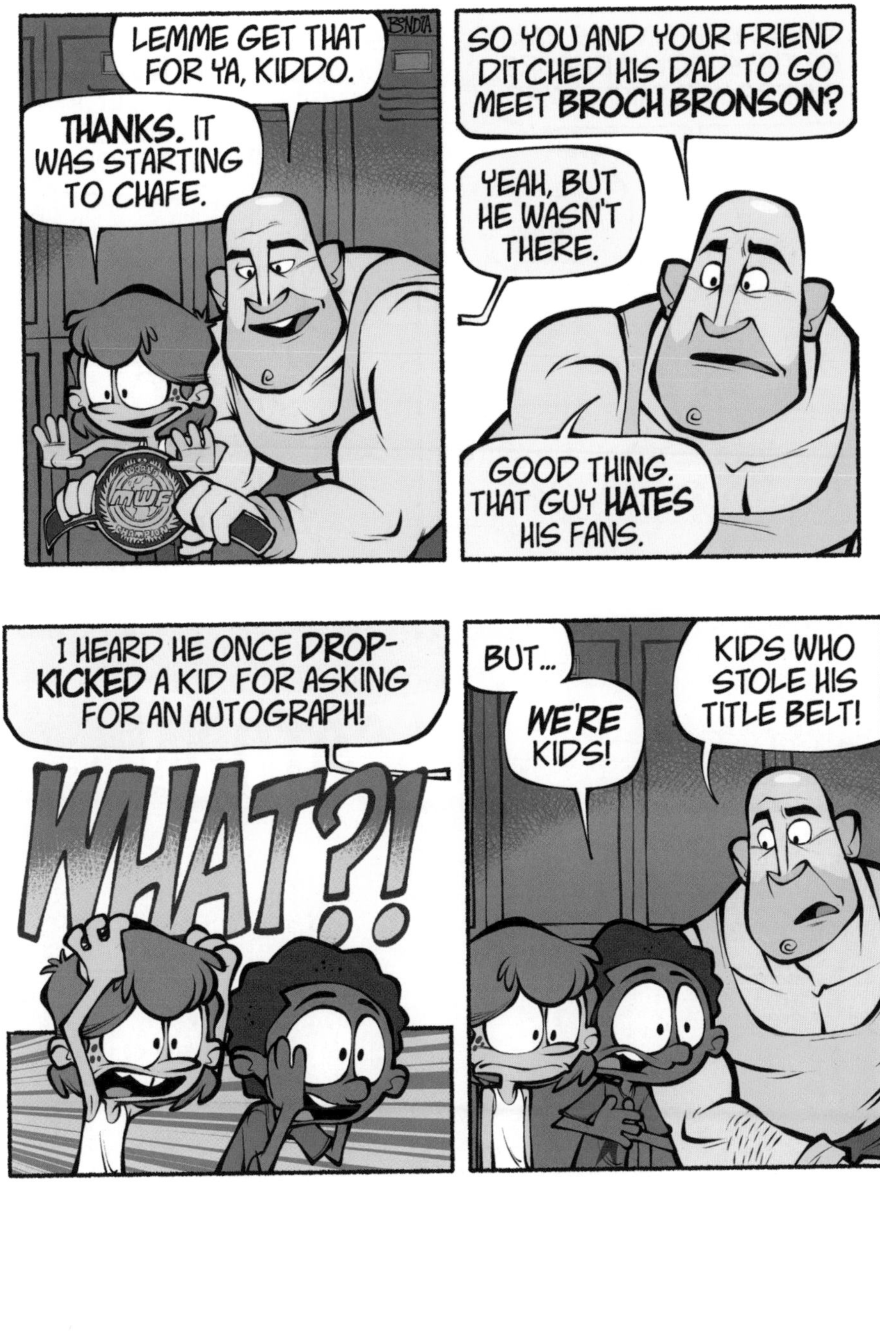
LEMME GET THAT FOR YA, KIDDO.
THANKS. IT WAS STARTING TO CHAFE.
SO YOU AND YOUR FRIEND DITCHED HIS DAD TO GO MEET BROCH BRONSON?
YEAH, BUT HE WASN'T THERE.
GOOD THING. THAT GUY HATES HIS FANS.
I HEARD HE ONCE DROP-KICKED A KID FOR ASKING FOR AN AUTOGRAPH!
WHAT?!
BUT...
WE'RE KIDS!
KIDS WHO STOLE HIS TITLE BELT!

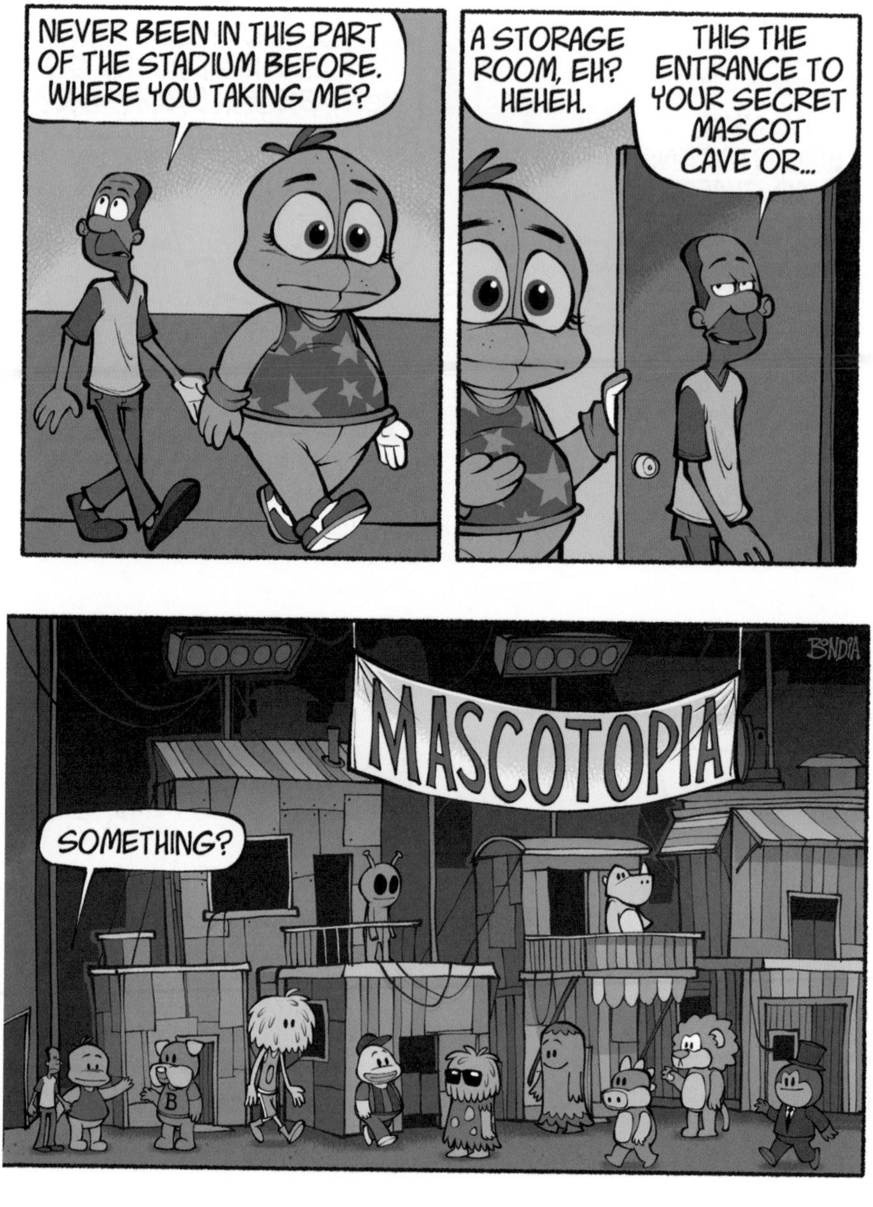
NEVER BEEN IN THIS PART OF THE STADIUM BEFORE. WHERE YOU TAKING ME?
A STORAGE ROOM, EH? HEHEH.
THIS THE ENTRANCE TO YOUR SECRET MASCOT CAVE OR...
MASCOTOPIA
SOMETHING?

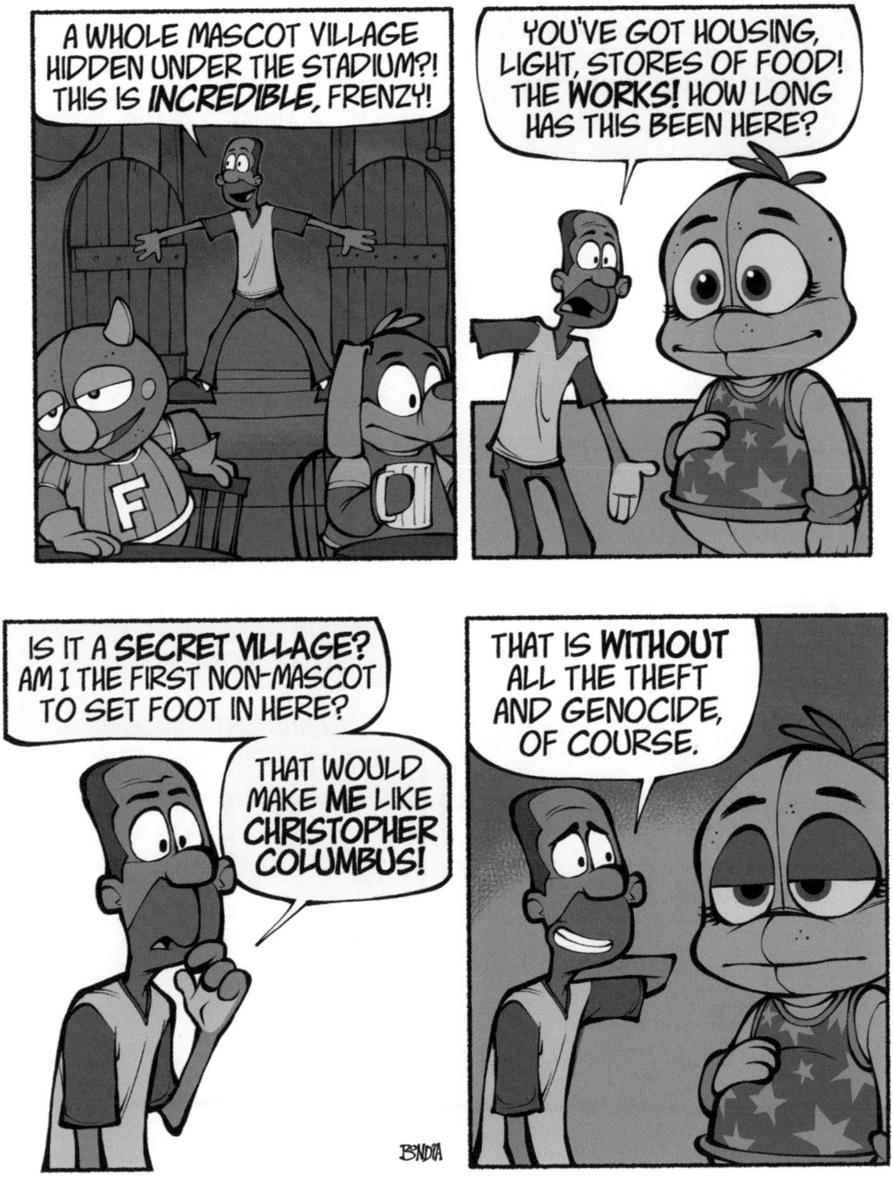
A WHOLE MASCOT VILLAGE HIDDEN UNDER THE STADIUM?! THIS IS INCREDIBLE, FRENZY!
YOU'VE GOT HOUSING, LIGHT, STORES OF FOOD! THE WORKS! HOW LONG HAS THIS BEEN HERE?
IS IT A SECRET VILLAGE? AM I THE FIRST NON-MASCOT TO SET FOOT IN HERE?
THAT WOULD MAKE ME LIKE CHRISTOPHER COLUMBUS!
THAT IS WITHOUT ALL THE THEFT AND GENOCIDE, OF COURSE.
BONDIA

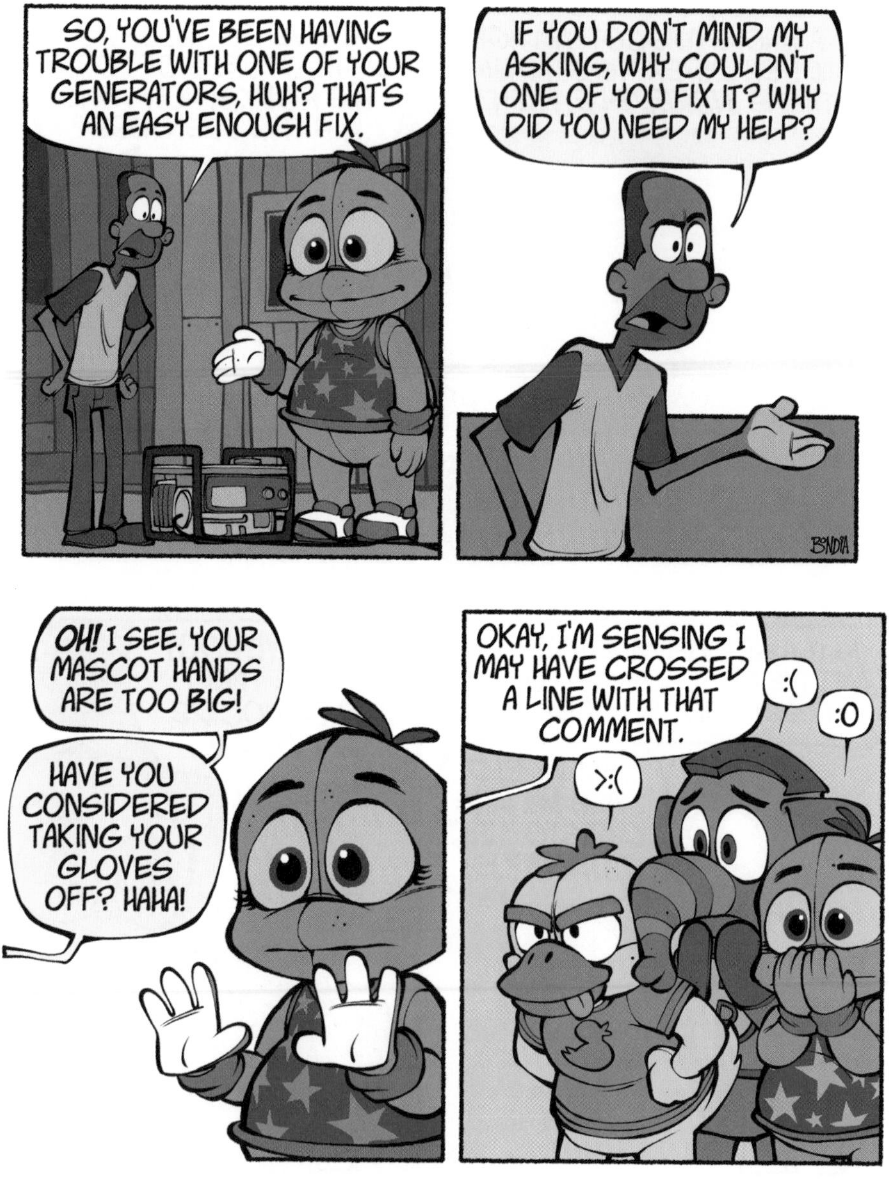
SO, YOU'VE BEEN HAVING TROUBLE WITH ONE OF YOUR GENERATORS, HUH? THAT'S AN EASY ENOUGH FIX.
IF YOU DON'T MIND MY ASKING, WHY COULDN'T ONE OF YOU FIX IT? WHY DID YOU NEED MY HELP?
OH! I SEE. YOUR MASCOT HANDS ARE TOO BIG!
HAVE YOU CONSIDERED TAKING YOUR GLOVES OFF? HAHA!
OKAY, I'M SENSING I MAY HAVE CROSSED A LINE WITH THAT COMMENT.
:(
:O
>:(

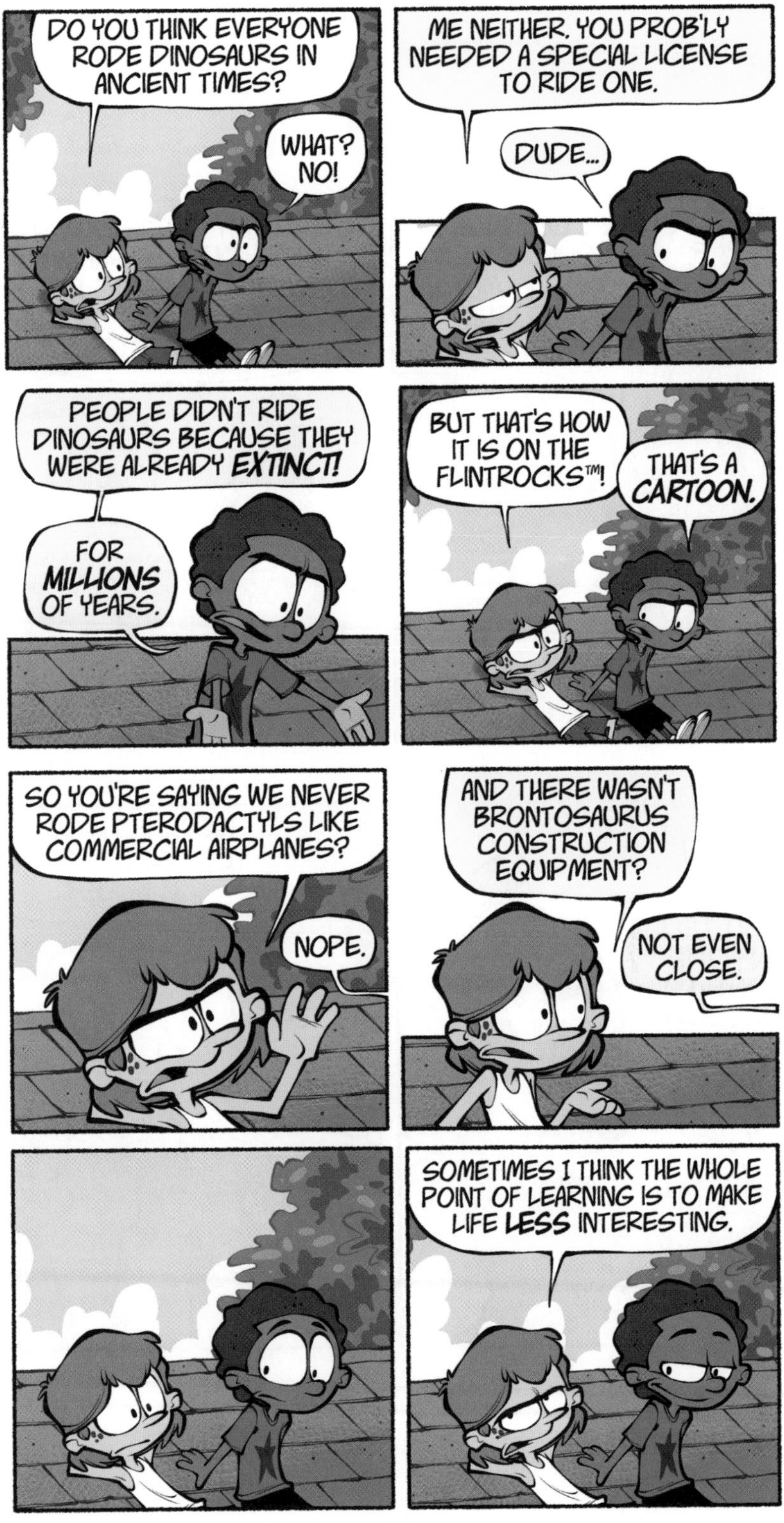
DO YOU THINK EVERYONE RODE DINOSAURS IN ANCIENT TIMES?
WHAT? NO!
ME NEITHER. YOU PROB'LY NEEDED A SPECIAL LICENSE TO RIDE ONE.
DUDE...
PEOPLE DIDN'T RIDE DINOSAURS BECAUSE THEY WERE ALREADY EXTINCT!
FOR MILLIONS OF YEARS.
BUT THAT'S HOW IT IS ON THE FLINTROCKS™!
THAT'S A CARTOON.
SO YOU'RE SAYING WE NEVER RODE PTERODACTYLS LIKE COMMERCIAL AIRPLANES?
NOPE.
AND THERE WASN'T BRONTOSAURUS CONSTRUCTION EQUIPMENT?
NOT EVEN CLOSE.
SOMETIMES I THINK THE WHOLE POINT OF LEARNING IS TO MAKE LIFE LESS INTERESTING.

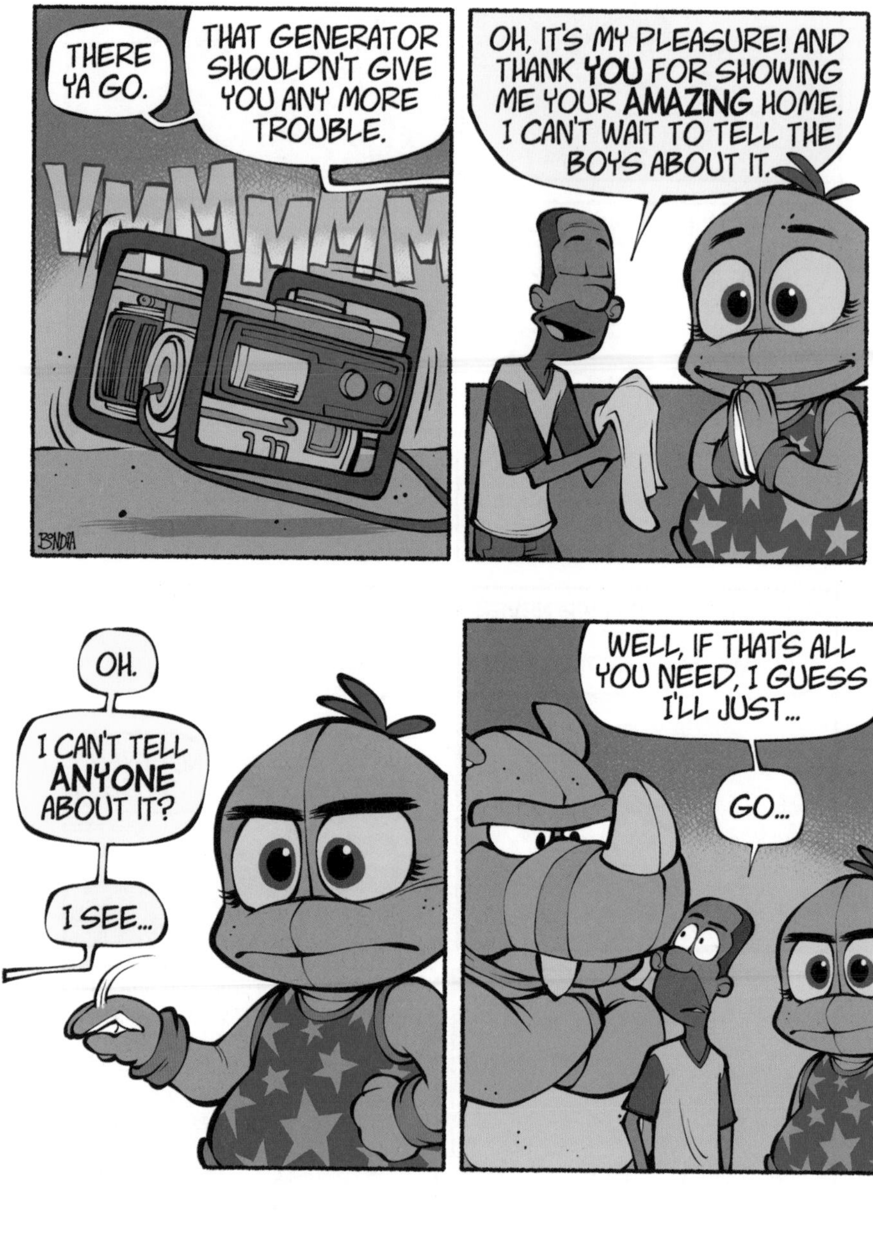
THERE YA GO.
THAT GENERATOR SHOULDN'T GIVE YOU ANY MORE TROUBLE.
VMMMMMM
BONDIA
OH, IT'S MY PLEASURE! AND THANK **YOU** FOR SHOWING ME YOUR **AMAZING** HOME. I CAN'T WAIT TO TELL THE BOYS ABOUT IT.
OH.
I CAN'T TELL **ANYONE** ABOUT IT?
I SEE...
WELL, IF THAT'S ALL YOU NEED, I GUESS I'LL JUST...
GO...

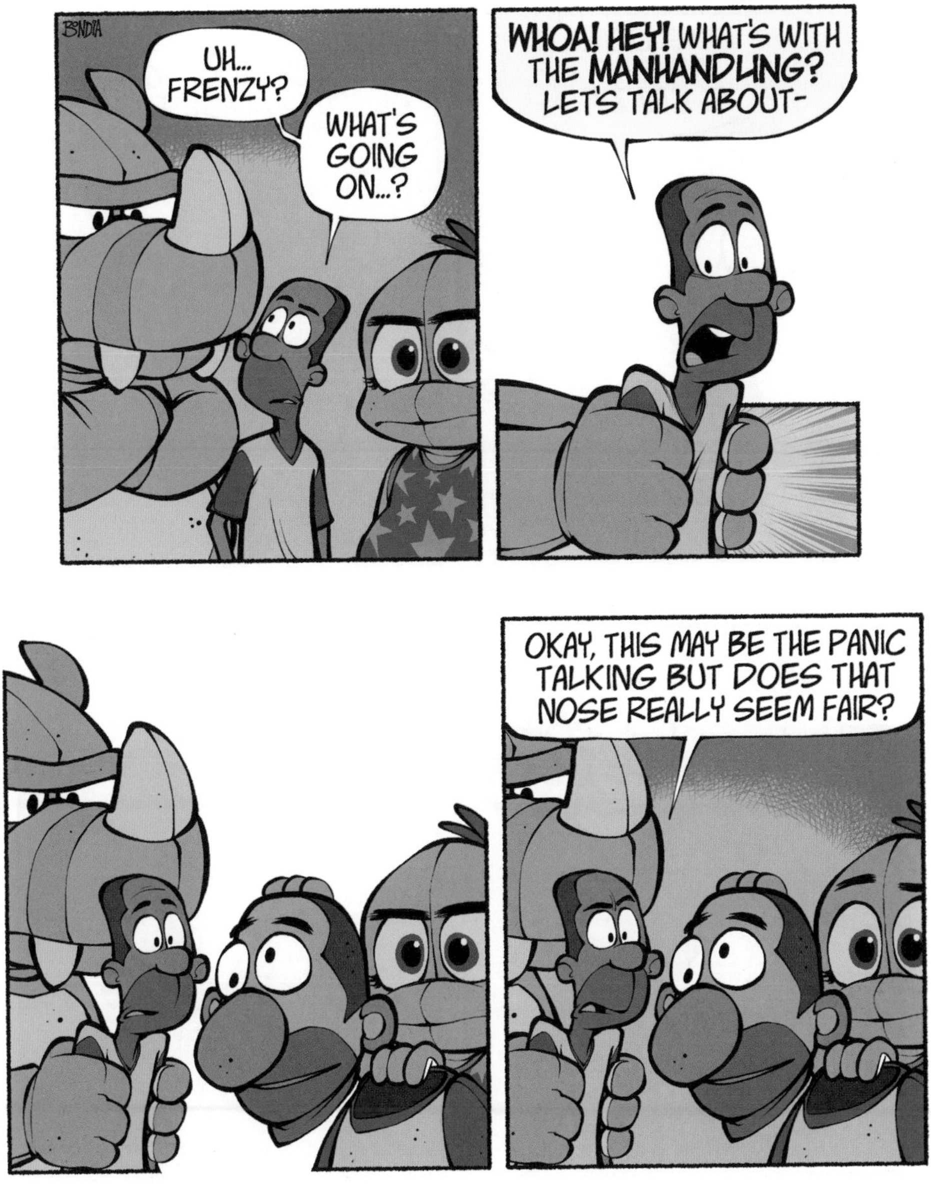
UH... FRENZY?
WHAT'S GOING ON...?
WHOA! HEY! WHAT'S WITH THE MANHANDLING? LET'S TALK ABOUT-
OKAY, THIS MAY BE THE PANIC TALKING BUT DOES THAT NOSE REALLY SEEM FAIR?

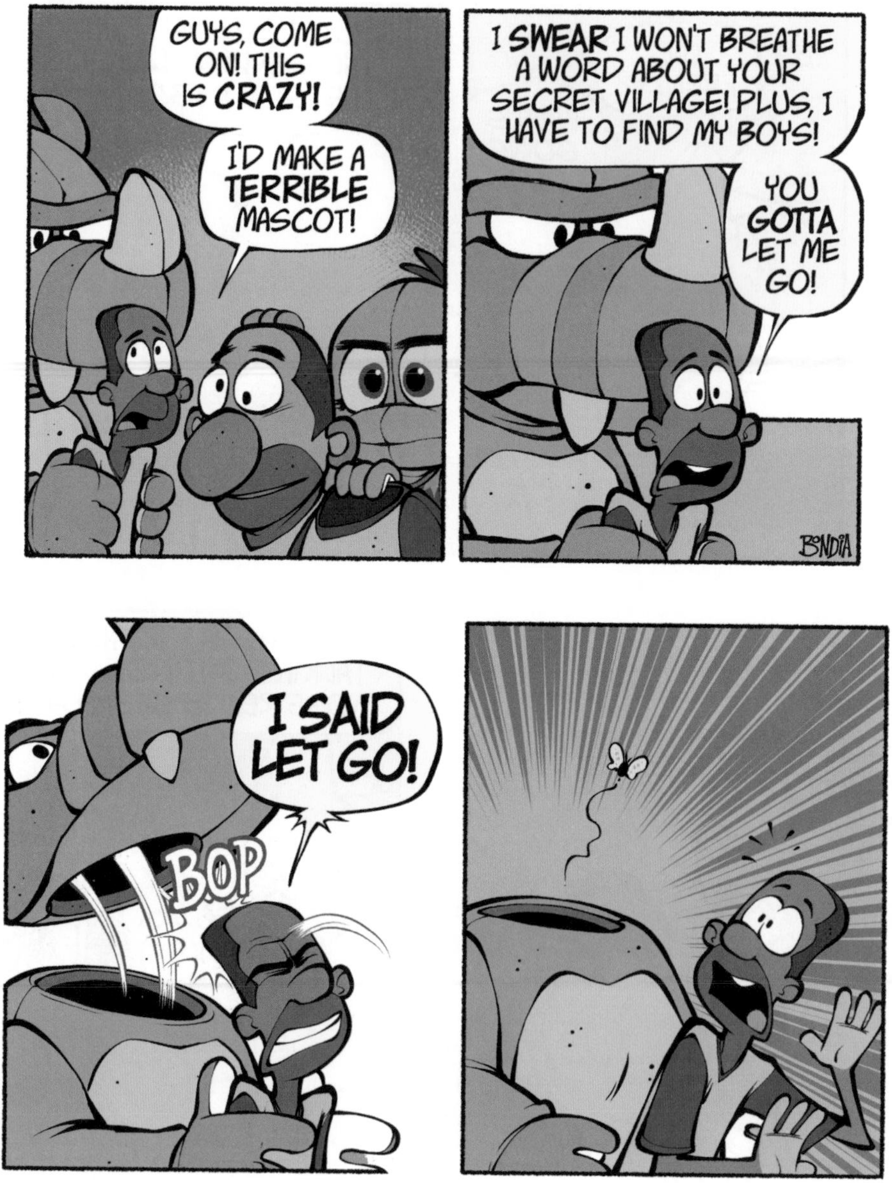
GUYS, COME ON! THIS IS CRAZY!
I'D MAKE A TERRIBLE MASCOT!
I SWEAR I WON'T BREATHE A WORD ABOUT YOUR SECRET VILLAGE! PLUS, I HAVE TO FIND MY BOYS!
YOU GOTTA LET ME GO!
BONDIA
I SAID LET GO!
BOP

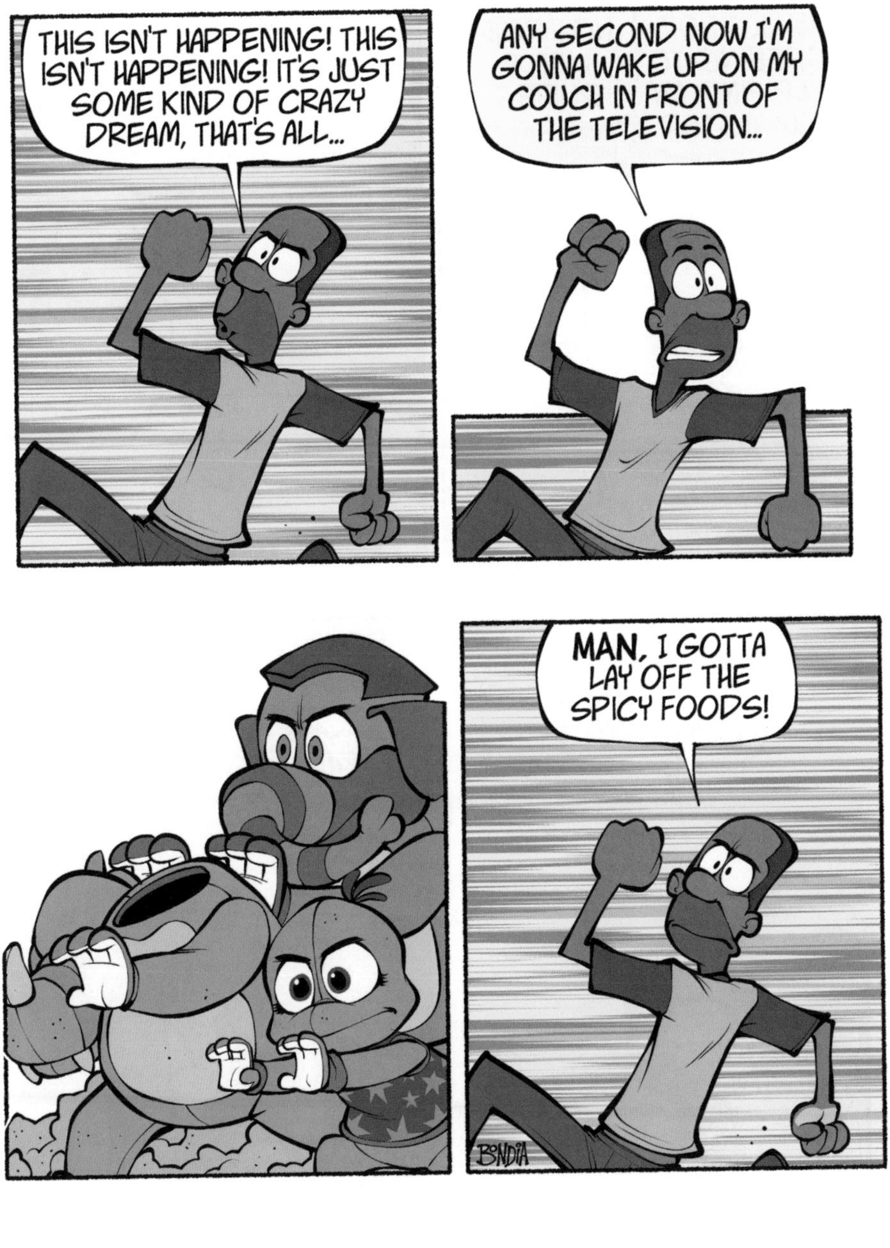
THIS ISN'T HAPPENING! THIS ISN'T HAPPENING! IT'S JUST SOME KIND OF CRAZY DREAM, THAT'S ALL...
ANY SECOND NOW I'M GONNA WAKE UP ON MY COUCH IN FRONT OF THE TELEVISION...
MAN, I GOTTA LAY OFF THE SPICY FOODS!
BONDIA

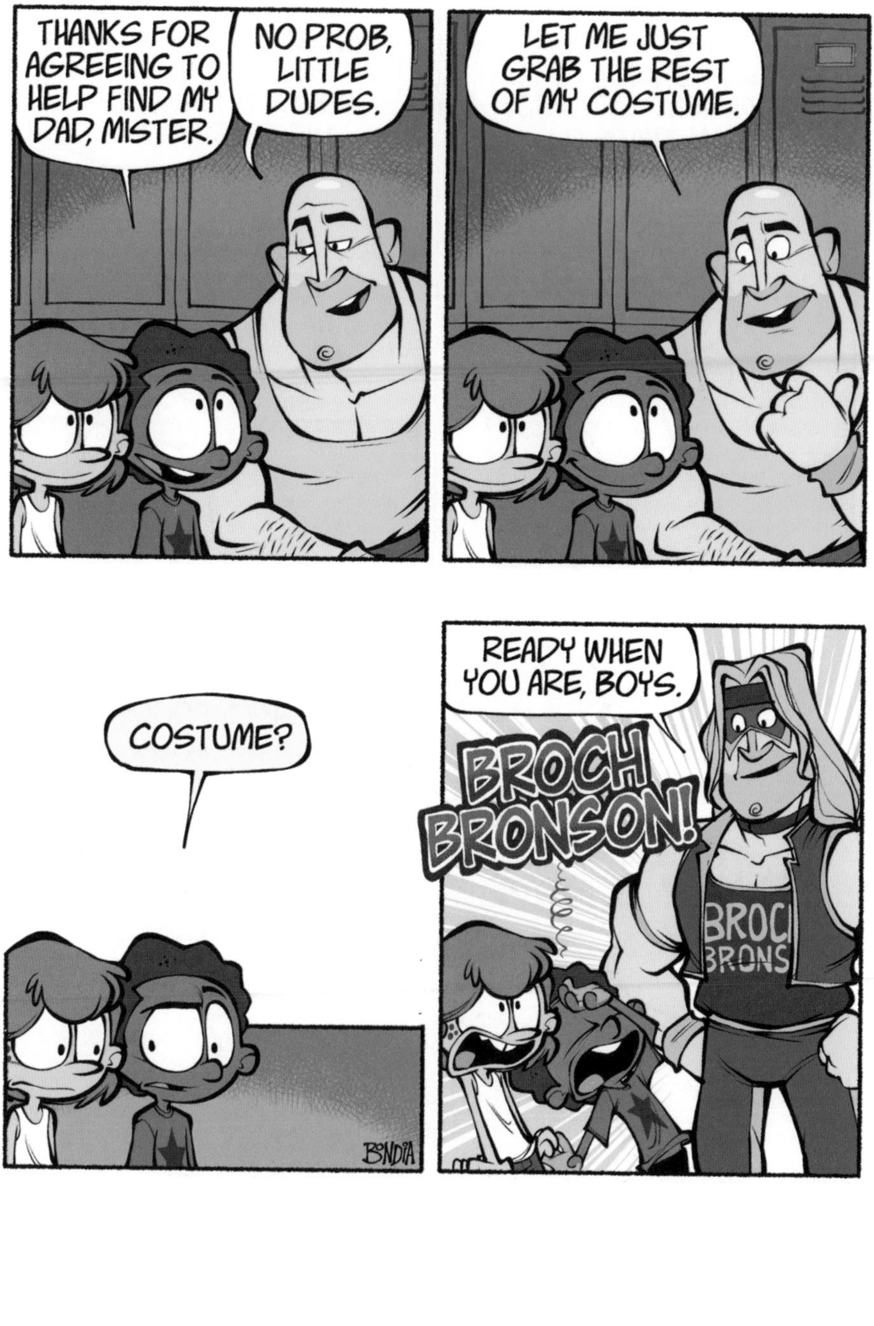
THANKS FOR AGREEING TO HELP FIND MY DAD, MISTER.
NO PROB, LITTLE DUDES.
LET ME JUST GRAB THE REST OF MY COSTUME.
COSTUME?
READY WHEN YOU ARE, BOYS.
BROCH BRONSON!
BONDIA

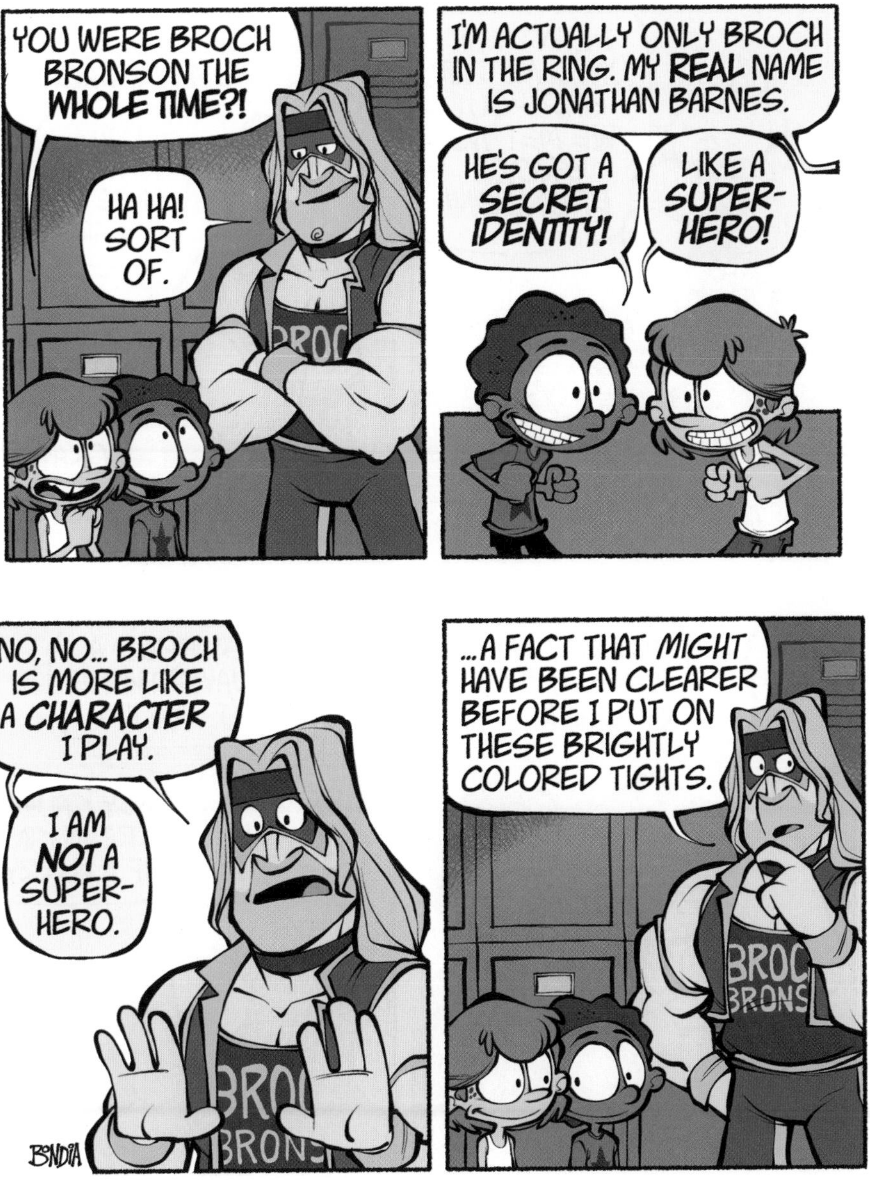
YOU WERE BROCH BRONSON THE WHOLE TIME?!
HA HA! SORT OF.
I'M ACTUALLY ONLY BROCH IN THE RING. MY REAL NAME IS JONATHAN BARNES.
HE'S GOT A SECRET IDENTITY!
LIKE A SUPER-HERO!
NO, NO... BROCH IS MORE LIKE A CHARACTER I PLAY.
I AM NOT A SUPER-HERO.
BONDIA
...A FACT THAT MIGHT HAVE BEEN CLEARER BEFORE I PUT ON THESE BRIGHTLY COLORED TIGHTS.

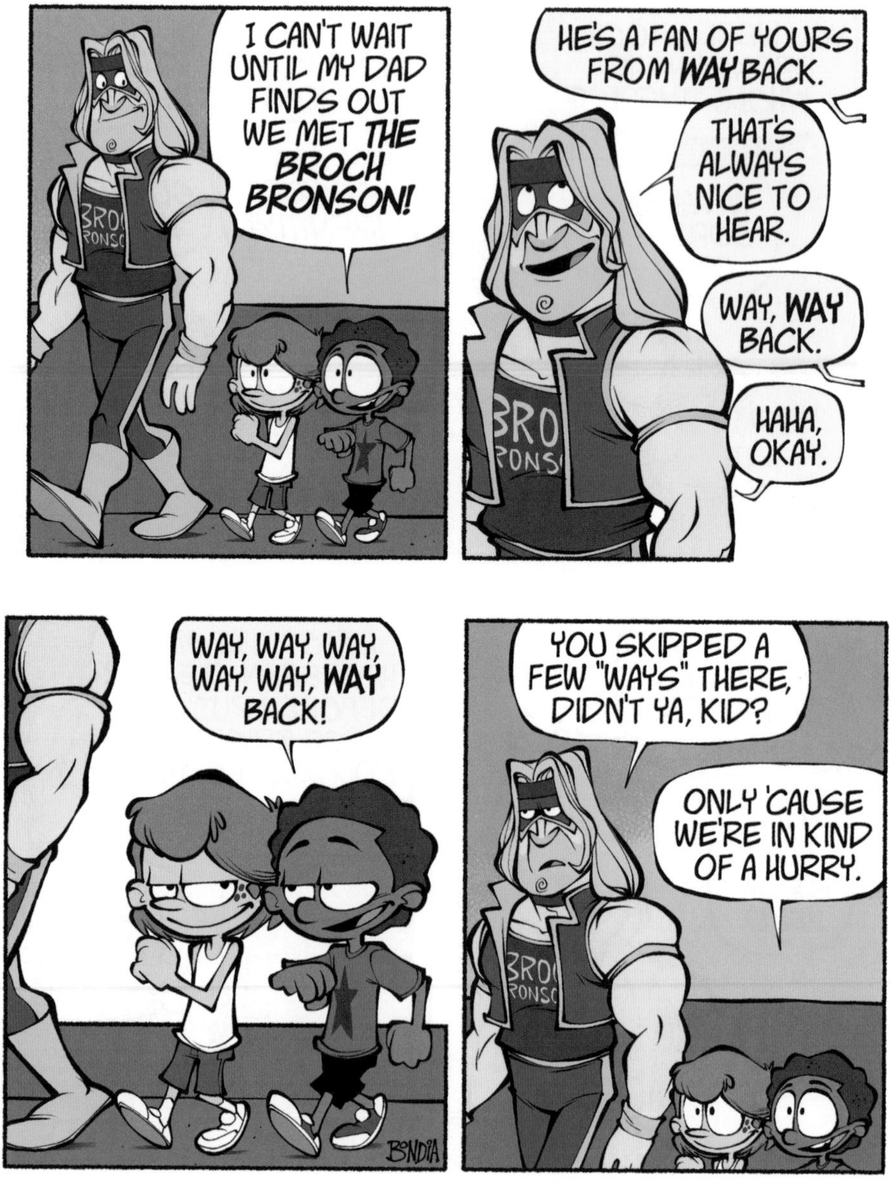

I CAN'T WAIT UNTIL MY DAD FINDS OUT WE MET THE BROCH BRONSON!
BROCH BRONSON
HE'S A FAN OF YOURS FROM WAY BACK.
THAT'S ALWAYS NICE TO HEAR.
WAY, WAY BACK.
HAHA, OKAY.
WAY, WAY, WAY, WAY, WAY, WAY BACK!
BONDIA
YOU SKIPPED A FEW "WAYS" THERE, DIDN'T YA, KID?
ONLY 'CAUSE WE'RE IN KIND OF A HURRY.

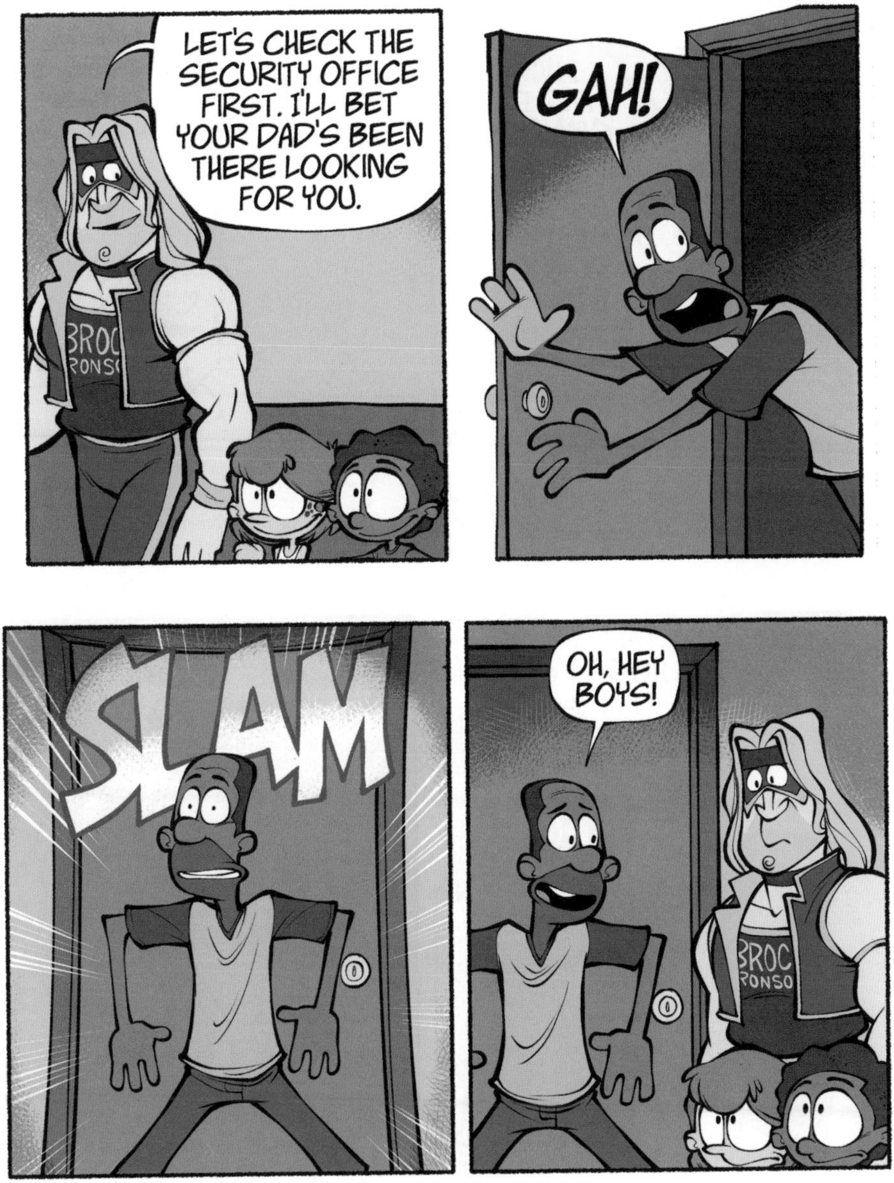
LET'S CHECK THE SECURITY OFFICE FIRST. I'LL BET YOUR DAD'S BEEN THERE LOOKING FOR YOU.
BROC RONSO
GAH!
SLAM
OH, HEY BOYS!
BROC RONSO

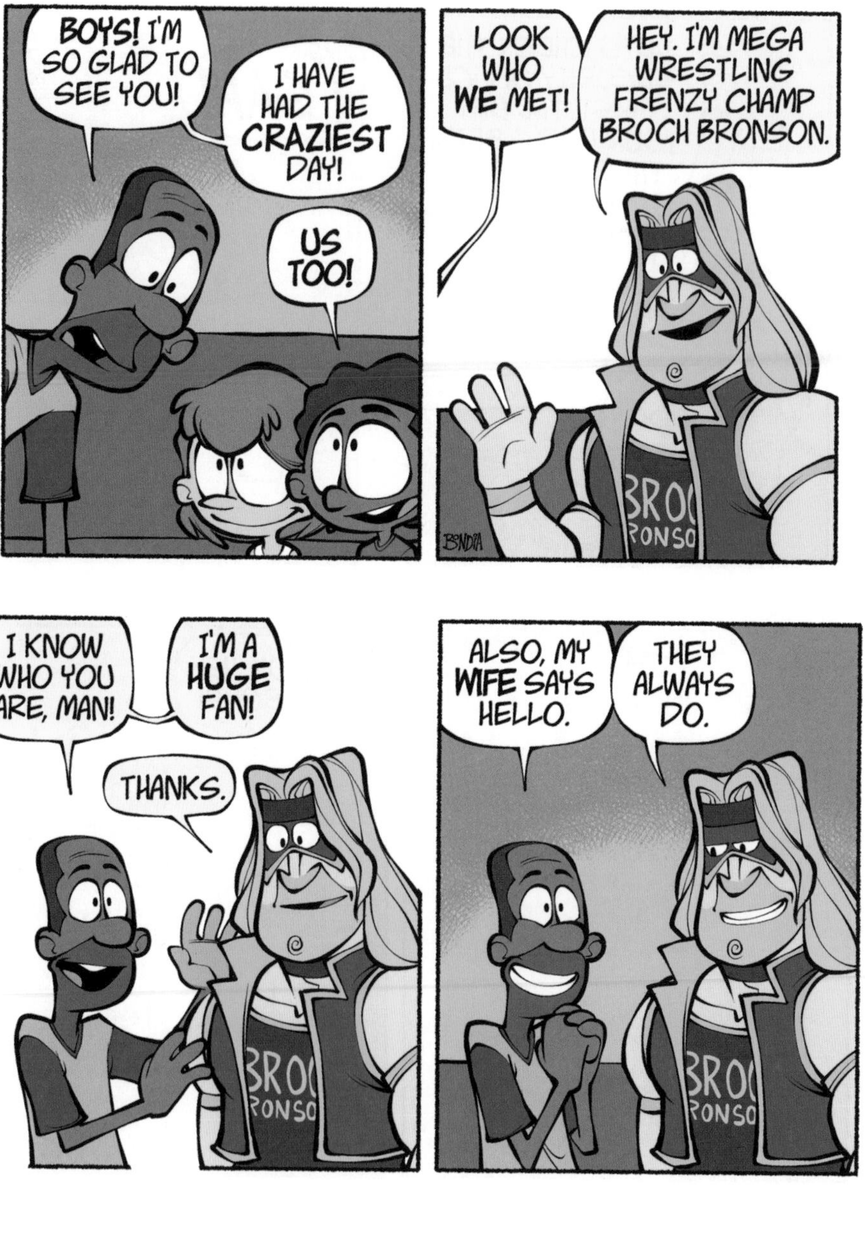
BOYS! I'M SO GLAD TO SEE YOU!
I HAVE HAD THE CRAZIEST DAY!
US TOO!
LOOK WHO WE MET!
HEY. I'M MEGA WRESTLING FRENZY CHAMP BROCH BRONSON.
BONDIA
I KNOW WHO YOU ARE, MAN!
I'M A HUGE FAN!
THANKS.
ALSO, MY WIFE SAYS HELLO.
THEY ALWAYS DO.

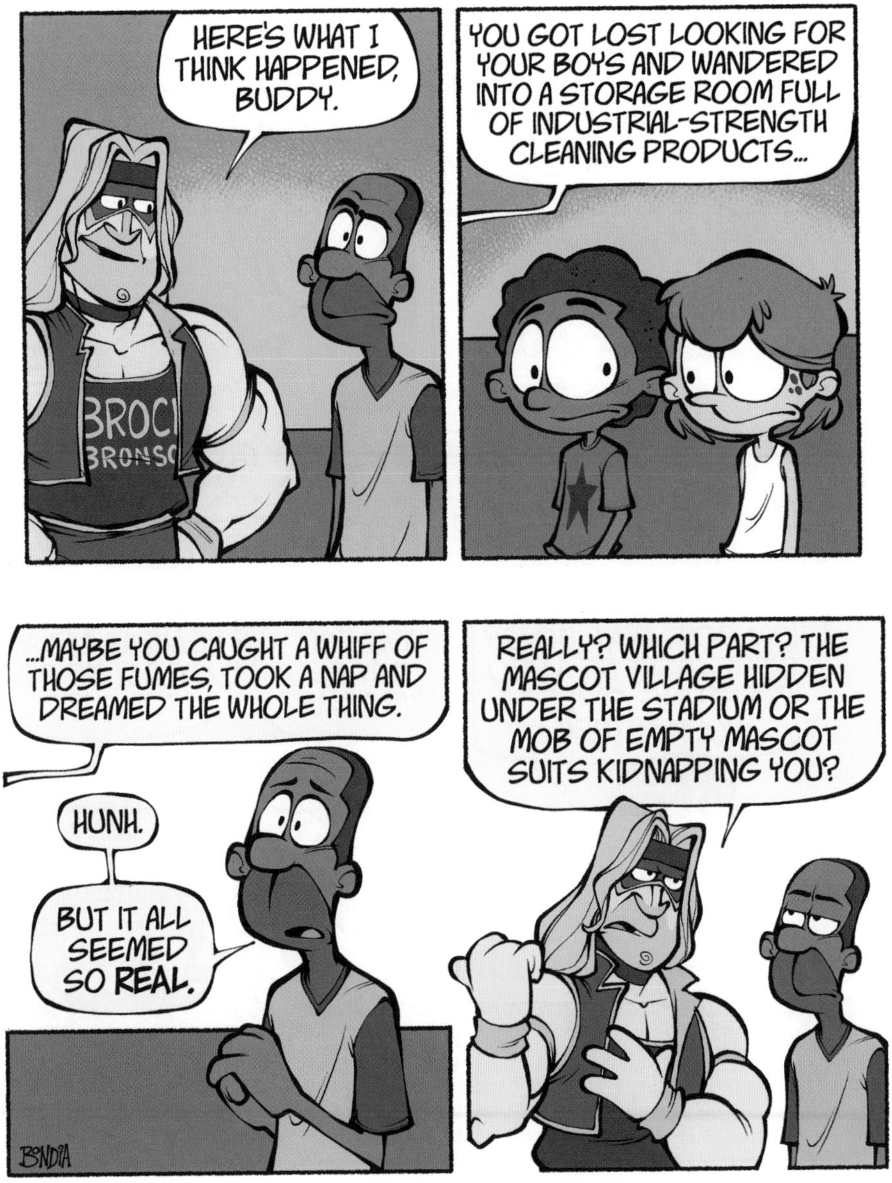
HERE'S WHAT I THINK HAPPENED, BUDDY.
BROCK BRONSO
YOU GOT LOST LOOKING FOR YOUR BOYS AND WANDERED INTO A STORAGE ROOM FULL OF INDUSTRIAL-STRENGTH CLEANING PRODUCTS...
...MAYBE YOU CAUGHT A WHIFF OF THOSE FUMES, TOOK A NAP AND DREAMED THE WHOLE THING.
HUNH.
BUT IT ALL SEEMED SO REAL.
REALLY? WHICH PART? THE MASCOT VILLAGE HIDDEN UNDER THE STADIUM OR THE MOB OF EMPTY MASCOT SUITS KIDNAPPING YOU?
BONDIA

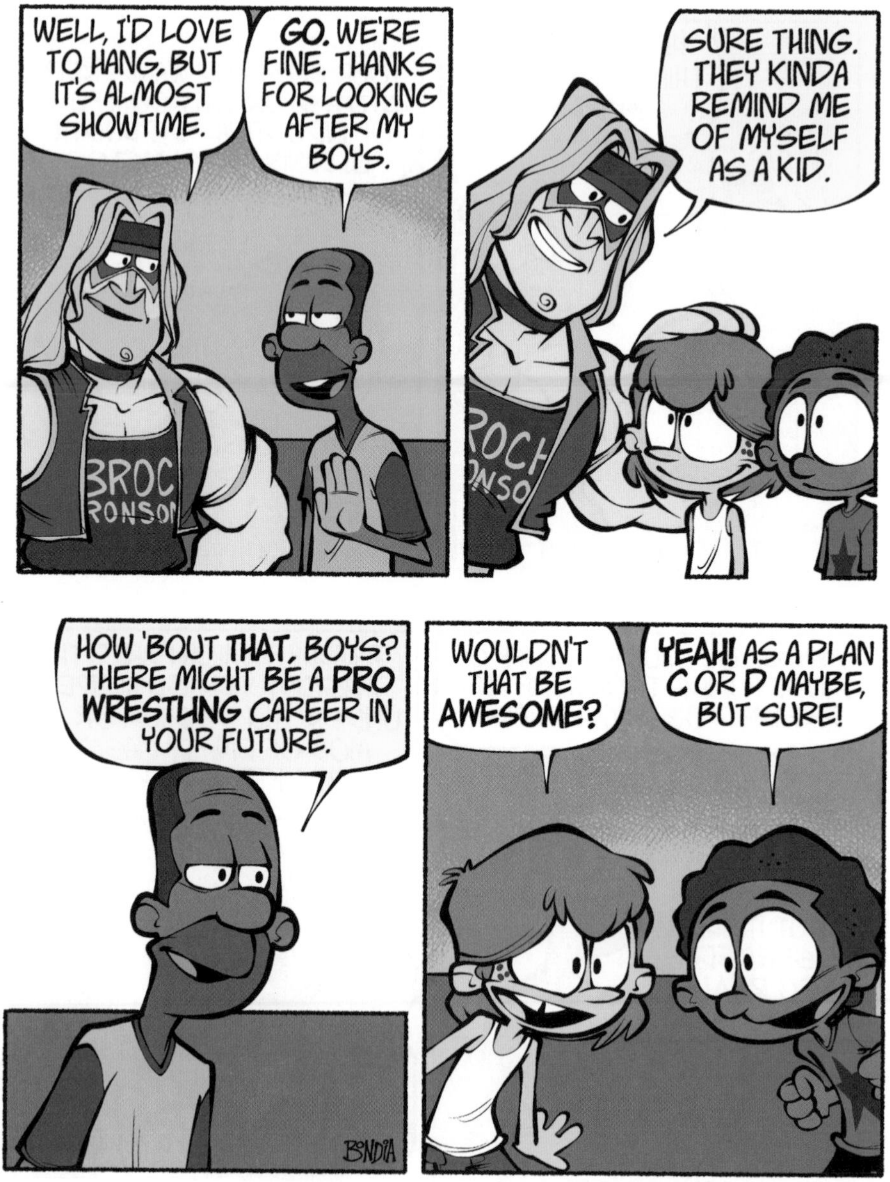
WELL, I'D LOVE TO HANG, BUT IT'S ALMOST SHOWTIME.
GO. WE'RE FINE. THANKS FOR LOOKING AFTER MY BOYS.
BROC RONSON
SURE THING. THEY KINDA REMIND ME OF MYSELF AS A KID.
HOW 'BOUT THAT, BOYS? THERE MIGHT BE A PRO WRESTLING CAREER IN YOUR FUTURE.
BONDIA
WOULDN'T THAT BE AWESOME?
YEAH! AS A PLAN C OR D MAYBE, BUT SURE!

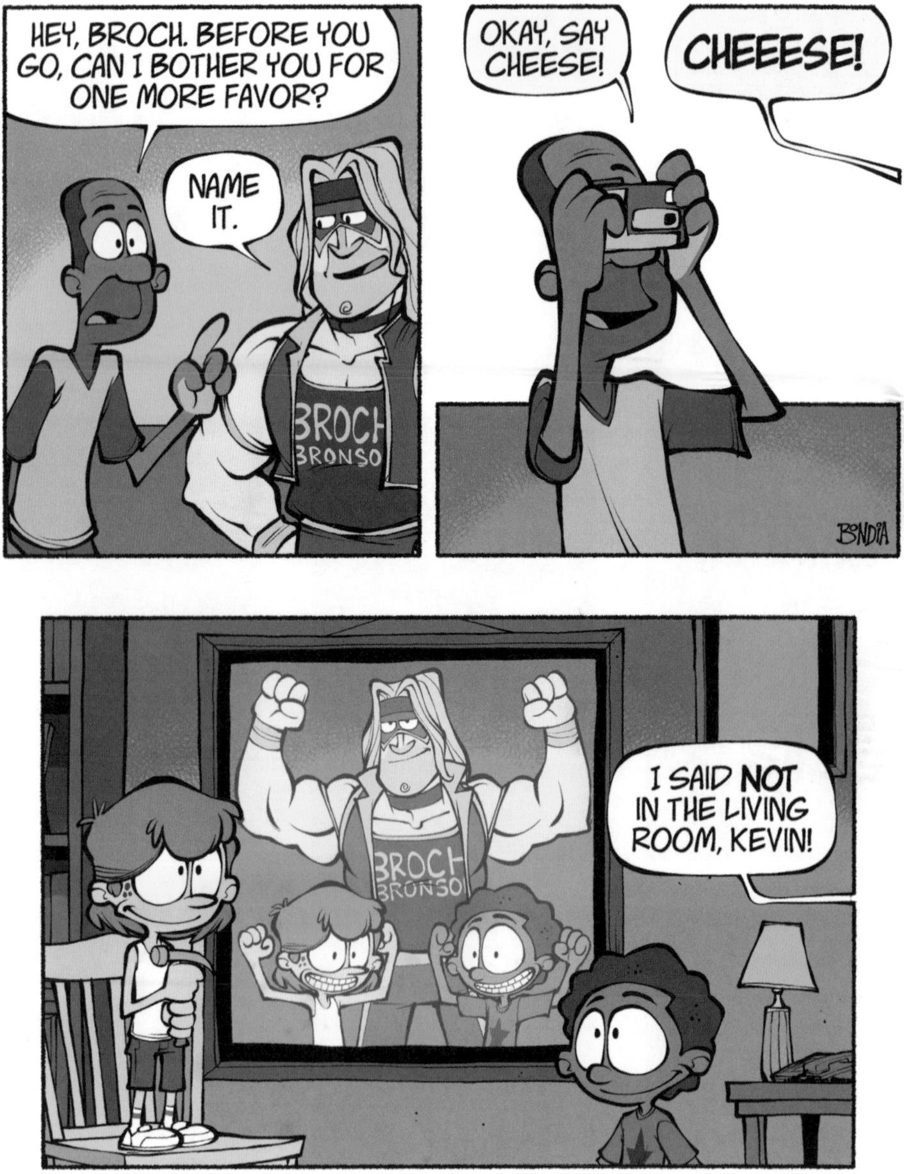

HEY, BROCH. BEFORE YOU GO, CAN I BOTHER YOU FOR ONE MORE FAVOR?
NAME IT.
BROCH BRONSO
OKAY, SAY CHEESE!
CHEEEESE!
BONDIA
BROCH BRONSO
I SAID NOT IN THE LIVING ROOM, KEVIN!

Look for these books!

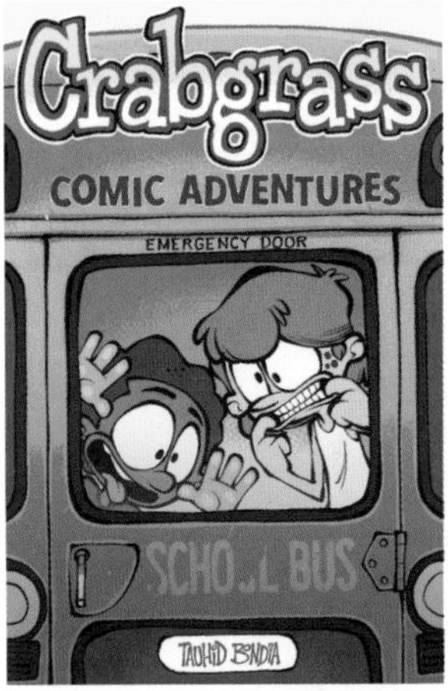
Crabgrass
COMIC ADVENTURES
EMERGENCY DOOR
TAUHID BONDIA

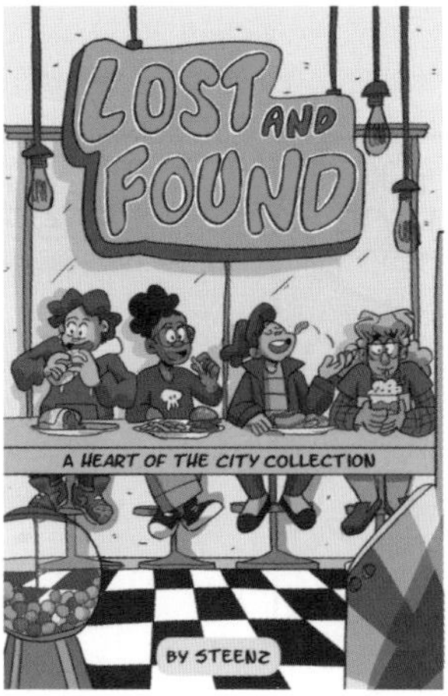
LOST AND FOUND
A HEART OF THE CITY COLLECTION
BY STEENZ

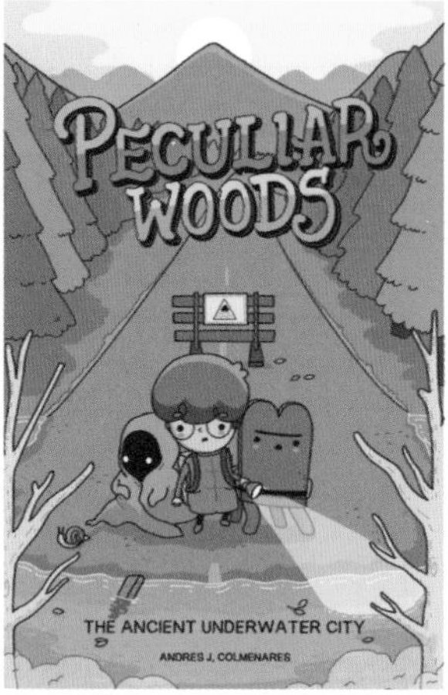
PECULIAR WOODS
THE ANCIENT UNDERWATER CITY
ANDRES J. COLMENARES

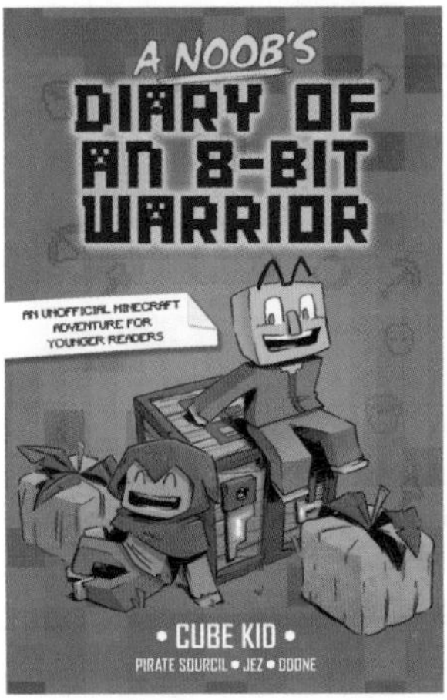
A NOOB'S
DIARY OF AN 8-BIT WARRIOR
AN UNOFFICIAL MINECRAFT ADVENTURE FOR YOUNGER READERS
• CUBE KID •
PIRATE SOURCIL • JEZ • ODONE

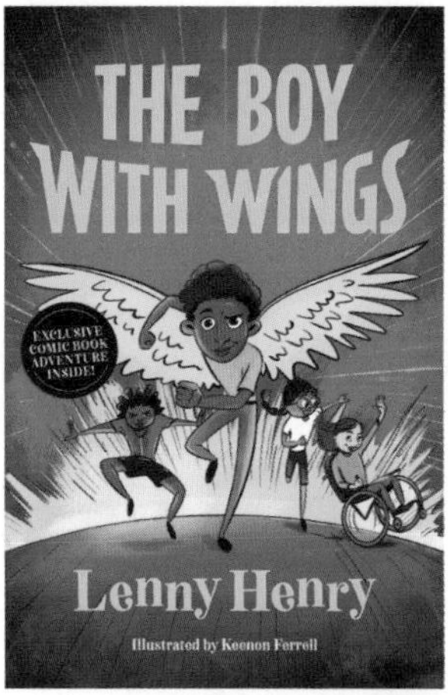
THE BOY WITH WINGS
EXCLUSIVE COMIC BOOK ADVENTURE INSIDE!
Lenny Henry
Illustrated by Keenon Ferrell

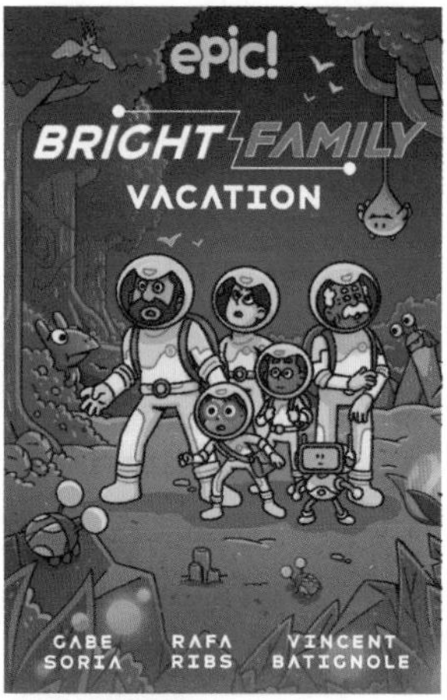
epic!
BRIGHT FAMILY
VACATION
GABE SORIA
RAFA RIBS
VINCENT BATIGNOLE

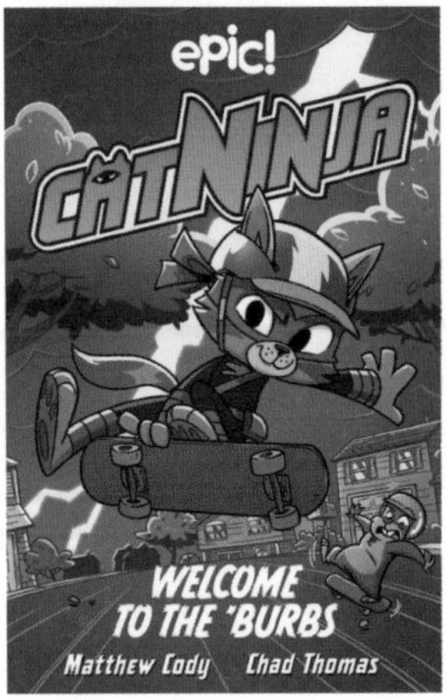
epic!
CATNINJA
WELCOME TO THE 'BURBS
Matthew Cody
Chad Thomas

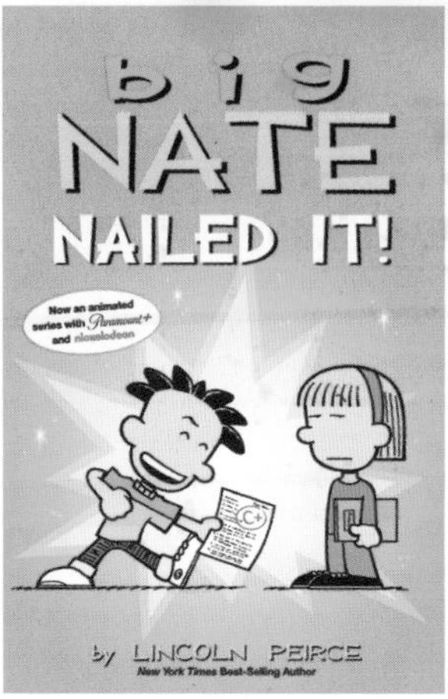
big NATE
NAILED IT!
by LINCOLN PEIRCE
New York Times Best-Selling Author

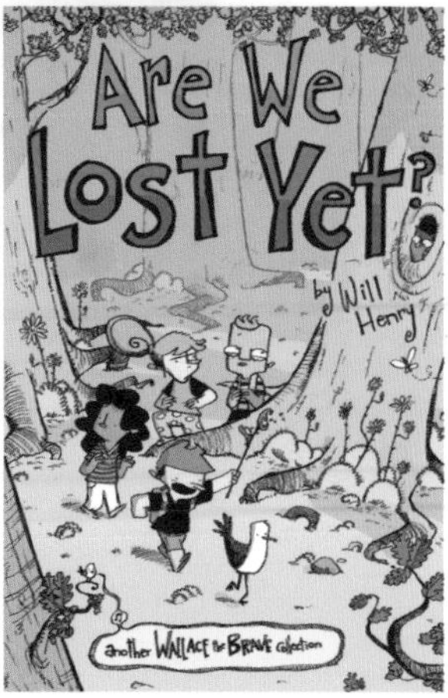
Are We Lost Yet?
by Will Henry
another WALLACE the BRAVE collection